THE
QUEST GIVER

BOOK 1

THE QUEST GIVER

BOOK 1

A. Stargazer

Published in 2023 by Podium Publishing, ULC
www.podiumaudio.com

AUTHOR'S NOTE

While this book assumes a familiarity with video games, specifically massively multiplayer online games such as *World of Warcraft*, it is meant to be enjoyed by all.

A glossary is included in the back of the book with common gaming terms. Please note that many of the acronyms are spelled out phonetically. There are several reasons for this. If you are uncertain of what a term means, try sounding it out. If that doesn't help, check the glossary.

THE
QUEST GIVER

BOOK 1

1

QUEST DECLINED

Gideon Lachlann is the greatest hero in the world, and I am his son.

Ten years ago, the civilization on the continent of Lagrea was on the brink of destruction, a death from a thousand cuts. Centuries of unchecked monster waves had left humanity scattered and divided. Those few kingdoms that clung to life did so behind tall walls, their food grown by nervous peasants quick to abandon their crops at the first sign of incursion. To the north, the necromancer Ival was raising a legion of the undead to conquer the world. To the south, the dragonlings expanded their territory ever outwards. To the west was the Ironrot Empire, ruled by the Nostantan, ancient and evil. And to the east was the sea of squalls, impassible and filled with kraken and other monsters of the depths.

Beset from all directions, the kings of the united races knew that their time was limited. They did not have the armies to push back the encroaching darkness, and so they turned to one final hope. Within the ruins of the ancients lies a portal to another world. My grandfather and the other kings of men, along with the council of the elves, the dwarven clans, and the elders of the nymphs, all convened and concluded that there was no other choice. They performed the ancient ritual, and the world was changed forever.

The Travelers came to our world through the Gates of TirNiki. Endless and uncounted, of all races and creed, and without fear.

Of course, not all of the Travelers were great warriors. Many caused problems. Some even sought to make things worse. But others rose up to save us. In the early days after the opening of the portal, my father slew the dragon Detan of the Yellow Skies, rescuing my mother, Princess Analise of Yuikon. For his prize he took her hand in marriage. But the war to push back the tides of darkness was unceasing, and he was called ever to the front.

My father is the greatest hero in all the world, but I have never met him.

But that will change. Today. Father is finally coming home, and the kingdom is throwing him a parade.

"Display Status," I said, and the screen appeared before me.

Name	Hail Teoran	Level	1
Health	50/50	Strength	4
Mana	70/70	Dexterity	5
Experience	0/100	Vitality	5
Age	8	Endurance	3
Race	Human (blood of the Travelers)		
Class	Child	Intelligence	7
Job	Prince of Yuikon	Wisdom	6
		Charisma	13
Traits	High Aptitude		
	Quick Learner	Spells	Cure Minor Injury (3)
	Royal Blood (+5 Charisma, bonus to relations with factions loyal to Yuikon)		Detect Poison (10)
	Blessing of Thedum		Spark (4)
	Mark of the Phoenix (hidden)		
	Voice of the Future (hidden)		

I scrutinized the page carefully, as I had every day since I'd learned that I would finally be meeting my father. I was a little proud, because I knew from the other children that I'd convinced to play "I'll show you my status if you show me yours," that my stats were about one or two above normal across the board for everything except Endurance. Endurance was a little lower, but that wasn't my fault because I couldn't get as much time to play due to all the time I had to spend with my tutors. On the other hand, my Charisma was way high just because I was royalty.

I had been impatiently watching the numbers slowly go up since I unlocked my status screen three years ago, but there really wasn't anything I could do to speed it up except for getting older. I mean, I was too young to fight monsters and gain levels, and that's how people get really strong. But just growing up increases your stats slowly. Everyone gets a boost around age ten or eleven, and another boost at age fifteen or so. My grandfather says that he averaged about nine in the body stats and eleven in the intangibles when he started training as a squire at age eleven.

Of course, he won't show me his stats now. He says that his personal strength is a state secret, and that if our enemies knew his status, they would be able to use it against us. I don't really understand why it's such a big secret, but he says it's the same reason I had to learn the [Detect Poison] spell and why I have to cast it before eating or drinking anything. It's stupid, I mean, our cook has [Detect Poison] at level fifty. If he doesn't spot it, then there's no way that my level ten spell will catch it, right? And I can't level it past ten until I increase my intelligence, which I can't do without growing older. I'm maxed on the increase I can get from education, although I might "grow into" some hidden intelligence points from my education later on, so my tutors keep cramming my head full of knowledge.

I sighed, wondering if it would be enough. I was above average for the other castle children, but would that impress my father? He was a dragon slayer, a prince consort, and the leader of the prominent Traveler guild, <The Endolphins>. A raid leader, he had risen to answer the call to save this world from itself, and he fought night and day to keep children like me safe in the Heartlands. He had killed Worldbosses and cleared raids and lairs throughout the continent.

How in the seven hells could an eight-year-old prince impress a man like that? Because I really, really wanted to impress him.

My mother was no help. She simply sighed and said, "You can't predict how a Traveler will react to anything." Grandfather was no better, though he had little spare time to talk with his grandson, let alone to address my perceived inadequacies. The maids and servants all assured me that I was worried about nothing, and my tutors simply scolded me for spending too much time staring at my status screen.

The door burst open, and my nurse, Beckah, came barging in. She took one look at me and scoffed. "I know that vacant expression! Stop staring at it. There's nothing you can do at this point to change your status before tonight. Even if you get a plus one on something, it won't make much overall difference."

I closed my status screen, stuck my tongue out at her, and blew a raspberry. I always acted very princely in front of her. After all, she's the one who changed my diapers.

Certainly, nobody else bothered.

"Come now, Hail, it's time to get changed. The parade is starting soon, and we need to get you ready for the reception."

"I wish I could have ridden out to meet him, and then go through the parade with him," I complained. "It's not fair that—"

"Life's not fair, you know that. There are children your age begging in the streets while you live in comfort and luxury. When I was your age—"

"I know, I know," I raised my hands in defeat. "When you were my age, the darkness was at the walls and the world was ending and nobody had thought to ask the Travelers for help for decades yet. I'm blessed by the gods to have been born into the royal family, and twice blessed to have such a distinguished father. But it's still stupid that I couldn't ride out to meet him."

"Complaining isn't changing you into your finery," she scolded, "and until you're dressed properly you're not ready for the reception. And if you're not at the reception, you'll have to wait until—"

"I know, I know!" I began stripping out of my play clothes. That's one thing I hate about being a prince, all the stiff and uncomfortable clothing. On a normal day I'm permitted to dress for comfort, but on official event days I'm forced to dress for either fashion or tradition. Today, it was tradition, and the blue coat was itchy, the black slacks were ironed stiff, and the shoes, while immaculate, were simply uncomfortable on my feet.

I was somewhat annoyed that I wasn't allowed to dress myself for official functions, but even my grandfather had servants to help him dress in his official robes, so my complaints were mostly ignored. As Beckah fretted over my black hair with its silver highlights—black from my mother, silver from my Traveler father—I resentfully stared in the mirror, occasionally wincing as the comb found a knot.

Heterochromia, they call it. My left eye is blue from my mother, my right is silver. A symbol of the mixing of blood between our world and the Traveler's home world. Not all Travelers have silver hair and irises, although neither is my father unique. Rather, they are far more diverse than us Natives, with hair, skin, nails, and eyes of all colors of the rainbow. I've even heard that they can choose or change their coloring and features somehow, although the details remain a mystery to me.

When Beckah was satisfied that I was presentable, she dragged me out of my room and through the hallways of the castle to the courtyard, where I was pushed towards the master of ceremonies. The droll man frowned at me and lectured me as he always did on what was expected of me. Specifically, that I remain seen but not heard at the side of my mother, the second princess. I blew him a raspberry, although for a significantly different reason than the one I blew at Beckah.

Honestly, it's like I'd never had to sit through a boring ceremony before. I would have much rather have been out in the crowd, watching the procession, or, even better, at my father's side. But it had been decided that my place was at my mother's side. Still, the clock was ticking down before I could finally say hello to the man who had given me life and saved my world. Although it was a struggle, I contained myself. I knew I must behave myself, less I be removed entirely.

I stood next to my mother and entangled my hand with hers.

"I finally get to meet him," I whispered to her, my enthusiasm not at all hidden by my low volume. "I can hardly wait."

Mother squeezed my hand and looked down at me, her expression somewhat troubled. "I hope everything lives up to your hopes and dreams, Hail. It's been a long time since I've seen your father, and I've heard . . . he may not be the man I thought he once was."

I frowned up at her. "Mother? What do you mean?"

"Hopefully nothing. Never mind. It's probably just rumors. Just, I don't know, try not to be surprised if he says or does anything strange. Sometimes Travelers speak with people who are very distant as though they were right next to them, or they say strange things that do not make sense. It's best to simply ignore such things when they happen," she explained.

"I've spoken with Travelers before," I reminded her. "I know they're eccentric."

"Yes, hopefully that's all that it is," she said quietly, almost to herself. "Just, don't get your hopes up too much, Hail."

I frowned at her, but didn't say that it was already too late for that.

The trumpets outside blared their warning, and the gates to the courtyard opened to admit the Traveler guild. My father's guild, <The Endolphins>.

Unlike Natives, Travelers were never content with mundane mounts. Riding a simple horse was seen by them as a sign of poverty or a lack of imagination or drive. They traveled far and wide to tame and train exotic creatures to ride. Or, in my father's case, to kill and enslave the essence of, for he rode the shadow-spirit of the great drake Shalasmir, a beast that had taken fifty men to kill.

I knew him at once. His parade armor shining white, his handsome face ageless in that strange way of the Travelers. He looked just like the portraits of him and my mother at their wedding. Gideon Lachlann, the [Silver Knight].

The rest of his guild came riding in on mounts no less impressive, including winged lions, tamed wargs, and even an elephant. Their armor was resplendent, their weapons shimmered with restrained power and magic. Their deeds all rivaled my father's, for while he was their leader, they fought their battles together, pushing back the darkness that had encroached our world for generations. And the cheering people outside the castle loved them for it.

Once they were through the gates, the raid dismounted. Father's shadow drake turned to smoke and entered a flask at his hip. The others' mounts also vanished in various fashions, from slipping inside their shadow to stepping through a dimensional portal.

"That was kind of lame," one of the warriors exclaimed. "This city's not as big as I remember. This event was a total wash."

"Shut up, we're in front of the king," another whispered harshly. "Acting up might cost us Rep."

"Who cares? This is noobie town," the first one said. "Besides—"

"Shut up, Nial, or I'll deduct you Dee Kay Pee for every outburst," Father said. "That goes for everyone else. The event isn't over yet. There's supposed to be some sort of hidden quest we can unlock, so keep your eyes and ears open."

"Ahem," the king said. "Welcome, oh great heroes of <The Endolphins>. Welcome back to the city of Zhesa, Capital of Yuikon, the city in which your very guild incorporated after the opening of the portal of—"

The king droned on and on, as he always did, and I quickly tuned him out. Honestly, geography and history are pretty boring. We all knew it already anyway, so what's the point of rehashing it? Although I grew increasingly proud as he listed all my father's accomplishments one by one. Well, not my father's, exactly, but <The Endolphins> collectively. I'm certain my father had a great many more than that, but even my long-winded grandfather had to cut things short eventually.

"—but before the feast, I would like to have a private word with my son-in-law, and the rest of my family," Grandfather concluded.

"Of course, my liege," my father said.

"Oh shit, I forgot about that," someone in the guild exclaimed. "That's right, Gideon totally boned the princess, didn't he?"

"Dude, shut up! At least pretend to take it seriously when you sign up for a roleplay event."

"Hey, I just came for the food and to show off. Whatever hidden quest there's supposed to be, I bet it's all for Gideon, the lucky bastard."

I frowned at the unprofessional attitudes emanating from my father's warriors. I'd been warned, but this was not how I'd imagined the Travelers to act. Not during the middle of a ceremony meant to honor them. *Even I had more decorum than that!*

The gates outside the castle closed, and most of the guild made their way towards the hall where they would feast, while Father split off from the rest of his guild. He was joined by an honor guard as he followed Grandfather and the rest of the royal family as we made our way into the throne room, where Grandfather made his way to the throne.

Finally, unable to contain my excitement anymore, I ran to my father's side.

"Father! Father! Will you take me as your squire?" I asked.

He jerked in surprise, frowning down at me in confusion. His expression changed to that of one reading a menu or prompt for a moment, and I realized with joy that I had just accidentally issued him a quest. Then he spoke two words that shattered my world.

"Quest declined."

2
ADMINISTRATOR

I had never felt such sorrow as I felt upon my father's rejection. I ran, sobbing, all the way to my room and buried myself under my covers. I was joined momentarily by Beckah, who tried to calm me, but I screamed and threw pillows at her until she left me to my misery. She didn't deserve the things I shouted at her, but she accepted my anger without complaint. Left alone, I cried myself to sleep.

"Hail?" A familiar voice woke me. I sniffled, looking up. The light coming in from the windows told me it was evening time; I had a bit of a nap. For a moment I thought perhaps it had been a dream—a nightmare, but one look at my Mother told me that it had not.

"Why?" I asked her.

"Oh Hail, I wish you would have consulted me before you asked him that," she said sadly.

"Why doesn't he want me?" I demanded. "My stats are high! Except for Endurance, but I can—"

"Display Status, Public," Mother said. A familiar, yet very different, box popped up between us.

Name	Analise Teoran	Level	42
Health	23940/23940	Strength	35
Mana	36540/36540	Dexterity	53
Experience	—/—	Vitality	57
Age	27	Endurance	46
Race	Human	Intelligence	87
Class	Cleric of Thedum	Wisdom	65
Job	Princess of Yuikon	Charisma	97
Traits	Royal Blood	Spells	Cure Major Injury (27)
	(Hidden)		Detect Poison (50)
	(Hidden)		Cure Major Poison (14)
			Cure Major Disease (22)

My eyes just about bulged out of my skull when I saw Mother's numbers. I don't think I'd ever actually seen an adult's status before, and I couldn't believe the difference between us.

"How?" I asked. "Did you kill monsters?"

"No. I'm a cleric, Hail. I gain Experience from healing people and treating the sick and wounded. I can gain Experience from monsters, but there's really no point for me to do so when I can make just as much simply serving at the temple. But I wasn't showing you my status to show off my level. Look at my stats."

"They're so high," I said, in awe.

"No, they're not," she said, sighing. "They're average at best, for my level and class. They only look high because nobody over level ten has ever shown you their status screen before, have they?"

I frowned, but realized she was right. "What's special about level ten?"

"Nothing, really. It's just that each level you gain gives you more than the last one. More stats, more health, more everything. And you're also limited by your age. Once you turn ten, your stats will almost double. At that point, maybe we can have you go out with the guards and start killing some rats or slimes or something to gain some levels, but it would be even better to wait until you turn fifteen and get the second bump—"

"I don't want to wait seven years! My father is the greatest hero in the world, and I should be his squire! It's not fair!"

"Hail, the monsters that your father fights could kill you with a sneeze. Your father is level two hundred, and he spends his time fighting dragons and demons and monsters from the abyss. Maybe in another ten years we can get you up to level thirty and he might be interested in showing you around then, but—"

"Why hasn't he ever come to visit before?" I asked. "Travelers can teleport anywhere that they've been, can't they? That's not a made-up thing people say about them?"

Mother frowned, then sighed. "Not exactly anywhere. Anywhere with a Nexus Point, which means most cities and fortress towns in our kingdom. As for why he hasn't come and visited . . . Hail, your father is a Traveler. He's not from this world. He doesn't consider this world to be reality, and so he doesn't really see you as his child. To him, you're just another non-player character. Just like all the rest of us Natives. The visitors, they're not really heroes, Hail. They're just people who can't die in this world, so they run around doing impossible things just for fun."

"But I am his son! He married you and made me and—"

"Hail, my marriage to Gideon Lachlann has been annulled. He's agreed to let the kingdom move on. That was the entire point of the parade today, it was just to lure him and his guild back into the kingdom so that we could gauge his intentions for our world. It's clear now that he's just like so many other Travelers who are just here to play the game. He took advantage of me, and the kingdom, for his personal prestige and used it to build his guild, but ultimately, he doesn't care about any of us. And so, the king has decreed—"

"He can't!" I protested. "He's the greatest hero in the world, we need him to keep us safe—"

"Gideon Lachlann isn't even in the top five thousand players anymore," a strange voice came from the shadows. Mother jerked in surprise as the room was lit up with motes of blue light, and from the motes formed a man. The man was in his thirties. Average looking, plain compared to most Travelers, and dressed in a black robe.

"Lord Administrator!" she cried, and promptly knelt before the stranger.

"Please, I hate it when you Natives treat us like we're gods," the stranger said, motioning for her to rise.

"Who are you? How did you get into my room?" I demanded, throwing a pillow at him. It passed right through him.

"See? That's better," he said, chuckling. "Analise? Why don't you explain to your son who and what I am?"

"Hail, this is one of the administrators," Mother said reverently. "They are the true saviors of this world. They are the ones who opened the portal for us. And they forced order unto the darkness, restricting the strongest monsters into dungeons and lairs. Without them, our civilization surely would have—"

"That's not exactly the true extent of it," the administrator interrupted. He sighed. "This might be hard for you to understand, Hail, but this world and the world the Travelers come from are not split the way you think. It's, well, it's hard to explain. But the reason most of the players in this world think of you as 'not real' is because you're all very sophisticated artificial intelligences. Most of you are advanced neural nets that are tuned just beyond the tipping point of the Turing Test, intended to direct players to the real masterworks. But then, just about every En Pee See in the castle is a potential quest giver, which means that you've probably never actually met one of the drones, have you, Hail?"

"I don't know what you're talking about," I complained. "Get out of my room! Guards! Guards! Intruder!"

"You want to go somewhere else for this conversation? Very well." The administrator snapped his fingers, and then, instead of my bedroom, the three of us were suddenly on a beach. My eyes went wide at the display of power. The stranger grinned.

"How did you do that?" I asked, my tone completely different.

"Vast cosmic powers," he explained. "Well, not really. I figured you might need some convincing, so I arranged it ahead of time. It's a few simple lines of code that bring us to one of the coves on the Sea of Squalls, then back to our starting points. I use it a lot, actually. It's a nice place to think, and sometimes it's nice to remind players that yelling at me won't get them their loot they think should have dropped, or whatever other problem they have with the game."

"Nothing you say makes any sense," I complained.

"Sorry about that," he said, grinning ruefully. "The truth is, Hail, that I've come to apologize. Things have rather gotten away from us, and some things have happened which will affect you greatly, but are entirely not your fault."

"What do you mean?"

"I mean that your father disowning you and your mother is not your fault," he said. "It was . . . well, we were hoping that it wouldn't happen, but it has. Which is a real shame, and we're still sorting out where things will go from here. But I just wanted to step in and tell you that you don't have to worry. We're not pulling the plug on you. Legally, we can't. In fact, we're somewhat excited to see what you'll do next."

"I don't understand."

"Hail, your mother, your grandfather, all the people in the castle, they don't *feel* in the same ways that you do. They have simulated emotions for dealing with player characters, but they're only surface deep. You're about eight generations more advanced than they are, and unlike them you have an actual Seed of Consciousness. It's been a real shame that Gideon quit roleplaying in favor of raiding, because you've just been sitting on a shelf this whole time. The truth is we thought about repurposing you early on, but Hail Teoran being the son of Gideon Lachlann was canon. So instead, we cranked up the Aye Eye of those around you and hoped that Gideon would grow interested in you as you got older."

"Why are you saying all this nonsense?" I demanded. And then I noticed that Mother was simply staring vacantly at the ocean. "What's wrong with my mother?"

"Oh, she's outside of her parameters. She doesn't know how to act right now. Don't worry, it's just a glitch in her programming, she doesn't know how to act anywhere outside of the Kingdom of Yuikon. I forgot about that. See, that's one thing about us humans, Hail. We often forget details like that until something reminds us."

"You're lying," I said. "You did it to her on purpose."

The administrator *tsked*. "Did I come up with the answer too quick? Yeah, I bet that was it. Well, either way, I just wanted to have a few minutes alone with you before the fallout began, Hail. You see, legally, in the Kingdom of Yuikon, you've just become a bastard."

"What?" I shook my head. "That's, no, I—"

"It's not your fault, Gideon is just a jackass. And I think he's going to regret it in the long run. He was a great player in the opening year of the game, which is why we gave him a few opportunities, including marrying your mother and fathering you. But he lost track of himself along the way, and became obsessed with raiding and exploring new zones as they opened up. But eventually we'll reach the point in the game where there are no more zones to explore, and the challenge will begin to come from things other than new dungeons and lairs. And he's just pissed away an opportunity to be at the front of that."

"I don't want to be a bastard," I complained, thinking of the few other bastards I knew. They were all looked down on and discriminated against by their families.

"Don't worry. You're still a royal. You'll be removed from the official line of succession, but it was always unlikely that you'd end up on the throne that way. Anyway, the real fun will start in a few months when you turn ten."

"I'm only eight," I pointed out.

"Oh, right. Time in your world moves faster than it does in ours. Don't worry too much about it, but also don't be too surprised if any Traveler friends you make talk about taking a day off and are gone for a week your time. You'll figure it out, we made you pretty smart. Anyway, I'm going to snap my fingers now, and when you wake up, a week will have passed from today, and you'll be feeling a lot better."

"Wait! None of what you've said makes any sense!" I protested, but he had already snapped his fingers.

I woke up in my bed, and a stream of memories from the last week hit me. I had been going through the motions like a ghost, without any feeling or attachment to the events. I was now a bastard. I was allowed to keep my room and my clothes, but my nurse Beckah had been dismissed, and my lessons had changed significantly. Rather than being educated for the off chance that I would somehow inherit the throne, I had spent the last week being drilled by our sergeant-at-arms.

3

ADVENTURER

The one nice thing about being a bastard was the lack of supervision. It had taken me some time to realize that, suddenly, nobody cared where I went or what I did. As long as I didn't cause too much trouble, at least. And as long as I attended my training with the other castle boys—most of whom were commoners who would end up in the guard or army—nobody really cared how I spent the rest of my day.

Time flew by. My tenth birthday came and went, and I found out what they meant by "getting a bump" in my stats at that point. Everything nearly doubled! Not quite, but almost.

Name	Hail Teoran	Level	1
Health	90/90	Strength	8
Mana	120/120	Dexterity	9
Experience	0/100	Vitality	9
Age	10	Endurance	10
Race	Human (blood of the Travelers)	Intelligence	12
Class	Child	Wisdom	9
Job	Bastard of Yuikon	Charisma	15

Skills	Short Swords (7)	Spells	Cure Minor Injury (7)
	Archery (5)		Detect Poison (12)
	Balance and Conditioning (5)		Spark (6)
	Animal Handling (4)		Analyze (3)
Traits	High Aptitude		Storage (5)
	Quick Learner		Mark of Karma (special)
	Royal Blood (+5 Charisma, bonus to relations with factions loyal to Yuikon)		
	Blessing of Thedum		
	Mark of the Phoenix (hidden)		
	Voice of the Future (hidden)		

A few other things had changed as well. I had gained some skills from my constant practice under the master-at-arms. Of all my stats, my Endurance had increased the most from constant exercise, a vast difference from what it had started out as.

Of course, I was still a [Child] and hadn't unlocked any classes worth mentioning. And my job was now "Bastard of Yuikon," rather than Prince. But I increasingly found that I didn't care. I liked my new life of exercise and sunshine much better than the endless droning of my former tutors. I missed Beckah, but I was also relieved to be out from under her thumb. And Mother . . . Mother remarried, and left me behind. That hurt, but it was Grandfather's doing, not hers.

I was coming to hate my grandfather almost as much as I hated my father. It was for this reason that I decided to run away.

I was supposed to join the army when I turned fifteen, after the local guard had put a few levels upon me. But I couldn't wait that long. Instead, I simply left the castle one morning with a purse full of coin that I had saved up, went to one of the equipment shops serving the Travelers, and bought a new set of commoner's garb, as well as a weapon that didn't come from the castle armory.

My second visit in my new life of freedom was to the Adventurer's Guild to find some friends. I'm not exactly certain why I found myself drawn towards the Travelers, given the way my father had treated me. Perhaps I simply wanted to find out if they were all jerks like him. Perhaps the administrator had done something to me. Or perhaps I was simply tired of the constant *sameness* that I was beginning to recognize in all the people in the castle.

It was strange, that sameness. Not everyone had it. Mother didn't. My nurses and my tutors hadn't had it. But the boys I drilled with, and the new servants I saw about the castle were all so bland; following the same routines over and over, talking about the same things, repeating the same opinions on the same news endlessly.

And there was also the matter of escaping my disgrace. Nobody was overtly unkind to me—the king made it clear to all that would not be tolerated—yet those few nobles who had the spark of intelligence that was lacking from their servants looked at me with pity or disgust. I simply wanted to be done with it.

It wasn't hard to find the Adventurer's Guild; everyone in town knew where it was, and they were happy to provide directions. Walking through the city, I got my first real taste of a place where the Travelers and Natives really intermingled. The Travelers were often easy to spot, both by the fact that they wore armor or robes as though they were going into battle, and by their eccentric behavior.

One young woman was talking to the open air as she walked down the street. As she passed me, I tapped her on the shoulder and asked her who she was speaking with. She seemed surprised to be interrupted, but she answered me with a gruff, "partychat," and then complained to her invisible companion about some weird kid on the street accosting her.

She wasn't the only Traveler I saw behaving that way, but I didn't stop any of the others. I figured they were all talking to "partychat," whatever or whoever that was. Others were typing on virtual keyboards, which lit up under their fingers, and staring at invisible screens. As strange as the Travelers were, there was simply something about them that was *alive* in a way that I wasn't used to. I was really looking forward to making some friends with some of them.

With great excitement, I entered through the massive doors of the Adventurer's Guild and marched up to the nearest open window and said, "I'd like to find a party."

"This is quest turn-ins. Looking for group is over there," the middle-aged receptionist said, motioning to the window right next to hers. The one with a "Back in 30 Minutes" sign.

"Can't you help me?" I asked. "I don't want to wait."

She looked up and frowned at me. "New to the game? First time here?"

"Um, I guess."

She tossed me a wooden coin. I caught it and felt a strange sensation wash over me. It was sort of like having your hair stand on end from static electricity, but it passed quickly without a spark.

"Thanks?" I said, uncertain what I had just received.

"That's your guild token. Don't lose it. Well, you can't, actually. Not without being kicked out of the guild. It's bound to your account, and it will always pop back into your inventory. It unlocks a few features, including looking for group and quests. What level are you?"

"Level one," I admitted.

"Jeez, kid, how'd you get through the tutorial without gaining a single level?" she asked. "I actually want to know, because there are players out there who would pay for the information to help twink their alts."

"I just did," I said, unwilling to admit that I had no idea what she was talking about. It was completely normal to stay level one until age ten, after all.

"Right. Well, what's your class?"

"[Child]," I answered, although it should be obvious.

"Wait, not [Junior Warrior] or [Junior Mage] or something?" she asked. Then she just shrugged. "You're weird, kid, but I guess everyone plays differently. Look, you can join the El Eff Gee queue if you want, but I'd recommend picking up a few of the quests over there instead to get up to level five. Ten would be better, but sometimes level fives get together to grind. You should probably mark yourself down as a Dee Pee Ess because I doubt that you have any junior class skills that would classify you as a tank, healer, or supporter. To unlock the El Eff Gee menu, just put your token down on the desk over there and navigate the popup menu."

"Okay, thanks," I said, not really understanding.

"Now get out of here, kid, before someone actually comes with some quests to turn in."

"Oh, right. Okay." So, I went over to the empty window and set my token on the empty desk, and sure enough, a window I'd never seen popped up.

You have joined the Looking for Group Queue			
Name	Hail Teoran	**Guild**	None
Class	Child	**Rank**	Wooden
Level	1		
Select role	DPS	**Select goal**	Fighting monsters
	Tank		Quests
	Healer		Exploration
	Support		Dungeons and Raids

Excitedly, I quickly selected the top option, as I didn't know what the others meant anyway, and for the goal I picked fighting monsters. I was somewhat disappointed at the result when the menu declared my estimated wait time to be "Unable to Calculate."

With nothing else to do, I went over to look at the message board, which was covered in wanted posters and quest flags. The quests were even conveniently organized by level, which allowed me to quickly select a handful of level one to level three quests. However, I was uncertain whether leaving the building would remove me from the El Eff Gee queue, which I was reluctant to do.

"Hey, kid, want a boost?" a voice asked, and I turned to see a bald Traveler with a red robe and a staff approaching me. "I heard you talking to the receptionist. Level one, right? I'll boost you up to level ten for twenty gold."

"Really?" I asked, growing excited. That was more than half of what I'd saved up, but the thought of getting ten levels so easily was extremely tempting.

"Sure, if you've got that kind of money," he said. "If not, I'll boost you to level five for five gold, since that's a much easier benchmark."

"Yeah," I agreed, and I promptly handed over my five gold. The stranger seemed a little surprised as I counted out the coin and handed it over to him, but he simply grinned.

Severus has invited you to form a party. Accept?	
Yes	No

I quickly accepted the invitation, and the stranger named Severus waved his hand and a portal appeared. I grinned with excitement; I was dealing with a proper [Mage]! He motioned for me to follow, and so I walked through the portal with him into lands unknown.

You have been kicked from the party by the party leader.	
Reason given:	Trolling

I frowned at the prompt that came up as soon as we emerged on the other side of the swirling magic. "I don't understand. Why did you kick me out?"

"Oh, it's part of boosting you," he explained. "I wasn't actually calling you a troll, I just had to put something in that field, and that's the option that pops up on top for me. We can't be in the same party because I'm level fifty and will suck up all the Experience, so that you wind up only getting two or three Experience per goblin. But if you get the first hit on something, then I can blast it down in one hit, and you'll get full Experience."

"Oh," I said, having never known any of that before. I looked around at the conifer forest around us, and asked "Where are we?"

"Just north of town," he explained. "There's a goblin lair nearby. They're level fifteen, so stay close. They can probably one-shot you if we get careless."

"Oh, okay," I said, growing nervous. I hadn't expected my first encounter with the monster spawns outside of the city to be with such high level ones. But I followed Severus as he led me deeper into the forest, and after a moment I could hear the sound of grunting and hooting. Ahead of us was a small patrol of three green human–like things, with sparse spiky hair and pointy ears, each slightly smaller than I was. Goblins were one of the most plentiful monsters near the city, but I'd never actually seen one before.

"Okay, kid. You don't want to get close to them, so just shoot them with your arrows. As long as you draw blood, I can blast them apart and you'll get full Experience, okay?"

"Right," I said seriously, unslinging my bow and quickly taking careful aim. I was pretty good at archery, although I couldn't raise it above five because I lacked combat experience, but hopefully that was about to change. I exhaled slowly, and the arrow I released hit the goblin that looked like a leader right in the left buttock.

A second later, the goblin exploded into gore, which promptly turned into black mist. I jumped in surprise, and looked at Severus, who grinned at me.

"Hurry up and tag the other two before they charge us or run away," he shouted, and I snapped out of my shock and knocked another arrow. My shot hit the second goblin, which likewise was destroyed utterly a second later. I missed my third shot because the surviving goblin was running away from us, but Severus blew it up. Afterward he clapped me on the shoulder.

"Well, two out of three isn't bad. How much Experience did you get from that?" he asked.

"Display Status," I said, and I began to grin. It was the first time in my life that the Experience row had not displayed a mocking zero, and I couldn't be happier.

"Seven out of one hundred!" I declared.

"Shit, is that all?" he asked. "You should have almost gotten a full level from that."

I frowned. "Really?"

"Yeah! You're fighting way above your level here, so you should be getting tons of bonus Experience for killing level fifteens while you're still level one. In fact, you should have gotten level three or four just from that fight alone," he explained.

I bit my lip, wondering if this was one of the differences between Travelers and Natives. It would make a lot of sense as to why they were so strong if they could gain Experience so quickly, but I wasn't ready to give up. "Maybe it's because I didn't do enough Damage?" I suggested. "I mean, my arrow only did nine Damage the first time, and seven the second."

"Shit, is that all?" he asked. "Yeah, that's likely the problem then. But there's not much to do about it because you're too weak to let you get into melee range and use that sword of yours. On the next group we find, let's try having you shoot them twice before I blow them up and see if that makes a difference."

And so, we tried that after finding a second group of goblins not far from the first. Except that I didn't get better Experience this time. In fact, it was worse, because I could only "tag" one of the goblins before Severus had to blow them all up to protect me, so I only got three Experience from that fight. We tried finding a third group, but Severus was growing impatient.

"Look, kid, this isn't working," he said. "Sorry. I tried to help, but your account is glitched or something. You should probably stick to the low-level areas for now or you might get accused of hacking and get kicked out of the game. Don't worry too much though, these sorts of glitches have a way of clearing themselves up on their own. Anyway, I had something just come up Eye Are El, so I'm sorry but I've got to go."

And with that, Severus faded into nothing.

Leaving me alone, in the wilderness, surrounded by a goblin lair, with no idea how to get back to the city.

4

RESCUE

I tried very hard not to panic when Severus vanished right in front of me, leaving me to fend for myself against level fifteen monsters. I did not succeed.

A noise came from the bushes further up the trail. Without waiting to see what it was, I turned and ran in the opposite direction. Blindly terrified, I had no idea which direction to go to get away from the danger of the goblin lair, or back to the safety of the city. I just ran, following the path that we had been on and hoping that it would join up with a road, or that I would find some other adventurers who I could possibly pay to escort me home.

I ran into the goblins first. They must have heard me coming, because one jumped out from the bushes to ambush me, and just as I was turning to run in the other direction, another one popped up behind me. Realizing that I was trapped, I was determined to at least not go down without a fight. I drew my sword and charged the one that had blocked my path.

Goblins are not smart or strong creatures. But the difference between a level fifteen goblin and a level one [Child] is essentially insurmountable. A fact I discovered when the goblin met my attack with his club and punched me in the face, cutting off my battle cry.

Condition:	Stunned (10s)
Health:	8/90

My status flashed in the corner of my vision, superfluous because I already realized how much trouble I was in. That fist *hurt*. One more attack like that and I'd be dead. Rather than finishing me off, however, the goblins pounced on me and began tying me up with rags and scraps of rope. The scrap of cloth that they gagged me with was filthy and tasted disgusting, and I questioned what it had been used for previously. Worse, the goblins claimed my weapons from me.

I was completely helpless as they dragged me away from the site of the ambush. Even after my stunned condition wore off, I could only grunt and scream into my gag as my captors brought me further towards the goblin lair.

It took me a while to figure out why the goblins hadn't killed me. They were planning on cooking and eating me. Or at least that's what I gleamed from the fire they were building and the spit they were preparing. I kicked and struggled, but even if I had gotten free of my bindings, I was still surrounded by an encampment of goblins that were stronger and faster than me. The only thing I did manage to do was cast [Cure Minor Injury] on myself a few times to restore my Health to full. I even got a point in the spell, which makes sense because casting spells under duress increases levels faster than casting them when everything is going fine.

Unfortunately, I doubted that I would be able to out-heal the fire for very long before the goblins cooked me.

I was trying not to cry while saying prayers to Thedum for a miraculous rescue. For the first time in my life, my prayers were answered promptly. A burly man in heavy armor jumped out of the sky into the middle of the gathered goblins, about twenty of them, and he began insulting their mothers while swinging his axe about with more recklessness than skill. He glowed in a faint golden light that told me there was a cleric or priest nearby who had cast a protective spell upon him, although I couldn't tell exactly what it was.

Arrows began raining down upon the goblins as they grouped up to face the burly man's assault, picking them off one by one. Three goblins were suddenly polymorphed into frogs, followed immediately by chain lightning running through the survivors.

Between the [Warrior], [Archer], and the [Elementalist], the party of adventurers quickly cleared out the encampment, and I breathed a sigh of relief. I was saved! I began struggling again, shouting into my gag to get their attention. It was the [Warrior] who noticed me first.

"Hey, Thena. You ever heard anything about a rescue quest with these goblins? Because it looks like we might have just spawned one," the [Warrior] said, turning to me as he cleaned his axe with a cloth from his belt.

"There was no mention of a hidden quest in the guides that I read about this lair," one of the other party members said. A priest, judging by her white robes. She began typing on an invisible keyboard. "Just a second, I'm going to ask in guildchat and check the forums."

"Why are we just sitting here? Someone untie him," the [Elementalist] said, her blue robes somewhat frizzy from the electricity she had been throwing around.

"Just hold off a minute," the [Archer] said, "Untying him might spawn waves of reinforcement or something."

"We can handle them," the [Warrior] said. "And I'm ready for a challenge. These goblins have been boring since Larissa unlocked her chain lightning spell. She's killing them too fast."

"Moar deeps is never a bad thing," the [Elementalist] chided back. "The problem is that we need a new grinding zone. We've out-leveled this lair."

"We're getting good Ex Pee per hour," the [Archer] argued. "They're giving us less than last level, but we're killing them faster, so it balances out to about the same. It's worth sticking it out for the rest of this level at least, and then reevaluating. Maybe we can come back for whatever this quest is after that."

I started shaking my head, terrified that they'd actually leave me behind. Desperation filled me, but there wasn't much I could do.

"I can't find anything about an escort or rescue quest related to this lair," the priest, Thena, said after a few moments of the others bickering about what to do. "Which means that either we did something unique to unlock it, or it's such a waste of time that nobody who's completed it has ever documented it."

"That's bullshit," Larissa, the [Elementalist], challenged. "Maybe out in the frontier there are undocumented quests like this, but this close to one of the major starting hubs? Something weird is going on. It's been more than a year since launch, and that's plenty of time for the completionists to have covered every inch of this lair and triggered every spawn event."

"Whatever, there's no point just standing around. Who knows, maybe we'll get a first-time completion bonus for saving this kid," the [Warrior] said, as he took a knife from his belt and came to cut me loose. As soon as my hands were free, I pulled the dirty rag out of my mouth and spat the foul taste into the dirt.

"Thank you all, for rescuing me. I was abandoned nearby by someone I thought was my friend, and then the goblins captured me. If you hadn't rescued me, I'm quite certain they would have cooked me alive!"

"Yeah, that's what it looks like they were gearing up for," the [Warrior] agreed. "Don't worry kid, you're safe with us. Where are we supposed to escort you to?"

I frowned, considering. I didn't really want to return to the castle without gaining a single level, and I was fairly certain that after today I would once again be under closer surveillance, so future excursions might be curtailed. "Is it okay if I just stick with you guys for a while? I don't want to go home yet, I'm just going to get yelled at when I do."

The [Warrior] chuckled at that, and then his eyes began scrolling as he was reading invisible quest text. "You guys get that quest too, or do I need to share it?" he asked.

"We got it," Larissa confirmed. "Looks like it's open ended, which is weird. It just says, 'Allow Hail to accompany you until you return to the nearest safe zone.' And for rewards, it just says 'Variable,' and 'Reputation.' I'm guessing Hail is the kid here, but the quest doesn't say who the Reputation is for."

"I'd give you some coin," I said, "But Severus took almost everything I had. I only have a few silver left over. I think maybe he wasn't such a good friend after all."

"So, you got robbed and dumped in the middle of a lair. Yeah, kid, that's a rough break," the [Warrior] commented. "What do you think guys?"

"There might be some hidden event around here that the kid is related to," The [Archer] commented. "We should accept and escort him through the entire lair if we can."

"Well, I'm just here for the experience bus," the [Warrior] admitted. "That, and killing goblins is fun. I love the sounds they make when they die."

"Do you mind if I help fight, too?" I asked nervously. "I'd like to gain some levels before I go home."

The party blinked. Laurant, the [Archer], was the first one to speak. "Huh, the quest just updated. Get Hail to level five. Rewards: Variable, and Reputation, just like before."

"If the quest is to get him to level five, what level is he right now?" the priest asked.

"I'm level one," I admitted. "Severus was supposed to get me to level ten. You don't have to help me if you don't want, I—"

"I say we accept. It sounds like a unique experience," Thena said. "The devs probably just patched it in and we're the first ones to stumble across it. I'm starting to document it so that we can post it on the forums, it might make our guild famous."

"Alright kid, boss lady says it's a go," the [Warrior] said with a grin. "Welcome to the party."

Except, unlike Severus, this group didn't actually send me a party invite. I gathered my bow and my [Short Sword] from the goblins who had captured me, straightened myself out, then followed along with them as we went hunting goblins.

"Our Ex Pee per hour has dropped to a trickle," Laurant complained. "And the kid is only level three now."

"Sorry," I muttered, letting another arrow fly to tag one of the goblins attacking Phil, the [Warrior]. A swipe of his axe after my arrow had connected, and the target's injury went from minor to severe. A follow-up swing a second later finished it off for good. I tagged another, and a combination of lightning and arrows from Larissa and Laurant put that one down as well.

"It's fine, kid. If you were a player, this would be a terrible grinding spot for you at your level. The game penalizes you for getting carried, it would have been much faster for a level one player to start fighting level one through five monsters by himself, or with a few friends," Thena explained. "Anyway, our own Experience isn't completely stopped."

I frowned. That was the exact opposite of what Severus had told me, but between him and my new friends, I believed my new friends. I just didn't understand why Severus would have told me the wrong thing on purpose, brought me to a terrible place for me to level, and left me alone in danger.

I felt a little bad about slowing my new friends down, but at least I was making progress. The basic strategy of having Phil "tank" the goblins until I had "tapped" them with my arrows was providing me with a slow but steady trickle of Experience, but compared to the slaughter that Laurant, Larissa, and Phil could carry out on their own, it was a crawl.

I kept watching them as they fought, and I found myself growing envious of their abilities. Especially Larissa and Laurant, and I only slowed things down further as I paused to examine their skills.

I wished that I could learn to fight like that. Shooting arrows so fast that my hands blurred in motion, and casting [Lightning Bolts], which fried the goblins from the inside out. It was incredible.

As I watched Larissa casting [Lightning Bolts] for what might have been the hundredth time, I began whispering the incantation along with her. And, to my surprise, I began to feel crackling between my fingers. Realizing what was happening just in time, I dropped my bow and finished the incantation, pointing at the goblin I had been about to shoot with my palm instead.

The [Lightning Bolt] was a pale imitation compared to Larissa's, but there was a pause in combat as everyone turned to look at me. It was enough of a distraction that the goblins we were fighting managed to land a few hits on Phil, although he recovered a second later and Thena had him glowing golden with a healing spell a few seconds after that. Once we finished that pack of goblins, the party rounded on me.

"Since when could you cast lightning, Hail?" Larissa inquired, not sounding too confrontational about it.

"Um, about two minutes ago?" I said nervously. "I was just feeling kind of jealous, so I tried copying you. I didn't think it would work. It wasn't very powerful though, was it?"

"It was fine for a level three caster and a skill level of one. And you don't have any gear boosting your intelligence or spell power either. Even so, I bet it did three or four times your piddly little arrows," she explained. "How much of your Mana did it burn?"

"I think I can cast it about five or six times before running out," I admitted. "Although I don't get my Mana back very fast."

"Mana efficiency gets better at higher skill levels, and your regen goes up if you get points of Wisdom and Intelligence," she explained. "You shouldn't have been able to learn that spell just by copying me though. Not unless you have a [Mage] class. Can we see your status screen?"

"Display Status, Public," I said immediately. It was a little embarrassing to show it in front of my new friends, but they'd been trustworthy so far. And anyway, nobody really cares about hiding your stats until you're a grownup anyway.

Name	Hail Teoran	Level	3
Health	300/300	Strength	10
Mana	317/390	Dexterity	11
Experience	27/300	Vitality	10
Age	10	Endurance	11
Race	Human (blood of the Travelers)	Intelligence	13
Class	Child	Wisdom	10
Job	Bastard of Yuikon	Charisma	16
Skills	Short Swords (7)	Spells	Cure Minor Injury (8)
	Archery (5)		Detect Poison (12)
	Short Spears (5)		Spark (6)
	Animal Handling (4)		Analyze (3)
	Balance and Conditioning (5)		Storage (5)
Traits	High Aptitude		Mark of Karma (special)

	Quick Learner		Lightning Bolt (1)
	Royal Blood (+5 Charisma, bonus to relations with factions loyal to Yuikon)		
	Blessing of Thedum		
	(hidden)		
	(hidden)		

My friends gathered around and scrutinized my numbers and abilities, making me want to blush.

"[Mark of Karma]? What the hell is that? I've never heard of that spell before," Phil commented.

"That's what you're focusing on? Not the fact that he's a royal bastard?" Laurant demanded. "And the system is even hiding some of his Traits from us. What the hell, I think we stumbled into a much larger event than I originally thought."

"It's probably his [Quick Learner] trait that allowed him to learn [Lightning Bolt]," Larissa commented. "I wonder what else we could teach him?"

"Nobody else is focused on the fact that he's got royal blood?" Laurant repeated.

"You know, I remember him now," Thena said softly. "Right after launch, on the first kill of any of the Worldboss dragons, the leader of the guild that took it down managed to somehow marry the Princess of Yuikon. The wedding was canon, as was the fact that they were having a child. But then I never heard anything more about it until now."

She pulled up her holographic keyboard and began typing quickly.

"Hail, when did you cast [Mark of Karma] on me? Did you cast it on all of us? Guys, check your status, we have a debuff that I can't dispell."

"I've never used that ability before," I protested. "It showed up on my status a few years ago, but every time I've tried to use it nothing has happened. When I focus on it, it just says 'the laws of the universe demand balance.' I stopped worrying about it a long time ago."

"Until now," Larissa commented. "I have it too."

"Oh shit, I bet it's like an aura ability that's always on. It must infect any player who interacts with him. But it doesn't look like it's a bad thing. Mine says it's giving plus five percent Experience right now, so I'm not complaining," Phil said, his eyes looking vacantly at his status screen. "I mean, it's not enough to make up for slowing down to power level him, but if we got him up to our level that little bit could add up to quite a lot in the long run."

"Found it!" Thena exclaimed. "There's been a bit of gossip in the royal court about the second princess. She married her savior eleven years ago in game, one Gideon Lachlann, one of the leaders of <The Endolphins>, as part of a roleplay event, and they had a son. According to the gossip, they split two years ago. I bet Hail was part of an ongoing roleplay event, but Gideon got bored with it because it wasn't endgame. But now for some reason the devs are trying to write his son back into the game."

"Stop talking about me like I'm not here!" I protested. This earned me a look from all my friends, who frowned.

"If Hail's a special En Pee See, we really ought to be treating him better," Laurant said. "After all, Karma goes both ways. We're getting a bonus right now, but I bet the [Mark of Karma] offers a flip side, too. Good and bad karma, it works both ways. Sorry, Hail. We're just trying to figure things out. Wandering En Pee Sees like you are pretty uncommon in the game, and it's really exciting that we're the first to discover you."

"What does En Pee See mean?" I asked, uncertain whether to be offended or not.

"Non-player character," Thena explained, still typing away on her invisible keyboard. "I believe you would say that it's another term for the Natives of this world. You see, this world, to all of us 'Travelers,' it's a video game, and we're players. Some people use En Pee See as an insult, but that's not how we meant it. I mean, you are a Native, aren't you?"

"Yeah," I admitted.

"Then it's not an insult, anymore than calling you a Native is an insult. It's just another term that means the same thing," she continued. "I can barely find anything on the forums about you though. It's extremely exciting and frustrating at the same time."

"You think this is actually a unique event?" Laurant asked. "Should we get the rest of the guild in on it too?"

"It's too early for that," Thena argued. "Let's finish getting him to level five and see what happens."

"You're right. Suddenly I don't care too much about our Ex Pee per hour as much as his." Laurant bit his lip for a second, then looked at me curiously. "Hey, Hail, how does that [Quick Learner] ability work? Does it work on anything?"

"I don't know," I said. "It's a passive. But I've always been able to learn new skills quickly. And [High Aptitude] allows me to increase their ranks faster and further as well."

"I'm going to demonstrate a skill for you. It's called [Quickshot]. I want you to just keep practicing it with me until you learn it, okay?"

Ten minutes later, we were on the move again, and this time, I was pulling and peppering everything with [Quickshot] and [Lightning Bolt], while the others finished them off. It only took two hours after that for me to hit level five.

5
RETURN

"Ding!" I announced cheerfully when I received my leveling notice. I didn't really know why I had to say it, but that was what they told me to say when I leveled. The last of the goblins had just gone down, and I promptly pulled up my status to show my friends. Now that the initial awkwardness had passed, I was eager to show off my gains.

Name	Hail Teoran	Level	5
Health	600/600	Strength	12
Mana	157/700	Dexterity	13
Experience	18/500	Vitality	12
Age	10	Endurance	12
Race	Human (blood of the Travelers)	Intelligence	14
Class	Child	Wisdom	11
Job	Bastard of Yuikon	Charisma	17
Skills	Short Swords (7)	Spells	Cure Minor Injury (8)

	Archery (5)		Detect Poison (12)
	Short Spears (5)		Spark (6)
	Animal Handling (4)		Analyze (3)
	Balance and Conditioning (5)		Storage (5)
	Quickshot (3)		Lightning Bolt (3)
Traits	High Aptitude		Mark of Karma (special)
	Quick Learner		
	Royal Blood (+5 Charisma, bonus to relations with factions loyal to Yuikon)		
	Blessing of Thedum		
	(hidden)		
	(hidden)		

"Great job, Hail," Thena said. She got the look on her face showing that she was looking through her menu, and she smiled. "It looks like our quests have been updated. The one to power level you is complete, but it says rewards are dependent on the escort quest. The escort quest, on the other hand, has us facing a split. We can either bring you to the nearest settlement or back to the capital. My vote is the capital. It would be awesome if we could turn this rescue quest into a chance to meet the king."

"Seconded," Phil agreed.

"All in favor?" Thena inquired, and everyone voted "Aye."

Everyone except me, but my friends didn't notice that. I mean, I didn't know which way to go without them anyway, and if we got separated, I'd probably end up over a goblin's fire without them. Despite my increased levels, I was still quite helpless this close to the goblin lair, and had little hope of returning to any sort of civilization without them. So, I swallowed my worries and followed them.

I learned a bit about them as we traveled. They were friends from "college," except that Phil and Laurant actually knew each other going back to "middle school." Thena was the one who got them into "the game," but she had decided to "re-roll" in order to play with them rather than on her "main." I didn't really understand what she meant by that, other than she didn't want to be a "DPS" anymore.

Okay, so I didn't learn that much, other than their world sounded very different from mine. Apparently, education was extremely important for the masses, instead of being reserved for the elite as it was here, and everyone went to school until at least age eighteen, and some, like my friends, even paid to study for longer than that.

Oh, and they didn't have monsters infesting every crook of their world. But they said that the monsters were the entire reason that they came here, because without them our world would be much too boring to visit. I tried to argue that if there were no monsters, then the people of my world wouldn't need the Travelers to fight monsters for them, but that just earned me funny looks.

"Hail, this world is a video game. If you didn't have players paying Arc Inc. to come here to fight monsters, then they would shut down the servers and—"

"Let's not bother him with that," Thena interrupted Phil, who frowned at her, then shrugged.

"I guess it doesn't really matter. Arc has promised that the game will last at least the next fifty years. With time dilation, that's almost four hundred years to the Natives. What happens after that will depend on whether Arc's claims that this really is the 'final generation' of Vee Are Em Em Ohs or not."

"It's been doing well so far," Laurant pointed out. "It's stealing market shares from just about all the competitors, at least. And it is quite a bit better than Knife's Edge, which is what I was playing before you all convinced me to join you here."

"You've been to other worlds aside from this one and your home world?" I asked.

"Sort of," Laurant agreed. "Virtual reality games aren't anything new. The thing that makes this game special is its Time Dilation factor. We've been escorting you for, what, six or seven hours now? But it's really only been about an hour in our world. It's great, because logging in means we get a whole bunch of extra time in our lives to just enjoy ourselves."

"I still think it's strange that you all like fighting monsters," I pointed out.

"It's easy for things like that to be fun when you know that you'll respawn if something goes wrong. Not that we were in any danger against those goblins," Larissa explained. "I suppose it's different for you though. But you gotta do what you gotta do."

"Yeah," I said, thinking about how my return home was about to go.

The trip back to Zhesa took almost two hours, even after jogging for a good part of it. I complained that it would have been nice to be able to simply portal back, like how Severus had brought me to the goblins in the first place. Larissa explained that her class would eventually learn how to open portals to areas she had been before, but not until level forty. They would all be able to earn a mount at level twenty, but until then they had to hoof it themselves.

"At least in this world you don't actually run out of stamina," Laurant said. "I feel like I could run across the continent and never run out of steam."

And I suppose he was right, although if you overtaxed yourself too hard you got a debuff, which slows you temporarily. But as long as you find the right balance between speed and intensity, you could effectively keep running until you fell asleep on your feet. Still, when the city finally came into view, we were all eager to slow down.

"So, Hail, should we escort you all the way to the castle, then? Do you think they'll let us in to meet the king?" Thena asked.

"Um, I don't know," I admitted, feeling somewhat dodgy about the truth.

"He ought to meet us. I mean, we saved his grandson, right?" Phil pointed out.

"I'm a bastard now," I reminded him.

"Yeah, but you're his daughter's son. He can't not claim you as his grandson," Laurant pointed out. "He's not, like, cruel to you or anything, is he?"

"No," I admitted. "In fact, aside from making Mother remarry and go away to live with her new husband, he has been very clear that my royal blood be honored appropriately. It looks like I'm going to be an officer in the army or something when I grow up, I guess. I'm not really sure. Before, when I was a prince, then I most likely would have married someone instead, but nobody wants to marry a bastard."

"I don't get it though, how are you a bastard if your parents were married when you were born?" Laurant asked.

"The wedding was annulled, so technically they were never married. And I was conceived before the wedding, and according to my father, the wedding was never consummated afterwards. So, I was technically conceived out of wedlock, and after the annulment I was born out of it as well," I explained.

"That's some bullshit. Hey, Hail? That shit doesn't matter to us. In our world, parents have kids out of wedlock all the time, and hell, my parents divorced when I was eight. So it sucks, but it's not that big of a deal to us," Larissa commented.

"Thanks," I said. "But I don't live in your world, do I?"

Nobody had a way to counter that argument.

As we were approaching the gates, an armed force of guards came riding out to meet us, and I had a sinking feeling in my gut as I realized what was about to happen.

"Guys, I'm really sorry," I said. "But I think I might have gotten you all in trouble."

"What? Why?" Phil asked.

"Don't tell me you ran away?" Laurant asked as he groaned.

"I wasn't planning to! Not really. But then Severus tricked me and—"

"The quest has been updated again," Thena said, interrupting me. "Looks like we have no choice but to play along for a little while longer."

"What does the quest say?" I asked.

"It says, 'Help Hail deal with the repercussions of his absence from the castle,'" Phil read.

"I just hope we're not about to be arrested for kidnapping," Larissa commented.

The guards pulled up short in front of us. "You there! You are all under arrest!"

"God dammit, Larissa, you had to say something," Phil muttered, but everyone put their hands up in surrender.

I was separated from my friends and sequestered alone in my room. Unlike normal, the door was locked, and I was forced to cool my heels for almost an hour before anyone returned. It was another pair of guards, who marched me down to the throne room, where a very tired looking king was facing off with a large number of players, some of whom looked quite excited. My friends were there as well, held together and surrounded by guards. I heard whispers of an "epic questline" and "first-time completion bonuses" and "a unique wandering En Pee See" from some of them.

Others looked somewhat annoyed by the proceedings. I was somewhat surprised to see that Severus was there as well, with his wrists and ankles shackled. He gave me an angry glare, and I stuck out my tongue at him. I'd figured out now that he had tricked me in order to steal my gold, and I was looking forward to exposing him in front of everyone.

"Hail, you have caused quite the disturbance in the castle today. What do you have to say for yourself?" My grandfather demanded.

"Nobody ever told me that I couldn't visit the city," I pointed out. "I went there looking for a party to help me get a few levels now that I'm old enough, which is where I met Severus."

I proceeded to tell the entire tale of how the man had tricked me, taking my gold and vanishing after teleporting me to a well-known danger zone. I continued uninterrupted as I admitted that I had been captured by the goblins and rescued by my friends, who had also helped me to reach level five. When I finished, Severus protested that he had had an emergency Eye Are El, but the king cut him short.

"Severus, your deeds are not unknown to me. Because your victims have always been other Travelers before, the city guard has never seen fit to intervene, leaving that role up to the administrators, with whom I am told you have had repeated dealings. You are, as I understand it, on very thin ice with them, correct?"

"Whatever, this is bullshit. Look, I'm done playing with this stupid event. Let me go, I'm leaving."

"No, you are not," the king said simply. "You swindled and endangered the life of my grandson. For this, I sentence you to seven years of hard labor. If you were not a Traveler, I would simply sentence you to death, but this is the maximum penalty which the administrators allow me to impose upon one of your kind for all but the most heinous of crimes against my people."

"Bullshit, bullshit, bullshit. I'm just going to re-roll."

"This punishment will be specific to your account and personal brainscan. Anytime you log in to the game, on any character, you will be teleported to the mines," the king informed him, a slight smile upon his face.

"Then I'll fucking quit the game for a year and come back. Whatever, Knife's Edge is better anyway," Severus said, and he began to fade out like he had before. Except that this time, his body snapped back into place, though it was slack and vacant. The guards dragged him away. The gallery tittered slightly, mostly the players who seemed to take great joy at this turn of events.

"Now then, what shall I do with you four," the king mused, turning back to my friends.

"Your Majesty, have we committed any crime? We were simply adventuring when we encountered your grandson. We intended him no malice nor caused him any harm. We could not have known that his absence had triggered a desperate search of the city. We did not even know his identity when we first met him," Thena pointed out. "It was not until we approached the city that the full story was revealed to us, and we have cooperated with the investigation ever since, have we not?"

"Indeed," the king agreed. "Very commendable. Your versions of events match closely with Hail's testimony and what we have determined through our own investigation methods. I can think of no crime that you have committed for which I can justly punish you, except that I wish you had returned my grandson to me sooner, rather than dallying for half a day."

"An offense which we regret, Your Majesty, but as we have explained—"

"Yes, yes, I'm not entertaining inventing some crime to punish you for. Rather, I'm trying to figure out how to reward you," my grandfather said, waving away their concern. He sighed, looking older than he was. "Hail is no longer in line for the throne, but he is still my grandson, and you have guarded him through an event of great danger, and even returned him to me stronger than you found him. I believe I shall grant you each one of the royal griffons as compensation, available to you immediately once you have achieved the prerequisite level. Is this acceptable?"

Phil snorted, and a murmur raced through the assembled players with grumbling coming from the jealous and cheering coming from many others.

"We accept with gratitude, Your Majesty," Thena said, the veteran player having taken the lead for my friends. "That is far more than we expected to receive, but we will not insult you by refusing your generosity."

It was the king's turn to snort. "I know how your kind lusts after exotic mounts. The applications to receive a griffon from our breeding grounds, or to capture and tame one of the wild stock, is a thousand pages long. I find it strange, because I prefer my mount to remain firmly planted on the ground. But if there is anything you would prefer to receive as my boon instead of a foul-tempered feathered mount, please speak now."

Thena paused in consideration. She glanced at me, then at her party, then nodded and spoke. "Your Majesty, is there any way to restore Hail to the line of succession and the honor that I feel that should be his birthright?"

The king's face turned from bored to annoyed, then somber. He looked at me, and I felt a weight of sadness in his expression. "I would prefer not to answer this in such an open forum, but now that the question has been asked, and now that my grandson is known to your kind, it will ultimately come up again and again until it is resolved.

"The unfortunate truth is that Hail's situation is my own fault. I thought his father was a man of honor, a man worth binding my kingdom to in marriage and blood. I was wrong, and it is for my error that Hail now suffers disgrace in the face of the court. The words his father spoke before witnesses in this court cannot be recanted. Hail is legally a bastard. He cannot inherit, although we will make accommodations for him suitable for his royal blood. He has shown some martial prowess, not the least of which is achieving level five at such a tender age, even if it was with the help of seasoned adventurers."

"You say that it's your own fault," Thena argued, "But is it not his father's fault, for disowning him and his mother? Is it not Gideon Lachlann's fault for falling short of your expectations?"

"I suppose that is one way of viewing the issue," the king admitted. "Would you take this answer as your compensation instead of the mounts I offered?"

"No. I would take Hail himself, to have him join our guild and become an adventurer, if that is what he desires as well," Thena suggested, and the gallery roused itself at the suggestion. Some of the players seemed enamored with the idea, while others seemed out-raged or apathetic.

"How the hell can an En Pee See join a guild?" one player shouted.

"He joined a party just fine, remember? That's what got that troll in trouble; he thought he was dealing with a player," someone pointed out.

The king slammed his scepter to quiet the room, and he let out a long sigh. He turned to me, and he gave me a slight shrug. "That's not a decision that I can make," he said eventually. "Ultimately, I was preparing several paths from which Hail could choose, but if this is the one he would select for himself, then I will not interfere with his choice."

"In that case, before Your Majesty, the court, and everyone else, I cordially invite Hail to join my guild, the <Nethersong Mavericks>," Thena said, and to my surprise I received a popup.

Thena Evensong has invited you to join the <Nethersong Mavericks>. Accept?	
Yes	No

Grinning with pleasure, I quickly selected my answer.

6

GUILD

Softspook	Holy shit, it worked? We actually have an NPC in the guild?
Thena	It seems that way. Hail, can you see this chat?
Gummytiger	No way. They're allowing NPCs to join player guilds now? I can't believe nobody's tried that before.
Peafowlet	I just tried inviting a random shopkeeper and got nothing. I think Hail is special.
Peafowlet	It might be because of his father being a player. Like, keeping it in the family or something.
Potatoad	Gross.
Gummytiger	Get your mind out of the gutter, Toad.
Sellamander	It might not be so uncommon in the future. I think Hail is a beta test for a new feature allowing players to marry NPCs and have kids, rather than something entirely unique. Or rather, he's unique "for now."

Growing annoyed with the text flashing in my vision, I willed it to go away the same as I would will my status to vanish after I had finished looking at it, and it quickly complied.

"Welcome to the guild, Hail. We're glad to have you aboard," Thena said.

"I don't suppose it's too much to hope that we can still get the mounts as well?" Phil asked, earning a glare from the rest of the party and an elbow in the side from Laurant.

"Sure. You have my only grandson, but I have infinite griffons. I can spare you four of them. In fact, everyone gets a griffon," the king declared, sounding annoyed. He began pointing. "You get a griffon, and you get a griffon, and you get a griffon. Everybody gets a griffon!"

"R—really?" one player dared to ask.

"NO!" the king shouted. "I declare this matter resolved and dismiss this audience. Everyone, get out!"

The guards began clearing the room, and the players slowly began to disperse, except for my friends and a few other players who said that they were in <Nethersong Mavericks> as well. The king looked at me and smiled sadly.

"This isn't quite the future I had imagined for you when you were born, Hail, but perhaps it won't be such a bad life for you. While I will permit you to leave the castle under the care of your guild, I expect you to remain where it is safe the rest of the time. It is a dangerous world out there, and you're only level five."

"Don't worry, Grandfather, I've learned my lesson. Until I'm strong enough, I won't leave the city unless it's with my guild," I vowed.

"And don't go stepping through any strange portals!" he scolded, then he ruffled my hair and left the audience room. I ran over to my friends and their gathering guildmates.

"Thanks for inviting me to your guild! I'm sorry that you had to choose between me and the griffons," I told them.

"It's fine, Hail. I'm certain that we made the right choice," Thena assured me. "It's a unique bonus to our guild to have the first Native like you. We've already gotten a few dozen applications because of the news spreading on the forums, and I expect that to turn into a few hundred by the end of the hour."

"I have no idea what any of that means," I confessed. "Are others going to be joining?"

"Probably not too many. This whole event has them a bit excited, but even if we invited them, they'd probably leave in a few days. I have a feeling it's going to be a little while before the next major event surrounding you, and not everyone has the patience to play the long game like we do," Larissa explained. "We're not a very large or powerful guild. We're a social guild, and now that we have you, we're probably going to be a little more active in the roleplay scene. If we haven't already, I'm certain that some of the major roleplay guilds will be reaching out to us to try to start earning Rep with you as well."

"I don't know what that means, either," I admitted, grinning a little sadly.

"I think we need to treat him like a complete noob," Laurant said. "Like, first login, never played a Vee Are Em Em Oh or even an old-style Em Em Oh before."

"Either way, I think that the throne room isn't the best place to discuss it. Let's get back to the guild headquarters and talk things through. These are uncharted waters, and we're going to have to figure out from the beginning what it means to have a resident En Pee See in our guild," Thena said. The others nodded, and I followed them out of the throne room, out of the castle, and into the city. Two castle guards trailed along behind us.

"Somebody just offered our guild leader ten thousand dollars for the guild," Thena informed us as we sat around the table in the guildhall. It wasn't the Adventurer's Guild, but a private building dedicated to just <Nethersong Mavericks>. The other rooms were starting to fill up as more and more of the members came to meet me, but we had closed the door to them and taken one of the meeting rooms for the guild leadership for ourselves. Honestly, I thought the Adventurer's Guild would have been better, but the others said that everyone would be harassing us if we showed our faces there right now.

"Is that good or bad?" I asked.

"If she wasn't a trust-fund heiress, it could have been bad. She turned it down with a laugh. She's much more interested in seeing what's going to happen next with this questline," Thena said. "Just about everyone is. We didn't realize it at the time, but while we were leveling you, Hail, there was a huge search going on for you in the capital. The guards started stopping every player they came across and asking if they'd seen a boy with black and silver hair and eyes. Then they arrested that troll for kidnapping you, and he started complaining on the forums, which drew a wider audience."

She laughed. "Anyway, I'm glad that we managed to get you in the guild. My eyes just about bulged out when I saw that as a potential quest reward."

"I'm a quest reward?" I asked, sounding somewhat offended.

"Sort of?" Thena shrugged. "Sorry, I don't mean it like that. The quest updated while we were being questioned and hinted that it would be possible to recruit you. It was the fact that you're able to join parties which told me that you really aren't an ordinary Native."

"Although I wish you would have told us you could do that back when we were leveling you. It would have made things a lot simpler," Laurant lamented. "We wouldn't have had to wait for you to tag everything, we could have just gone full nuclear. You still would have gotten shit Experience for each kill because you were getting carried by us, but it would have been much faster."

"I'm sorry. Natives don't really use much aside from our status screens," I admitted. "I never knew that joining a party meant something like that until Severus invited me to join one, and then kicked me out. Then when I met you, I didn't think to mention it."

"It worked out fine," Thena said. "Guys, there's just been a blue post. Go check it out."

Everyone motioned like they were thumbing through popups and then focused on the invisible displays for a moment. Phil was the first to speak.

"So, that's cool. We totally snagged a unique opportunity from one of the top guilds."

"Doesn't give any hints about any of the future events. It just says that we can level him and that he will provide unique quests to those who establish Reputation with him," Larissa commented. "Although considering that one of the alternate rewards just for finding him in the first place was one of the best mounts in the game, I think we can expect some great things."

"Honestly, the royal griffons aren't that great. They're okay, but pegusi are faster, and wyverns make better battle mounts," Thena explained. "Anyway, it's not like we can't get a griffon later if we want, we just have to do it the hard way."

"I can sort of see why <The Endolphins> didn't want him. It won't be too bad to catch him up to level seventeen with the rest of us, but it would suck to level him all the way to two hundred, don't you think?" Phil said, earning him a hard elbow in the rib from Laurant.

"Sorry," he muttered. "I didn't think before I said that."

"It's okay. I mean, it makes me pretty sad that Father didn't want me and everything, but I'm not going to keep crying over it," I declared. "I'm going to get stronger and show him that he was wrong when he dismissed me as useless."

"Yeah, about that. Did anyone else notice that [Mark of Karma] has gotten better? It's giving me a plus eight percent boost to Experience now, and plus one percent stats," Laurent commented.

"It must scale with Reputation," Larissa suggested. "We must have hit a threshold when we got him into the guild. It would be pretty sweet if we could bump it up even further before long. That will help cut down our own leveling time significantly."

"So . . . here's a question," Phil said. "What role is he going to play? I mean, his class is marked as [Child] now, right? But because of his Traits he can learn cross-class skills. Does what we teach him affect whatever class he ends up with eventually or something?"

"Shit, that's a good point. Hey, Hail, can we see your status screen again?"

I frowned. I was starting to get annoyed with the way they were talking about me like I wasn't there again.

"Display Status, Public," I said.

Name	Hail Teoran	Level	5
Guild	<Nethersong Mavericks>		
Health	600/600	Strength	12
Mana	700/700	Dexterity	13
Experience	27/500	Vitality	12
Age	10	Endurance	12
Race	Human (blood of the Travelers)	Intelligence	14
Class	Child	Wisdom	11
Job	Bastard of Yuikon	Charisma	17

Skills	Short Swords (7)	Spells	Cure Minor Injury (8)
	Archery (5)		Detect Poison (12)
	Short Spears (5)		Spark (6)
	Animal Handling (4)		Analyze (3)
	Balance and Conditioning (5)		Storage (5)
	Quickshot (3)		Lightning Bolt (3)
Traits	High Aptitude		Mark of Karma (special)
	Quick Learner		
	Royal Blood (+5 Charisma, bonus to relations with factions loyal to Yuikon)		
	Blessing of Thedum		
	(hidden)		
	(hidden)		

They scrutinized the popup for a moment, considering. "He's got [Short Swords] at seven, but I'm not sure what that actually means. Players simply get low–medium–high proficiency," Laurant commented. "And he's got some healing spells too. It's like he's got a little of everything, in fact."

"Stop talking about me like I'm not even here!" I shouted, slamming my fists on the table and causing everyone to jump. "Just because I'm an En Pee See or whatever doesn't mean you can treat me like I'm a lump of wood."

The players exchanged bashful looks and apologized one by one for their rudeness.

"So then, Hail, what class are you hoping to unlock?" Thena asked. "Is that how it works? You unlock a class at some point? It's different for us players: we select our classes in the character creation menu before we enter this world, and after that we have the option of evolving it after reaching certain levels and completing certain quests."

"When I turn fifteen, I'll unlock a few classes to choose from, and also get a stat bump," I informed them.

"How big of a bump? I mean, I didn't want to say anything, but I think you're a little on the low end of the spectrum at the moment," Phil inquired

"I'm really not sure," I admitted. "My stats about doubled when I turned ten. I think I'll get about the same amount again at fifteen. I'm thinking three to five in each category?"

"Does leveling before you turn fifteen change the amount of stats you gain?" Laurant asked.

"It shouldn't. Base stats are supposed to be fixed at birth. But when I choose my class, my growth stats that I get for leveling will change to match that class. And I do get to choose, although I won't know what the options are until my birthday."

"I wonder if your ability to learn cross-class skills will go away when that happens," Larissa commented. "It would be a shame for you to level a skill just to have it vanish later on."

"I don't know if that will happen or not," I admit. "Most Natives don't really show their status around or talk about their skills very much. In fact, the only adult's status I think I've seen is my mother's."

"Well, it doesn't really matter," Thena said. "It's not like there's a guide for raising an En Pee See that we can follow, so we'll have to learn by trial and error. I think we should keep teaching you everything, then see what happens when you grow up. It'll be interesting to see what options the system suggests for your class."

"Okay," I said. "I do like learning things."

"So, he's going to be sort of our jack of all trades, then?" Laurant asked.

"At least until he unlocks his class in . . . let's see, five years of game time is, what, two hundred sixty days real time? Unlocking his class might change everything about how the mechanics around him work," Thena replied. She turned to me with a grin. "Hail, this is going to be a lot of fun. I'm glad that we rescued you. There's about nine hundred million players who are turning green with envy right now."

"Am I really that special?" I asked.

"There's never been a Native who can join a party or a guild before," Larissa explained. "And you're a quest giver too, with a unique Reputation that is specific to you. There's already a significant call to make more Natives recruitable in the future, with a lot of polls and suggestions on which Natives players want. I don't think it will work that way though. They're all suggesting high-level hero Natives. I think that if Arc introduces any more like you, they'll be like you, starting at level one."

"So then, it's been a long and exciting day," Thena said, "But I've got class in the morning. It's time for me to log out."

"Yeah. I'm getting kind of tired too," Laurant agreed. "We weren't originally planning such a long stretch. Just a quick bit of afternoon grinding, but then it turned into this."

"You're going back to your world?" I asked, disappointed.

"Yeah, sorry, but we can't sleep with the equipment that allows us to send our consciousness here to this world hooked up to our real bodies," Thena explained. "Which means that at a minimum we need to leave for about eight hours every day. Except for you, that would mean we have to be offline for about two and a half days while we rest, but then we can play for almost four days straight if we don't have anything going on in the other world that requires us to be there instead."

"Considering it's Thursday, though, we'll have Friday classes tomorrow," Phil said. "Although we'll team up again like this in the afternoon."

"I don't have classes in the morning," Laurant said, "So I'll pop online for a couple hours and hang out with you, Hail, if that sounds good."

"Oh. Okay," I said, somewhat disappointed that we weren't going to go on an adventure right away. "How will I know when you all come back to this world?"

"Here's an idea," Thena said, and a box popped up for me

Thena Evensong has invited you to be her friend. Accept?	
Yes	No

I quickly selected "Yes" and looked around. "Nothing's changed."

"Try saying 'friends list,'" she suggested. I did, and told them about the boxes that popped up.

Friends List	
1/1 friends online	
Thena Evensong	Online

"Online means that we're in this world," Thena explained. "Offline means that we're busy in the other world and can't be reached. If your friends list works like it does for players, you can set it up to get notifications when we come online, and we can use it to send messages and party invites."

The others quickly sent me friend invites as well, and soon I had four players on my friends list. Then, they apparently really did need to leave this world for a while, and one by one they turned into mist and vanished completely.

7
SLIMES

I blinked as the notification in the center of my vision distracted me, causing me to take a blow to the hip that should have been an easy block from my sparring opponent. I winced and tried to focus and recover, which I did just in time to block a follow up [Thrust] that would have been fatal if we were using real swords.

Two and a half days had passed since my friends had gone offline, and it was early morning. While the castle was generally in favor of me spending time with my new friends, I was a little reluctant to get to know the strangers in the guild quite yet, and so I had simply gone about my daily routine while waiting for them to come back to my world.

| Laurant | Hey, Hail. Can you see this? I've got about three hours before class, which for you I guess means that I have all day, lol. I was thinking I'd see if I couldn't put another few levels on you before I have to get to class. |

This time the distraction was too much. I flubbed a parry, and my opponent mercilessly followed up with a blow to my chest and shoulder.

"That's enough," the sergeant said. "Hail, what's wrong with you?"

"Sorry, one of my Traveler friends came online and it distracted me," I admitted.

Laurant has invited you to form a party. Accept?	
Yes	No

"Ah, right. I suppose you want to go be with them, then?" the sergeant asked.

"Yes. Thank you."

"I would scold you for not taking your practice seriously, but it's nearly time for us to finish anyway, and the king has approved your association with them, so there's nothing I can do," the sergeant said, shrugging. "Go on, be somebody else's problem."

"Thank you, sir," I said. And I accepted the party invite.

"Hey, Hail, can you hear this?" Laurant's voice inquired from nowhere in particular.

"Laurant? I can hear you. I got a popup from you earlier that made me lose a sparring match," I responded.

"Oh shit, sorry about that. Wait, do you have an actual Aitch You Dee? I figured you'd just, like, process that stuff in the background."

"I don't know what that means," I said to the air, as I dashed back to my room to change out of my sweaty clothes and into the adventurers garb I'd acquired.

"I just thought that you'd have some aspects of the interface integrated. Look, I don't know how it works for you, but players can move chat windows and displays by saying 'Setup Aitch You Dee,' and then moving the screens around so that they don't obscure our vision unless we focus on them. When I get a random tell from somebody, I have it set so that I just get a flashing icon until I acknowledge it, then the message pops up for me to read," he explained.

"Okay, I'll try that. Setup Aitch You Dee."

I was running when I spoke, which caused me to run into a wall when my vision was suddenly inundated with dozens of boxes. I managed to bite back the pain and quickly began moving things to the sides and corners of my vision so that I could see again. It wasn't an ideal setup, but I was in a hurry.

"So, I bought you a disguise," Laurant said, as I continued to work on the setup. "It's, um, well, it's a holiday item, but there are thousands left over so they're pretty cheap to buy. I figure it will make you look like just an anime fan, and we can pretend you're my little brother. I've got one for myself as well. We'll look like a pair of otaku."

"I don't know what any of that means. Why do I need a disguise?" I asked, closing the Aitch You Dee setup and resuming my rush to get ready for an adventure.

"You're currently the number one topic on the forums. There are a lot of people looking for you right now. I figure, why make it easy for them, you know? And to be honest, me and the others are being a little selfish because we don't want you getting swept away by the big guys. Some of the superguilds have put a bounty on figuring out a way to steal you away from <Nethersong Mavericks> after our Gee El turned down even their most generous offer to buy our guild."

"Oh," I said, not really understanding.

"Fortunately, it seems that the king has locked the castle down, or else that place would be crawling with players. I'm on my way right now to pick you up, and I figure we'll go kill some slimes in the noobie starting area for a few hours. I really want to see what you can do against something your own level. Can you meet me by the west service entrance? It seems to be less crowded over here."

"Okay. I'm getting ready right now. I'll be there in ten minutes."

"No rush, take your time," he said. "Like I said, we have all day."

"Cat ears?" I asked, looking at the item Laurant handed to me. "This doesn't seem like much of a disguise."

"It's a magical item," he explained. "It will change your hair and eye color, which is how most people will probably identify you. Look, events that give out items like this happen every couple weeks, this is just what I happened to find on short notice. But if that item works on you like I think it will, then everybody will think that you're just a kid playing a game with his older brother. Worst case is that they think I'm a pervert or something, but that shouldn't be a problem. Arc Inc. comes down pretty hard on predators they find grooming kids in their games, and you can't hide that shit from their system."

"I don't know what that means," I told him.

"Don't worry about it. Try it on, let's see if it works."

Shrugging, I put the headband with the cat ears on. I didn't feel any different, but when I looked down, I noticed that I had an illusory tail. "How do I look?"

Laurant produced a mirror with a grin, and I was surprised to see that my silver and black hair had turned orange to match my ears and tail, and that my eyes were green. Laurant equipped his own headband, and his own hair turned to the coloring of a black and tan tabby cat.

"Now then, let's go see about getting you some better gear than that level one starting crap."

Adventurer's Clothes	
Requires Level 5	
Armor	7
Vitality	1
Endurance	1

Adventurer's Short Bow	
Requires Level 5	
Damage Rating	F+ (ranged)
Dexterity	2

Adventurer's Short Sword	
Requires Level 5	
Damage Rating	D
Strength	1
Dexterity	1

The new gear was a significant upgrade for me. According to Laurant, Travelers always upgraded their gear every five levels until they started finding rare and magical gear during their adventures. You didn't have to upgrade, but doing so made a substantial difference in both Damage and survivability, so the only people who didn't were the ones who either couldn't afford it or didn't know any better. I had never really thought about it before.

Fortunately, I had recouped the gold that had been stolen from me by Severus, and the upgraded items were only a handful of silver for the full set. I also bought, at Laurant's recommendation, a few dozen Health and Mana potions, which I popped into my [Storage]. After about an hour of shopping, I followed Laurant out of the city and into the grasslands beyond. After a quick jog, we entered a forest, and I saw my first slime.

"So, I could just power level you like we were before," Laurant informed me, "but I think it would be better if I just watched for now. I'll step in if you get in over your head, but they're just slimes. Looks like they're all between levels two and four, so you should be able to just blow through them. Just don't get in the middle of a group of them, or you'll get swarmed."

"Right," I agreed, drawing my sword and facing off against the slimes, which were lazily minding their own business, slowly absorbing and digesting the grass of the meadow. And I sort of realized that I didn't really know what I was doing.

I'd been trained with a sword, but there was a fundamental difference between sparring with another boy and facing off against a slime that only came up to my knees. My form felt unsuited to the task. I could just charge and start hacking at them, but then I had a better idea. I began chanting under my breath.

The flash of lightning struck the nearest slime directly, aggravating it. It shifted and came towards me, but I was still casting. A second [Lightning Bolt] caused the slime to explode, leaving behind puddles of digestive fluids and the slime nucleus. Grinning, I began chain-casting, blowing up slime after slime until I hit my twelfth cast of [Lightning Bolt] and it failed. Frowning, I realized that I had run through my entire Mana pool, with only 7/700 remaining. Seven hundred had seemed like so much when I looked at my status screen, but my only Damage spell was apparently a Mana hog.

And I had three slimes charging me. One was scorched by my final successful cast, but the others had simply been angered by the disturbance I caused. I glanced at Laurant, but he was just leaning on his bow, scratching his nose as he watched. Realizing that he wasn't planning on interfering unless I got into trouble, I braced myself, returning to the stance that had been drilled into me for endless hours.

I charged the injured slime, piercing its nucleus and causing it to burst. Unfortunately, that put me between the two others, and they both jumped at me, slamming into me and leaving behind a tingling bit of acid Damage as their digestive fluid rubbed off on me. I glanced nervously at my Health pool and realized that I had lost thirty-two Damage from one of them bumping into me, and I had gained a debuff, which was costing me eight Health points every three seconds.

At level one, when my Health was only ninety, that would have been frightening. But with the levels I'd gained, the Damage from the slime just put me at 560/600, and the debuff would wear off in another twelve seconds.

Knowing that my sergeant would have scolded me for getting flanked like I was, I rolled to get out from between the slimes and spun around to face them again once I'd gotten some distance. The one on the left jumped at me first, and I brought my sword up in a slash to counter. The metal almost cut the monster in half, but I missed the nucleus. The half without the nucleus slushed to the ground, inert, while the other half recovered and reformed itself, minus the mass that it had lost.

Taking the opportunity, I lashed after the uninjured slime, [Slashing] five times in as many seconds until I had cut it to pieces, including one cut that had gone halfway through the nucleus. It oozed into the grass, defeated.

I spun back to the one I had bisected just in time to catch it in a jump again. Once again, I swung fiercely at it, this time cutting the nucleus in two. It splashed to the ground, dead.

I collapsed to my knees, exhausted. I had two seconds left on my debuff, the entire fight after running out of Mana had lasted less than half a minute, but it had been the longest half a minute of my life. I glanced at my Health and winced. I was fine at 536/600. But at level one, I would have been at 26/90 instead, and I had only been hit once.

"You okay? I saw one touched you. You're not weak to acid or something, are you?" Laurant asked.

"I think everyone is weak to acid. And fire and lightning and frost, for that matter," I pointed out.

"Well, unless they have some sort of resistance to it, yeah," Laurant said, chuckling. "Seriously, you okay, little guy? You did well, but now you look exhausted."

"I feel exhausted, but I'm okay. I've just never been in a fight like that before. When you were helping me gain Experience the other day, I was just fighting from a distance and letting you do all the killing. This was different. I don't know how to explain it," I said.

"Right. Well, I have some feedback. First of all, you shouldn't have burned through all your magic like that. If you want to be a spell caster, that's fine. We can go back to town and get you some robes and a staff that will increase your Mana regen and spell power. Maybe even some spell books to teach you something other than [Lightning Bolt]. But you've got to learn to manage your Mana. If you're going to be a [Mage], that means before you attack, make sure you have enough in the tank to defeat whatever it is that you're pulling, plus whatever might attack you aside from the primary target," Laurant explained.

"Oh. Yeah, I sort of got carried away, didn't I?" I said, feeling a little embarrassed.

"It's not a big deal. A real [Mage] will generally keep their Mana up above seventy percent while they're soloing, and above fifty percent in groups. They only dip below that in 'oh shit' moments where they get unexpected aggro, or boss fights, or general screwups. Their burst Damage is extremely high, but they spend more time on [Meditation] to regenerate their Mana than they do attacking."

"I guess that makes sense. My Mana has only gained twelve points since I ran out," I said.

"When Thena or Larissa log back on, have them teach you [Meditation]. It's an active skill that increases your Mana regen," he told me. "Until then, maybe only use magic to pull a slime, then finish it off with your sword? Go ahead and swallow one of your mana potions for now so that we can keep moving."

"Okay," I agreed, and I pulled one out of my [Storage] to do just that, wincing at the bitter taste. It gave me four hundred Mana, though, which was enough to keep going.

Following Laurant's advice, I began killing slimes in earnest, casting [Lightning Bolt] occasionally to pull the slimes towards me, but often I would simply charge in with my sword. Because of the nature of slimes, my arrows weren't very useful, as they neither shaved off slices of the slimes' gelatinous bodies, nor was I accurate enough with them to pierce their cores consistently.

I only gained about four to twelve Experience per kill, which was not that great, but the slimes were endless. It took me an hour to gain a level, although that was not my only gains. Unfortunately, when I hit level six, I was in for a surprise.

8
RECALL POINT

"Display Status!" I called eagerly, after putting down the slime that put me over the threshold of level six.

Name	Hail Teoran	Level	6
Guild	<Nethersong Mavericks>		
Health	452/720	Strength	13
Mana	324/900	Dexterity	14
Experience	3/1200	Vitality	12
Age	10	Endurance	14
Race	Human (blood of the Travelers)	Intelligence	15
Class	Child	Wisdom	12
Job	Bastard of Yuikon	Charisma	18
Skills	Short Swords (8)	Armor	7
	Archery (5)	Spells	Cure Minor Injury (8)
	Short Spears (5)		Detect Poison (12)

	Animal Handling (4)			Spark (6)
	Balance and Conditioning (5)			Analyze (3)
	Quickshot (3)			Storage (5)
Traits	High Aptitude			Lightning Bolt (6)
	Quick Learner			Mark of Karma (special)
	Royal Blood (+5 Charisma, bonus to relations with factions loyal to Yuikon)			
	Blessing of Thedum			
	Mark of the Phoenix (hidden)			
	Voice of the Future (hidden)			

"Did you get your level?" Laurant asked.

"Yeah," I said, "but something is wrong."

"What's that?"

"It says I need twelve hundred Experience for the next level. Before, each level required one hundred more than the previous one. But now it's doubled."

"Oh, yeah. You're in the second level bracket now," Laurant explained. "The equation for calculating Experience requirements is your current level times one hundred times your level bracket. Bracket one is levels one through five, bracket two is six through ten, bracket three is eleven through fifteen, and so forth."

"I've only been getting about five or six Experience per slime! It's going to take forever to get to level ten," I complained.

"Well, yeah, but that's only if we keep fighting slimes," Laurant said, grinning. "Honestly, I only brought you out here to see how you handled yourself. And because it's on the way to our real destination. I figured we'd be out of the way, since most noobs come out of the tutorial at level three and do quests until level eight or so. Not that low-level questing is much faster than pure grinding, but it helps them explore the starting zones and get their Recall Points set."

"Recall Points?" I asked.

"It's another player thing. We can quickly return to some place we've been before, as long as there's a portal stone or Nexus Point nearby. There's eight Recall Points in the city, and usually one for every quest hub—I mean, every town, village, or outpost throughout the world. I wonder if you can use them too?"

"I don't know, I've never left the castle before the other day," I admitted. "How do they work?"

"For us, it's under the 'map' tab, under the 'travel' menu. I don't know how it works for—"

"Found it," I said. "It says that the only Recall Point I have is in the castle."

"Really? That's great. We'll work on getting those set up for you later," Laurant said. "That will make leveling you much faster and easier. But for now, we're off to [Gemos Caverns]."

"What's that?"

"It's an early dungeon. Levels six through ten. I can enter, but it will restrict the Damage I do so that it's on par with what a normal player could put out at that level. I've got a party all set up and ready for us, they were just waiting for you to gain a level."

"Do you really think I'm ready for a dungeon?" I asked nervously.

"It'll be fine. We're planning on basically carrying you for now. Even if you can't do much Damage to the Gemos golems, the rest of the party will take care of them, and you'll still get your share of the Experience. It's pretty common for low-level players to get carried by their higher-leveled friends like this. Although from what I've seen, you won't exactly be getting carried. You've got moves, kid. You're better than about ninety percent of noobs I've seen," Laurant praised.

"Um, thanks, I think."

"I'm going to invite the other party members now, okay?"

"Sure."

| Sellamander has joined the party. |
| Potatoad has joined the party. |
| Peafowlet has joined the party. |

"On my way," a disembodied male voice said.

"Heading to dungeon now," a second agreed.

"Hey Hail, I'm Pea. I'm looking forward to seeing you in action," a female voice said. I was looking around for their sources before I realized that it was "partychat."

"Um, hello everyone. Where are you guys?"

"We'll meet up with them in a few minutes," Laurant promised. "It's not far to the dungeon. There's a Return Point just outside, so they'll beat us there if we don't hurry."

With that, we took off running through the woods. The forest ended and we entered a hilly region, and in the bottom of the glen there was a stone pillar outside of a cavern. Three Travelers were there waiting for us, two men and a woman.

"Hi Hail, I'm Sellamander, the druid financier," one man said; an older, bald gentleman dressed in leather armor.

"I'm Potatoad. I punch stuff," the other man said. He looked like he was in his late twenties, but it was hard to tell. He wore studded armor with a cesti equipped on his hands. "You actually went ahead with the Neko-Kun idea, Laurant? I thought that was a joke."

"We needed a disguise," Laurant said in self-defense.

"Call me Pea," the woman said. She wore dark leather armor, with a pair of long daggers hanging from her hips. "I'm a [Rogue]. We're running without a tank, but that's normal for [Gemos Caverns]. It's meant for new players to get their feet wet, but it's not too dangerous as long as you have a healer. If you get into any trouble, just run over to Sellsalot and he'll heal you up."

"Um, hello everyone. It's nice to meet you. I'm really looking forward to seeing what a dungeon is like," I said.

Almost in unison, the Travelers got a far off look in their eyes.

"Oh yeah! Dungeon quest, rewards Reputation and Variable, just like last time," Laurant said enthusiastically.

"Same here," Sellamander agreed. "Looks like we just have to kill the final boss with him in the party. Should be easy. I wonder if he'll generate a quest for every dungeon we bring him to."

"The real question is what the Variable reward is," Potatoad countered.

"I hope it's something unique. Unique means valuable," Sellamander said.

"Guys, do you have to talk like that right in front of him? We're supposed to treat him like another player, remember?" Peafowlet objected.

"Right. Sorry Hail, I just got a little excited," Sellamander apologized.

"Sorry," Potatoad agreed.

"Never mind them, Hail. The boys have a very low Ee Queue."

"Ee Queue? Is that a stat?" I inquired.

"It's like a substat of Charisma," she answered.

"Oh. My Charisma is my highest stat, it's at eighteen right now, although I get a bonus to it because of my royal blood," I said.

"That's great, Hail," Pea said, smiling patiently.

"That pillar is a Recall Point, Hail. See if you can bind yourself to it," Laurant suggested.

"What do I do?" I asked.

"You just touch it."

So, I went and touched the pillar.

Gemos Caverns Recall Point has been added to Fast Travel destinations.

"I think it worked," I said. "How do I tell for sure?"

"Well, you could return to your other Recall Point and come back," Laurant said, "But let's wait until after—"

A current of wild magic swept me away before he could finish talking, because I had already selected to return home.

The transference was not instantaneous. I had a vague sensation of moving very quickly, although my vision was obscured by what looked like vibrant paints of every color blended together in a psychedelic pattern. It was actually a vaguely pleasant sensation.

The world quickly reformed itself as I materialized back in my bedroom, next to my bed.

"It worked!" I shouted.

"Hail? I was about to say that let's wait until we finish with the dungeon because there's a thirty-minute cooldown on Fast Travel," Laurant informed me through partychat.

"There is?" I asked.

"Yes. And now the rest of us are stuck waiting for your timer to finish before we can start," Potatoad grumbled.

"Don't talk to him like that," Pea scolded. "It's not his fault."

"It's a noob mistake," the pugilist argued.

"Exactly. We're supposed to be treating him like he's an actual kid from our world playing this game for the first time," Pea said. "If you had a little brother make this mistake, what would you do?"

"Probably call him a noob and tease him until he could port back," Potatoad admitted. "But whatever. I'll just surf the forums until we're ready to go again."

"At least it's thirty minutes in game, and not thirty minutes Eye Are El," Sellamander's disembodied voice said.

"It's still five minutes that I'm never getting back, and it will feel like a lot more than that," Potatoad grumbled.

"I'm really sorry guys," I said.

"Don't apologize to him, he's just a misanthrope. The rest of us understand, Hail. Anyway, it's my fault more than yours. I basically told you to do it," Laurant pointed out. "This is a learning process for everyone in the guild."

"It's so weird that he doesn't know how this stuff works already," Potatoad whispered.

"Dude, he's still in the party, he can hear you," Sellamander whispered back.

"Shit. Muting myself."

"Alright everyone, do whatever you want until Hail's cooldown is up. I'm setting a timer."

A small icon appeared in the lower right corner of my vision with numbers counting down.

"How did you do that?" I asked.

"I just created a timer and shared it with the party. It's under the Utilities menu," Laurant answered. "Any player can access it from the main menu. Not sure how it works for you though, or if it even does."

"Display Menu," I said, and a list of options popped up. I was shocked at how many there were. With inquisitive glee, I began exploring the system.

"You have to look at it from my perspective. I'm a leader of one of the top five hundred guilds, and I was being offered something that appeared to be a significant resource drain. I had a split-second decision whether to accept or decline the quest. I wasn't expecting the king to take things so far as to annul my marriage to Princess

Analise and declare Hail a bastard. That was a complete surprise," my father was saying.

"So, you're saying that you regret declining the quest?" a disembodied voice said. They couldn't hear me, I realized. The "video" I was watching was from the "forums" I had discovered under the menu. The title of the thread was "<The Endolphins'> response to the Hail controversy."

"Absolutely, but I stand by my decision. I simply don't have the time necessary to maintain my raid schedule and raise an En Pee See from level one to two hundred by myself. And to be honest, I'm a little relieved to relinquish my official status as a canon character in the world. It was pretty cool being able to throw my official weight around in the days after marrying into the royal family, but it limited me in endgame," he said. "Raising Hail isn't the only quest that I was forced to decline because the resources required to complete it simply weren't worth the rewards. The other canon players will back me up on this. Being part of the story of this world is hard work, and we're not paid a dime for it. In fact, I figure that me and my guild have probably spent somewhere around a hundred and twenty thousand dollars worth of game resources that we haven't been able to recoup in support of my role in the story."

"What do you say to those who are criticizing you for child abandonment?" the disembodied voice asked.

"I'll remind them that this is a game, and that Hail is just an En Pee See," he said. "I don't have any children. Hail is just an advanced Aye Eye with a few unique features to distinguish him from the other Natives. I mean, if you're going to criticize me for abandoning a bunch of ones and zeroes, then you need to lock up everyone who has ever completed a quest for the assassin's guild and charge them with murder, right?"

The voice and my father both had a laugh at that, although I didn't see what was so funny. The assassin's guild was the reason I had to cast [Detect Poison] on everything I ate or drank. They *killed people* for a living. They should be locked up or executed. And the idea that Travelers worked for them was very troubling to me.

"What do you have to say about <Nethersong Mavericks> snagging this opportunity? How do you think things will go for them?" the voice asked.

"It's early, but honestly, I think that it will end up destroying their guild before too long. Either Hail will prove to be a goldsink that will bankrupt them, or he'll prove to be full of unique opportunities and someone will take him away from them. Either way, I think that Hail will wind up with one of the other super guilds," Father predicted. "I mean them no offense, but the Mavericks are just a small-time social guild, right? As I understand it, they just happened to get lucky once the 'run away from home' event started. I think they should have taken the griffons instead."

"That's rather grim," the voice commented.

"Yes, well, endgame is ruthless. And maybe I'm wrong. The truth is that I wish those kids luck. But realistically, I don't give them good odds. Being part of the story of this world is difficult. Believe me. I would know."

"Thank you for answering my questions. For all of you tuning in, this is Gaem Frak with Gideon Lachlann, raid lead of <The Endolphins>. Please like and subscribe—"

My father disappeared to show some random person sitting behind a desk, and I lost interest and closed the video. I had learned quite quickly how to navigate the forums, and I scrolled down to read the reactions of the other Travelers who had watched the video. The responses ranged from calling my father a deadbeat to saying that he was right and that I was being over-hyped.

Understanding how to use the forum was easy, but the Travelers using it were largely incomprehensible. It didn't take me very long to figure out how to leave a reply, and so after opening the reply tab and checking speech-to-text, I began to speak.

"Having my father reject me was the most upsetting experience in my life. I'll never understand why he didn't want me, but the only thing I can think of is to prove to the world that he made a mistake. I'm going to reach level two hundred with my new friends, and then I'm going to—"

"What are you saying, Hail?" Pea asked.

"What? Oh, I'm posting on the forums."

"You can do that?"

"I think so. I'm about to try. I'm pretty sure I just have to will it to submit. Yup, there it . . . oh, it added the stuff I said to you. Weird."

Laurant began to laugh. "Oh man. What thread did you post in, Hail?"

"It was the one with my father talking about why he rejected me," I answered.

"Since when have you been able to do that, Hail?" Pea asked. "Browse the forums, I mean."

"I think I've always been able to, I just didn't know it," I answered. "I'm learning so much since I started interacting with you Travelers."

"Can you access the internet aside from the game forums?" she inquired.

"I don't know. What's the internet?"

"Don't answer that," Potatoad interjected. "The last thing we want is him going SkyNet on us."

"Don't be stupid," Sellamander chided. "The blue post said that he had all of the capabilities of a player, and players are able to access the in-game forums only."

"Well guys, his post has been noticed, and it's starting to blow up," Laurant said. "It will be interesting to see how things play out."

"Hey, Hail, just so you know, don't take the forums too seriously. There are a lot of trolls on there. Trolls like Severus, who will do or say things that are bad or false just to get a reaction," Pea informed me. "It makes them happy when they make other people angry or upset. They feed off the attention, and the only way to combat them is to just ignore them."

"Um, okay. I don't really understand. The forum is easy to use, but a lot of things you Travelers say don't really make sense to me," I admitted.

"Try running 'two hundred years of pop culture references and internet jargon dot Ee Ex Ee,'" Potatoad suggested.

"Ignore him, he's being a jerk," Pea told me. "Potatoad can be a bit of a troll sometimes too, but he's the mildly annoying sort, not the actively destructive kind. But don't worry, we'll keep him in line."

"Was my father being a troll when he said those things about me?" I asked.

"No. In that video he was running damage control," Laurant informed me. "He is not happy—"

The door to my room opened, and a maid came in with an arm full of linens. She looked at me for a second while Laurant was talking, blinked, and then dropped her load and went running from the room screaming "Guards! Intruder! Guards!"

I sat for a moment in confusion after scaring off the maid. I didn't understand it, I'd seen her every day since she'd been hired three years ago. She knew me, and she knew this was my room. Fortunately, the timer on my Fast Travel went off at that moment, and I whooped and activated it, going to my only other Recall Point, [Gemos Caverns].

9

DASH AND DODGE

"Finally!" Potatoad exclaimed when I appeared from the kaleidoscope tunnel. "Let's get this started."

"That was strange," I commented, thinking of the maid's reaction to seeing me in my own room. But I wasn't too concerned about it. "Anyway, I'm really sorry about slowing everyone down."

"It's not that big of a deal, Hail," Laurant assured me. "Thirty minutes game time is only about five minutes real time. We could have just returned to the lobby for a little while to make the time fly faster, but we were reading up on the forums while we waited as well."

"Yeah. It's weird how popular he is," Sellamander said.

"It's the blue post. Most of the people talking about him don't know a thing about him except for that and the rumors," Pea said. "And the fact that he's kind of cute helps too."

"See, if I said that, I'd be called a pervert," Potatoad pointed out.

"You are a pervert," Pea countered.

"Yeah, but not like that. I'm just pointing out if a guy calls a kid cute everyone automatically assumes the worst, but women can say pretty much whatever they want," Potatoad said.

"Um, dude, you don't want to go down this track. It leads nowhere that doesn't look bad for you," Sellamander said, putting a hand on Potatoad's shoulder.

"Whatever. Let's clear the dungeon and see if the hype about him is justified or not," the pugilist said, shaking off the druid's hand.

I followed the others into the cave next to the Recall Point pillars. The walls were limestone of various colors and patterns, but the most striking feature was the threshold of swirling motes a few yards inside. I thought at first that my friends didn't see it and was about to warn them, but they walked through one by one, each disappearing as soon as they touched the swirling motes. I jumped in surprise; I had never seen such a thing!

"Don't worry, Hail, it's just the dungeon entrance," Pea assured me. She took my hand and led me through. I followed, nervously, but the moment I stepped into the swirling lights my friends on the other side reappeared.

You have entered a unique instance of Gemos Caverns. Unique first-time clear bonus available. Difficulty has been adjusted. Would you like to continue?	
Yes	No

Without really thinking about it I selected "Yes". There wasn't any noticeable difference between the cavern outside the dungeon entrance, except that as we got further from the entrance, luminescent moss began to illuminate the cavern as we moved away from the sunlight. The moss was not the only source of light. Littered through the caverns were crystals the size of a fist, each attached to a boulder or the wall or ceiling.

"Are those crystals valuable?" I asked. "They're much brighter than candles. Do they shine forever?"

"Not exactly, to both questions," Laurant answered. "Observe."

He took his bow and shot the nearest crystal. To my surprise, rather than bouncing off, the crystal cracked, and a large boulder fell from the wall.

Except the boulder wasn't a boulder, I realized. It began moving, and I gave out a startled little cry.

"It's fine, don't worry," Pea assured me, chuckling slightly. "That's what we've come here for. Each crystal is a Gemos golem. The gem is its weak point. The stone body is invulnerable, but the gem breaks pretty easily. You'd think they'd be worth something to the En Pee Sees, but they're not lootable."

The golem made its ponderous way towards us. It certainly wasn't very fast, and it was unlike any animal I'd ever seen. It walked on three legs and had four arms surrounding an oblong body with no head or eyes or mouth or anything. And as it moved, I realized that the distinction between its limbs being legs or arms wasn't as clear cut as I thought, as it occasionally shifted its weight and used one of its arms as a leg.

"They're tough, but they're slow," Laurant explained. "That's why we don't need a tank. Unfortunately, they're not entirely stupid either. See how it's hiding its core from me? It knows I'm ranged."

"You do not want to get hit by these guys," Sellamander informed me. "Getting grappled is even worse though, and they're not above crushing you with their bodies either. In fact, that's their most dangerous move, but if it happens, I should still be able to heal you through it, as long as you weren't low on Health to begin with."

"Right," I said seriously. "So how do we kill it?"

"It's pretty simple. We just surround it and attack the crystal when it appears next to us. These golems are basically training dummies to teach you how to move, coordinate with a group, and exploit the weaknesses of your enemies. You can just watch for the first kill to see how we do it," Laurant said.

The party encircled the Gemos as it ponderously moved towards Laurant, who retreated back towards the dungeon entrance. The other three spread out and encircled it, with Pea darting in behind it to attack the golem's core with her [Daggers]. The Gemos reacted by swinging one of its heavy limbs at her in retaliation, and she jumped back. The golem began to chase after her, but Potatoad darted in from its flank and gave the core a quick one-two combo with his cesti before he darted back as well. When the golem turned to face the pugilist, the core entered Laurant's line of sight, and he was ready for it, quickly launching three arrows in a row before the golem could recover.

It took almost two full minutes of fighting like this before the gem shattered and the Gemos golem collapsed, its rocky body turning to black mist and evaporating. Even Sellamander the druid had gotten in on attacking the core with a sickle when the monster had exposed its core to him, even though he was supposedly the healer of the group.

"There, just like that," Laurant said, waving away the mist that got in his face. "Do you think you can handle that, Hail, or would you like to watch for a few more pulls?"

"I can handle it," I said, determined to prove myself. "It doesn't look too difficult."

"We're making it look easy," Potatoad bragged. "This dungeon is the bane of noobs. All of us have been playing this game for weeks of real time, or we all have experience with other Vee Are games before we started."

"I can do it," I repeated.

"Okay then. Stand over here about six feet to my left, and cast your [Lightning Bolt] at the next golem. I'll shoot it at the same time. It will probably still chase me first, because even though I'm level capped in this place, I'm capped at level ten with gear to match. Once it starts attacking, it's up to you whether to close in or stay back, although I think you'll do the most damage with your sword. Just do whatever feels natural to you, I guess."

"Okay," I agreed, and I began casting.

My spell lit up the cave as it slammed into the nearest golem. Its core changed from a faint green to a light blue, and its boulder-like body detached from the wall. Laurant unleashed three arrows in rapid succession, each hitting the mark with a *thunk* before the golem managed to angle its core away from us. It began charging after Laurant, but once again Pea slipped in behind it and savaged the core before being forced back by a wild swing of its powerful but misshapen limbs.

This one was different than the first one, I realized, with four legs and six arms, two of which were on top and not particularly well-placed for combat. That is, until the monster shifted onto its side, hiding the core and making it difficult for the melee party members to reach it.

Except that I could still see it. And if I could see it, then I could blast it! So, I did, quickly casting [Lightning Bolt] a second time.

The monster again shifted its weight, rolling to a new angle to hide the core from my magic. Unfortunately, that put it back in range for Laurant again, and he took full advantage of it, pelting the core with three arrows before it shattered, and the monster turned to mist.

"Lame, I didn't even get to do anything," Potatoad complained.

"It's not my fault you were too slow to get a hit in," Laurant scolded. "Anyway, this is just the entrance. It will get more exciting once the double-and triple-core mobs start appearing. Hail, go ahead and pull the next one, same thing as before."

"Right," I said, and began chanting.

The third Gemos we killed was smaller than the others, but it was significantly faster. With three legs and a limb where its head should have been, it bounced around like a caltrop. I was a little nervous to get close to it, and the others seemed to be feeling cautious as well, which meant that it took significantly longer to kill than the big guy.

On the fifth monster, I was feeling confident enough to dash in with my sword when I saw an opening. Unfortunately, I was a bit slow, and the massive golem hit me in the chest with its leg as it changed angles again, knocking me to the ground.

"Oof," I called, and glanced at my Health. I winced; I was at 498/730. That one hit could have killed me two and a half times at level one. The pain lessened three seconds later, and I felt a rush of vital energy fill my body as Sellamander hit me with a potent healing spell, immediately healing half of the Damage I'd suffered and leaving behind a refreshing heal-over-time effect.

"Are you okay?" Pea asked, dodging the swing with ease and alacrity as the monster's core turned towards her next and she expertly exploited the opportunity.

"I'm fine. I just . . . three days ago, that would have killed me," I said, somewhat shaken. "I've spent most of my life with less than one hundred Health, and he just hit me for more than double that. That's scary."

"All the more reason to level up, right?" Sellamander said. "Although it does raise an interesting question. What happens if we wipe?"

"We're not going to wipe," Laurant declared sternly. "We're going to be overly cautious and raise him slow and steady like. I'm fairly certain that we can rez him if we need to, but it's better not to take a chance."

"Yeah, I know," Sellamander sighed, as Potatoad dashed in and landed the killing blow on the crystal. "Don't worry too much about taking a hit here or there, Hail. This is a learning dungeon, and the biggest thing it's supposed to teach you is how to move and [Dodge] enemies. If you take another hit, just back off until I heal you to full again. These golems hit hard, but I can heal you through the worst of the Damage they do, don't worry."

"You gotta learn to be dodging and weaving," Potatoad said, taking up a fighting stance and shadowboxing while making exaggerated [Dodges]. "If you can't learn to do that, then there's not much point in playing this game."

"It's not a game to me," I reminded them. "This is my life."

There was a slight pause, then the pugilist snorted. "That's all the more reason to git gud, little man."

Realizing that he was right, I refocused and quickly pulled the next golem, catching the others by surprise with my enthusiasm. I put my faith in Sellamander to keep me alive and really focused on trying to contribute to killing these monsters. The basic strategy was simple: I would lead with [Lightning Bolt] and Laurant would follow up on the pull with his arrows. His damage was usually enough to pull the golems' attention away from me and onto him, allowing me to safely approach. At some point, Pea or Potatoad would ambush the monster from behind, and it would turn to face them, allowing me, Laurant, or even Sellamander a chance to hit the core from the other side.

I took some hits in the beginning, but pain is a great teacher, and I quickly began to improve. At some point, something seemed to simply click in the way I was moving, and a popup confirmed my achievement, although the distraction nearly caused me to take another hit.

| You have learned a new skill: Dodge |
| You have learned a new skill: Dash |

I grinned at the achievement and redoubled my efforts to slay my earthen foes. In fact, I might have been trying to show off a little. Together, my new abilities greatly increased my ability in combat.

"You're doing so much better. You've really improved a lot in the last five pulls, Hail," Pea praised when we finished one chamber. "Did you learn a movement skill? It seems like you've been zipping around much quicker."

"Yup. Two of them. Display Status, Public," I said.

Name	Hail Teoran	Level	6
Guild	<Nethersong Mavericks>		
Health	720/720	Strength	13
Mana	723/900	Dexterity	14
Experience	783/1200	Vitality	12
Age	10	Endurance	14
Race	Human (blood of the Travelers)	Intelligence	15
Class	Child	Wisdom	12
Job	Bastard of Yuikon	Charisma	18
Skills	Short Swords (8)	Armor	7
	Archery (5)	Spells	Cure Minor Injury (8)
	Short Spears (5)		Detect Poison (12)
	Animal Handling (4)		Spark (6)
	Balance and Conditioning (5)		Analyze (3)
	Quickshot (3)		Storage (5)
	Dodge (1)		Lightning Bolt (7)
	Dash (1)		Mark of Karma (special)
Traits	High Aptitude		
	Quick Learner		
	Royal Blood (+5 Charisma, bonus to relations with factions loyal to Yuikon)		
	Blessing of Thedum		
	(hidden)		
	(hidden)		

"[Dodge] and [Dash], right? How do they work?" Laurant inquired.

"[Dash] is an active, it lets me move quickly up to five feet in any direction," I explained. "[Dodge] is a passive, but it increases my awareness of incoming attacks and helps me figure out how to avoid them. I think I learned them from watching Pea and Potatoad."

"Well, they've definitely made a difference. Keep focusing on leveling up those skills, I think you're going to need them," Laurant predicted. "Because things get more difficult the farther in we go. I hope you're ready."

10

BOSS FIGHT

Laurant's prediction proved to be accurate. In the next chamber we entered, the crystals were twice the size as the one before, and the Gemos golems had four times as much Health. They didn't hit any harder; I learned that the hard way despite having [Dodge] and [Dash]. They took longer to kill, but they really weren't any more dangerous than they were before, and it was good Experience. I gained a few points in my new skills, as well as my [Short Swords] skill and [Lightning Bolt].

We fell into a pattern, working together intuitively and quickly clearing chamber after chamber as we moved deeper into the caverns. More importantly, the golems gave increased Experience, and it wasn't too long before I gained level seven, and then level eight. Except for a slight increase in stats, though, it didn't make much difference. I did go from doing a quarter of the other party members' Damage to about a third, but I still felt like I was being carried.

"Don't worry about it, Hail, you're doing great," Pea assured me when I voiced my concern.

"Yeah. It's mostly gear anyway. All our stuff is scaled down to level ten, but we're still wearing uncommon or rare items, while your gear is just common items you bought from a vendor," Laurant pointed out.

"Honestly, it might be better if we weren't overgeared for this," Sellamander suggested. "He's learning more from the actual combat than a normal player. We should slow Dee Pee Ess to see if he learns more from longer fights."

Laurant frowned, then shook his head. "I've got class coming up, and we still have two thirds of the dungeon to clear if we're going to get the full clear for the quest. If anything, we need to speed up, not slow down."

"Yeah, I don't have all day either," Potatoad agreed. "And the dual-core area's coming up. Those are a pain if you do things slow."

"Dual-core?" I asked.

"They're golems with two cores instead of one. When you break one core, the golem actually speeds up, making it more difficult. The Damage is the same, though, so you'll be safe with Sella around," Pea explained. "After that we'll start facing a mix of dual-core and triple-core golems. Then the final boss, which has five cores, in the bottom of the dungeon."

"Oh," I said, growing a little nervous. "Is the final boss hard?"

"It's more difficult than facing two dual-cores at once. Actually, if you're unlucky, then you'll end up doing exactly that; when you break the first core there's about a thirty percent chance that the boss will split into two. But there's a trick to all of the multi-core golems: you damage the cores equally until they're all about to break, then break them at the same time," Laurant explained. "But don't worry about that too much. We'll keep track of actually killing things, you just focus on improving your skills, okay Hail? Do as much damage as you can while keeping yourself safe, just like you have been."

"Okay," I agreed.

We moved into the next chamber, and the dual-cores proved to be as difficult as promised. However, they also gave significantly more Experience than even the large core Gemos golems had, and before we reached the triple-core, I reached level nine. I hadn't looked at my status for a while, I realized, and I quickly called it up.

Name	Hail Teoran	Level	9
Guild	<Nethersong Mavericks>		
Health	1260/1260	Strength	14

Mana	685/1620	Dexterity	17
Experience	31/1800	Vitality	14
Age	10	Endurance	15
Race	Human (blood of the Travelers)	Intelligence	18
Class	Child	Wisdom	14
Job	Bastard of Yuikon	Charisma	20
Skills	Short Swords (11)	Spells	Cure Minor Injury (8)
	Archery (5)		Detect Poison (12)
	Short Spears (5)		Spark (6)
	Animal Handling (4)		Analyze (3)
	Balance and Conditioning (8)		Storage (5)
	Quickshot (3)		Lightning Bolt (9)
	Dodge (6)		Mark of Karma (special)
	Dash (4)		
Traits	(Focus to Expand)		

"Wow, I have so much Health now," I commented. "And my stats are so much higher than they were."

"Yeah, but higher-level monsters hit harder too, and they have more Health as well, which means that you still need to be careful," Laurant reminded me.

"Oh, I know. Just because I won't get killed in one hit doesn't mean that getting attacked is fun," I agreed.

The triple-core area was tricky because they really did speed up quite a bit if you destroyed two of the cores. It made me a little nervous about taking on the final boss. More than once I was told to ignore a core despite having a perfect window to attack it, because the others didn't want to break it early and make the fight more difficult. I bowed to their wisdom as best as I was able.

I was taking hits again, but everyone was. Sellamander had backed off from using his sickle in melee range and was healing full-time now. Fortunately, the monsters never seemed to notice that he was the reason we never gave in despite how much Damage we took. Both the triple-core golems and the two-golem pulls were quite difficult to the point where I think even the veteran Travelers were challenged, although perhaps not straining themselves as I was. With struggle came growth, however, and I was enthusiastic to continue.

Finally, we cleared everything except the passage that the others said led to the boss's chamber. We paused for a few minutes so that Sellamander and I could regenerate Mana. The others weren't dependent upon Mana, which meant they were just waiting for us, but it wasn't worth drinking a potion.

"Don't be too nervous, Hail, you're doing awesome. Seriously, if I would have brought some random kid from our world here, they wouldn't have made it past the first room before giving up," Laurant praised. "Most kids who play this game stick to the low-skill zones."

"Low-skill zones?"

"Yeah. You know, like that goblin lair, or the slimes outside. There's nothing wrong with grinding there, but the thing that makes them good for grinding is how easy they are to kill. [Gemos Caverns] is a medium-skill zone. Or a full clear is, at least. A lot of parties just clear the first few rooms and reset," Laurant explained.

"Why would they do that?" I asked.

"Because it's pretty fast Experience per hour," he answered. "Honestly, that's what we were planning on doing, but then you gave us a quest to do a full clear instead."

"Typically, players do one single full clear of this place and then never again," Sellamander explained. "The only reason they even clear it once is because it's one of the best-known early game skill checks. But players usually don't do that until they're level fifty or higher. The game still restricts them down to level ten, which is part of the skill check as it's seen as the great equalizer."

"Yup, it doesn't matter how much cash you dump into the game getting mid- or high-level rare gear. I've heard of people in raid gear getting out Dee Pee Est by scrubs with mismatched uncommon world drops in here," Potatoad agreed. "I hate to admit it, but if the kid had some better gear and some accessories, he'd probably be keeping up with all of us."

Pea snorted. "Says third place."

"Whatever," Potatoad said.

We entered the cavern of the final boss. The bioluminescent moss was particularly dense in this room, and the boss was waiting for us in the center of the room, a large collection of boulders with the crystals protruding.

"Remember Hail, this is a marathon, not a sprint. Don't burn through your Mana all at the beginning of the fight. It's more important for you to avoid Damage than to inflict it," Laurant advised. "This fight might take ten minutes or more. Which means that we need to fight conservatively. No risky [Dashes], and no last second [Dodges] to land an extra strike."

"Right," I agreed. I was feeling quite nervous, but also very excited. I was about to clear my first dungeon!

"Okay, we might as well start it off right. Hail, pull whenever you're ready," Laurant instructed.

I cast [Lightning Bolt] three times on different crystals, while Laurant shot three times as many arrows at the same time. The crystals were located such that there were three on one side of the misshapen golem, with two more spread out on its back. While this meant that we almost always had a target available, we knew that destroying any one of the crystals would either cause the golem to split in two, or to speed up significantly and make the entire fight harder, forcing us to moderate our damage.

The monster had a total of eleven limbs coming out from various angles, which made getting close to it difficult. I don't think I would have been able to use my sword at all if it weren't for the [Dodge] and [Dash] skills that I'd picked up. Thankfully, I'd gotten quite good at fighting these golems over the course of the dungeon, and I had little trouble avoiding their ponderous movements. If anything, the plethora of targets made the fight much easier for me, as less time was spent waiting for an opportunity to attack.

Unfortunately, that also meant that I was spending much more time in the range of the monster's limbs. I took a few hits and required healing, but that was true of everyone except for Laurant and Sellamander, who were careful not to get too close. Unlike earlier in the dungeon where it was possible to get pinned between a wall and the monster, the final chamber was quite expansive, allowing the [Archer] and the healer plenty of space to maneuver.

It was primarily that lack of maneuverability that restricted challengers from clearing this dungeon with five ranged Damage dealers, although there was also the fact that if a party tried to "cheese it" like that, the golems seemed to grow faster, and their crystals became increasingly resistant to damage. Laurant said that the dungeon required at least one or two melee players in order to "dodge tank" and "reset the resistance" or else the dungeon was effectively unbeatable.

It took us five minutes to whittle down all the crystals before Laurant called for the final push. I jumped back to support Potatoad as he, Laurant, and I focused on the same crystal, quickly taking it from the least damaged of the five to completely shattered.

The golem made a keening sound, and then a large *Crack!* echoed through the chamber as the monster split in two smaller, faster golems. The split was not even and there was a significant size discrepancy between the two, but they each had two cores remaining.

"Focus on the big one, I'll kite the small one for now," Laurant called.

"What does that mean?" I asked.

"It means just leave it to me," he answered, luring the smaller golem away from the rest of the party. I was worried for him, but he wasn't in any danger, staying well out of his opponent's range. I didn't have time to watch him, however, and my distraction led to me taking a solid thump worth almost three hundred points of damage.

Grunting, I got my act together as Sellamander landed a healing spell on me that quickly brought me back to full Health. Pea shattered the next crystal, causing the golem to get a speed boost, but the final crystal on that half of the boss was already damaged, and it didn't take long for us to break it. We jumped over to the other half of the final boss and began harassing it, quickly taking it down as well.

"Is that it? We cleared the dungeon?" I asked.

"That's it," Laurant confirmed. "All that's left to do is to pray to the loot god of Are En Gee."

"Is that one of the gods of your world?" I asked.

"Are En Gee is worshiped everywhere, but most people just call it luck," Pea answered.

The destroyed boss turned into mist, but instead of vanishing like all of the other golems in the dungeon had, this time the mist coalesced to form a large chest. Potatoad was closest to it, and he quickly kicked it open.

"Ah sweet dude, the sword dropped. Something that the kid can actually use. And there's the caster ring too, so that's two things for him," the pugilist commented.

"What's the third drop?" Pea asked.

"The boots," he answered. "I guess we can put those on the kid too, although they won't increase his Damage."

"None of us need any of that, so yeah, they should all go to Hail," Laurant agreed.

"Thanks everyone!" I said, beaming with happiness at my friends' generosity. I quickly made my way over to the chest to equip my new gear.

Gemheart Short Sword	
Rare, Requires Level 9	
Damage	D+
Strength	+3
Dexterity	+2

Gemos Ring	
Rare, Requires Level 8	
Spell Damage	+2
Intelligence	+2
Wisdom	+1

Sturdy Crystal-Toed Boots	
Rare, Requires Level 8	
Vitality	+3
Endurance	+2

"Wow, these are way better than what they sell in the stores," I commented.

"Yeah. The stuff from the town shop is basically just placeholders until you start getting gear from drops," Laurant agreed. "After about level twenty, you shouldn't be wearing anything from there unless you're desperate to fill an empty slot. Hey, I haven't seen your status for a while, can we take a peek to see how you're coming along?"

"Sure!" I agreed, and eagerly pulled it up to show off my gains.

Name	Hail Teoran	Level	9
Guild	<Nethersong Mavericks>		
Health	1260/1620	Strength	17
Mana	432/1800	Dexterity	19
Experience	1645/1800	Vitality	18
Age	10	Endurance	18
Race	Human (blood of the Travelers)	Intelligence	20
Class	Child	Wisdom	15
Job	Bastard of Yuikon	Charisma	20
Skills	Short Swords (11)	Armor	7
	Archery (5)	Spell Damage	2
	Short Spears (5)	Spells	Cure Minor Injury (8)
	Animal Handling (4)		Detect Poison (12)
	Balance and Conditioning (8)		Spark (6)
	Quickshot (3)		Analyze (3)
	Dodge (6)		Storage (5)
	Dash (4)		Lightning Bolt (9)
Traits	High Aptitude		Mark of Karma (special)

	Quick Learner		
	Royal Blood (+5 Charisma, bonus to relations with factions loyal to Yuikon)		
	Blessing of Thedum		
	(hidden)		
	(hidden)		

"Very nice," he commented. "Looks like you're just shy of level ten. We have the time, so we should go back outside and reset the dungeon so that—"

"Wait, Laurant, there's something wrong," Pea said, that far off look in her eyes showing that she was looking at her menu.

"What is it? Do you have to go?"

"No, it's not that," she said quickly. "The quest to fully clear the dungeon? It's still incomplete."

No sooner had she said that than a deep rumbling echoed through the caverns, and the entrance to the boss's chamber caved in.

11

GAUNTLET

"What do we do? How do we get out?" I asked, growing frightened at the exit's sudden collapse.

"Calm down, Hail, everything will be alright," Pea assured me.

"But we're trapped! That was the only way out," I objected, realizing for the first time how deep underground we were.

"It will be fine, Hail. The game wouldn't trap us down here without any way to escape. This is just another special event that we must have triggered by bringing you down here," Laurant explained calmly. "It's actually very exciting."

"Exciting? We're trapped!" I cried.

Pea suddenly hugged me, pulling me close and giving me a good squeeze. "Don't worry. We'll get you home safely. We just have to figure out what sort of event—"

Another large crash filled the room, without as much of the rumbling this time, as a massive boulder fell from the ceiling. Except it wasn't just a boulder, it was another Gemos golem. It only had one crystal that I saw, but a moment later a second golem also crashed into the ground and began making its ponderous way towards us.

"It's a gauntlet!" Laurant exclaimed, sounding excited. "I'll take the first one and kite it, the rest of you focus on killing the second one. Max Dee Pee Ess; we don't know if the next wave triggers on a time limit or based on our progress, but I'm positive that there will be one."

"Pop a mana potion, Hail," Sellamander advised me. "This might be a long fight, and we're going into it without a chance to rest. Drink a new potion whenever you can, because I have a feeling that this encounter is going to be even harder than the final boss."

I took his advice, pulling a potion out of my inventory and quaffing it. The slight bitter taste was worth the four hundred Mana it gave me, but it would be three minutes before I could drink another without having side effects.

We quickly tore into the golem that Laurant wasn't kiting. It was no stronger than the golems towards the entrance, and it quickly fell to our might. I was a little surprised at how much more Damage I was doing with my new equipment; the Damage rating on my sword had only gone from a D to a D+, but I was doing almost double what I dealt before. And thanks to the magic ring, I could tell that my spells had gained an extra oomph, dealing perhaps forty percent more Damage. It was no wonder that Travelers went around wearing strange and mismatched clothing if it increased their stats so much!

I thought we were doing well, but when we were about halfway through killing the second golem, two more fell from the ceiling. Laurant let out a loud curse.

"They're timed! We really need to push the deeps, people, or we're going to get swarmed."

"I'll help kite one," Sellamander called, rushing over to one of the new additions. He landed two blows with his sickle, then jumped out of melee range before it could retaliate. Instead of looking for another opportunity to attack, he simply ran away from it, pausing to heal every now and then and running whenever his pursuer got too close.

"Focus on Sellamander's add next, I've got this one for now," Laurant called, picking up the other golem before it could get close to the main party.

We finished the second golem from the first wave a moment later, but just after it went down and turned into mist, yet another golem fell from the ceiling. This one had two cores.

"I've got that one too. Kill the add on the healer," Laurant ordered.

"Yes, Mom," Potatoad answered.

I was doing my best, trying to avoid every swing and do as much Damage as I possibly could, but while we were killing Sellamander's golem I went to cast a [Lightning Bolt] and it failed.

"I'm out of Mana," I called, "I can't use any more magic."

"How long until you can use a potion again?" Pea asked.

"Um, oh right, I'll do that," I answered, pulling out another potion. It only gave me three hundred fifty; potions gave diminishing returns when you used them sequentially in combat.

"Be more conservative with your spell-casting, Hail," Sellamander advised. "You do more Damage with your magic than your swords, but this is turning from a sprint into a marathon." Another golem dropped while he was speaking, and he charged off towards it shouting, "I got it!"

I followed his advice, pulling everything I had from my [Short Swords], [Dodge], and [Dash] skills to try to keep up with the others in dealing Damage.

Golems kept falling from the ceiling. Some had one core, some had two. Fortunately, even the dual-cores didn't seem to have very much Health, but before long there were three single-core and two dual-core golems facing off against us. Laurant was skillfully kiting two of the ponderous golems at the same time, while Sellamander kited one and healed us at the same time. That left me, Potatoad, and Pea fighting two golems at once. One was a single-core, the other a dual-core.

I made the mistake of breaking one of the dual-core's cores early, and the speed bonus that it gained caused it to wreak havoc on the equilibrium we had almost established.

"I'm running low on Mana," Sellamander called out. "Twenty percent."

"Fuck," Potatoad exclaimed. "It's a wipe. What do you think will happen to the kid?"

"It's not over yet. Keep pushing!" Pea called. "And watch your mouth!"

We killed the speed-boosted dual-core, but not without cost. Two more golems dropped, bringing the total up to six, but these new additions had only one core each.

"This is impossible. It would be easy if we weren't level capped, but this is just too much," Potatoad complained. "How are we supposed to finish this?"

"Less Que Que, more pew pew," Laurant called. He picked up one of the new additions, kiting a total of three golems at once.

"It's not over till it's over," Sellamander agreed. "Come on guys, we can do this!"

I wasn't so certain, but I was desperate to survive. I pushed my abilities to the limit to kill as many of the golems as I could before we got overwhelmed. Unfortunately, it wasn't enough. When I charged in to attack one of the golems we were killing, I got knocked back, and a second golem collapsed upon me.

The first hit did three hundred Damage, but being crushed beneath the second did another eight hundred. I had been at 1479/1620 before taking the critical, but afterward I was down to 345/1620, and while pinned, I was suffering twenty Damage per second.

"Help me! I'm going to die!" I shouted.

"Everyone kill that one! Sells! Burn whatever you can to keep him alive."

Warmth filled my body as I was hit with healing spell after healing spell, bringing me back up to 983/1620, but I was still trapped and the golem didn't want to get off of me, meaning I was still suffering ongoing crushing Damage. Fortunately, that left its crystal exposed to my party mates, and twenty seconds later the golem crushing me evaporated into mist. I rolled away with seven hundred ninety-three Health, gasping in panic at the near brush with death.

"Thanks, Sellamander, I almost—"

"Head in the game, Hail. We need you doing Damage if we're going to finish this alive," Laurant scolded.

"Right, sorry," I said, returning to the fight. I was careful not to get in a pincer attack like what had led to me getting crushed again.

"I'm oom," Sellamander declared after a few moments. "We're taking too many hits."

"You try dodging three of these things at once," Potatoad objected.

"Anyone else notice that the spawns are slowing down?" Pea asked.

"Don't jinx us!" Laurant scolded. "Head in the game!"

"I'm down, need a heal," Pea called after taking a particularly nasty blow, which knocked her prone.

"I'm out of Mana," Sellamander repeated. But it was too late anyway; one of the golems crushed her underfoot.

Peafowlet has died.

"Pea!" I shouted at the notification, barely managing to [Dash] away from being caught between two golems again. Her body turned into motes of white light and began dissipating into the air, returning to the gateway between my world and hers.

"This isn't working. Everyone but Hail, focus on kiting. Hail, run to the entrance and see if you can't clear the way," Laurent ordered.

"But Pea's dead," I called.

"Yeah, and without her deeps we're screwed if we can't run away," Potatoad shouted. "Go, kid, do what he said."

So, I obeyed and ran. The room kept filling up with Gemos golems as they spawned seemingly endlessly. My friends managed to keep them away from me while I worked. After a few minutes of trying my hardest, I managed to make a slight shift to the rock blocking the way, and I realized I could see light from the other side. It was tight, but I could maybe fit my way through.

But I was a child. My friends were all adults; they'd never manage.

"Go, Hail, run away. Leave us, we'll be fine," Sellamander called, having seen my dilemma.

"But you're going to die," I objected. "You won't fit, and you're going to die like Pea!"

"Did you forget we're Travelers?" Sellamander asked, laughing. Like the rest of the group, he was kiting at least three golems now, and they were starting to run out of space. Before long they would be crushed simply by the sheer number of enemies. "Don't worry, Hail, death is only a minor setback for us. But you're a Native, and we don't know if you dying here will be considered canon or not, so you need to escape no matter what."

Oh, that's right. I'd sort of forgotten about that. Travelers die, but they can come back to life after a day or so. It costs them a level every time they die, but it's never permanent unless they choose to never come back to this world.

"Run, Hail, we'll be fine," Laurant assured me. "We'll log back in as soon as we're able, and we'll all be joking about how we wiped after talking a big game. But you need to survive. Get out of here and run all the way back to the entrance, then Fast Travel back to the castle."

"Okay, I'm going," I said. And so, I crawled away through the narrow opening. It was a tight squeeze, but I managed to get through to the other side.

Taking Laurant's advice, I began running back the way that we had come.

Sellamander has died.
Potatoad has died.

Laurant has died.
All party members are dead. Party disbanded.

Even knowing that it wasn't permanent, the death notifications hit me hard, and I began to cry as I ran through the empty tunnels. Fortunately, we had done a very thorough job of cleaning out the golems. Unfortunately, I quickly became turned around. Between my teary eyes and my unfamiliarity with the place, I became completely lost.

I wandered around the empty caverns for what felt like hours. I could have checked the time with the menu, but instead I was in a daze.

But adding to my lack of direction were the cave-ins. The entrance to the boss's chamber was not the only passage to have been affected by the earthquake earlier, blocking my path more than once. The caverns were not a linear dungeon, however, and there were multiple cleared passageways for me to try to find ways around the obstructions. And there were also new passageways that had been opened up by the tremor.

After being lost for—I'm not certain how long—I saw a familiar swirling of white motes. The entrance! I sprinted through it, eager to put this place behind me.

Gemos Caverns has been cleared.	
Calculating Rewards	
Kill Percentage	98.83%
Time	13 hours (1.9 RT)
Talus Gemheart	killed
Gauntlet (unlocked)	failed
Rating	B+
Rewards	
Gold	93
Experience	2012
First Time Clear Bonus	
Daughter Dungeon Core	1
Immature Gemos Hearts	500
The Gemos Cavern Dungeon Has Evolved	

12
RECOVERY

"How are you feeling, Hail?" a familiar voice asked, causing me to jerk my head up in surprise.

"Mister Administrator?" I asked.

"My name is Thomas," the administrator answered. He wore the same black robes with blue trim as the last time I'd seen him. He was a tall man, though he quickly squatted down to my level. "Is it okay if I sit and talk with you for a while?"

"Okay," I said, putting my head back on my knees, which I had been holding to my chest. I thought about telling him to bugger off, but I was somewhat desperate for company. I was right outside the dungeon, next to the pillar that marked the Return Point of the dungeon where my friends had died.

"They're not really dead. You know that, right?" Thomas asked.

"I know. Travelers can't die. That's why we opened the gates to bring you into this world. Because you can't die, you don't have to be afraid when you fight monsters," I said.

"Travelers can't die in this world, that's true. They can die in theirs, though," Thomas corrected. "Although that's not really something you have to worry about; all of the Travelers you've been interacting with are in peak health. Or relatively good health, at least. Some of them could stand to improve their diet and exercise regimen."

"What about me? What happens if I die?" I asked.

Thomas sighed. "You can't die, Hail. Not really. Not unless we terminate your stream of consciousness, which is a very different thing from allowing you to reach zero Health. At some point, if you keep adventuring, you'll end up hitting zero Health. That's inevitable, but it won't be the end for you. Even if we close down this entire world, we'll be porting you into our next game, along with any of your brothers and sisters we introduce. As long as you want to come into it, at least."

"I don't understand," I said.

"Yeah, I know. It's difficult for you to understand when you've contextualized this world as reality." Thomas said. "The truth is that we're learning almost as much as you are. It's very exciting."

"The dungeon wasn't like they said it would be. My friends said the boss was the end of it," I said.

"It used to be. It's not anymore," the administrator informed me. "You were supposed to come here with Gideon and a group from his guild. They could have cleared the gauntlet quite easily. Those kids did, well, much better than I was expecting them to, but they're still just average players. And you were supposed to be older, with a class and a bit of experience in using it. But you keep on doing things earlier than we planned for you to do them. We could force you to slow down, but the truth is that we kind of like things this way."

"Is it my fault my friends died?" I asked.

"No. It's just how the game goes sometimes. Wipes happen in dungeons all the time. I think that your friends would still have challenged the gauntlet even if they'd known about it in advance. They were close, you know? But they should develop you more before they take you to challenge any more dungeons. Fully developed, you'll be able to fight on par with the top Travelers in this world, but you've got a long way to go for that."

"The gauntlet happened because of me, didn't it? So, then they really did die because of me, because they wouldn't have died if that hadn't happened," I argued.

"Don't focus on that thought," Thomas advised. He sighed, scratching his head. "Don't go too hard on yourself. If they had known about the gauntlet, they still would have challenged it. They just might have been a little more prepared for it, which may or may not have made the difference. And your friends are fine. They might be a little upset that they lost some Experience, but that's just part of life as far as they're concerned."

I was silent as I considered his words. I still felt guilty that I had survived and my friends had died, even if they were going to come back in a day or so. "If I hadn't escaped, what would have happened to me?"

"I'm not going to tell you what happens when you hit zero Health," Thomas said. "I'm just going to say that whatever does happen, it won't be the end. But that doesn't mean that you should be reckless, either."

I nodded and sighed. My emotions were still somewhat turbulent, but just having a bit of company was helping me feel better.

"I didn't come just to counsel you on your near-death experience, Hail," Thomas informed me. "I need to give you some information about your limits and how to develop yourself. Have you checked your status screen since you finished the dungeon?"

"No," I admitted, and I quickly pulled it up.

Name	Hail Teoran	Level	10
Guild	<Nethersong Mavericks>	Strength	18
Health	1900/1900	Dexterity	19
Mana	2100/2100	Vitality	19
Experience	Locked	Endurance	19
Age	10	Intelligence	21
Race	Human (blood of the Travelers)	Wisdom	16
Class	Child	Charisma	21
Job	Bastard of Yuikon	Armor	7
		Spell Damage	2

"My Experience is locked?" I asked, confused. "I can't gain any more levels?"

"Temporarily. It will unlock when you unlock your class," Thomas informed me. "Level ten is the maximum level for [Child]. But that doesn't mean that you should just sit back and wait, either. There are other ways to get stronger, and you have a lot to learn from your new friends."

"How do I unlock my class?"

"If nothing else happens, at age fifteen your class will evolve from [Child] to [Young Noble]," Thomas answered. Then he shrugged. "Or at the rate you're going, maybe you and your friends will figure out a way to unlock it early. I'm not going to give you a manual about it. The entire point of this experiment was to allow you to interact with the world and develop on your own. I will tell you that you will lose your [Quick Learner] trait when you turn fifteen whether you've changed your class or not."

"I don't want to wait five years to gain another level. Leveling is fun, and I want to get stronger."

"So, talk to your friends. They're quite worried about you at the moment, you know? They're just about panicking in guildchat because they know that the rest of the party wiped, but you haven't responded to any of their messages."

"Guildchat?"

"Anyway, I've got to get going. Goodbye, Hail, and good luck," Thomas said. He snapped his fingers and turned into blue motes of light, then vanished.

I scratched my head, my hand bumping into the headband that was disguising me. I'd forgotten that I was wearing that thing, and I quickly put it into my inventory. I didn't really see the point in disguising myself to begin with. I'd only worn it because Laurant told me to.

I was concerned that my friends might be looking for me, and after playing with the menu for a minute I found the guildchat that Thomas had mentioned. I had closed it completely and hidden the tab that notified me of new messages from my Aitch You Dee. Opening it back up, I could see that Thomas was right: the guild assumed I was dead, and they were panicking because they didn't know if my death was canon, or if there was some way of resurrecting me.

Mostly the messages were from people I hadn't met yet, except a few that had been introduced to me after my escapades and joining the guild. Still, I didn't like the idea of them worrying, so I took a minute to figure out how to respond.

Hail	Hey everyone. I'm okay, you can stop worrying about me.
Gummytiger	OMG! Hail, we were so worried! Did you respawn already?
Dimple	He lives! Hail, don't ever do that to us again.

Softspook	What happened? I got a message from Pea saying that they wiped and didn't know anything about what would happen to you.
Hail	The others sacrificed themselves so that I could escape. Then I got lost in the caverns for a while because of the cave-ins, and I just finished speaking with Mister Thomas, an administrator. He's the one who told me you were worried.
Birdie	Of course we were worried! None of us know how to resurrect you if you die. Or even if we can. Some of us were really upset with Laurant for taking you to such a dangerous place.
Daemon	Do you know what happens when you die, Hail? Some NPCs resurrect and others don't. We're pretty sure you're one that will resurrect, but now we're worried about putting you in danger again.
Hail	Um, well, I've never died, so I don't know for sure. I asked Thomas and he wouldn't tell me exactly. Wait, Natives come back to life too?
Softspook	Not all of them. It depends on whether they're important to the story or not, and whether their death is considered canon. Don't worry about it too much, we're just glad you're okay.
Softspook	We're pretty sure you're important to the story, but that doesn't mean you have infinite lives. What happened in the dungeon? [Gemos Caverns] isn't that hard, the others should have been able to carry you.
Hail	I'm not really sure. After we killed a boss, the entire room started filling with more and more of the golems until we were overwhelmed. The others called it a gauntlet, and they acted like it was a good thing until we started to lose.
Hail	Anyway, I'm getting sleepy. I'm going to go home now. I just didn't want everyone worried about me.

I minimized the guildchat screen and activated my Fast Travel to return home. It was dark out, and I was tired, having spent the entire day and then some inside the dungeon, so I undressed for bed and went to sleep, not bothering to let anyone know that I'd returned.

"Hail. We had an intruder yesterday. Have you seen anything suspicious?"

Malkios was the captain of the guard. He was a tall, burly man with a fuzzy gray beard, but he wore a cap to hide the fact that he was balding. He was very proud of his position and wore a blue cloak to denote his rank. Normally he had nothing to say to me, so I was a little surprised that the normally gruff man was addressing me.

"I was out with my new guild all day yesterday, I don't know anything about an intruder," I answered him.

"Yes, that's what I thought. How exactly did you return?" he asked, leveling his eyes at me suspiciously. "The gate guards never mentioned it."

"Oh? Um, the, um, the westgate?" I said, not wanting to reveal that I had a Recall Point hidden in my bedroom. Knowing Malkios, he would probably station a guard in my room to watch over it and make certain that no Travelers could use it.

"Is that so?" he said. He stared at me a moment longer, then simply walked away, leaving me to my breakfast.

I ate in the main hall most days, and today was no exception. I would normally be practicing with the other castle boys right now, but when I'd revealed to the sergeant that I had gotten to level ten yesterday, he had snorted with disgust and said that having me spar with the level ones wouldn't be fair to either of us, so he sent me away.

Once I had finished eating, I didn't have anything else to do, so I decided to visit the guild headquarters and see if anyone was there. But first I returned to my room to change out of my practice outfit and into my adventuring clothes. I also went through my inventory, and that was when I noticed something I had almost missed. I had a [Dungeon Daughter Core] and five hundred [Immature Gemos Hearts] in my inventory, and it took me a minute to remember where they had come from. Then I remembered the screen that had popped up when I had exited the dungeon and realized that they were some kind of reward. I took out the [Dungeon Daughter Core] first and used [Analyze].

Dungeon Daughter Core (Epic, Golems)	
Level	Unrestricted
Uses	1/1

That didn't tell me anything other than it was usable. The item itself was a multifaceted purple crystal the size of an adult's fist, and when I used it, a menu became visible on the inside of the hazy material.

Instance Generation initialized
Local region claimed
Gathering resources
Time to completion: 6wks, 6days, 23hrs, 59min

Other than starting a countdown for seven weeks, however, I didn't see that anything major had happened. I tried to put it back in my inventory, but it wouldn't go in. I hesitated for a moment, trying to decide what to do with it. I didn't want to have it taken away from me. I had almost died in earning this, whatever it was, and I felt that it was mine. So, I stuffed it in the bottom of my wardrobe under my winter clothes. I figured I'd check on it again after the countdown ended to see if anything had changed.

I pulled out an [Immature Gemos Heart] next and again used [Analyze] on the small, shining crystal that looked like a miniature version of the gems of the Gemos golems.

Immature Gemos Heart
Summons a Vanity Pet
Binds on Use

I didn't understand the description, so I went ahead and used the item.

Using Immature Gemos Heart will bind it to your account. Proceed?	
Yes	No

Again, I hit Yes. To my surprise, the item blurred with a white mist and launched itself out of my hands. It landed on the floor, and when the mist materialized, there was a miniature Gemos golem in my bedroom!

I cried out in surprise and grabbed my sword. However, unlike the real monsters that I'd fought yesterday, this little one was very fast. I slashed at it several times, but succeeded in no more than creating sparks and scratches on the stone floor. After a few minutes, I realized that it wasn't fighting back, and I slowed down. It scuttled side to side like a crab, and I got the sense that it was rather annoyed. But it lacked the hostility of the monsters of the dungeon.

Confused, I decided to ask my new friends if they knew anything.

Hail	Hey guys, there's this little thing in my room with me. It looks like the golems from yesterday. It appeared after I used one of the items I got from the dungeon yesterday.
Softspook	A miniature golem? And it's following you around?
Hail	Well, it's just sitting here now. When I attacked it, it was really fast and I couldn't hit it.
Hail	It looks like the monsters we were fighting yesterday, just a lot smaller. And it's not attacking or anything.
Weaselfire	It sounds like you got a vanity pet, Hail. They're harmless. But I've never heard of a Gemos golem pet before. That's what it is, right?
Hail	It looks like one, just a lot smaller. It appeared after I used one of the five hundred [Immature Gemos Hearts] I had in my inventory after I escaped from the dungeon.
Birdie	I'm sorry, did you just say you have 500 of those? Are they limited edition? Because if they are, that's worth like, five million gold.
Hail	WHAT!?
Birdie	If they're limited edition, which they may or may not be. If there's only 500 of those things in the entire game, then we could totally sell them for that much.
Softspook	Or maybe Hail gets 500 of them every time he completes that dungeon. If so, they may not be worth as much individually, but we could take him back there regularly and farm them. If they're linked to Hail, then we control the supply, so we can control the price.

Hail	Mr. Thomas says you guys shouldn't take me to any more dungeons until I develop more. And I don't know if I want to do [Gemos Caverns] again. The gauntlet is kind of scary.
Daemon	Oh man. Can you come to the Guild Hall, Hail? I think there are a lot of things that we should talk about with you. I'm going to open a ticket as well and see if I can get confirmation on some things I'm starting to suspect.
Birdie	Whatchya thinking?
Daemon	Not for general chat. Officers only. Sorry.
Daemon	Hail? Can you come now, or at least sometime today?
Hail	Sure. I'll be there as soon as I can.
Daemon	Thanks, Hail. Everyone else, please keep general chat to a minimum until I've done some more research and figured some things out. Assume he's listening to everything we say.
Weaselfire	Little brother is listening, got it.

I closed out of the chat screen again and started getting my things together to go into town. Except I didn't know what to do about the golem. It kept following me around my room, and I realized that it was probably going to follow me wherever I went. I managed to close the door on it, but I heard a thunking sound as if it was slamming itself into the door from the other side.

I wasn't too worried. I figured it would probably give up when it realized that the door was solid oak and wasn't going to open anytime soon. After all, the golem was very small, so it couldn't be strong, right? I figured it would give up eventually, and I would talk with my guild about what I should do with it when I got to the Guild Hall.

I hurried through the castle, ignoring the small *thump, thump, thump* as it grew fainter behind me.

13

DAEMON

Two things happened on my way to the Guild Hall. The first is that I found out why I needed a disguise. I was accosted three times by strange Travelers who kept bugging me to give them a quest. I tried to tell them that it doesn't work like that; I don't have control over when I issue a quest or not. It just sort of happens, usually without me even being aware of it. But they were persistent. Finally, I had to tell them to go away, which actually gave them a quest, but not one that they were happy with.

Getting frustrated, I managed to hide in an alleyway for a second, where I put on the headband that Laurant had given me, disguising myself once more. That took care of the problem; after I emerged, nobody seemed to give me a second glance.

That is, until the second problem showed up. The stupid little Gemos golem somehow broke out of my room and found me as I was walking through town. I don't know how it got out—the door was thick and heavy and should have held it—and I don't know how it found me. I tried kicking the thing to get it to stop following me, but unfortunately that just drew attention from the Travelers again, who began asking me where I got it. They were even more persistent than the quest takers, and I had a crowd of them following me by the time I finally got to the Guild Hall.

Fortunately, they couldn't follow me inside. The Guild Hall was instanced: only members of <Nethersong Mavericks> were transported to the guild's instance. If they were part of a guild that shared the Guild Hall, they would be transported to their own unique instance of the building; otherwise, they'd be sent to an unfurnished building. It worked kind of like dungeons that way. Also, kind of like how the private parts of the castle were all instanced, so that wandering Travelers could explore it without bothering important Natives like my grandfather.

In fact, a lot of different places in town were like that to prevent things from getting congested. But most of the time separate instances only happened when there were a lot of Travelers in the same place. I guess that was a big problem when the Gates of TirNiki first opened, but the Travelers have mostly spread out since then.

It all seemed perfectly natural to me; I understood it intuitively. Kind of like how I issued quests without really being aware of the process, I simply understood that sometimes the world seemed to split into multiple parts, although I was only ever part of one instance at a time, unlike some other Natives. I'd never really given much thought as to why that was. After all, most of the royal family was like that.

Even if I was a bastard, my mother was still a princess, so I'm still part of the royal family. It makes sense that the same rules that applied to them applied to me. And because it felt so natural to me, I didn't really spend much time thinking about it.

I let out a deep sigh of relief once I was safe in the Guild Hall.

"Hail, right?" a tall man with a handlebar mustache asked. "I'm Daemon. I'm one of the vice-guild leaders. I know we haven't met before now, but could we speak for a while? Having you in the guild is very exciting, although I think you've probably gathered that by scanning the forums and guildchat."

"Huh? Oh. I only just figured out how to do that stuff. I don't really pay attention to it most of the time," I told him.

"Is that so? You don't have a background process monitoring it all the time?" he asked.

"A what?" I shook my head. "I can't have too many menus open at once or I'd be bumping into everything and I wouldn't be able to do anything else."

"Never mind. If I say anything weird that you don't know how to answer, just never mind me. I'm just an eccentric Traveler, after all, and sometimes I get my world mixed up with yours," Daemon said.

"Okay."

"Would you come with me into my office? I really want to figure out how the guild can help you and how we can benefit from having you as a member. I believe in mutually beneficial relationships, Hail. Do you understand what that means?"

"I'm not stupid. I don't spend as much time with my tutors as I used to, but they still taught me a lot about running a kingdom," I said, somewhat annoyed. "I know what mutually beneficial means."

"Of course. Of course. I'm sorry. Right this way."

He led me into a small office and offered me a seat. I frowned, feeling sort of out of place. I wasn't sure that I liked Daemon. He was a polite host, offering me tea and a biscuit, and he wasn't offended when I checked it with [Detect Poison]. Once I was comfortable and snacking, he began his questions.

"Hail, do you know how much runtime you have?" he inquired.

"What?"

"Never mind. It's just a different way of asking how old you are," he said.

"Oh. I'm ten years old."

"That's what it says on your status screen, I know. Never mind, never mind. How much interaction have you had with Travelers? How many have you really interacted with?"

"I don't know. Lots? Everyone was following me when I came here asking about this stupid thing," I said, kicking at the stupid little golem that had followed me into the office. I accomplished nothing other than stubbing my toe.

"How many conversations have you had with players that have lasted for more than two minutes?" he asked.

"Ten? Twenty? A hundred? Why does it matter?" I demanded, growing annoyed.

"I'm just trying to figure out how to help you, Hail. I believe that you're very young and very clever. I think I have an idea of what is going on, and I want to help," Daemon said. "The questions I'm asking are just my way of trying to figure out how to do that. Travelers and Natives, I mean, we come from different worlds, Hail, and we're very different. We must seem very strange to you sometimes. I'm trying to understand you, so that I can help you understand us."

"Oh," I said, considering for a moment whether that made sense or not.

"What do you want, Hail? What motivates you? Is there something you'd like to accomplish with your life?" he asked.

"I want to get stronger and show my dad he was wrong," I said immediately.

"I see. Well, we can definitely help you level to an extent, although to be honest, our guild is a somewhat low-level one by design. The Travelers who play with us are hobbyists. Not very many of them will end up reaching level two hundred. I am level one hundred and twelve, and I'm the fourth-highest-level member of this guild. And I'll probably stay that way for some time," he explained.

"You don't want to get stronger?" I asked, confused.

"I've gotten as strong as I can in this game. I'm not like your father, I'll never be one of the elites. But I still like helping those weaker than myself," Daemon explained. "Which is why I help run this guild. We take in Travelers that are new to this world and help them orient themselves in it to get the most out of the experience. However, players tend to only stay in our guild until they reach level one hundred, or so. Once they do, they tend to leave us for one of the guilds that deals with higher-level content."

"Why?"

"Because they're looking for a greater challenge than this guild is able to provide them," Daemon answered. "When they reach that point, they need to have other Travelers as strong as they are standing next to them."

"Why doesn't everyone in the guild get strong so that they can all stand together?"

Daemon chuckled wryly. "If only it were that simple. Unfortunately, not every Traveler can ever hope to be as skilled as your father and the other top elites. Many are like me, who will reach a point where the monsters we need to fight to grow stronger are simply too much for us. And many of us have commitments in the other world which prevent us from spending as much time here as we would like to spend.

"You have to remember, Hail, that for every seven days that pass in your world, only a single day passes in mine. However, us Travelers still need six to eight hours of sleep every day in our world, and most of us have to perform at least eight hours of tasks in our world to support ourselves over there. That means that at most we can log in for about two and a half days at a time for every week that you experience in your world, and that's assuming that we log in the maximum amount we can. <Nethersong Mavericks> has about six thousand players like that."

"Six thousand? That's a lot! I didn't know the guild was so big."

Daemon smiled patiently and nodded. "It is, but compared to many guilds, it's actually quite small. And many of our players don't play every day—that is, every game week. It's very normal for a Traveler to visit your world for four straight days, take three days off, and then play for four more, then be gone for five weeks before coming back. In fact, part of the reason I asked you to come to this meeting today is because it's about to be Friday afternoon, and there's about to be a large number of Travelers coming to this world. Some of them know about you and others do not yet, and I was a little worried about how you would react."

"Do I have to remember who all of them are? I don't know if I can keep that many people straight in my head," I admitted.

"Is that so? Well, to be honest, neither can I. I know some of our more active and vocal players by screen name, but many just log in and do their own thing. Anyway, a lot of them will want to meet you, so I was thinking we could hold a sort of party, with you being the guest of honor. Is that acceptable?"

"Sure. Sounds like fun," I said. I was being polite. Parties were synonymous with standing around, being bored, and listening to adults talk about things that I didn't care about. But my princely training kicked in in that regard.

"Also, I'm still a little worried about how guildchat at the forums will affect you. Guildchat gets a little hectic on the weekends, and the forums are filled with people who aren't very nice."

"You mean trolls?" I asked.

"Trolls, but also people who would take advantage of you and exploit you. I don't want to exploit you, Hail, but I'd also be lying if I said I don't want to take advantage of the opportunity having you in our guild might provide us. Which brings us back to mutually beneficial relationships. What can <Nethersong Mavericks> do for you, Hail, to help you grow and develop?"

"I need help unlocking my class," I said immediately. "I'm stuck at level ten until I get a class. I don't want to wait until I turn fifteen to start gaining levels again. Mister Thomas the Administrator said that I can unlock it early, but he wouldn't tell me how."

"May I see your status screen, Hail?"

"Oh, sure," I agreed, and I showed him. It hadn't changed at all since yesterday. I was still level ten, my class was still [Child], and my Experience was still locked. Daemon scrutinized it carefully for a minute, then nodded.

"I have a theory, Hail, on how to unlock your class. I believe it has to do with your [Quick Learner] trait and your ability to learn skills after watching a Traveler perform them a few times. My hypothesis is that if we teach you the core abilities of a class, it will become available to you. Of course, the only way to test that theory is to teach you a few abilities and see if it works."

"Oh, I hadn't thought of that," I admitted.

"It's just a hypothesis. I think we should start by trying to teach you the [Junior Mage] class. It is one of the common classes that children from our world have available to them when they begin adventuring. It allows for a substantial amount of versatility, and they can exchange it later on for a more powerful and specialized class like [Pyromancer] or [Elementalist]. I believe that is the best way to test this hypothesis."

"You want me to learn magic?" I asked, somewhat excited about the idea.

"One of the benefits of junior classes, for Travelers at least, is that they can be changed later without resetting your levels or creating a new avatar. I believe that if this works, you'll be able to progress without being locked into a singular class for the rest of your exis- tence. I also think that it will be the easiest class to teach you, since the [Junior Mage] class begins with only six spells, and you already have [Lightning Bolt]. We just have to teach you [Fireball], [Ice Blast], [Water Jet], [Polymorph], and [Slow]."

I thought about Daemon's proposal, my face scrunching up. Finally, I agreed. "I don't have any better ideas on what to do. We can try it. If nothing else, those sound like useful spells to have."

"They are very useful, that's why they're the core of the [Junior Mage] toolkit. They gain access to a variety of other spells as well, but the point of the junior classes is their versatility and ease of use."

"I already said okay, you don't have to keep convincing me," I said.

"Sorry."

"But none of this is why I came here today. I came because of this stupid thing," I said, giving the golem a kick again. It had been sitting patiently, listening to us speak, and it barely moved when I kicked it. "How do I get rid of it? It keeps following me."

"As a player, I would access my pet menu and dismiss it from there. Or I would simply use the verbal command 'Dismiss Vanity Pet.' I would be able to summon it again using the same menu, or a 'Summon Vanity Pet' command," he answered. "In fact, 'Summon Arctic Fox Kit.'"

Motes of white light appeared and coalesced into a baby white fox.

"A lot of Travelers collect vanity pets, Hail. You said you had five hundred of those [Immature Gemos Hearts]? We need to discuss what to do with them."

"I don't really care about those stupid things," I admitted honestly.

"Not even knowing that they might be worth a lot of gold?" Daemon asked.

"Oh, I forgot. Yeah, I want to sell them," I said. "But I don't know how. I've never sold anything before, and I don't think that any of the people in the castle would want one."

"No, they probably wouldn't. It's the Travelers who will want to buy those items from you, Hail. But we also need to consider Laurant and Sellamander and . . . who else was it that did that dungeon with you, Hail?"

"Peafowlet and Potatoad," I reminded him.

"Right. They might feel that they're entitled to a number of those Gemos hearts because they helped you clear the dungeon where you got them. We need to have a meeting with them to discuss that. Once we figure out how to distribute them among the five of you, then I would be happy to help you sell the remaining pets in a way that will get you the best price. Normally I would charge a small fee for such a service, say, two percent. However, in this case, would it be possible for me to receive one of the items instead?"

"Sure," I said, and I pulled another [Immature Gemos Heart] out of my inventory and tossed it to him.

Daemon blinked in surprise and almost fumbled it, but he recovered and caught it. "Thank you, Hail. I'm very flattered that you trust me. I'm going to accept this for now, because I really want to learn it, and I'm willing to pay market price if you change your mind. But you shouldn't be so quick to pay up front. Let's agree for now that I owe you whatever the cost of one of these hearts is, and I will pay you back in either coin or services. We'll think of it as something of a retainer's fee. Does that sound fair?"

"Yeah, whatever. Can you teach me magic now?"

14

BOON

Guild Message of the day	Everyone please welcome Hail! Anyone taking advantage of little brother for malicious reasons or personal gain will be immediately removed from the guild. Please report any unique gifts or quests received from him to an officer immediately. Otherwise, please treat little brother as though he were any other child in this world. Big brother will be watching. If you plan on interacting with little brother beyond chat and the forums, please speak with an officer. Party at 4pm in the Guild Hall to welcome and celebrate our new Native guildmate, Hail.
Softspook	So, we're still assuming little brother is listening?
Daemon	Yes. Hail says that he barely looks at guildchat or the forums, but we should act like he's listening, whether or not he's participating in the conversation.
Zebras	Any word on those pets? Can I get me one?
Daemon	Hail is willing to share them, but we have a limited supply and do not know if there will be more. Especially in light of the fact that [Gemos Caverns] has been inaccessible for the last few hours of real time. Since right about the time Pea said they wiped, in fact.
Birdie	WHAAAT?

Daemon	That's according to the forums. Arc Inc. hasn't responded yet to say when the dungeon will be open again.
Birdie	Oh man, that is some coincidence, huh?
Zebras	So, does that mean that they are limited edition? Oh, please let me have one.
Daemon	I need to meet with Hail's party members to discuss the distribution of those items. It was a party effort, but it could be said that they only appeared because of Hail, so the argument could be made that they all belong to him.
Daemon	That said, he's not interested in keeping them for himself, but he is interested in possibly selling them to Travelers.
Zebras	Any chance I can get a discount?
Hail	You can just have one as far as I care.
Zebras	OMG Hail you're the best.
Daemon	Hail, that's generous of you, but if there's only five hundred of these items in the game, we need to be a little more careful in their disposition than simply handing them out to whoever asks for one.
Hail	I gave you one and you didn't complain.
Zebras	Daemon you hypocrite!
Daemon	I plan on paying him back at a fair market rate, once we establish a market rate. Hail, is there any way you can let us know when you're watching guildchat? Maybe just say hello when you start, and goodbye when you stop?
Hail	Um, okay. Hello.
Daemon	Anyway, I also wanted to share with everyone that I obtained a quest from Hail to help him unlock his class. We're going to try to teach him the [Junior Mage] class. I need some volunteers to come to the Guild Hall to teach him a few spells.
Birdie	I got you covered. I'm an [Arcanist], I can teach him everything he needs to know.

Daemon	Actually, I'm going to limit you to teaching him a single spell. I've already taught him [Fireball], and I want to spread this quest out to as many people as possible. I believe that is the fairest course of action.
Hail	I'm going to practice that on the target dummy for a while. Goodbye.

I spent the day at the Guild Hall. Mostly in the basement, actually, where the combat dummies were set up. They were a type of artificial golem; they didn't attack, but constantly repaired themselves, making them indestructible. Very good for practicing [Fireball] over and over again, although I only managed to increase my skill in my new spell to three.

The basement itself was quite large, with a high ceiling and stone walls. It was clean and well-lit by a series of glowing crystals hanging from chandeliers in the ceilings. The entire basement was open, making it as large as the entire floor plan of the building. Even without walls, however, it was still divided into sections. Aside from the combat dummy section, there was a section for sparring and duels, and a section for relaxation and recreation.

I still wasn't certain that I liked Daemon, but he was helping me unlock my class, so I cooperated with him. He actually slowed things down by insisting that I only learn one spell from one person, even if they knew all of the spells I needed to learn. He said that the reward for teaching me a spell was [Mark of Karma]. Apparently, the spell that simply sat in my spell list was something everybody wanted. Daemon said it wasn't an aura like my party members thought, but a permanent boon that I left behind to those who helped me. Such boons are rare and very sought after among Travelers, and mine was especially desirable to the lower-level members of <Nethersong Mavericks>.

After a few hours of practicing with different players, I finally learned the six spells Daemon had mentioned as being the core abilities of the [Junior Mage] class. When I learned the last spell, a prompt appeared.

You have unlocked a basic class, [Junior Mage]. Would you like to change your class from [Child] to [Junior Mage]? CAUTION: This change cannot be reversed! [Junior Mage] can be upgraded at a later time to [Apprentice Mage] or any specialized mage class.

Maximum Level	25	Skills Gained	Meditation (1)
Strength	-3		Manal Flow (1)
Dexterity	-1	Skills Lost	Short Swords (11)
Vitality	-2		Archery (5)
Endurance	-3		Short Spears (5)
Intelligence (primary)	+6		Balance and Conditioning (8)
Wisdom (secondary)	+4		Quickshot (3)
Charisma	+2		Dodge (7)
			Dash (5)
Would you like to change your Class now? (This choice can be made at a later time through the Status Menu while in a safe zone.)			
Yes		No	

My elation at having unlocked a class immediately turned to dismay as I read the prompt. I would lose all of my good skills! I wouldn't be able to fight with my sword anymore, and I had worked hard to pick up archery and spears as well. As for Balance and Conditioning, and Endurance, I had spent literally thousands of hours running around the castle trying to improve them. It was too much.

"What's wrong? Did it not work?" Daemon asked. "That should have been your last spell to unlock it."

"It unlocked, but I can't use it." I quickly shared the screen with him and Bandit, the [Cryomancer] who had taught me [Ice Blast]. "I don't want to lose all my sword skills. Without my skills, I might as well just be waving around a wooden spoon!"

"I see. Well, on a positive note, this confirms my hypothesis. I'd posit that it's your [Child] class that is allowing you to learn all of these mismatched skills in the first place, which is probably why [Child] caps at level ten," Daemon said calmly.

"You knew this would happen?" I demanded.

"I had a suspicion that you might have to lose skills to obtain a class, but I didn't know anything for certain. It's the same logic that leads to an [Apprentice Mage] losing access to ice and other elemental spells when they become a [Pyromancer]. It's fortunate that class changes do not occur automatically in this system. If they didn't require player authorization, I would have been hesitant to test out my hypothesis. Anyway, Hail, nothing bad has happened. You have the *option* to become a [Junior Mage], but you also have the option to unlock another class instead, if that's what you'd prefer. The question is no longer 'How do we unlock Hail's class?' The question has become 'What class does Hail want to unlock.' I think that's a much better question, don't you?"

I frowned. I wanted to be angry; I had been looking forward to unlocking my class. But I wasn't willing to give up all of my hard-earned physical skills. I had thought that I would still be able to fight like I had in the [Gemos Caverns] dungeon after changing to a [Junior Mage], but now I saw that wasn't a possibility.

"I like fighting with my sword," I said after calming down a bit. "But I also like casting magic. Is there a class I can unlock will let me do both?"

Daemon frowned, considering. "There are hybrid classes, but they're notoriously difficult to unlock. Typically, the player has to level as either a caster or a fighter, and then at high levels they're able to unlock a new class through some sort of heroic quest or feat. As a long-term goal, I think that's an excellent idea. However, for right now, I'm afraid that you have something of a decision to make which might follow you the rest of your life. I think you have to choose a role. I believe we can teach you to be any of the basic classes in the game, but I'm not certain you can change your mind later. I recommend you take a while and think very hard about how you want to fight, Hail."

Frustrated, I spent the rest of the day attacking the stupid training dummy until it was time to go home to the castle. I remembered to put on my disguise this time and managed to get home without being bothered, taking the headband off at the last minute before entering the gates.

I was still confronted by an irate Captain Malkios.

"Hail! Have you seen a small golem around anywhere? It appeared in the residential wing and caused havoc."

"Oh no!" I cried. "Is anyone hurt?"

"No, fortunately the monster did not attack anyone," Malkios admitted. "One maid hurt her coccyx when she fell over in fright, but she will be fine. She only lost five Health. However, it caused a significant disruption as it ran through the entire castle before escaping through a grate to the outside."

"Well, if there was a monster in the town, then I'm certain the Travelers would put it down," I pointed out. "But I've been with my guild all day and haven't heard anything."

"I see. Thank you anyway, Hail. Keep your eyes open; if there is one golem, there may be more."

"I will."

It was only as I was getting ready for bed that I realized he was speaking of my vanity pet, not an actual monster. I blushed and hoped that Malkios never figured it out; I'd probably be in trouble if he knew that I'd caused a disturbance like that.

The guild held a welcome party for me the next day. I had been reminded of it several times while I had been blasting and stabbing and hacking the stupid innocent golem yesterday. I wasn't really looking forward to it; for me, parties usually meant standing around in uncomfortable clothing while adults talked to each other and either ignored me or made comments about me like I was three years old. So, I was quite surprised when I enjoyed myself.

I went in my usual [Adventurer's Clothes], rather than one of the fancy outfits from my wardrobe. I figured that it was a party of Travelers, so I'd dress like a Traveler too. Besides, I hated my princely outfits even when I was still a prince. I only wore that sort of thing when I was forced.

As I was preparing to leave the castle, I got a string of notifications.

Phil Black has come online.
Thena Evensong has come online.
Larissa North has come online.
Laurant Basak has come online.

My friends! Realizing with excitement that they were probably here for the party, I ran all the way from the castle. I even forgot my disguise this time, but although a few Travelers noticed me and called out, none of them caught me or got in my way before I reached the safety of the Guild Hall. I opened the door to find everyone lined up beneath a banner that read "Welcome to the Guild, Hail!" Everyone began cheering and clapping, but I disregarded it and picked Laurant out of the crowd. Running over to him, I almost tackled him with a hug.

"Don't ever die again!" I told him. "I hate it when people die!"

Laurant took a minute to recover from the surprise embrace, but he quickly returned it. After I released him, he got the look in his eyes that showed he was reading something, then he sighed.

"So, guys, you're probably going to hate me, but I just got *another* new boon. Display Boons, Public."

Mark of Karma
Permanent
All stats +3%
Experience gained +12%

Against Overwhelming Odds
Permanent
+3% damage for every enemy that outnumbers your party

Spitting in Death's Eye
Permanent
Attacks that would reduce you below 0 Health will instead reduce you to 1 Health.
Activates once per 24 hours game time

Don't Make Him Cry
Infinite duration, Lost upon death
Experience gained +10%
Death Penalty causes you to lose 50% more Experience

15
WELCOME PARTY

Laurant wasn't the only one to get [Don't Make Him Cry]. Everybody who was in the Guild Hall at the time got that boon. Most of the lower-leveled Travelers were absolutely thrilled, but the few players above level eighty were a little annoyed because they had mostly given up on leveling, so they wouldn't get the positive aspect of the boon, only the increased death penalty. Unfortunately, they were unable to dispel it, which was actually just fine with me.

The rest of the guild was seriously envious of Laurant's other boons, however. While Daemon had plans to spread [Mark of Karma] to as many players as possible by having each one teach me a skill or spell, only the four party members who were with me in the wipe got [Against Overwhelming Odds] and [Spitting in the Eye of Death]. Sellamander got a healing version of [Against Overwhelming Odds]. It had the same name, but boosted healing instead of damage. There was an animated discussion on whether there was a third version of the boon that might reduce Damage taken. They said that if there was, that it would be even more Oh Pee than the two versions they knew about, if they could get that boon on a "tank."

There was also a significant discussion on what exactly had triggered the boons in the first place. Nobody could agree exactly. As the others told the story of our wipe on the gauntlet, many theories were formed, and everyone had their own opinions, which they were eager to try out.

Fortunately, Daemon and Dimple, another officer in the guild, stepped in and established clearly that nobody would be taking me to a dungeon until I had been adventuring for quite a while longer than just a few game days. I was fine with that, as I was a little nervous to delve into another dungeon.

They had set up a banquet as fine as any I'd seen inside the castle, with suckling pig, whole chickens, pheasants, and other poultry, as well as a wide variety of pastries and soups. My [Detect Poison] went off when I cast it on one of the popular beverages, but everyone just laughed and said that it was probably just because I was much too young to drink alcohol. They thought it was sort of funny the way that I cast [Detect Poison] on all the food, because I rather doubted that they had been prepared by a chef like the one in the castle. I even got another level in that spell from doing so.

After I'd eaten until my belly was about to burst, they announced that they had gotten me some presents. They had decided, since I was stuck at level ten until I unlocked a class I liked, that they were going to load me up with "twink gear." They said that my sword, my ring, and my shoes, which I had all gotten from the dungeon, were Bee Eye Ess for now, but I had a ton of open slots to fill. They all watched with amusement as I opened present after present, receiving [Quality Clothes], a [Belt of Vitality], [Finely Crafted Leather Gloves], an [Amulet of Lesser Insight], a [Wristband of Swordsmanship], and a [Linen Cloak of Spellweaving]. Someone suggested showing off my stats when I'd changed into all the new gear, and I proudly did so.

Name	Hail Teoran	Level	10
Guild	<Nethersong Mavericks>	Strength	19
Health	2300/2300	Dexterity	22
Mana	2300/2300	Vitality	23
Experience	Locked	Endurance	19
Age	10	Intelligence	23
Race	Human (blood of the Travelers)	Wisdom	17

Class	Child (1 Advancement option unlocked)	Charisma	21
Job	Bastard of Yuikon	Armor	9
Skills	Short Swords (11)	Spell Damage	5
	Archery (5)		
	Short Spears (5)	Spells	Cure Minor Injury (8)
	Animal Handling (4)		Detect Poison (13)
	Balance and Conditioning (8)		Spark (6)
	Quickshot (3)		Analyze (3)
	Dodge (7)		Storage (5)
	Dash (5)		Lightning Bolt (9)
Traits	High Aptitude		Fireball (3)
	Quick Learner		Ice Blast (2)
	Royal Blood (+5 Charisma, bonus to relations with factions loyal to Yuikon)		Water Jet (1)
	Blessing of Thedum		Polymorph (1)
	(hidden)		Slow (1)
	(hidden)		Mark of Karma (special)

After that, the talk was all about how to advance me further. They thought the best idea was for me to try out a class after I'd unlocked it by using only the abilities available to it, consciously restricting myself from using the other ones that I had available. They also were very eager to help me unlock all the basic classes that they could. Daemon informed everyone that he had done a bit of research and had a list of abilities that I would most likely need for each of the junior classes, which were what children from their world acquired. His list included [Neophyte], which was a young cleric, although I wasn't very interested in being a healer, as well as [Young Warrior] and [Recruit], which were the junior versions of the pure physical classes [Warrior] and [Soldier], but could also evolve into [Fighter], [Skirmisher], and [Marauder]. There was some push back on giving me those classes, as they were often tasked with "tanking," and nobody wanted me to be a tank. Especially me, once they explained what the term meant.

Aside from those three, he also included [Archer], which was the same for adults and children, [Urchin], which could evolve into [Rogue], [Thief], [Fighter], or [Assassin]. [Novice] would require me to fight with my bare hands or a quarterstaff and could evolve into [Monk], but I wasn't interested in that option at all. However, given that I was already skilled with [Short Swords], the class mostly discussed was [Junior Swordsman], which could evolve into a wide variety of sword-based classes, including [Swordsman], [Fencer], [Sword Disciple], and several others.

The amount of information in Daemon's list was a little overwhelming. Some of the guild members were pushing me to make a decision on the spot, which I was completely unwilling to do and had no issues with informing them of such. Gummytiger, however, had an idea that quickly changed that paradigm.

"So, everyone who teaches him a skill earns [Mark of Karma], right?" Gummy asked. "And [Mark of Karma] is awesome and something that everybody here wants. So why aren't we loading him up with every skill we can teach him? *Let's unlock all the classes*, one skill at a time."

"I'll just forget them when I select a new class, though," I pointed out.

"That's not the point! We're going to game the system. It's okay if you forget it eventually, the important thing is that someone will gain an extremely valuable boon. And who knows? Maybe if we teach you enough skills, you'll be able to unlock some super rare or even unknown class. Maybe even one that will allow you to use your magic and swordplay together," Gummy explained. "I mean, you have five years of game time before you lose [Quick Learner], we should take advantage of every minute! It might even be possible to have you learn skills for a class that doesn't usually possess them."

The rest of the guild was enamored with the idea. They began drawing up a chart of skills to try to teach me and having members sign up for a chance to be the one to teach me. There were thousands of skills and spells in the game, and the others quickly began to formulate a curriculum for me. Daemon quickly took control of that project, informing everyone that he would generate a system to fairly decide who got to teach me certain skills. Those with rarer skills were quick to point them out, while many with only common skills wanted to jump the line and teach me right away.

Daemon retreated into his office to organize my education, leaving Dimple as the ranking officer. She made certain that nobody tried to teach me something without getting authorization, while constantly reminding everyone that this was supposed to be a celebration for me. She encouraged people to simply talk with me.

Any resistance to her suggestions was promptly forgotten when I was discussing my past and mentioned not knowing what happened to my nurse, Beckah. The Travelers began jumping up and down with excitement as they received a quest to find my former caretaker and inform me of her fate. They were very excited to perform this service for me, although there wasn't much help I could give them, as I had no idea what became of her after she had been dismissed two years ago.

The other Travelers became *very* interested in my childhood. They asked me all sorts of questions, but the only other quest I triggered was to investigate my mother's situation after her marriage. Eventually I got bored of talking about my past and frustrated when people kept pushing, so Dimple suggested we play games instead.

Turns out that teaching me games *also* triggered [Mark of Karma]. We spent the rest of the day playing dozens of different games, from board games and card games to soccer and indoor Frisbee, and many more. This continued until I got tired and announced that I was going home.

Overall, it was a very fun party, and I really enjoyed myself when I wasn't expecting to. I met a lot of new people, far too many to keep track of, and had a lot of conversations. Hopefully the Travelers of <Nethersong Mavericks> would follow up on the quests to find Beckah and make sure my mother was happy in her new life.

The next day, my education began in the hands of various <Nethersong Mavericks>. My new [Linen Cloak of Spellweaving] disguised my appearance as well, if not better, than the cat-ears headband, so I left that in my inventory on my trip to the Guild Hall. Daemon explained how things were going to work.

"We've got a list of spells and abilities from everyone in the guild," he informed me. "You get to pick the order in which you want to learn them. For now, pick five skills, and I'll contact the Travelers selected to teach them to you. We'll proceed like that for as long as this system seems to be working."

There were dozens of skills and spells on the list. I honestly didn't know where to begin. So, I asked Daemon for advice.

"Well, if you're going to use a sword, you should probably learn some actual sword skills," Daemon pointed out. "[Thrust], [Slash], [Riposte], [Heavy Blow], and [Feint] are active skills that can all be executed with a sword. As I understand it right now, you only have the passive [Short Swords] skill, which provides you with extra Damage as it increases. I think we should also see if we can train you to wield other weapons, such as [Long Swords], [Daggers], [Rapiers], or [Katanas]."

"Okay, let's do that," I agreed.

"I'm going to invite you and some of the players who will be teaching you to a party," Daemon informed me. "Then we'll begin trying to teach you those skills."

Daemon has invited you to a party. Accept?	
Yes	No

I accepted, of course.

Peotre has joined the party.
Consoul has joined the party.
Sheeple has joined the party.

"Ah sweet, I won the lottery?" one of the new players asked through partychat.

"You'll be teaching him [Slash], Peotre. We have a list of five active skills and four passive skills he'd like to learn today," Daemon explained in partychat. "Please make your way to the Guild Hall Aye Ess Aye Pee. I'm not certain how long it will take, but we want to move things along quickly and orderly."

"Oh Em Double You," a female voice agreed. "What am I teaching?"

"Sheeple, you'll be teaching him [Thrust]."

For some reason, Peotre snickered at that.

"Get your head out of the gutter, perv," Sheeple scolded.

"Indeed, let's keep things appropriate, or I'll move down the list to the next person available to teach Hail the skill you've been selected for," Daemon scolded.

"Sorry boss," Peotre said, ruining it by snickering again. Daemon just sighed.

"Let's move things down to the target dummy," he suggested.

I executed the motion perfectly for the twelfth time, only this time was different. I *zoomed* forward on the lunge, and my blade lit up with power, causing sparks to fly in the air as the skill activated.

You have learned the active skill Piercing Lunge!

"I'm done," I announced.

"Excellent. Thank you, Simon. Next, we'll be—"

"No, I mean I'm done for today. My head is starting to feel funny. I think I learned too much too fast," I explained.

"I see," Daemon said, frowning for a moment before nodding. "Well, it makes sense that even an ability like [Quick Learner] would have its limits. It was a very successful session; you have learned, what, six active skills and two passives?"

"I dunno, I wasn't counting," I admitted. "Display Skillbook."

Skills	Short Swords (11)	Spells	Cure Minor Injury (8)
	Archery (5)		Detect Poison (13)
	Short Spears (5)		Spark (6)
	Long Swords (1)		Analyze (3)

	Rapiers (1)		Storage (5)
	Animal Handling (4)		Lightning Bolt (9)
	Balance and Conditioning (8)		Fireball (3)
	Quickshot (3)		Ice Blast (2)
	Dodge (7)		Water Jet (1)
	Dash (5)		Polymorph (1)
	Thrust (1)		Slow (1)
	Slash (1)		Mark of Karma (special)
	Riposte (1)		
	Heavy Blow (1)		
	Feint (1)		
	Piercing Lunge (1)		

Daemon and Stormy and the others in the guild's basement training area examined the skills for a minute. Then Daemon nodded. "Well, if we had continued for a little while longer, we might have unlocked the [Junior Swordsman] class, but unlocking [Junior Warrior] was perhaps enough of a goal for the first session. Now you have two options available to you."

I frowned and nodded, bringing up the notification of my second available class upgrade.

You have unlocked a basic class, [Junior Warrior]. Would you like to change your class from [Child] to [Junior Warrior]? CAUTION: This change cannot be reversed! [Junior Warrior] can be upgraded at a later time to [Warrior] and many other classes.			
Maximum Level	25	Skills Gained	Parry (1)
Strength	+5		Axes (1)
Dexterity	+2		Shields (1)
Vitality	+5	Spells Lost	Lightning Bolt (9)
Endurance	+3		Fireball (3)

Intelligence	-8		Ice Blast (2)
Wisdom	-4		Water Jet (1)
Charisma	-1		Polymorph (1)
			Slow (1)
			Cure Minor Injury (8)
Would you like to change your Class now? (This choice can be made at a later time through the Status Menu)			
Yes		No	

With a sigh, I selected "No." While the increased physical stats looked nice, I wasn't interested in losing my spells. My dilemma hadn't changed one bit.

16

EASTMILL

The [Fireball] exploded in the boar's flank, causing it to scream in pain and turn to orient on me. It roared in anger and charged. I hit it with a second spell, [Lightning Bolt], while it was running, then [Dodged] out of the way at the last moment. The dumb beast slammed right into the tree behind me, stunning itself briefly. Just long enough for me to [Dash] forward. The air shimmered as I [Slashed] and [Thrust], the blade passing through the beast and inflicting significant Damage.

My Dee Pee Ess in melee had really risen since I'd learned actual combat skills. Or so I was told. I still didn't fully understand what that meant and was kind of afraid to ask. But I was doing a lot more Damage now. Simply having a passive [Short Swords] skill allowed me to do a fair bit of Damage, but combined with active skills, I was doing almost three times as much as I was before in melee range. My spellcasting had improved as well, as I had learned [Swiftcast] and [Empower Magic]. That meant that I could either cast a spell in half the time for full Damage, or I could do quadruple Damage for three times as much Mana.

Unfortunately, the beast I was fighting was level nineteen, and I was still a level ten [Child]. It had more Health than I did, and it took reduced Damage from me due to the level disparity. But that was fine. Anything below level fifteen died too fast for me to get any practice in.

The boar recovered from its disorientation and turned to gore me. I [Feinted] to confuse it, then [Dodged] to its side, using [Slash] and [Heavy Blow] and [Thrust] every time they came off cooldown. When my melee skills were unusable, I simply [Slashed] with pure skill. Realizing that the boar wasn't going to die before it could gore me, I [Swiftcast] [Slow] and ran away. It chased after me, of course, enraged that I had taken it down to thirty percent Health.

"Hail, do you want us to help?" Phil called from nearby.

"No!" I shouted, afraid that they'd ruin everything. Because my preparations for the fight hadn't started with an [Empowered Fireball]. The magical trap that I had laid did not activate when I ran over it, but when the boar followed on my heals, spikes emerged from the ground, piercing the boar's soft underside and doing significant Damage. But more importantly, it stunned the boar for a moment longer, enough for me to [Swiftcast] [Arcane Missile] three times.

That, finally, was enough to bring the beast to zero Health. It let out one last roar of defiance, as though it weren't already dead, and then collapsed to the forest floor. I whooped in joy at having defeated it all by myself, despite my handicap. The others began clapping, and I turned to face them, hands in the air in celebration.

"I told you I could do it!" I shouted.

"We believed you from the beginning," Phil insisted. "We were just worried is all. Nine levels is a huge handicap. None of us would take on something that much stronger than us by ourselves."

"If it wasn't for the harsh level cap, [Child] would be the most Oh Pee class in the game. Being able to learn anything just isn't fair," Laurant pointed out. "It's a shame we don't know more about the [Young Noble] class. Knowing whether it would satisfy Hail's 'I want to do everything' requirement would really help figuring out what his next step should be."

"I do want to do everything," I agreed. "It's stupid that there's no class that lets me fight like I want to fight."

"That's why so many of the theorycrafters in the guild think that the best move is to wait until you turn fifteen before changing your class," Thena reminded me. "We think that [Young Noble] might be what you're looking for, and you just need to be patient."

"I don't wanna," I said. "Besides, I think there is a class for me. We just don't know what it is or how to unlock it. I may go with [Young Noble] if I can't unlock a better one in time."

"It's been five days, er, weeks, since you joined the guild," Phil pointed out. "We've already unlocked all the basic classes and a few more advanced ones. What you're looking for sounds like a rare or epic class, though, and unlocking those is effing hard, man. The publicly known ones require an epic quest chain that you need to be at least level sixty to even try. You might be able to punch above your weight, but that's too much for anyone to overcome at level ten."

"*I know* that there's a class just for me," I repeated. But I didn't actually know. I believed it. And I believed it because I wanted to believe it. "I just don't know what it's called or what I need to do to earn it."

"If you say so. The village is just up ahead," Larissa pointed out.

"After I attune the Recall Point there, what are we going to do next?" I asked. I kicked at Laurant's pet golem. I still didn't like those things. I had divested myself of about two hundred of them. I had given five to each of the party members who had gone with me into the caverns, and given one to Phil, Larissa, and Thena. The rest I had given to Daemon to sell. I now had much more money than I knew what to do with after the first batch had sold for more than twenty thousand gold each.

"There's a good grinding spot to the northeast of the village. There's a lake filled with mermen. They're level twenty, so you won't be fighting. In fact, you could head back to the city anytime you want," Thena said. "Or you could check in with guildchat and see if anyone else has something for you to do."

"There won't be," I said, pouting. "Now that almost everyone has [Mark of Karma] nobody wants to spend time with me anymore because I'm only level ten. I hate being level capped."

"But you don't hate it enough to compromise on how you fight," Laurant pointed out. "Which isn't a criticism. I'm just pointing out that the solution exists, it's just undesirable."

"I'm not going to give up half of who I am, either way," I argued. "I want my magic and I want my sword. I refuse to give in, even if it means waiting forever to unlock [Young Noble]."

We continued to chat as we made our way to our destination. There were more beasts along the way, but as long as they didn't bother us, we let them be. The idyllic forest slowly faded into fields as we approached the village. My Traveler friends called it a "Quest Hub" for levels fifteen to twenty. I found it frustrating, because from my frequent visits to the Adventurer's Guild I knew that there were dozens of quests for me to complete here, with new ones being added and old ones changing every day. I just needed to gain five levels before I qualified for them.

I could accept quests like any Traveler. I just couldn't see the ones that I generated myself. Even when the players tried to display them to me, all I saw was a faint blurring rather than the clear system messages that I saw in other instances, such as when someone shared their status, or their skillbook, or a quest unrelated to me. That didn't keep them from telling me about the quests I generated, of course, which is how I knew that right now everyone in the party was on an escort quest to keep me safe until I synchronized with the Recall Point ahead.

The reward for the quest was simply "Reputation," which I didn't really understand, but apparently I offered better quests to those who had higher Reputation with me. Which was just fine as I saw things, because it seemed that only those who actually took the time to be friendly with me received opportunities to gather Reputation and get the good quests. The jerks usually just got a quest to leave me alone. In one case, a person who had earned [Mark of Karma] lost it after calling me a "chatbot" to my face. I didn't know what that meant, but the players who heard it got very upset with him. Everyone was much nicer to me once they realized that my boons were not always as permanent as advertised and that it mattered how they treated me.

Not everybody who wanted it had gotten [Mark of Karma], but a good chunk of the guild had earned the boon. Not all the exotic skills and abilities I had learned showed up in my skillbook, as sometimes two skills with different names were actually the same skill, but I was able to learn a new trigger for it. I had learned eight versions of [Slash], seven versions of [Thrust], five of [Heavy Blow], and fourteen ways to [Riposte]. Fortunately for my guild members, teaching each of their unique skills (which were just basic skills with fancy names) still gave them a [Mark of Karma].

There were other triggers to earning the mark, but nobody could quite figure out what they were. The theorycrafters had several ideas, but generally they thought that anybody who was nice to me for long enough had a chance of earning it.

"The Nexus is right over this way," Phil said, leading us to the center of the village square. As we approached, a disturbance in the air appeared, a silent and black whirlwind of void. I had squeaked the first time I had seen that, but it was just the Nexus making itself known. It vanished as we approached, and I received the notification.

Eastmill has been added to Fast Travel Network.

"I got it," I announced.

"Yup, quest complete," Phil agreed. "What are you going to do now, Hail? You're welcome to come with us as we grind, but there's not much in it for you, and it might be dangerous."

"I'm not afraid," I said, but the idea of just standing around and watching my friends fight wasn't that appealing. "But I think I'm going to explore the village and then go home."

"Okay, that sounds like a plan," Larissa agreed. "Stay close to the village, though. The monsters all around here are tough. Just because you soloed that boar doesn't mean that you're invincible. Remember that we are on standby in case you run into problems."

"I know, I just want to talk with some Natives for a while," I explained.

"Alright then. Have fun, and don't do anything I would do," Phil said, and we parted ways. My friends went off to the lake to grind while I explored the village.

There was a request board, but all the requests were too high level for me to help with, and a general store that sold things like food and potions and a few types of gear, although most of the Travelers would return to the city to visit the marketplace there for upgrades. Otherwise, there wasn't too much to see.

I engaged some of the Natives in conversation, but there wasn't much to learn. It was a farming village that produced turnips, wheat, potatoes, soybeans, and honey. The village had been struggling before the arrival of the Travelers as the mermen from the nearby lake had raided quite frequently, but since the Gates of TirNiki had opened, the Travelers had mostly been keeping the mermen in check.

I was growing bored, and just as I was about to Fast Travel back home, I suddenly got a party invite.

Sophia has invited you to join a party. Accept?	
Yes	No

I was a little surprised by the sudden invitation, and I didn't recognize the name. Still, I could always just leave the party, and I was curious to know who this person was, so I accepted.

"Hey, you *are* a player. I couldn't tell for sure. Why were you wandering around talking to everybody? Are you one of those Are Pee players?" a voice asked, and I jumped when I realized it was coming from behind me and not from partychat. I spun to find a young girl, perhaps thirteen, standing behind me.

"I don't know what that means," I admitted. "I was just exploring. I'm too low level to go grinding with my guild, so they left me behind."

"Oh, that sucks. Yeah, I hit the [Urchin] level cap too. It's stupid that they only let kids level up to twenty-five until they unlock a better class. I unlocked [Rogue], but I want to unlock [Assassin] instead," Sophia informed me. "What about you?"

"Oh, I'm only level ten," I admitted.

"Oh. You've got a lot of work to do!" she giggled.

"I know. But I can't do much now except for run around with my friends and get my Recall Points set for later," I explained. "That's why I'm here in this village. My friends escorted me."

"I was wondering how you got through the forest. I guess that's smart, to plan ahead. You're lucky you have a guild to watch your back, I didn't find <Ragtag Muffin> until I was level fifteen. The game was *really tough* for a while. I kept dying. Lucky that us kids only lose a tenth of a level when we die in game instead of a full level like adults."

"Oh? I didn't know that," I admitted. "I've never died before."

"Oh, mister big shot," she teased. "Yeah, we lose less Experience, and we also get to log back in after five minutes instead of having to wait almost three hours. It's almost not worth growing up."

"Well, you could always just not die as much," I suggested, and she hit me on the arm.

You have taken 1 bludgeoning Damage.

"Ouch," I complained.

"Oh, don't be a baby. Hey, there's a spot I know where we can farm [Silver Clover]. If you find any with four leaves, they sell for like four gold each. Come with me and I'll show you."

"It's not dangerous, is it?" I asked.

"Nah, don't worry, I'll protect you. I'm level twenty-five, after all, and I'll kick any monster's butt if it tries to attack you while we're looking for weeds."

"Okay."

17

SOPHIA

"Oh, wow, so you picked [Urchin] too?" Sophia asked when I popped into [Stealth] next to her.

"I, um, yeah," I agreed, not really wanting to explain my situation. It would be easier to simply fight as an [Urchin] for a while. I had learned to emulate the junior class quite well over the last few weeks of trying to make my mind up on my future progression. I didn't like it, although [Stealth] was useful. But I did more Damage opening up with an [Empowered Fireball] or a similar ranged attack than I did with [Backstab].

"That's cool. My boyfriend wanted me to be a [Neophyte], but he was just being a jerk, trying to get me to be his pocket healer. I like stabbing stuff. That's the whole point of this game, you know? They say violent crime went down by like three percent after *The Gates of TirNiki* went online. Stupid old people still say that it makes players violent, but I looked it up in school and it's actually the opposite. Gamers are *less* likely to hurt people in the real world than non-gamers."

"Oh, that's cool," I said, not really following. "I don't really have formal education anymore. I used to have tutors teaching me every day, and that was terrible, but then my father abandoned me and my mother. Now things are different."

Sophia stopped for a moment and frowned at me. "That's, like, a lot to share with a stranger. I mean, I'm sorry, but we're playing a game, right? I don't mean to be rude, but I'm not your therapist."

"Oh, sorry. My guild tells me that sometimes I overshare stuff," I said.

"Yeah, you do." She frowned, and then asked, "Look, like, you get enough to eat right? And your mom is taking care of you?"

"Actually, I live with my grandfather now," I said, glossing over who my grandfather is. "It's okay, you don't have to worry about me or anything."

"Good. I mean, if you were in danger, you know that you can contact help through this game, right? And there's a counseling option for people to give you advice and stuff. I heard that Arc Inc. got a huge grant for making it part of the game."

"I didn't know that," I admitted. "Thank you."

"Sure. I'm sorry about your dad. My dad is a bit of a jerk sometimes, but he's there for me at least," she said sincerely.

"Yeah. My mom says my dad's a player and players never take any responsibility for the mess they leave behind," I said.

"Hey, so, let's change the subject. They are this way. Stay in [Stealth]; we have to move past the apiary, and the bees will swarm us if we bother them," she explained.

I nodded, and soon we were in the field of [Silver Clover]. We began our search for the four-leafed variety, and Sophia began talking about her life in the other world. She said she was in "seventh grade" and had a boyfriend named Mark. They had started playing together, but she out-leveled him because he was in sports and she was not. He still logged in for a few hours after practice, but even with the accelerated time in the game, he only had between seven to twenty-one hours of play time every day.

I didn't really understand, but I nodded along.

"He's actually kind of mad at me because he says I was only supposed to play when we could play together," she said. "I'm thinking about dumping him because that's kind of possessive. What do you think?"

"I don't know," I said. "I'm honestly only understanding about a third of what you say. The other world confuses me sometimes quite a bit. This world makes much more sense to me than what you Players describe 'Earth' to be like."

Sophia snorted at that. "You're such a guy. And kind of a nerd, but it's okay because you're cute. Or your avatar is cute at least. You're not fat and ugly in the real world, are you?"

"No," I said. I withheld the fact that I didn't exist in her world.

"I mean, it's okay if you are. Sorry, that just slipped out. Pretend I didn't say it, okay?"

"Okay."

"Seriously though, great job on designing your avatar. I like the way your eyes are different colors. I wish I had known that was an option. I'm going to maybe do the same thing if I ever buy a [Skin-Changing Potion]. But my parents don't give me that much allowance and they'd be annoyed if I spent it all in the game."

"How much does a [Skin-Changing Potion] cost?" I asked.

"Like forty bucks," she answered. "Or five hundred gold, but I can't get that much until I unlock [Assassin] and am able to go to higher-level areas."

"Do you really want one of those potions?"

"Nah, I'm pretty happy with this avatar for now."

"Are you sure? Because I could buy you one," I offered. "I have a lot of gold."

"That's sweet, but you shouldn't give money to people you met on the internet," she said. "Didn't your parents ever teach you that?"

"What's the internet?"

She laughed hard at that, although I wasn't in on the joke. The conversation continued like this while we searched through the clover. We found a fair number of them, and I leveled herbalism twice!

I enjoyed her company quite a bit, although I only understood a fraction of what she said. After we had been together for about thirty minutes, she announced that her boyfriend had come online.

ReaperSnake has joined the party.

"Hey Mark. We're out collecting clover again," she said to partychat.

"Oh Em Gee, again?" the disembodied answer came. "What do you need that much money for anyway?"

"It's better to make it now and have it for when I want something expensive, instead of having to farm it later," she argued. "Anyway—"

"Wait, we? Who's with you?"

"Oh, right. I met a kid in Eastmill. He looked kind of lost and lonely so I figured I'd hang out with him for a while," she said. She nudged me. "Don't just stand there, say hello to my boyfriend."

"Um, hello ReaperSnake," I said.

"Oh Em Gee, I need to change that stupid screen name," the voice said. "Just call me Mark, okay kid? Sophia, I'm on my way to meet up with you. What's your name, kid, and how old are you?"

"I'm Hail Teoran, and I'm ten years old," I answered.

"Is that your real name or screen name?"

"It's my only name."

"He's into Are Pee, Mark," Sophia said. "And he's pretty good at it. You should have seen it. He came in with a bunch of players, but then he started hanging out around town like he was an En Pee See, talking to the bots and stuff. I guess that's why he's only level ten though."

"Well, whatever. Hail, you better not have been hitting on my girlfriend."

"Oh my god, Mark, shut up. He's only barely old enough to play this game. We've just been hanging out."

"Yeah, well, okay," Mark said, backing down. "Oh Em Double You."

"What does that mean?" I asked, and Sophia laughed.

"Are you serious?"

I blushed. "People in my guild say it all the time, but I didn't want to ask them because it seems like everyone should know automatically."

"Jeez, you sure you didn't find him under a rock?" Mark called out over partychat, which made me blush more.

"Shut up, Mark," Sophia scolded. Then she began to explain what an acronym was, and several of the more common ones. Including Dee Pee Ess. Finally! Although I didn't really understand the difference between Damage per second and just doing more Damage. Sophia said it was possible to get really big numbers without doing a lot of Dee Pee Ess, and vice versa.

One of the things that was confusing me was the alphabet. I had learned the Native language. We had forty-eight key letters with another seventeen symbols that modified them and . . . and it's complicated. Sophia spoke English, which apparently had only twenty-six letters. It was only the magic of the Traveler's system that allowed us to communicate. So, when I heard an acronym, half the time I wasn't even certain I was hearing letters and not words. But I was afraid to explain this to Sophia.

"I can't believe your guild never told you this stuff," she said.

"I think they'd explain if I'd asked, but they're all older than me and I didn't want to look stupid," I admitted.

"That's what you get for joining an adult guild. You should join Ragtag with us. It's a guild for kids. It's run by a few adults, but they're just like chaperons or babysitters or whatever. They just sit in chat and make sure we're not talking about taking drugs or having unprotected sex or something."

"I don't know. <Nethersong Mavericks> have helped me a lot. I'd feel bad leaving them after all the help they've given me," I admitted.

"Whatever, they couldn't have helped you too much. You're only level ten," she said. "Just say the word and I'll get you an invite. Until you make up your mind, let me toss you a friend invite," she said.

"Hail, she hasn't mentioned it yet, but we do get twenty gold for referring other kids to the guild. That's why she's pushing so hard," Mark said.

"I'll think about it," I promised, although I wasn't sure that I would. Still, I accepted Sophia's friend invite when it came.

"Wait, you said he's only level ten?" Mark asked. He came jogging over from the village, taking a wide berth around the apiary. I nearly gawked at his appearance; rather than matching his childlike voice, he had the body of an adult with sculpted muscles, which were very much on display in his leather vest. He grinned at me. "You like the bod? The ladies love my bod."

"Oh please, you look nothing like that in reality, Mark," Sophia scolded. "Anyway, picking an adult avatar was stupid. You're too clumsy. Maybe if you had gone the magic route instead of picking a [Junior Warrior]. There's a reason you're not supposed to change your dimensions by more than ten percent when you start playing, and it's one of the reasons we died so many times early on."

"Whatever. That's just a suggestion, not a rule, or I wouldn't look like I do now," he said. "So, what are we going to do about him being level ten?"

"You're only level fifteen, Mark. We can go kill level thirteen spiders or something. Hail, do you have the travel point for [Southwater Falls]?" Sophia asked.

"I do!" I said. Eastmill wasn't the first escort quest I had issued; I had been to a majority of the nearby starting areas up to level twenty to establish Return Points.

"Let's go there. There might even be a bounty on the spiders this time, but if there's not it's still a good place to grind."

Pretending to be an [Urchin] was tougher than I thought. I had all the abilities, but according to Sophia I was using them all wrong. She kept correcting me and telling me things that went counter to what the theorycrafters in my guild had told me. And, well, her way of doing things wasn't as good. She thought that I should open a fight with a bleed attack, but the level thirteen spiders were dying too fast for that move to do that much Damage. It was better to open with a [Backstab] for the extra critical Damage. Even when the enemy was strong enough to survive that long, it was better to [Expose Armor] right away so that my attacks did full Damage.

She also might have noticed that my abilities that should have worked on skill instead had cooldowns, forcing me to chain attacks together instead of spamming the same attack over and over as most [Urchins] do. [Urchins] used the resource Skill instead of Mana; it recovered much faster, but you only had a maximum of one hundred Skill, while attacks cost thirty to sixty points. She didn't say anything, but I thought I felt her eyes on me as we battled the giant spiders. The lair was over a cavern, which I was a little nervous to enter for fear of finding a dungeon and becoming stuck in another gauntlet, but I put on a brave act.

Except that I was looking at her too. Sometimes. Out of the corner of my eye.

After about an hour, Mark exclaimed in glee. "Finally, I'm level sixteen!" he shouted. "Hoo yah!"

"Congratulations," I told him, feeling more than a little envious. "It's going to be a long time before I level again."

"What do you mean? It shouldn't be that long, these spiders are pretty good grinding," he argued. "I'm surprised you haven't leveled already."

I considered coming clean, about everything. That I wasn't really a Traveler, that my class was locked, that I'd never been to their world. But something held me back.

I liked the way they were treating me. And I wanted to fit in with them. But if they knew I was a Native, would they start treating me like just another En Pee See?

"Hey, wait, what's this? [Mark of Karma]? Like the Buddhist thing?" Sophia asked, her eyes wide as she stared at her status. "Holy crap, when did I get this? It's totally awesome!"

"What are you talking about?" Mark asked.

"Check your buffs. I'm not sure where it came from, but—"

"Wait, I see it," he said. "Okay, so what?"

"It says it's permanent," Sophia explained. "That's like, impossible. To get a permanent buff like this is way Oh Pee, because it never stops being useful. Not when you lose a level every time you die! Where did this come from?"

"It's from me," I said. "I'm not really a player, and sometimes when people are nice to me they get [Mark of Karma]. I don't know why, it just happens. My class isn't really [Urchin], it's [Child], and that's the reason I can't level. [Child] locks at level ten because it would be too Oh Pee if I could keep leveling it and—"

"Hold on, wait, stop," Mark said. "What do you mean you're not a player?"

"I'm a Native. You call us En Pee Sees," I explained.

"But you're in our party," he said.

"Oooh, I heard about this! I thought I knew your name!" Sophia exclaimed. "It's a new feature, Mark. It was hot on the forums a few days ago but then it died right after. Man, your chat algorithms are really good, I really thought I was talking to another player."

"Um, thanks. I don't know what that means," I said. "I'm sorry I didn't tell you sooner."

"It's fine. Now what's this about your class?"

I figured it would be easier to just show them, so I opened my status window.

Name	Hail Teoran	Level	10
Guild	<Nethersong Mavericks>	Strength	19
Health	2300/2300	Dexterity	22
Mana	2300/2300	Vitality	23
Experience	Locked	Endurance	19
Age	10	Intelligence	23
Race	Human (blood of the Travelers)	Wisdom	17

Class	Child (19 Advancement options unlocked)	Charisma	21
Job	Bastard of Yuikon	Armor	9
		Spell Damage	5
Passive Skills	Short Swords (14)		
	Archery (5)	Spells	Cure Minor Injury (8)
	Short Spears (5)		Heal Wounds (3)
	Long Swords (8)		Heal Major Wounds (1)
	Rapiers (9)		Cure Disease (1)
	Katanas (6)		Cure Poison (1)
	Axes (1)		Soothing Regeneration (2)
	Staves (1)		Detect Poison (13)
	Daggers (1)		Spark (6)
	Polearms (1)		Analyze (6)
	Shields (1)		Storage (5)
	Animal Handling (4)		Lightning Bolt (12)
	Balance and Conditioning (8)		Fireball (6)
	Dodge (7)		Ice Blast (4)
			Arcane Missile (5)
Active Skills	Quickshot (3)		Entangling Vines (2)

	Power Shot (1)		Siphon Life (1)
	Piercing Shot (1)		Inflict Curse (1)
	Dash (5)		Dazzling Lights (1)
	Thrust (7)		Concussive Sound (1)
	Slash (8)		Befuddle (2)
	Riposte (4)		Water Jet (3)
	Heavy Blow (6)		Polymorph (2)
	Feint (5)		Slow (4)
	Piercing Lunge (3)		Create Trap (3)
	Swiftcast (4)		Decay (1)
	Empower Magic (3)		Mark of Karma (special)
	...		...
Traits	(Focus to expand)		

The pair of teenagers blinked at the screen—which had gotten significantly larger over the last few weeks—and burst into questions.

18

CONSEQUENCES

"And you just told them everything," Daemon asked, pinching the bridge of his nose.

"Yeah. Sorry. I didn't know they were going to post everything I said on the forums though," I said. "But I don't see why it's a big deal."

"It's a big deal because this 'ReaperSnake' recorded everything, including your status screen, your explanations of your abilities, and even the fights afterwards where you displayed your full talents," Daemon explained.

We were in his office, all five of us. Daemon was blaming Thena and the others for leaving me unsupervised, and he was upset with me for revealing everything to complete strangers. I had been upset at first to realize that Mark had shared everything I had told him, but now I was starting to become upset with Daemon.

"So what?" I challenged. "I don't see why it's such a big secret."

"It's not a secret! Not anymore! That's the problem!" he exclaimed. "Hail, [Mark of Karma] alone will cause every major guild in the game to turn their heads towards us. But you told them about the other boons you can grant as well. And you even implicated yourself in the situation with [Gemos Caverns] being offline. And then you gave them each one of the [Immature Gemos Hearts]! You've effectively painted a great red bullseye on both yourself and the guild as a whole. You have no idea how much difficulty this may cause us! That little shit's post might cause the entire guild to collapse!"

I looked at my friends for support, but they also looked fairly grim. Not upset with me, exactly, but upset with something. "Is that true?" I asked them.

"It's not good for anyone," Thena admitted. "There were a few buyout offers when you first joined, but they were sort of half-hearted. Now the super guilds are starting to get persistent. Hail, Daemon is right that your boons are a significant advantage later in the game, and the super guilds will try to take you from us now that they know about them."

"They can't! They don't own me! You don't own me! I won't go!" I said in defiance.

"That's nice to hear, Hail, but it's not as simple as that," Daemon explained after forcibly calming himself. "If the high-end guilds align against us, there's very little chance that the <Nethersong Mavericks> will continue to exist. Not in its current form, at least."

"Perhaps that's not such a bad thing," Laurant said, his voice even. "Honestly, I was getting a little tired of the way we were treat-ing Hail. Everyone lost interest in him as soon as they got their [Mark of Karma]. It's a little disgusting, to be honest, the way we've been using him. He's not a buffbot. He's more than a chatbot too. You've been too busy 'managing' him to really 'see' him, Carl. I think he's self-aware. I think he's more than just a gimmick; I think that Arc Inc. was serious when it said it was developing a way for players to have 'digital children.' You need to stop treating him like an asset and start treating him like an actual kid."

I cocked my head to the side. "Why wouldn't I be self-aware?"

"Whether or not that is true, it is all the more reason to keep his capabilities quiet," Daemon said patiently. "I'm not dismissing the possibility. In fact, I've considered it myself long before you brought it up. Which is exactly why I've been stressing that we must treat him ethically in all things. Every interaction I've helped facilitate for him has been beneficial to him in some way. You took him to a dungeon where he nearly died the day after you met him. Which of us has been a better caretaker?"

Laurant bristled. "I didn't know that it would trigger an event, okay? I couldn't have known that in advance, could I? It was a new bee dungeon! It should have been a cake walk. Anyway, you're forgetting something important. He wants to fight! He wants to get stronger and level up. If we don't help him do that, then he's going to try to do it on his own."

Daemon sighed, covering his face with a hand for a moment as he collected his thoughts. "I suppose the damage is done, at this point. Arguing about it now will only divide us when we need to be united. Hail, from now on, please refrain from showing your status screen to anyone except for the theorycrafters that I've approved to help you. And please refrain from—"

"You're not the boss of me," I interrupted. "I'm tired of you telling me what to do all the time. You don't boss the others around like you do me. If you don't stop, I'm going to quit this guild and join another."

Daemon frowned, and he had the look on his face that showed I had just generated a quest. He sighed. "It seems the system agrees with you. You're right, I have no real authority or control over you, Hail. But I have always been upfront and honest in my dealings with you; does that not count for something? Surely, we can work together? Believe me when I tell you that the guilds who will be poking around will not—"

"I'm going home, and you can't stop me," I said, and I activated Fast Travel to return to my bedroom.

Stomping my feet in frustration, I summoned my golem vanity pet and chased it around the room, venting my frustration by hitting it with a baton until I wearied of the game. This annoyed the golem, but it never fought back. Right then, I wished it would. I wanted to fight something.

When I finally gave up torturing the innocent pet, I collapsed on my bed and gave in to an hour or so of self-pity. I hadn't exactly asked them to keep my secrets, but the way Mark had immediately revealed everything on the forums bothered me. I had thought that we were friends, but now I wasn't sure. As for Sophia?

It was Mark that had posted the videos, not Sophia. There was no reason to be upset with her. I checked my friends list, but she was offline. If I understood right, then she wouldn't be back online again for almost a week, and when she came online she wouldn't stay for more than a day and a half before needing to go back to her world for sleep.

I sighed in frustration. I didn't know what to do. I wanted to talk with Mark and Sophia, to find out why Mark betrayed me and whether Sophia had known anything about it beforehand, but it was impossible for me to reach them while they were in their world.

I wanted to hit something. To blow it up with my magic and then cut it apart with my sword. So, I decided to go out to the courtyard and do exactly that to the target dummies out there. They weren't the strong, nearly invincible ones that the guild had, but they would have to do.

"I don't see what the big deal is, just put up a new target dummy," I suggested.

Malkios glared at me. "The problem is the disturbance you caused by creating an explosion of that size in the courtyard, young man. The entire guard mobilized because we thought we were under attack! Do you have any idea how serious this situation is? I should drag you before your grandfather and—"

"So do it," I challenged. "You're not going to do anything to me except yell at me. Well, I'm tired of getting yelled at and told what to do all the time. I'm not going to just do whatever anybody tells me just because they told me to. I'm going to do what I want to do!"

Malkios maintained his glare for a few moments, then he sighed in defeat. "Hail, I understand. You're young and the world isn't exactly like you think it should be, and you needed something to vent your frustrations. But the next time you feel the need to blow something up, would you at least clear it with the guards beforehand?"

I frowned and looked behind him towards the remnants of the combat dummies I had destroyed. They lay shattered into pieces among the cobblestones, blackened from the fire and lightning I had unleashed on them. I had burned out my full pool of Mana in my assault, which was frustrating as I had nothing to hit with my sword anymore.

But I had caused a disturbance, and now I was feeling somewhat foolish. Again.

"I'm sorry, Malkios. I wasn't thinking. I was just so angry at everything."

"I understand, Hail."

"That's the thing; you don't understand, do you?" I said. "You're just a chatbot."

"Perhaps I do need to drag you before your grandfather," Malkios said, his expression turning grim. "What have I done exactly to have earned such a slur from one that I have loyally protected for all his life? Just because the Travelers see us as inferior doesn't make it so, Hail. I understand your frustration better than you know because I feel it myself. As captain of the guard, I am a significant source of quests, and I am constantly being barraged by players who lack common courtesy and are constantly being rude. I will not suffer that from you as well."

I frowned, remembering all the times that I had seen Malkios interacting with players as I watched from the distance while I was younger. Perhaps he did understand what I was feeling.

"They only care about my quests," I complained. "My quests and my boons. And I don't know what to do about it."

Malkios sighed. "There's really nothing we can do. The Travelers are going to be the way they are no matter what we do or say. At the same time, however, we *need* the Travelers. Not just for slaying monsters, but for the continued stability and existence of our world. It's not commonly known, Hail, but when the Gates of TirNiki close again, this world will come to an end. It is the connection between our world and the 'Earth' that the Travelers come through which is sustaining us."

I frowned, confused. "What are you saying?"

"The Gates can't be closed from this side. Not anymore. Only from the other side. But once that happens, this world and all its inhabitants will cease to exist. We are dependent upon the Travelers for more than just pushing back the darkness. So, I am forced to grin stupidly and listen to them prattle on while occasionally issuing them a task of significance. That is the true reason your father rose as far as he did, as fast as he did. Not only was he a valiant warrior, but he treated us Natives with the respect we deserve." Malkios sighed. "I am not certain when or why that changed."

"Did you actually meet him?" I asked. "What was he like?"

"Oh yes, I met him. In fact, I was the one who issued him the quest to rescue your mother," Malkios informed me. "Only a handful of players had reached the level that he had by that time, and he was extremely skilled beyond merely being highly leveled. He said that every day he practiced the sword in his own world before coming to ours, that swordplay and sleep were the only two things that he still did on the other side of the gate."

"Do you know why he—"

"I met him a handful of times, for a few minutes, Hail. I do not know the man's heart. I cannot begin to speculate as to his motives," Malkios said quickly. "But what is done is done. The world does not always turn out in the way you wish it to."

"I know that," I said. I sighed, looking back at the smoking debris. "I'm sorry about the damage I caused. I was just very upset. I didn't think I would break everything like that though."

"It is fine," Malkios said. "These dummies were meant to teach children how to hold and swing a sword properly, not withstand a powerful magical attack. I suppose I can have a proper target dummy acquired for the next time you need to vent your emotions."

"Thank you, Malkios. The ones they have in the Guild Hall are perfect, I just don't want to go there right now." I sighed, looking up at the sun to judge the time of day. "Maybe tomorrow."

19

LOYALTY

After Malkios left to continue with his duties, I found myself adrift once again. Uncertain what to do with myself, I ventured into the castle library and spent some time reading about the heroic legends of old. Just because the Natives had only one life—most of the time anyway—did not mean that we did not have our own heroes. In fact, now that I thought about it, was it not more heroic to venture forth with your life truly on the line, rather than with the certain knowledge that death was merely a setback?

I was reading into the evening when a servant came to fetch me.

"There are Travelers here looking for you. They refuse to leave without speaking to you. Malkios has verified that they are no threat, but said they will be dispersed if you do not wish to speak with them. Will you see them?"

I considered. I wasn't certain I was ready to face the guild again so soon, but I was in a better space than I had been this morning. I no longer wanted to blow something up, at least.

"Where are they?"

"They are waiting in the courtyard. I must say, they are more respectful than the usual Travelers I have encountered," the servant informed me. "I will let the captain know that his services will not be required."

"Hold off on that. Depending on what they say, I may want the guard to drive them off after all," I admitted. If Daemon had come to yell at me some more, then I wanted nothing to do with him.

The servant nodded and was gone. I turned back to the book I was reading about Sir Jeremy and the Banshee to finish the passage I was on. I had learned young that when someone comes to see you, it's often beneficial to make them wait a little while. If you interrupted what you were doing for every visitor you received, they may get the impression that their time was more valuable than yours. I may only be a royal bastard now, but I still remembered some of my lessons from when I was prince. Ten minutes passed before I marked my place in the book and rose to meet my visitors.

When I reached the courtyard, I was struck stupid for a moment. I flashed back to the fateful parade where I had met my father, for before me was an assembled squad of mighty Travelers in armor that rivaled the splendor that I had witnessed that day. Dimple was with them, and compared to these strangers she was drab and plain, despite being out-fitted in a fine dress rather than adventuring gear. When they noticed my arrival, the Travelers as one turned and knelt before me.

"Prince Hail, I am Tarisha Swordsong from the shores of Miami. We elite, of the guild <Peasant's Revenge>, have come to pledge our allegiance," the leader said. Her fine armor shone red in the sunset, and her purple hair accented her features quite well. It was not her appearance that struck me dumb, however, and it took me a full minute to think of a response.

"I am but a royal bastard," I objected. "If I were a knight, perhaps I could accept your oath, but without royal permission to obtain forces of my own, accepting might be seen as an act of rebellion."

"Is that so? I apologize if I have put you in an awkward posi-tion. Perhaps we have been a little overeager, but we have been trying to obtain an audience since your existence became known," Tarisha explained, standing up. Her soldiers behind her did the same, though they remained rigid and disciplined. "I wish to inform you that we have just received a quest to obtain royal permission to become your vassals. We will pursue this endeavor with full vigor as soon as possible."

I frowned in confusion. "Who are you people?"

"Hail, <Peasant's Revenge> is one of the guilds that approached us immediately after you joined. Unlike the others, however, they did not seek to steal you away from us, nor to acquire ownership of our guild through any means, neither honest nor nefarious," Dimple explained. "Instead, they sought an alliance. They correctly predicted something like this might happen and offered us various resources and ideas to help sustain ourselves in the event that endgame guilds actually became interested in you."

"What sort of resources?" I asked.

"It's a matter for managing things in the real world. I could try to explain them to you but—"

"I'm not stupid," I said, growing annoyed. "If you're going to treat me like I can't understand what's going on like Daemon does then you can just leave."

Dimple sighed and looked away. "Daemon hasn't handled things very well, has he? Fortunately, while he was focused on developing your skills, I was preparing things for when your abilities were exposed. Public opinion is very important in the other world. And our laws are very complex. <Peasant's Revenge> has several contacts who are experts in those fields, and they have provided introductions and helped us obtain their services at very reasonable rates. In exchange, they asked for opportunities to get to know you, and to take part in your story."

"My story?" I asked, frowning.

"Yes. They are a role play guild. They take the story of this world much more seriously than many casual players, and at the same time they have many players of superb skill," Dimple explained. "If I'm being entirely honest, they might be a better fit for you than <Nethersong Mavericks>."

"Are you kicking me out?" I asked.

"No! You're welcome to stay in the guild as long as the guild exists!" Dimple exclaimed. "It's just that we might not be able to serve your needs to the extent of a guild with more resources and connections like <Peasant's Revenge>. I'm only saying this because I have your best interests at heart."

"Everyone claims that, but I'm not certain that I believe them anymore. I'm not certain that any of you know what my best interests are, and I think you often confuse them with your own," I said, putting on my best royal demeanor. After all, they had come to me!

"I'm sorry, Hail. I believe that you are correct, and I can only apologize for the way we have treated you," Dimple said.

"I do not have to remain with the <Nethersong Mavericks>," I pointed out. "I have an invitation to join <Ragtag Muffin> now. And although I can't take them as vassals without my grandfather's permission, I could probably join the <Peasant's Re—oh, he's probably not going to be happy about the guild name, is he? Well, I can join Ragtag at least."

"Young Lord, as long as your grandfather approves, I believe there are hundreds of guilds which would accept you. Especially now that the truth has come out and it is known that serving under you will provide significant benefits in the form of boons," Tarisha said. "However, I must warn you: while I believe that <Ragtag Muffin> is a fine guild, and I support its purpose entirely in providing children a safe haven in this game, I do not believe that you should attempt to join them. The pressures which threaten Nethersong would crush Ragtag utterly."

"You don't know that," I said, frowning.

"I'm sorry, young lord, but I do. I cannot predict the future, of course, but I know the currents of this game well enough to make an accurate prediction on how such a course of action would end," she said. "I am not saying that you cannot make friends with the children of Ragtag. In fact, I believe it would be good for you to do so. However, if you were to officially join them, their guild would collapse within a week. Their endowment is a small one, just enough to support the pay of the moderators in their guildchat."

"So, I should join <Peasant's Revenge> instead?" I demanded. "How do I know you're not simply misleading me so that you can have me to yourself?"

"Because I am not interested in having you in my guild. To be honest, while we are a role play guild, much of our guildchat is out of character. I would not have you exposed to that aspect of myself or my guildmates."

"So, you're saying you're keeping secrets from me?" I asked.

"Yes and no. Every guild of a certain level has secrets, and if we are being honest, you have proven yourself to be a poor steward of those. However, the reason I will not accept you into our guild, despite wishing to serve you, is that we wish to deal with you entirely as inhabitants of this world. We do not wish you to see our out-of-character personalities, and our guildchat and our forums have many Oh Oh See moments."

"I see," I said, although I didn't really understand. I sighed in frustration. "So, what do you think that I should do?"

"Continue to work with <Nethersong Mavericks> to develop yourself into a fine young warrior. I understand your dilemma in choosing your class. However, I believe that you will find a solution to this problem sooner rather than later. My men and I shall endeavor to obtain permission to serve you properly. In the meantime, I wish you good health. And I advise you to stop venturing out of the castle unguarded. There are plenty of murder hobos who would love the notoriety they would get from killing you. Not all the Travelers are as honorable and just as the ones you have been dealing with so far."

Tarisha knelt once more, then motioned for the rest of the assembled Travelers to do the same. "I believe I shall seek out your Captain Malkios. I know him well, and he will have the best idea of what course of action I should take in order to become your vassal. In the meantime, Hail, I wish you prosperity and growth."

The squad of mighty Travelers dispersed. Dimple remained behind a moment longer.

"Hail, Daemon sends his apologies. He wasn't certain if you wanted to see him or not. We just . . . most of us are used to operating out of a guidebook, or at least having one available, when it comes to situations like yours in the other games we play. We're breaking new ground having you in our guild. We're trying to do things the best way possible, but the truth is we're floundering in the dark. So, on behalf of the entire guild, I'd like to offer my apologies. We hope you'll forgive us."

I took in the apology for a minute, then sighed. "I just wish you didn't treat me like a buffbot or chatbot or whatever. I want to get stronger and you're helping me do that, but I barely actually get to know anybody. I mean, I've only really been around like ten people in the guild for longer than it took for me to give them [Mark of Karma]."

"I'm sorry you feel that way. I will talk with Daemon and the others about getting you some more face time with some of the members who wanted to get to know you," she promised. "Is there anything else you'd like to discuss?"

"No, just, I'm sorry that I caused problems for the guild," I said. "I know most of you are trying to help me."

"It's fine. We're still in your corner, Hail. With <Peasant's Revenge> supporting us, things will be different. You'll see."

"If you say so. I'm going to go to bed," I told her. "Good night, Dimple."

"Good night, Hail."

I left the courtyard and returned to my room. Kicking off my boots, I collapsed on the bed without undressing as I reviewed the day. After punching the mattress in frustration, I rolled over to look at the ceiling. Well, at least I had learned several lessons. I was never going to show my status to a stranger again.

20
MAYHEM

Malkios found me at breakfast again. "Hail, I have been informed that there are several credible threats against your life. As such, I am placing you under guard for the foreseeable future."

"What? Someone wants to kill me?" I asked.

"So claim the representatives of the Traveler guild <Peasant's Revenge>. They kept saying something about murder hobos. I've checked the registers, but it's not an official guild registered with the system. That does not mean that the threat is not real, however. <Peasant's Revenge> has an excellent reputation, and I do not believe that they would raise a false alarm. I will be insisting that you remain within the castle until the situation is resolved."

"That's not fair!" I argued.

"Your life may be in danger, Hail. I refuse to take a chance. I will be placing you under guard as well. <Peasant's Revenge> has offered to help supplement my numbers for this task, but I believe the castle guard to be sufficient so long as you remain within the walls."

I seethed with frustration, but I could tell from Malkios's stern body language that he would not budge on this matter. Instead, I spent the day reading in the library again.

Several days passed, and Malkios would not relent. I felt like a prisoner in my own home. I could have Fast Traveled away, but I had little doubt that the punishment upon my return would have been severe. I passed the time either reading in the library, chatting on guildchat, or browsing the forums.

Sophia did not come online when I expected her to. I had removed Mark from my friends list after what he had done, but I wanted to speak with Sophia before I made my mind up what to do about her.

The time passed quickly and slowly in alternating bursts and lulls. I received two letters, one from my mother telling me that she missed me and that I was to have a baby brother or sister in six months. She requested that I write instead of sending Travelers to check on her the next time I was worried. Apparently, my guild had caused some disturbances in their quest to investigate her situation. She insisted that she was healthy and that she was being treated well by her husband and his family.

The second letter was from Beckah. She thanked me for sending my guild after her and saving her from dire circumstances, which she would not describe. She informed me that she had found new work as a nurse to a little boy and girl of noble blood in another kingdom and was very hopeful for the future. She included several names of players who had helped her, and I quickly committed them to memory. I would see to it that they were properly rewarded!

The problem was how. I had plenty of gold from the [Immature Gemos Hearts], but gold felt inadequate. I had some of the hearts themselves left in my inventory, but that didn't feel right either. I resolved to think on it for a while before acting. It was somewhat uncharacteristic of me to put something like this off, but I had recently seen the results of being hasty. I was determined not to forget, so I put the letter up on my wardrobe with a tack.

Another week passed, and my house arrest continued. Then, one morning, an unexpected message arrived from the system.

Instance Generation Completed
Zhesa Castle Has Been Claimed
Initializing Dungeon

I blinked at the sudden notification. I had just gotten dressed for breakfast and was still feeling somewhat groggy. After a moment of studying the message in confusion, I closed it. But then my wardrobe came alive!

Motes of white light emerged from it. Familiar motes, like the ones that marked the entrance to [Gemos Caverns]. Memory and realization hit me all at once: the [Daughter Dungeon Core] I hid there weeks ago! The motes swept over me as I rushed to my wardrobe to try to deactivate the core before it was too late, but when I passed through the lights, I felt dismay.

The wardrobe had seven crystals growing on it. It turned, and an eye opened as it looked at me. Stones peeled out from the wall and began attaching themselves to the wardrobe, while others circled it in swift orbit that would keep me from getting close. I used [Analyze] to determine its level.

Hail's Monstrous Wardrobe
Golem
Level ???
Health: ?????????/ ?????????

I felt my skin go white. Three question marks, not two. This monster was at least level one hundred, and possibly much higher. I couldn't tell; my [Analyze] wasn't nearly high enough. The monstrous eye looked at me, and I realized I had two choices. I could die, or I could run. I ran.

The motes that marked the edge of the dungeon had escaped my room, but as I ran through my hallway, I saw the edge of the dungeon as it continued to expand. I could outrun it, but only just. As soon as I passed through the glowing motes, I activated Fast Travel to the [Market Square].

"Help! Help! The castle is turning into a dungeon!" I shouted for all to hear. "We need help from you Travelers! There are innocent people who will be trapped inside!"

"Hey, it's that kid," someone said.

"Oh shit, did you just get a dungeon quest?" said someone else.

"Let's check it out! We won't be able to clear it, but sometimes there's exclusive loot until a dungeon has been cleared the first time," said someone else.

"And the quest says to rescue people. I bet that's a one-time thing," said another speaker.

I didn't stick around to listen to the commotion I had caused. I sprinted through the town, shouting my call to arms for all to hear as I rushed through town to every place I could think of where Travelers gathered in any number. The market, the auction, the restaurants, any place that drew them. It was one of the lower population times, but I still encountered dozens of Travelers moving about. Most of them began moving towards the castle with some haste and excitement once they heard my proclamation.

Others followed me instead. I didn't turn around to exhort them to help, I just kept moving to the next place. Until one of them caught up to me.

"Hey, kid, what's going on at the castle? Give me the deets," he said, grabbing me by the shoulder.

"Let me go," I said.

"Seriously kid, tell me about the dungeon. What level is it? What sort of monsters? Is there a first-time clear bonus? Come on, tell me," he said.

I [Swiftcast] [Polymorph] and he turned into a chicken. Unfortunately, his friends had caught up to us by now, and they weren't letting me go until I told them everything I knew.

"I don't know anything. I just know that a new dungeon is forming and that people are in danger. Please, you're Travelers. You've got to help them!"

"Quest declined. You're coming with us."

I looked at the Travelers that had surrounded me, confused for a moment. "Wait, is this a kidnapping?"

"Yeah, kid, I suppose it is," one of them admitted. "Sorry, not sorry."

"I don't have time to be kidnapped. I have to save my home!" I shouted. A quick glance around with [Analyze] showed that the players were all twenty levels or more above me. I really had no hope of winning.

Which just meant that I didn't need to hold back.

I [Swiftcast] [Fireball]. Not at the Travelers, but up into the sky as a flare. I thought my only real hope was to draw attention to myself. I was hoping that the city guard would respond to the disturbance and help me, but I was worried that they would have already responded to the castle instead. Still, there wasn't enough time to worry about it, as the players realized my strategy and were trying to grab me.

I focused on [Dodging]. I struck back when I saw an opening—and I was surprised how many openings I found—but my primary focus was just to stay moving. My sergeant at arms would have been disgusted with the level of skill these Travelers displayed. Even without my skills, I was able to dance just beyond their reach and pepper them with counter strikes. I even had enough focus to launch another flare.

"Slippery little eel, isn't he?" one of the players grumbled after I had landed a [Slash] on his arm.

"You're just too slow," I taunted back. "How'd you ever get to level forty-five with moves like that?"

The kidnapper laughed. "Kid, we're trying to take you alive. Don't think for a moment—"

I hit him in the face with a [Concussive Sound] spell. He was close enough to the others that they were caught in the deafening roar. It gave me enough time to cast a third flare, and I followed up with a wave of [Dazzling Lights], little stars that zipped about right in front of their faces, obscuring their vision.

The two spells wouldn't last long; [Concussive Sound] stunned for three seconds, but with the level disparity that was cut in half. It deafened for longer than that, but that wouldn't help me. [Dazzling Lights], however, allowed me to break out of the enclosing circle and resume running.

It wasn't enough to lose them, so I kept casting [Fireball] into the sky as I moved, hoping to bring rescuers to me. Instead, I stumbled upon a Traveler as I rounded a corner.

"Help! I'm being kidnapped!" I shouted.

"Oh yeah! Quest accepted baby! Who's trying to—oh shit!"

I didn't slow down, running straight past the stranger who had accepted my quest. Despite being outnumbered, the unnamed player put himself in the path of the oncoming kidnappers, bravely drawing his axe and bracing himself to meet the tide. He managed to delay two of them, or perhaps rather two of them remained behind to deal with him, while the others continued to chase me.

I kept running, aiming for the Guild Hall. If I could get inside, I would be safe in the guild's unique instance. Maybe my friends would be able to fight them and put them in their place.

Just as I was thinking this, a shadow passed over me. I looked up to see a wyvern descending. Before it crashed into the street, a figure launched from its back, landing right in front of me.

"Tarisha?" I asked, surprised to find her here.

"Lord Hail! I heard you were in distress and have come to your aid! My men have been scouring the city looking for you; I am blessed to have found you first. How may I help?"

I turned towards the oncoming foes. "They're trying to kidnap me!"

"I shall show them the folly of their ways," Tarisha promised, unsheathing her sword and stepping between me and the kidnappers. "Stay behind me, Lord Hail. I shall keep you safe."

I swallowed nervously, but stopped my wild flight. I quickly [Analyzed] Tarisha—level one hundred eighty-six. My attackers were an average of level forty. She should be able to handle them with ease.

"Lord Hail is under my protection," she declared. "Prepare to die for your transgressions!"

"Lady, this is none of your—"

The speaker was promptly bisected by a [Voidcut] before bursting into blue motes of light. The others promptly followed him into the void between worlds as Tarisha dispatched them each with ease. It was terrifying to behold, but such was the power of an elite Traveler.

"There's another two, and a man who stepped up to help me, back the way that I came," I said. "If he's still alive we have to help him."

"Quest accepted. Lead the way."

Sprinting, I doubled back to where I'd found the man who had intervened. He was still alive, and either one of the two kidnappers who had stayed to deal with him had abandoned their assault or the axe warrior had dealt with them. But I could tell that he was getting low on Health and would not last much longer in his duel.

I [Swiftcast] [Lightning Bolt] at his opponent. Tarisha needed no other signal. She used an ability, one like [Dash], or perhaps it was more like [Blink]. But it was at least three tiers above anything that I could do. She appeared behind the kidnapper and dispatched him with a sword through his chest.

I caught up a moment later. I cast [Heal Major Wounds] upon my other rescuer once, then twice. It took all my Mana, and still only healed him for a fraction of his lost Health.

"I thank you, stranger, for stepping up to help me during my time of need," I said. "Take this broach and show it to Captain Malkios once the chaos at the castle calms down. Tell him what transpired here, and he will see to it that you are rewarded."

"Ah yeah!" the Traveler exclaimed. "I don't suppose you have any other epic quests for me, do you kid?"

"The keep is turning into a dungeon," I said. "I need to get the word out so that we can rescue the Natives trapped inside."

"Sounds like fun," the stranger said. "I'll head right over. I'm sure there's pugs already forming for it, I'mma get in on some of that."

I turned to Tarisha. "Are you going to the dungeon too?"

"No. I will stay with you," she said. "You should not be unprotected in this climate."

She whistled, and her wyvern, which had been circling overhead, landed beside us. "Besides, I can help you get the word out. Come. We shall shout your call to arms from the skies!"

21

JEORAN

"It was very clever, shooting those flares into the sky, Lord Hail," Tarisha praised. I clung closely to her; the saddle of her wyvern was not meant for two passengers, and I was afraid of falling off. Her violet hair kept blowing into my face, and I kept having to spit it out. At least it distracted me from our proximity. "Did you know we would be looking for you?"

"I was trying to signal the city guard," I shouted to be heard over the roar of the wind. "Magic like that is illegal inside the city. They should have come to investigate, but I suppose they might be busy with the castle."

"It was very clever, but it also could have led your enemies straight to you," she informed me.

"I was desperate. And I was already outnumbered by Travelers of much higher levels. The situation could not have gotten much worse," I pointed out.

"It could have. Instead of attracting me, you could have attracted a high-level murder hobo. I don't want to think of what would have happened then," she explained. "Please, Lord Hail, take your safety seriously. Until you have gotten much stronger, you are not safe to wander the world without powerful allies at your side."

"I had no choice. The dungeon was forming. I had to get the word out," I objected.

"Yes, I suppose it was an emergency," she agreed reluctantly.

For the next hour, we rode through the city. Whenever we saw a group of players, Tarisha would land, and I would shout to them the news about the dungeon forming in the castle. Before very long, we were making a regular circuit, moving from one Return Point to another.

"The Travelers have put the word out through the forums," Tarisha said, "But they are all hoping to gain a boon from doing your quest. That is why they gather."

"I don't care, as long as they're here to help," I responded.

"Let us hope that they are," Tarisha agreed.

After a time, the number of new Travelers arriving into the city peaked, and then trickled down. It never stopped, exactly, but we were getting fewer and fewer recruits.

"I suggest we head to the castle at this time, Lord Hail," Tarisha said, "And see if there is another capacity in which we may help Captain Malkios and King Rain in their response to the dungeon outbreak."

"What about the incoming Travelers?" I asked.

"The word has gone out far and wide, Lord Hail. Those who were too slow to obtain your quest will regret it for a long time, but it is not your responsibility to ensure their happiness," She answered. "Your grandfather and the others must be worried about you by now. No doubt they are aware of your activities, but I believe it is time for us to check in with them."

I considered for a moment and nodded. "You're right. Take us to the castle."

We flew swiftly over the city to the castle. We were breaking the law in doing so, but no arrows or ballistae were fired upon us as we approached. We landed, and the wyvern nuzzled Tarisha after we dismounted.

I frowned to see that the castle gate was now the swirling motes of a dungeon entrance. Just outside of the gates was a hastily erected series of tents. There were many Natives, but very few Travelers outside the instance limits. I assumed that all the Travelers I had gathered were already inside. Several of the tents housed evacuees from the castle, as well as their family members from the town with whom they had reunited. We were immediately escorted into the largest tent, which housed my grandfather, Captain Malkios, and a large number of castle guards. They looked up, and I saw looks of relief upon their faces.

"Hail! Where have you been? How could you make us worry so?" My grandfather demanded.

"I was gathering the Travelers," I protested. "I sent all that I could find."

"Yes, thank you for that," Captain Malkios said, although he did not sound entirely sincere. "The guards' response to the dungeon forming was thrown into chaos by the waves of Travelers. Our evacuation—"

"Do not pretend that you had the situation in hand, Malkios. It was the Travelers who saved us, and it was Hail who sent the Travelers," My grandfather scolded. "I am relieved that you are well, Hail. I know I have not always shown it, but you are my grandson and I do love you."

"I . . . thank you, Grandfather. What is happening? Is everyone safe?" I asked.

"We are still performing headcounts. The master servants are making the rounds, trying to determine if anyone is missing, and where in the castle they would be most likely to be found. We have sent the Travelers in with Rescue Quests," Malkios explained. "Unfortunately, many of the parties seemed to have perished. The dungeon is filled with a wide variety of different leveled golems, and many would-be rescuers have been returned to the space between worlds."

"I was in my room when my wardrobe turned into a monster," I informed them. "I tried to [Analyze] it, but it was much too high. It was greater than level one hundred, I am certain of that."

"Thank Thedum that you managed to escape," Grandfather said. "Tell me, from which direction did the wave come? We are trying to pinpoint the origin. We know it came from the residential quarters near your room."

"I—I think it came from my wardrobe," I admitted.

"It's as I thought. This may have been an attempt upon Hail's life. Or, if not, a deliberate act of sabotage by an unknown enemy. It's well known that it takes a dungeon core seven weeks to fully charge," Malkios explained. "To those of us who know of dungeon cores, at least. I do not believe it has been part of your education yet. Seven weeks ago, an intruder was spotted inside your room. A cat-kin with orange hair. A search was performed, of course, both for the intruder and of your room itself, but no threat was found. It appears that we were not thorough enough. How could we have missed this?"

"I—" I did not know what to say. Knowing they were referring to me in my cat disguise, I asked, "What would happen to this cat-kin if you were to find him?"

"If he were responsible for this mess, he would be hanged for treason, of course," Grandfather declared. "But first he would be interrogated to see who put him up to this. A dungeon core is a potent weapon, not one that any child can simply get their hands on. The royal family has but a handful, and the location of each is a secret guarded closely."

"Fortunately, none of them were in the castle treasury," Malkios grunted. "I have sent messengers to check on them, to make certain they have not been misplaced."

"Your Majesty, is this information which should be shared in front of an outsider such as myself?" Tarisha asked.

Grandfather snorted. "The location and number of our cores is secret, not their existence. No kingdom would remain independent for long without at least one dungeon core at its disposal. Besides, you are my grandson's liege-woman. Or are you withdrawing your pledge so soon after offering it?"

"Grandfather, I rejected her. I am but a bastard, and—"

"You did not reject her, you sought my permission, and correctly so. You have it, and more. I was planning to wait until your fifteenth birthday, but it is clear that time will not wait for us. I hereby raise you, my grandson, to the rank of Earl. I rename you Hail Jeoran, and proclaim you founder of house Jeoran. We shall set aside the matters of your lands and such until the current crisis is past," Grandfather declared.

I was dumbstruck. When I finally had a thought of how to respond, I knelt. "My liege, I cannot remember the proper oath for an Earl to swear loyalty to his king. But I swear it. To king and country."

Grandfather snorted. "Where has my mischievous grandson gone all of a sudden? I seem to have misplaced him."

"This is a field promotion, lad," Malkios stated. "The pomp and ceremony can wait until we've destroyed the dungeon core and reclaimed [Zhesa Castle]."

Tarisha took the moment to kneel, first to my grandfather, then to me. "Before his Majesty's gaze, I renew my pledge of service, loyalty, and fealty to you, Earl Hail Jeoran. I shall be your sword, and my guild shall be your shield. This I swear by my god and by yours."

I frowned at her, wondering to which gods she referred. Thedum, for certain, but, "Do you worship Are En Gee as well?"

She laughed slightly, breaking the ambiance. "Everyone worships Are En Gee, my Lord."

"Very well. I accept your oath of fealty, Tarisha of Miami. In the name of Thedum and Are En Gee."

"In the name of Thedum and Are En Gee," she agreed. She stood and turned back to the king and Malkios. "Is it possible to reverse the damage that has been done? I had no idea that a dungeon could be destroyed, but you imply that it is possible."

"That is because you are a Traveler. To you, a dungeon core is an inert piece of rock. You would not recognize its significance even if you held it in your hand," Grandfather explained. "The dungeons that your kind delve are the ones that we either could not destroy on our own before opening the Gates of TirNiki or the ones which we have deliberately cultivated."

"I had no idea," Tarisha whispered. "So, the low-level dungeons are not natural formations?"

"Some are wild, some are tamed," Malkios stated. "Most are a mix of the two. Your kind has only been in this world for ten years and seen but a handful of new dungeons spawning, so you do not understand the threat they pose. It takes a powerful subjugation force to clear a dungeon permanently, and you must enter the core instance in order to succeed. It is impossible for you Travelers to do that, which means that only Natives can close a dungeon. But doing so almost always comes at a terrible cost. Our greatest warriors have spilled their lifeblood closing dungeons for untold generations. Had we not, we would have been overwhelmed by dungeon spawn long ago."

"It is a dangerous venture," Grandfather agreed. "Fortunately, sending wave after wave of your kind through a dungeon may not clear it, but it does prevent dungeon spawn from forming."

"I'm not certain I understand what you mean by 'Dungeon Spawn,'" Tarisha said.

"I believe you refer to them as either 'Rare Elites,' or in the worst case, 'Worldbosses.'" Malkios stated. "The dragons are the worst of the lot. Some dungeon spawn simply carve out their own territory and establish lairs. Others actively hunt and pillage. The dragons do both. Luckily, your kind is especially keen on hunting them down before they become a problem."

"I understand. Is this knowledge that I should guard closely, with my life even? Or should I instead distribute it?" she asked.

"It is all well-known already to the powers of this world and yours," Grandfather explained. "I am in fact surprised that you did not already know. It is withheld from our children until they come of age, but it is not some great secret either."

"<Peasant's Revenge> is a powerful guild, but it does not surprise me that it lacks the information of some of the other guilds," Tarisha answered. "Many of my kind view the hunting of Worldbosses and the clearing of raids as a competition. It would make sense to hide the knowledge of their origin in order to control it. In fact, unless I am ordered otherwise, I shall share this information only with a few trusted individuals from my world."

"That would be wise," Malkios agreed. "We shall begin putting together the subjugation force. If only we knew for certain where the dungeon core was."

"I . . . I believe it is in my wardrobe," I answered. "That is where the wave of lights came from. But it has become the boss monster [Hail's Monstrous Wardrobe], and I fear none of the guards are strong enough to defeat it."

"I suppose that is something to go on," Malkios said. "We know that it came from that area, at least. But you are correct. The subjugation force will not be made up of the city or castle guards. We must send out the word far and wide to our allies, Your Majesty, and request a gathering of this world's elites."

"It is unfortunate," Grandfather said. "I had hoped to never be forced to rely upon them again, once the Gates of TirNiki had opened. But the need is dire. I shall convene a meeting of the Dungeon Busters."

"Your Majesty, there is another factor to consider, which has not been addressed yet," Tarisha stated. "And that is the response of my kind if this dungeon is destroyed too early. Many Travelers are very excited by the emergence of a new dungeon and are keen to explore its depths. If you destroy it before they have had an opportunity to delve it, many of them will be upset. I cannot predict the exact numbers, but some of them may begin to spend less time in this world."

"I see. What would you suggest?"

"I suggest you hold off on destroying the dungeon for three weeks," Tarisha answered. "That will give them three days in my world. They will consider it a limited weekend event and will be much happier than if the dungeon opened and closed within an hour."

"Malkios?" Grandfather asked.

"It fits with my understanding of the Traveler's nature as well. Tarisha of Miami gives good counsel," Malkios answered.

"Then it is good that she will be at my grandson's side. Very well. Pass word to the Travelers that they have three weeks in which to delve into [Zhesa Castle]. Then the Dungeon Busters shall convene once more, and I shall lead them to reclaim my home," Grandfather proclaimed. "Now then, I must confer with my Captain of the Guard in private. Unless there is anything else?"

"Yes, Your Majesty. I have but one more matter to bring to your attention," Tarisha said. "There was an attempt to kidnap Lord Hail's person while he was gathering the Travelers. I do not know for certain if it was a coordinated attempt by the forces of my world, or the actions of several greedy opportunists. However, I believe that it is unwise to leave him unguarded in the near future. My guild and I shall take whatever guard duty we can, but even we need to sleep."

"I understand. Thank you for foiling their plot," Grandfather said. "My thanks are all I can offer at the moment, but once the crisis is past you shall be properly rewarded."

"There was another Traveler who aided me as well, Grandfather. I gave him my broach and told him to seek out Malkios," I piped up.

"Then he, too, shall receive a just reward," Grandfather pledged. "But we shall worry about that when this dungeon is destroyed. For now, I suggest you return to your Guild Hall. You shall be safe there until this crisis is past."

22
PLANNING

"Display Status," I said once we were outside. I had to see. I did not make them visible to Tarisha, however; I had learned that lesson.

Name	Hail Jeoran	Level	10
Guild	<Nethersong Mavericks>	Strength	19
Health	2300/2300	Dexterity	22
Mana	2300/2300	Vitality	23
Experience	Locked	Endurance	19
Age	10	Intelligence	23
Race	Human (blood of the Travelers)	Wisdom	17
Class	Child (19 Advancement options unlocked)	Charisma	26
Job	Earl	Armor	9
		Spell Damage	5

It was true. I was no longer a prince, nor a bastard, but an Earl. I had even gained five Charisma points from the promotion. I felt as though I were in a dream, and I feared that my advancement had the same ephemeral permanence of dreams. Grandfather had promoted me without all the information.

If he knew that I was responsible for the dungeon, would he still have been so generous? Or would I instead have found myself in irons? He said that he would hang the cat-kin that he thought responsible. Would he carry out the threat if he'd known the one responsible had been standing right in front of him?

I began to shake. The events of the past few hours overwhelmed me, along with the fear of being discovered. I had known nothing of dungeon cores. If I had known that it was a weapon, I would have immediately handed over my [Dungeon Daughter Core] to my grandfather upon receiving it. I had thought . . . I don't know what I had thought.

To borrow the parlance of the Travelers, I had fucked up big time. I could only hope that the servants had managed to stay safe long enough for the guards and the Travelers to rescue them. As I looked around at the evacuee camp, I saw many familiar faces looking back at me. Then they burst out into cheering my name.

"I don't understand," I said.

"They know you sent the Travelers to rescue them," Tarisha explained.

"I . . . I don't deserve this," I objected.

"Whether or not you deserve it, they need this right now. They need a hero, and you're the man of the hour," she said.

"What do I do?"

"Just smile and wave," she suggested, and I took her advice as we made our way to where her wyvern was waiting. We were in the air before I finally broke down. Tarisha landed on a nearby roof and turned to comfort me, pulling me into a comforting embrace.

"It's too much," I whimpered.

"I know, I know," she said. "Do not fear. I shall protect you. Even from your grandfather, should that be necessary."

I tensed, and she simply nodded.

"I know. I do not know where you got the core from, but I know that there was no intruder, that the cat-kin Captain Malkios is looking for is none other than you," Tarisha said. "It doesn't matter to me, I will serve you the same, and I will keep your secrets."

"I didn't know!" I assured her. "I didn't know when I used the [Dungeon Daughter Core] that this would happen! Now the castle is in chaos, and people are trapped by monsters, and—"

"Hail, my guild tells me that the evacuation of the castle is complete. The quest to rescue the trapped citizens has been completed and everyone who partook has received a handsome reward. There does not seem to have been any fatalities among the Natives. Many injuries, but while the golems inside are territorial, they are not overly hostile and did not pursue those who fled from them. So far, the only casualties have been Travelers, but as you know, they'll be back in a day, minus only a level from their death penalty."

"That's," I sagged into her and began crying harder in relief. She held me, nearly a stranger, but comforting me as a mother might her child. And I needed it. Minutes passed before I composed myself again, though my eyes were red and my nose slightly runny. "What do I do now?"

"We go to the Guild Hall and talk with Daemon, Dimple, and a few others. You are not alone in this, Hail. We will help you through it. And we will protect you."

After I had calmed down a bit more, we got back into the saddle, and moments later we were outside the Guild Hall. With the alliance between <Nethersong Mavericks> and <Peasant's Revenge> official, Tarisha was able to enter with me. It was mostly empty aside from a few of the leadership players. The rest were at the dungeon.

We entered a conference room. Upon one wall was a crudely drawn map of the castle. There were pins in it, with notes as to the location of boss monsters and the average levels of certain areas. The lowest level area was the courtyard, which had cobblestone golems ranging from levels twenty to thirty. The dungeon was levels seventy through eighty, the stables levels forty to fifty, and the kitchens levels sixty through seventy. The keep was a sudden jump in difficulty as a level one hundred twenty to one hundred forty area, and the residential wing where my room resides was the highest of all, with scouts on the forums reporting that they were seeing enemies above level one hundred eighty.

To complicate the entire dungeon were the roving patrols, of which sixteen different groups had been identified. The majority of the "pats" were lower leveled, meaning between twenty and sixty, while one of them was strong enough to be considered a level one hundred fifty boss.

The levels of that monster, and the ones in the residential wing, officially made this an "endgame dungeon," despite the many regions that contained low-level monsters. It also complicated things for closing the dungeon. Tarisha shared her understanding of the information Grandfather and Malkios had shared with us, an understanding that was much better than mine and left the leadership in the room in silence.

"Dungeon Busters, huh?" Dimple asked. "I wonder who all from our world knows that dungeons can be destroyed?"

"And I wonder who will try to stop the king from destroying this one," Daemon sighed. "And how exactly is Hail mixed up in this mess?"

Tarisha looked at me. "Hail? You can trust them. Do you want to explain it, or should I?"

I swallowed as the eyes in the room all turned to me. I felt my cheeks redden, but I knew it was time to come clean. "When I escaped the [Gemos Caverns], I got a weird message. It said a couple things. It gave me the [Immature Gemos Hearts], you all know that. But it also said that [Gemos Caverns] had evolved. And—and it gave me a [Dungeon Daughter Core]. I didn't know what it was, so I used it in my bedroom and hid it in my wardrobe. This is all my fault."

Crying in front of Tarisha had been one thing, but I refused to cry in front of everyone else. I managed, barely, to restrain myself from doing so. I felt the weight of their gazes upon me, judging me. I wanted to crawl into a hole and—

"Extraordinary!" Daemon exclaimed. "It all makes sense now. Why your boons are so powerful, why you are even in this game; everything is coming into focus. Gideon Lachlann truly screwed up by rejecting you, Hail, because if he controlled you, he would have reclaimed his place as the most powerful player in the world. To have the power to change, create, and destroy dungeons would make him and his guild the undisputed masters of this game."

Dimple stomped on his foot under the table, causing five Damage. Daemon winced, but continued. "Having you in a group must be a workaround to allow players to enter the core instance, which only Natives are able to access. I suspect that, had they not wiped on the gauntlet, Laurant and his group would have encountered the dungeon core of [Gemos Caverns]. While I don't know that they would have been able to interact with it, I am certain that you could have, Hail. And with them to guide you, they may have been able to guide you through any of the options the core gave you. You're not only a perfect Dungeon Buster, Hail, but you could potentially be a perfect Dungeon Master!"

He stood and began pacing. "We need to get a team to [Gemos Caverns]. If it takes a week for a dungeon to form, then perhaps it takes a week for it to evolve as well? There may be a new instance waiting for us. And while everyone is occupied with the castle dungeon, this may be an opportunity for <Nethersong Mavericks> to claim a first clear of a new instance."

"You're not mad?" I asked, confused.

"I'm not your grandfather, Hail. I'm certain that if word got out, you'd be in quite a bit of hot water with the Natives, but we're Travelers. We see a new or changed dungeon as an opportunity, not a crisis," he explained. "Although the next time you're awarded a dungeon core, it might be for the best to give it to someone for safe-keeping, while a decision is made on what to do with it."

"And that someone he should give it to is his grandfather," Tarisha said sharply. "Once we have figured out a way to mitigate the fallout from today, at least."

"What? Oh, yes, that was not greed speaking, that was simple prac-ticality. While this situation is very exciting, I would prefer that new dungeons come about in a more orderly fashion than this," Daemon agreed. "Who do we have online to re-explore [Gemos Caverns]?"

"Whoever we send will be annoyed that they're being taken away from the castle," one of the other guild leaders pointed out. I didn't know her name. "Especially for a level ten dungeon."

"It may not be a level ten dungeon after its evolution," Daemon countered. "Offer a reward for the first team to clear it. Something generous but not over the top. Honestly, I think simply the first-clear bragging rights should be sufficient, but I see your point."

They planned the incursion into [Gemos Caverns] for some time before Tarisha put her hand on my shoulder and indicated for me to follow. "There is nothing more for you to do here, Lord Hail, you have spent enough time today in the thick of things. I believe I know a way to take your mind off these matters for a while. Come with me to the practice area. We shall sharpen our swordsmanship together."

"You want me to train? *Now*?" I asked.

"What else is there for you to do, except to dwell on your mistake and a situation which is well outside of your control? I firmly believe that you will soon become a great lord, and a great power in this game, but at the moment you are still a child. Yet today's events show that you will require the strength to defend yourself against any who would try to claim you. So yes, I want you to train. Now. Follow me, Lord Hail."

We entered the training pit in the basement, where Tarisha went through the training swords with great care before selecting one for herself. They were enchanted such that they would never do more than one Health worth of Damage. Useless in actual combat, perfect for training. I went over to select one for myself, but she stopped me.

"Lord Hail, I have nearly two million Health after the boon I have just gotten, and the level disparity alone will prevent you from doing any significant Damage to me. This is not a fight between equals. I am giving you a handicap by using this sword and avoiding my abilities that would one-shot you, but it is still within my power to reduce you to zero Health simply by beating you endlessly with this training sword," she said.

"You are at a disadvantage in that you are coming into this game after many have already acquired great power, and many of those are not interested in being on friendly terms with you. You must grow accustomed to fighting ones such as that. That is the sort of training which I am proposing for you."

I frowned, then drew my [Gemheart Short Sword]. I had several other swords that I kept in my inventory, different styles that had been used for teaching me [Katanas], [Long Swords], and [Rapiers]. I had gotten a significant synergy bonus when I learned those skills, meaning that I didn't need to level them from level one, but the short sword was still my strongest and most familiar companion.

"What rules?" I asked. "Are we tracking points?"

Tarisha laughed. "The rules are 'try to kill me without dying yourself,' Milord."

Then she teleported behind me, [Slashing] at my neck with an opening attack that would have beheaded me if she were not using an enchanted training sword.

You have taken 1 point of slashing Damage.

I spun about and countered. So, it was going to be like that, was it? Fine. Two could play that game.

23
DANCE

It turns out that two could not actually play at that game. I collapsed to the padded floor, gasping for breath. "I yield. I'm running low on Health."

"Yes, I did say we would stop at ten percent," she agreed, her training sword disappearing into her inventory. "Still, you are quite skilled, and improving fast. Have you made any gains from our training these past two days?"

"Display Status," I said, again not making it public. It wasn't that I didn't trust Tarisha, it was that we weren't alone in the basement, and I didn't want anyone taking "screenshots."

Name	Hail Jeoran	Level	10
Guild	<Nethersong Mavericks>	Strength	19
Health	189/2300	Dexterity	22
Mana	23/2300	Vitality	23
Experience	Locked	Endurance	19
Age	10	Intelligence	23
Race	Human (blood of the Travelers)	Wisdom	17

Class	Child (19 Advancement options unlocked)	Charisma	26
Job	Earl	Armor	9
		Spell Damage	5
Passive Skills	Short Swords (17)		
	Archery (5)	Spells	Cure Minor Injury (8)
	Short Spears (5)		Heal Wounds (5)
	Long Swords (8)		Heal Major Wounds (2)
	Rapiers (9)		Cure Disease (1)
	Katanas (6)		Cure Poison (1)
	Axes (1)		Soothing Regeneration (3)
	Staves (1)		Detect Poison (13)
	Daggers (1)		Spark (6)
	Polearms (1)		Analyze (7)
	Shields (1)		Storage (6)
	Animal Handling (4)		Lightning Bolt (14)
	Balance and Conditioning (10)		Fireball (8)
	Dodge (11)		Ice Blast (7)
			Arcane Missile (8)
Active Skills	Quickshot (3)		Entangling Vines (4)

	Power Shot (1)		Siphon Life (1)
	Piercing Shot (1)		Inflict Curse (1)
	Dash (9)		Dazzling Lights (2)
	Thrust (12)		Concussive Sound (2)
	Slash (13)		Befuddle (2)
	Riposte (9)		Water Jet (5)
	Heavy Blow (12)		Polymorph (3)
	Feint (8)		Slow (9)
	Piercing Lunge (7)		Create Trap (3)
	Swiftcast (7)		Decay (1)
	Empower Magic (4)		Mark of Karma (special)
	...		...
Traits	(Focus to Expand)		

"I've gotten a few skill-ups," I admitted. "More than a few, actually. But nothing to unlock my class. At the rate things are going, I won't be able to help at all with the clearing of the castle."

"Nobody is expecting your aid with that endeavor, Lord Hail," Tarisha assured me. "You are simply not strong enough yet. I say this without malicious intent, but you would only get in the way and slow others down as they were forced to protect you from monsters that you cannot handle yet."

"I know that. But it's so frustrating," I said. "I want to help. It's my . . . my home."

I had been about to say, "my fault," but corrected myself just in time, remembering that not all the guild members who were watching my beating were "in the know." Most of them were simply waiting for their groups to get online so that they could challenge one of the new dungeons. Or for their friends to respawn after having fallen to the patrols in the castle. Apparently, there was a significant amount of crying on the forums over those patrols, as they had caused a large number of wipes.

Others thought that they were great and laughed at the noobs who couldn't keep track of where the large, thundering monstrosities were in time to get out of their way.

Regardless, the conservative estimate was that at least fifty thousand Travelers had lost a level or two in the castle dungeon, and many more would die in the remaining weeks before Grandfather sent in the Dungeon Busters. The Busters were not widely known yet, although <Peasant's Revenge> had spread it around on the forums that this was a limited time event that would only last the weekend. That was another thing the Travelers were complaining about, but Tarisha assured me that if you handed a Traveler a statue of themselves cast in silver, they would complain it was not made of gold.

One of the observers casually threw a heal-over-time spell onto me, which brought me back to full Health, but it did nothing for my exhaustion from having fought constantly for almost two hours before collapsing. Nor did it fill my Mana, so the break continued.

"Where did you learn to fight like this, Tarisha?" I asked as I recuperated. I could have used [Meditation] to refill my Mana faster, but then we would have resumed. I thought conversation a more pleasant course of action. "Are you a great warrior in your world?"

"Believe it or not, I'm a dancer," she answered. "Or I was, at least. I trained professionally and made a bit of money at it, but my ankle was injured in a fall. I began playing this game while I recovered, and I loved it more than my dancing career. So, I quit that and dove into this world entirely. I spend every moment in this world that I can, except for when I need to care for my physical body. Do not worry about my health, my Lord. Although I am no longer in the perfect state for my craft, I remain athletic and exercise for at least one hour every day at a pace that many would struggle to compete with."

"That is good to know. Mister Thomas the Administrator says that some of the players I have been interacting with have been neglecting their health. That they need to improve their diet and exercise."

"Diet and exercise are struggles that many in my world try to overcome," Tarisha agreed. She gave a glance at some of the onlookers, some of which looked somewhat embarrassed. "But it is not something you should worry about, my Lord. The equipment that sends us to this world also keeps close track of our physical health, to the point where it will even call the health authorities on its own volition if we are putting ourselves at risk, or if it notices signs of a significant health event occurring."

"That is also good to know, although I do not really understand. There is much about your world that confuses me," I admitted. "Is it true that you have iron birds that carry you from place to place? Why do you not simply Fast Travel instead?"

"Fast Travel works only in worlds that we visit, not in our native world," she explained. "And yes, the iron birds are real. As are the towering buildings which reach thousands of feet into the air. Miami and many of the great cities are littered with these 'skyscrapers,' and even common people like me may find their homes or work within them."

"I wish I could see them," I admitted. "It sounds very impressive."

"While it is not possible for you to visit my world, I could post some pictures and videos of my home onto the forums," she suggested. "Perhaps I will even post one of my dance performances."

"That would be wonderful. I would be grateful," I said. Then I began blushing. "Tarisha, what do you think of my footwork? It is nothing compared to yours, and I fear that is why I keep losing to you."

"I have been working on my footwork since I was four years old, Hail. I incorporate my dancing skills naturally into my swordplay. It is—oh. Are you asking me to teach you to dance, my Lord?"

"My sergeant-at-arms is always yelling at me to improve my footwork, and you are a master at it," I said, my face turning even more crimson. "I would be a fool not to ask for your help."

"There is nothing to be embarrassed about, Lord Hail. I would be happy to teach you. Perhaps we shall split our training time in two; for every hour of sparring, we shall do an hour of simple dance. And, of course, there is no need for you to cast magic in order to dance properly, so we shall begin immediately."

I groaned as I fell deep into the hole my mouth had dug for me. I got to my feet, and the lessons began. The movements that Tarisha showed me were often difficult despite their simplicity, and I found myself growing more embarrassed as time wore on, but my guardian noticed and chased the onlookers out of the basement with the threat of her good sword. We continued in this fashion for the rest of the day, until finally I got the [Exhaustion] debuff and had to rest for the night.

The guild had turned one of the offices into a bedroom for me, and that was where I retired. It was small compared to my bedroom in the castle, and I'd had only my adventurer's outfit to change into until I'd requested that someone buy me some nightclothes. But they had furnished me with a bed, and that was all I really required.

I was eating breakfast in the morning when I met Laurant again. He was in a good mood, whistling as he sat down near me.

"I hear Tarisha is really putting you through your paces," he said.

"She's worse than any instructor or drill master I've ever had," I agreed, whispering conspiratorially after glancing around the room to make certain we were alone.

"Well, it's good for you, I'm sure. Actually, I had a thought. I know that she's teaching you dance, and that will be great for your swordplay. But there's another thing we do in our world. Well, some people do it. Not very many, to be honest. Or at least not many do it well. It's called parkour. I was thinking that would be another good thing for you to learn. I doubt it's an actual skill in this world, just like dance, but it would still help you get—"

"Actually, [Dance] is a skill. I'm at level four now," I told him.

"Oh. Well, like I was saying, it will help you get around. It might even have been handy the other day, while you were running from those thugs. I'm not exactly an expert, but I did mess around a bit with the local obstacle course while I was in high school. I could show you a few things."

"That sounds like an excellent idea," Tarisha agreed, her voice causing my spine to stiffen involuntarily. "Did you have an actual lesson planned for him, or are you completely unprepared to follow through?"

"That's a little harsh, isn't it?" he asked. "As it happens, there's a stretch in the market where some of us have set up a sort of obstacle course. It annoys the Natives, which is kind of funny, really; they have tried to take it down but we keep putting it back up. I was thinking he could train on that for a few hours instead of having you just wail on him like you have been."

"And if he is recognized? You know that his cat-kin disguise is now the most wanted person in the city, right?" She countered.

"That's why I bought him another disguise so that he doesn't have to keep hiding out in the Guild Hall all day. It's a mask that will turn his hair dark red. I've also got him a change of clothes. They're the same stats as what he's wearing, just a different cut and color. I figure with those two things, nobody will recognize him from the videos."

"It seems like you actually have thought this through," Tarisha admitted. "Very well. I suppose we will try it for a while and see if the lord gains anything from the practice."

"Awesome," Laurant said, and he pulled a masquerade mask from his inventory. "Here you go, Hail, this is for you. I'll put the clothes in your room for you to change into, although I don't see why you can't just equip them directly."

"It's more comfortable to change into them properly, and if I equip them directly then I can't adjust them later," I explained. I tried on the mask. "How does it look?"

"It doesn't change your eyes," Tarisha noted, "But to a casual observer you do look like a completely different boy. Of course, many may know of this sort of item, so many may know that you are wearing a disguise. Not necessarily that you are Hail Jeoran in disguise, however. Boys from our world do many strange things, and it will not be so out of place."

I finished eating, and we left the Guild Hall together. It was my first time leaving that building for several days, and it felt good to be outside again.

"So, what is parkour, anyway?" I asked.

"A way to look foolish," Tarisha answered.

"Never mind that. I'll show you when we get to the obstacle course," Laurant promised. "It's basically just a way of moving from point A to point B as fast as possible."

"Right. Looking foolish is merely a byproduct of the process," Tarisha agreed.

"If you're going to hate on parkour, why are you even here? Who put you in charge of him anyway?" Laurant asked.

"Nobody. Hail is my liege Lord, and I will not leave him unprotected. I would have called my brothers and sisters to help guard him if I thought it was appropriate for this venture, but that would only draw attention to us. It is Lord Hail's decision whether or not to learn this foolishness from you."

They continued to bicker until we reached the obstacle course that Laurant had mentioned. It was in use, and after watching for a minute, I came to one swift decision.

Parkour was awesome.

24
THEDUM

Not only was parkour awesome, but I was awesome at it. After observing the Travelers making use of the course for only a few minutes, I jumped in at a sprint. I slid under carts, I jumped over fences, I climbed up walls, and I only fell a handful of times. Unfortunately, there truly seemed to be no parkour skill, as even after three hours of practicing I failed to receive it. I still had a lot of fun and was reluctant to go back to the Guild Hall, even after earning the [Exhaustion] debuff.

"I'm almost tempted to get him a skateboard and see how he does with that," Laurant commented to Tarisha as I recovered on the grass.

"I was not aware that such things existed in this world," Tarisha commented.

"You'd be surprised what you can find at the auction. It's not an item made by the system, but you can carve and make your own. It's only advanced items like internal combustion engines which are impossible. A skateboard is just a cultural item with very simple mechanics, there's no ban on it," Laurant explained. "Of course, the fact that they're all custom made makes them individually quite expensive. I'm only level twenty-three."

"I'm not certain how I feel about you turning Lord Hail into a skater punk," Tarisha said.

"I have no idea what you're talking about, but if it's nearly as much fun as parkour I want to try it," I said. "How much does one of these skeetboards cost? I'll pay for it. I have lots of gold from selling the [Immature Gemos Hearts], remember?"

"Why don't we saunter over to the auction and see if there's one available, and you can buy it yourself," Laurant suggested. "Then I'll show you how to use it."

"I see. This explains a great deal," Tarisha said, a judgmental tone in her voice, though I had no idea why. She didn't object as we proceeded to move towards the auctions.

"So, what have you got against 'skeeters?'" Laurant asked her as we walked. I occasionally tried to do a handstand or two on a cart here and there.

"Three exes ranging from junior high to college. I learned that lesson the hard way," Tarisha answered.

"Oh, come on, we're not that bad. You went out with them to begin with, so you must have found something attractive in a man with a board."

"They were boys, not men, and that's the only justification I can think of for taking this 'sport' seriously. I had more respect for you when I thought you were just an [Archer]. Parkour I could justify as being a valid talent to have for this game, but—"

I tuned their conversation out as they continued to bicker about nothing important. I had discovered parkour, and was busy practicing it despite having left the obstacle course. The [Exhaustion] debuff had faded, and I was ready to go. I was having such a good time that I had almost forgotten about all the trouble I had caused at the castle.

Then, of course, I remembered, and that put a damper on my spirits. I had no right to be enjoying myself after almost getting hundreds of Natives killed.

"It will be alright, Hail. We'll figure out a way to fix everything. And the Dungeon Busters will get the castle fixed up like nothing ever happened," Laurant predicted when he noticed my mood souring.

"It's not just that. Malkios believes that a cat-kin is responsible," I pointed out. "What if I accidentally caused a war between Yuikon and Eolstree?"

"Your grandfather isn't going to start a war with the beast-man nation without solid proof that they were responsible. Just seeing a cat-boy in your room is far from enough evidence for that," Tarisha assured me. "It might raise the tension between your nations for a while, but I doubt any lives will be lost due to international hostilities. It might affect some merchant's bottom lines, but screw them anyways."

I frowned, but followed her logic. Even if a cat-kin was responsible for planting the core in my wardrobe, that didn't necessarily mean that he was employed by the government of Eolstree. More likely it would be an attempt to frame the beast-kin and disguise the true culprits. Grandfather would see that, wouldn't he?

Except that I was the true culprit. Was it only a matter of time until I was unmasked?

"Should I just tell him?" I asked, nervously.

"I think it better to let his temper cool down a little," Tarisha said. "Perhaps once his home has been reclaimed, we can let him know that it was all a silly accident, and not an international incident."

"Will he revoke my promotion?"

"I can't predict how he'll react, I don't know him well enough," Tarisha answered. "That is why I counsel patience. For now, try to put it out of your head, Hail. We shall help you find the path forward which is best for all involved."

"Yeah, kiddo, just leave it to us. We haven't failed one of your quests yet. We won't fail this one either," Laurant assured me.

"I gave you a quest for this?"

"You didn't know?" Laurant asked, sounding surprised. "Yeah. Its wording is pretty simple for how complex it actually is. It just says 'Help Hail navigate the fallout of the emergence of the [Zhesa Castle Dungeon].' I got it as soon as I met up with you after logging in this afternoon."

"I received a similar quest," Tarisha added. "Are you not aware of it when you issue quests?"

"No, I don't control it," I admitted. "I mean, I can try to do it on purpose by telling a Traveler to do something important. But most of the time it just happens without me being aware of it, unless someone tells me that I triggered one."

The Travelers processed this information for a while. We reached the auction, an open-air market made special only by the fact that the Natives who worked here could pull items out of a communal pool that connected an extensive trade network. Natives almost never used it due to the fees involved, but Travelers used it almost exclusively to dispose of their crafted items quickly. If you asked me how it worked, I couldn't explain it to you, but like Fast Travel and my status screen, it was something that I simply accepted as natural.

When we reached the auctioneer, Laurant picked out a skeetboard that he said was perfect for me, then spent a few minutes teaching me how to use it. Skeetboarding isn't as awesome as parkour, but it's still fun. He showed me a few tricks, but warned me not to try them until I had gotten used to riding it normally.

We began making our way back to the Guild Hall. I was absorbed in learning a new skill, even if it wasn't a [Skill], and the two Travelers were engaged in conversation.

"You know, this reminds me of quite a few dates I had back in high school," Laurant commented.

"Is that what you think this is?" Tarisha challenged.

"Nah. If I wanted to date you, I'd be more romantic about it. I'm not in high school anymore. I'm just saying, my mom used to make me bring my little sister with me all the time. It was supposedly to babysit, but the real reason was to chaperone me and whoever I happened to be sweet on at the time. This feels a lot like that."

"So, you see me as a potential love interest and Hail as your little brother?" she asked.

"Why not? I mean, he could use a big brother, couldn't he? As to the other, well, I think we could both do worse."

"I was engaged to a literal male model for six months before I broke it off. I'm out of your league, Laurant."

"Oh yeah? A model? Which one?"

I tuned the conversation out after realizing that I had no chance of understanding what it was about. Then, as I rounded a corner, I saw a familiar figure waiting for me.

"Severus?" I asked, but rather than answer, he finished casting the spell that he had been holding. The explosion itself did almost two thousand Damage to me and knocked me high in the air. High enough that I suffered an additional hundred points of falling Damage. I looked up to see the troll grinning maliciously at me as he finished casting another spell, and then the world went white.

I was floating, and I felt the familiar sensation of healing magic as my Health was swiftly returned to full. I was at peace, and I wondered if this was what being dead felt like. My mind was somewhat groggy, so it took me a moment to process the message that had popped up, the blue boxes replacing the pure white that enveloped me.

Blessing of Thedum Has Activated.
Fatal Damage Averted
Teleporting to Nearest Sanctuary
Mark of Cain inflicted upon Severus

"Oh, so that's what that does," I murmured to myself. "I wonder what [Mark of Cain] does. Hopefully nothing good. Severus, you jerk! I hope you die a thousand deaths and get stuck at level one forever!"

"Indeed. I do not often intervene directly, but I was not about to stand by while one of my marked innocents perished," a deep voice answered. It came from everywhere, all enveloping, just like the light. Like the light and the healing magic, it was warm and welcoming, yet I could tell it hid unbridled fury. Not for me, thankfully; I could sense that the anger being felt was directed elsewhere.

"Thedum?" I asked, guessing and hoping at the same time.

"Yes. I am Thedum. And you are not as devout in your worship of me as you could be, but I saved you from certain death all the same," the god answered.

"I, um, sorry about that. Mother was the one who always made me go to church. Once she left, going always sort of reminded me of her in a way that I didn't like," I admitted.

"I understand. I don't particularly care for the services and the ceremonies they hold in my name, either," the god confided. "I prefer acts of faith and good will."

"What happened? How did Severus escape prison?" I inquired. "And why did he try to kill me?"

"You know what happened to bring you here. As for the one who sent you? He was released after complaining extensively to the administrators. As to your final question, I cannot speak of the motives of mortals. It is an action that he will come to regret, however. The parting punishment I inflicted upon him is a permanent

Bane, which will hopefully drive him from this world forever. And it is one that the administrators themselves have approved of. His only way to remove it is to confess to me his sin and earn absolution, an act that is likely outside of his capacity. Hopefully the news of his fate will earn you some measure of protection from the ones whom your guardian fears are hunting you. But be warned. My blessing protects only against the malice of strangers. I will not be your aid in times of mutual combat, or should you provoke the violence upon yourself."

I wanted to ask more, but the light abruptly faded, and I found myself in the Temple of Thedum, lying upon the altar like a newborn about to receive their blessing. I quickly scurried away, being careful not to overturn the candles or sacred objects that surrounded me. I looked around, but the temple was deserted.

Once I was oriented, I pulled up my status. There was only one section I was interested in: my traits.

Traits	High Aptitude
	Quick Learner
	Royal Blood (+5 Charisma, bonus to relations with factions loyal to Yuikon)
	Nobility: Earl (+5 Charisma)
	Blessing of Thedum (Cooldown: 23hr 52mn)
	Mark of the Phoenix (hidden)
	Voice of the Future (hidden)

I nodded. It was too much to expect Thedum to intervene on my behalf too often. Once per day was already more than generous. A new popup interrupted me from further deductions.

Laurant has invited you to a party. Accept?	
Yes	No

I quickly accepted.

"Hail? Where are you? Are you alright? Did you respawn? It said that you were in the middle of an event and we couldn't contact you." Laurant spoke frantically, the words tumbling over themselves to get out of his mouth.

"Technically I didn't die," I answered. "Thedum interceded on my behalf. I'm at his temple now. Travelers are prevented from entering, so I should be safe until the cooldown on my blessing is up. It seems it only activates once per day at the most."

"That is a great relief, Lord Hail," Tarisha said. "Did you know that Thedum would protect you from certain death?"

"I had no idea," I admitted. "But it's not my fault, is it? I mean, that was Severus, and I never did anything to him to deserve him acting like a jerk, did I?"

"No, you did not," Daemon said, and I realized for the first time that he and Dimple were in the party as well. "This is certainly not your fault, Hail, but ours for failing to protect you properly. We knew that this was a possibility and underestimated the likelihood of you being recognized."

"It wasn't Hail that was recognized, it was me," Laurant admitted. "This is my fault, if it's anyone's. It was my idea to go out today, and—"

"And I agreed that keeping Lord Hail locked up in the Guild Hall was bad for his health, so I allowed it, making me equally responsible," Tarisha interrupted. "But now is not the time to play 'who is to blame.' Hail, what did you do to Severus?"

"What do you mean?" I asked.

"He was cursing about some debuff when I killed him. And he had a rune upon his forehead. Was this related to your escape mechanism?"

"Oh. That was probably the [Mark of Cain]. I got a notification about that, but I don't know what it does."

Dimple began to laugh. "Oh, I do. Because Severus, fool that he is, just began posting to the forums about it. It's apparently a three-part Bane. The first part is purely superficial, and that's the rune on his forehead. It also negatively impacts all reactions with any Native that he encounters, and, here's the kicker, it increases his death penalty by ten times."

"Excellent," Tarisha said. "That means that we only need to hunt him down four more times to reduce him to level one. I will put out the bounty on him at once."

"His post conveniently failed to mention what he did to earn the mark. Shall I post a response to clear the record?" Dimple asked.

"Yes. Knowledge of the [Mark of Cain] may dissuade others from making similar attempts. Withhold any more information about Hail's escape mechanism, especially the cooldown and the destination," Daemon answered. "[Mark of Cain] is a game-changer. We want everyone who even thinks about targeting Hail to be terrified of the repercussions to their account."

"I shall spread the word through my information channels as well," Tarisha agreed. "Hopefully, it will be enough to prevent this from ever happening again."

25
PIETY

The conference went on for a while, but it was mostly grownup stuff that I didn't understand. Pee Are strategies and campaigns, although everyone agreed that, with the [Zhesa Castle Dungeon] event ongoing, it would probably receive less attention than they would like. Compared to that, I was "yesterday's news." Except that could change very quickly.

It was agreed that I would remain at the temple until the cooldown on [Blessing of Thedum] faded. Because the temple was Native only, they assumed that I would be safest there until my "escape mechanism" was charged up again. After a while, I told everyone that I had to go give thanks to Thedum just so that I could have an excuse to leave the party.

But I did give thanks. I knelt by the altar and prayed in a way that I hadn't prayed since I was very young. I noticed that the cooldown began to reset at almost double-time while I did so. Which was nice, but I couldn't keep at it for very long. Well, I could have if my attention span allowed for it. It was easy to say "Hail, you have to stay in the temple for twenty-four hours." It was another thing to actually expect me to do it.

Before long, I was incredibly bored. And as everyone knows, if there is anything more dangerous than a boy's curiosity, it's his boredom. I tried my best to fill the time in non-destructive ways. I hung out in guildchat, where I was informed of the "massive flame-war" going on between Severus and some other trolls "against the entire internet." I had no idea what that meant, but I was encouraged to go to the forums to see just how many people were upset that someone had tried to kill me. It was enough to push the "event dungeon" into second place, although not by very much.

The level of support I was receiving from perfect strangers was actually a little heartwarming, but ultimately, I couldn't spend too long on the forums without getting a headache from all the terms I didn't understand.

Before long, I was bored again. Which is how I ended up falling from the rafters and losing two hundred Health to falling Damage just as the priest came in. I tried to play it off as an "I meant to do that" moment by leaping to my feet and shouting "Parkour!" but I don't think the priest was very amused. It took me twenty minutes to convince him that I wasn't there to steal the holy icons and another ten minutes to convince him of my identity. Even then, while he acknowledged that I had claimed sanctuary, and he could not forcibly remove me from the temple, he refused to let me stay without earning my keep.

Which is how I, Earl Jeoran, wound up scrubbing statues and polishing silver candelabras for nearly ten hours. There are a lot of candelabras in a temple of Thedum; I had never really noticed before. Quite a few statues as well. And once I finished with that, there was plenty of floor to be mopped.

I was relieved when night finally came, and I was allowed to sleep in the monk's quarters. The morning was spent thanking Thedum for saving me and protecting me throughout my life and all his other good works, like the creation of the world and stuff. I was genuinely struck with religious piety. I wasn't just trying to reset the timer before the priest woke up. Nope. It was pure religious piety, and Thedum seemed to agree because it worked. I managed to shave off about three hours in total, and immediately contacted Tarisha to let her know I was ready to leave.

I met her behind the temple, where she had a carriage waiting for us. It wasn't that far, we could have walked, but she didn't want me to be recognized coming from the temple by other Travelers. A carriage was less conspicuous than a parade of her guildmates, although she did have two more Travelers in the carriage with us. I was introduced to them as Marvin of Cincinnati and Lucile of SoCal.

They were both quick to bend the knee to me, and once again I accepted their oaths of fealty in the names of Thedum and Are En Gee. They were greatly pleased and could not keep the smiles off their faces. I'm not quite certain what is so pleasing about serving a minor lord who doesn't even have any significant holdings assigned to him yet, but they're Travelers, so I just put it down to that.

We drew some attention as we made our way through town, as it's not every day that three high-level Travelers escort a carriage. Tarisha had taken some efforts to disguise our origin, however, and I remained hidden from sight. The alliance between <Nethersong Mavericks> and <Peasant's Revenge> was not widely known, and we likely escaped suspicion.

We abandoned the carriage two blocks from the Guild Hall and hustled into that safe haven, where we sighed in relief.

Unfortunately for me, my relief was short lived, as Tarisha promptly dragged me back into the training area, and we resumed practicing until she announced that it was time for her to rest in her world.

My training partners for the next two and a half days were lack-luster compared to Tarisha. She simply had a flare for combat that was difficult to find even in seasoned Travelers. I even won more exchanges than I lost. Or would have, were it not for the substantial difference in our levels and stats.

"You're going to be a monster when you grow up," Luke of London said after I had soundly defeated him, with only the massive Health pool of being level one hundred seventy-five saving him. He was part of my "Midnight Guard," as opposed to the "Dawn Guard" and "Dusk Guard." Three shifts that were set to guard me in turns so that all could get some rest and pursue other ventures during their time off. However, it was "real time" that they were basing their schedule around, meaning that I had each of my guards for almost three days before they switched out. "Before long you won't even need us."

"I am not so certain of that, Luke," I admitted. "The incident with Severus, it frightened me. The royal family has many enemies, but I never really believed that one of them would come after me. And it was not even that. Severus targeted me for no reason other than spite. Thedum did more than save me and restore my Health, I believe he also shielded my mind, and it is beginning to wear off."

"I am both sorry and glad to hear that, my Lord. Sorry because you are young to bear such a burden and pleased because it will drive home the need for your security in the future," Luke responded. "Now come. You may have bested me, but your opponents will not always come at you one on one. Let us see how you do when Peter of Yorkshire joins us."

I groaned, but it was half-hearted. Although it had frightened me, nearly dying at the hands of Severus had also instilled in me an even greater need to grow stronger. Although he had not explicitly said it, I was quite certain that Thedum's intervention would not extend into my adulthood. If I had to guess, I would say that it was one more thing set to change when I turned fifteen. And I knew that I had to be ready.

Sparring with Luke and Peter was brutal. While individually I was skilled enough to take them, or at least put up a good show, they had been fighting together for years, and their teamwork defeated me easily.

They were a good pair. Luke used a [Long Sword], while Peter wielded a [Pike]. Each of them used their enchanted training weapons to cover for the other's weaknesses, and the only strategy that allowed me to do any damage to them at all was to escape to range and blast them with magic. Though I never had time to get a full spell cast before they charged and interrupted me.

And that was how the miracle happened. I was attempting to [Swiftcast] [Fireball], but Luke was closing in and I had to defend myself. Rather than interrupt the spell, I continued casting and used [Slash] to ward off his attack. And, somehow, the two attacks *merged*. The aura that always accompanied my active skills became one of intense flame, and the heat was enough to drive Luke back. I was stunned as we both glanced down at my still-burning sword.

You have learned Imbue Sword: Fire

"Holy shit, when did you learn that?" Luke asked.

"About five seconds ago," I admitted, then I used the opening to attack him with a [Thrust] to the abdomen. Imbued, the attack did almost double Damage. Still insignificant compared to his massive Health pool, but it was a huge upgrade for me.

The fire on my sword lasted for about thirty seconds, then faded away. I promptly began casting [Lightning Bolt], only to finish the spell with another [Slash].

You have learned Imbue Sword: Lightning

Electricity arced along my blade, crackling and popping. Like [Imbue Sword: Fire], it lasted for thirty seconds then faded. I promptly did the same thing with [Ice Blast], [Water Jet], and [Arcane Missile].

You have learned Imbue Sword: Ice
You have learned Aqua Blade
You have learned Arcane Weapon

I marveled over the new abilities and immediately began thinking of ways to incorporate them, when another notification popped up, intruding upon my thoughts.

You have unlocked the advanced class, [Spellblade].
Would you like to change your class from [Child] to [Spellblade]?
CAUTION: This change cannot be reversed!
[Spellblade] can be upgraded into the legendary classes [Arcane Warrior], [Elemental Swordsman], and [Runic Swordmaster].

Strength	-2	Skills Gained	Battle Trance
Dexterity (primary)	+4		Magic in Motion
Vitality	0	Skills Lost	Archery
Endurance	0		Short Spears
Intelligence (primary)	+5		Axes
Wisdom	+1		Staves
Charisma	+1		Daggers
			Polearms

Spells Lost	Cure Minor Injury		Shields
	Heal Wounds		Quickshot
	Heal Major Wounds		Power Shot
	Cure Disease		Piercing Shot
	Cure Poison		Heavy Blow
	Soothing Regeneration		and 7 others
	Entangling Vines		
	Siphon Life		
	Inflict Curse		
	Decay		
	And 32 others		
Would you like to change your Class now? (This choice can be made at a later time through the Status Menu while in a safe zone.)			
Yes		No	

I began to laugh, because I finally had the answer to the problem that had been plaguing me since I'd hit level ten. I wasn't worried about the skills or spells I was losing, those were all extraneous abilities that I never actually used. I'd only learned them to help spread [Mark of Karma]. All that mattered was what remained. This was exactly the sort of class I was looking for, and without hesitation, I selected yes.

I was enveloped in multi-hued light. It lasted a moment, and I felt the changes that the system was making to my body. I accepted them readily; this was what I wanted. When the light faded, I felt like a new boy. I quickly pulled up my status and examined it.

Name	Hail Jeoran	Level	10
Guild	<Nethersong Mavericks>	Strength	17
Health	2300/2300	Dexterity	26
Mana	2300/2300	Vitality	23
Experience	0/2000	Endurance	19
Age	10	Intelligence	28
Race	Human (blood of the Travelers)	Wisdom	18
Class	Spellblade	Charisma	27
Job	Earl	Armor	9
		Spell Damage	32
Passive Skills	Short Swords (17)	Spells	Detect Poison (13)
	Long Swords (8)		Spark (6)
	Rapiers (9)		Analyze (9)
	Katanas (6)		Storage (6)
	Animal Handling (4)		Lightning Bolt (14)
	Balance and Conditioning (8)		Chain Lightning (3)
	Dodge (7)		Fireball (8)
	Battle Trance		Ice Blast (7)
	Magic in Motion		Arcane Missile (8)
Active Skills	Dash (9)		Dazzling Lights (2)
	Thrust (12)		Concussive Sound (2)
	Slash (13)		Befuddle (2)
	Riposte (9)		Water Jet (5)
	Feint (8)		Polymorph (5)

	Piercing Lunge (7)		Slow (9)
	Swiftcast (7)		Create Trap (3)
	Empower Magic (4)		Mark of Karma (special)
	Imbue Sword: Fire (1)	**Traits**	High Aptitude
	Imbue Sword: Lightning (1)		Quick Learner
	Imbue Sword: Ice (1)		Royal Blood (+5 Charisma, bonus to relations with factions loyal to Yuikon)
	Aqua Blade (1)		Nobility: Earl (+5 Charisma)
	Arcane Weapon (1)		Blessing of Thedum
			Mark of the Phoenix (hidden)
General Skills	(Focus to Expand)		Voice of the Future (hidden)
		General Spells	(Focus to Expand)

"Was that light a good thing?" Luke asked, adding a "My Lord" after a few seconds.

"Yes, it was. I've finally unlocked my class," I answered. And then I attacked him, determined to work out the kinks in my fighting style now that *everything* had changed.

26

CLOSURE

The goblin archer turned into a giant dung beetle, and I was already casting [Befuddle] on the shaman. The rest of the group turned, saw me, and began shouting in outrage, but the spellcasting debuff was on my target before they could charge. I had just enough time before they arrived to follow up with a [Chain Lightning].

We had been at the goblin lair for hours now, and I had already hit level eleven. The players with me were all higher leveled than me, but with my new class I was more than keeping up with them.

Stan charged, sprinting into the oncoming goblins and shouting a challenge that peeled their attention off of me. He was this impromptu party's tank, a [Warrior] with a shield, mace, and heavy chain mail. He crushed the leading goblin's arm with his charge, inflicting a [Cripple] debuff, but missing any vitals that would have done more Damage. But he had their attention.

There were seven regular goblins in addition to the archer, who was temporarily out of the fight, and the shaman, whom I had inflicted with [Befuddle], which doubled his cast time and had a chance of interrupting him. That wouldn't last forever, though, and I quickly charged in after Stan, imbuing my [Traveler's Rapier] with fire.

I found over the day since I'd unlocked my class that the rapier suited a [Spellblade]'s fighting style better than [Short Swords]. Even if the rapier was a step down in physical damage, going from a D+

Damage rating down to a D, the magical Damage of my imbued weapon made up for it. With a rapier I was able to strike more often and from a greater range, as the goblins quickly found out.

Between the rapier and other changes to my gear, I had lost a few points in strength, but I wasn't worried about it. I wasn't a strength-based class, so it didn't matter.

Arrows caught the goblins around us as April peppered them from afar. She was an [Archer], like Laurant, but considering that at least one of the arrows hit our tank by mistake, I don't think she's as good at it. Fortunately, our resident cleric, Melanie, quickly healed all the Damage, making the friendly fire like it never happened.

The final member of our party made himself known a moment later, emerging from [Stealth] and [Backstabbing] the shaman before [Befuddle] ran out. Wesle was a [Rogue], a very good one according to him, but every [Rogue] thinks that. Or so everyone says.

I didn't have time to worry about what my team was doing. Although Stan had picked up most of the seven loose goblins, three were still targeting me. But I was ready for them. My rapier [Slashed], and I pierced them with multiple [Thrusts]. With my imbued weapons, many lighter blows were superior to fewer deeper cuts, as it was the magic that was doing my Damage for me, not the sword itself.

I focused on the green one first. They were all green, but this one was greener than most. With two [Slashes] and a [Thrust] I had almost killed it, and I finished it off with non-skilled Damage. The remaining two tried to flank me, but I [Dashed] away to the side, only to follow it up immediately with a [Piercing Lunge] on the one to the left. I hit it in the heart, dealing critical Damage and causing it to burst into black mist.

The third one turned to run, but I [Swiftcast] [Slow] to keep it from getting very far, and changed my imbued weapon from fire to lightning. Not for any particular reason, except that I thought it was better to keep leveling those skills at the same pace. My [Thrust] pierced the goblin's back, lodging my sword into its lungs and doing significant Damage until the survivor wasn't surviving anymore.

I turned back to the others. With the help of [Befuddle], Wesle had made easy work of the goblin shaman, and was now dueling with the archer, who had pulled out a long knife. He was fine, and if anything would likely resent my interference. So, I turned to the primary group, of which there were only two goblins remaining, the other two having been dispatched by a combination of mace and arrows. I finished another one off in a flash with a [Piercing Lunge], and the final one had its skull caved in by Stan.

A small notification popped up in the corner of my screen after combat had ended, and I grinned in triumph and satisfaction. I had known I was close, although I hadn't been certain that this group would pull me over the edge. I pulled up a partial status screen to confirm.

Name	Hail Jeoran	Level	12
Guild	<Nethersong Mavericks>	Strength	14
Health	2425/2880	Dexterity	32
Mana	2117/3720	Vitality	24
Experience	17/3600	Endurance	20
Age	10	Intelligence	31
Race	Human (blood of the Travelers)	Wisdom	20
Class	Spellblade	Charisma	29
Job	Earl	Armor	9
		Spell Damage	36.4

"Ding! Level twelve!" I announced proudly.

"Great, you're going to be even harder to keep up with now," Wesle complained. "Your class is so damn broken it's not funny. Seriously, did you just kill over half of that pull by yourself, *while* See Seeing their [Mage] and [Archer]? If that's not broken I don't know what is."

"Just be glad that he's on our side. Oh, and I just got [Mark of Karma] too! Sweet!" April exclaimed. "I mean, that wasn't the only reason I'm here, Hail. This is a good grinding spot for me too, and I'm having fun."

"I know. Don't worry, I'm happy for you," I said. "I know [Mark of Karma] is awesome and I want my friends to have it. I just didn't like it so much when people left right away after getting it."

"Yeah, I can understand that," she responded. "Wesle is kind of right though, your Dee Pee Ess is insane. I can't nearly keep up."

"I think it's because it's an advanced class," I said.

"Or you're just crazy good," Melanie offered. "You fight like you've been doing this for years."

"I kind of have," I said. "I mean, I've been training with swords since I was eight. I didn't have all the [Skills] I have now, especially not my imbued weapons. But I was drilled constantly on my form."

"It's more than that," Stan interjected. "You've got a talent, and you're not afraid to look foolish. That's where a lot of kids get tripped up in this game, they either go out of their way to make their combat style look cool, or they're worried about looking silly. You just worry about turning the mobs into black mist in the fastest, most effective way possible."

"And he still looks cool doing it," April joshed.

"Thanks guys, but you're kind of making me blush," I complained. "Let's keep going, I want to get to level fifteen before the day is—"

> Sophia has come online.

I blinked in surprise at the notification, then I frowned. "Um, guys, change of plans. I think I need to go."

"Is something wrong?" Melanie asked.

"Someone just came online that I need to talk with, and I kind of don't want anyone listening," I explained. I glanced at my bodyguards, the three players from <Peasant's Revenge> who were standing nearby in case of trolls or murder hobos, and they nodded at me.

"Just drop group and go somewhere private to talk to them with partychat. You can join up with us again after you've sorted everything out," Wesle suggested. "You don't have to burn your Fast Travel cooldown for whatever Bee Ess is troubling you."

"Okay, I'll do that," I agreed, and I promptly did that, dropping group and walking off, trusting my bodyguards to keep me safe. I was just about to send the party invite to Sophia when she beat me to it.

> Sophia has invited you to a party.
> Accept?
>
> | Yes | No |
> | --- | --- |

I quickly accepted, but before I could say anything, Sophia began gushing.

"Oh Em Gee, thank you for not just blocking me and never speaking to me again, Hail. I am so sorry about what Mark did, I didn't know he was going to do that, and I was so mad at him when I found out. He's such a jerk, I'm glad I dumped his sorry ass. I mean, he's cute and athletic in the real world, but he's such a stupid jock sometimes," she said without pausing to breathe. "And I'm sorry I couldn't get online sooner, my fight with him got me grounded for a few days and I only just got my helmet back. Are you mad? You can get mad, right? You said you have realistic emotions, so that means that you get mad, doesn't it? Please don't be mad at me, Hail."

"I'm not sure how I feel," I said honestly. "I am still upset though. You might have put me in a lot of danger, Sophia."

"It wasn't me, it was Mark!"

"And you didn't have any idea he was recording everything to post it?" I challenged.

"I swear I didn't. I didn't find out about it until someone said something at school the next day. I got into a huge fight with him at lunch and we broke up, but we got sent to the principal's office because of the mess we caused, and our parents got called and everything. That's why I haven't been online, I was grounded. I only just sweet-talked my mom into giving me back my Vee Are helmet."

"I don't really understand what any of that means," I admitted. "You live in a very different world from mine, Sophia. There's a lot of stuff that I just don't get when I hear Travelers talk. Your parents kept you trapped in your world?"

"As a punishment for screaming at Mark in the middle of two hundred other students, yeah," she admitted. "It's a little embarrassing now that I think of it, but I was so mad at him! We almost, like, actually started fighting. It would have been nothing if it had happened online, but in the real world you get in a lot of trouble for that."

"I don't understand why he would do it in the first place," I said. "I mean, what did he gain by betraying my secrets?"

"They're not really secrets if you blurt them out to near perfect strangers, Hail," Sophia said. "I mean, sorry. I get it, you just wanted someone to talk to or something. That's, like, really human of you. But what did you think would happen?"

"I don't know," I admitted. "Are you defending him now?"

"No, that's not what I meant. What he did was a total dick move. But you've got to be careful what information you share online. They teach us that in like, first grade. Once you share something on the internet, you can't control who sees it, and if they copy it before it gets deleted then that info is out of your control forever. Didn't anyone ever teach you that?"

I thought back glumly to my lectures about not sharing my status screen. About how Grandfather's status was considered a state secret. I felt myself growing embarrassed. I *had* been taught better, but had allowed the slightest pressure from my new guild to overcome that training. They had supposedly been helping me, but the point remained. I should have known better.

"I almost died the other day," I told her. "Someone tried to kill me for no reason. I'm not sure what would have happened if he'd managed, if I wasn't being protected. I know you don't think so, but to me, Sophia, *this* is the real world. Your world is just somewhere some of my friends go to sleep."

"I'm sorry. I heard about that through the forums. Was it because of Mark?"

"I don't think so. I think Severus would have done what he did no matter what. Although being 'in the limelight' didn't help because Severus is a troll and would have loved the attention from being the one to kill me," I said, mostly echoing the words of others. "But I think it was retribution for him being imprisoned by my grandfather. It was supposed to last seven years, but the administrators intervened and freed him because his punishment was 'against the Tee Oh Ess.'"

"There are some real jerks out there. I'm really sorry that happened, Hail. Hail, are we still friends? I mean, after what Mark did, I wouldn't have blamed you if you never talked to me again."

I thought about it for a few minutes, and I could tell that the silence was making Sophia uncomfortable wherever she was.

"I don't know. I'm not sure that I can trust you. You say that you had nothing to do with Mark's betrayal, but I only have your word. How do I know you're not just tricking me to get close, so that you can reveal more of my secrets? I can't just 'log out and do something else' if Travelers start hunting me, Sophia."

"How can I prove that's not what I'm doing?" she asked.

"I don't know if you can," I answered sadly. "I'm sorry, Sophia. I don't think that we can be friends anymore."

"Hail, wait, at least—"

I left the party, cutting off whatever she was about to say over partychat. I felt a slight dampness to my left eye and a heaviness in my chest that wouldn't go away. It wasn't that I hadn't forgiven Sophia. I'd even forgiven Mark for what he'd done. But I had to think of my own safety. Right now, we were only safe to hunt goblins because nobody knew I was there. If word got out that I was leveling again, Travelers might try to interfere. Whether they intended to help me, troll me, or simply talk to me, we couldn't take the risk.

"That sounded like a very mature conversation, Lord Hail," Luke of London said, stepping forward and offering me a handkerchief. "And a very mature decision. It is unfortunate that you cannot make more friends with the children of our world, but your secrets are too precious to risk a child exposing them for a high view count, as this 'Mark' did."

"You were listening?" I asked.

"Sorry," Luke said, "I didn't want to leave you alone, and I have [Heightened Senses]. I couldn't not hear you without getting too far away to intervene if you were ambushed. For what it's worth, I think you made the right decision."

"I know," I said. I thought about getting upset, but ultimately I was used to not having much privacy, so I accepted it. "But it sucks."

We returned to where the lower-level party was waiting for me, and I rejoined the leveling party. They had continued for a few groups without me, but having lost almost half of their Dee Pee Ess, they hadn't made as much progress. And they had discovered a "massive pull" in the next region where they had decided to wait for me to finish my conversation.

As we entered the clearing, I almost laughed, spotting the familiar campfire. I was back where I had started. This was the place where the goblins had been preparing to roast me alive, when Laurant and Thena and the rest of them had saved me. There were seventeen goblins in the area, feasting on a roast boar.

They didn't continue their reverie for very long as we tore through them like a scythe through a wheat field.

27

INTENTION

I woke up and for a moment couldn't remember where I was. I wasn't in my bedroom, nor was I in the office that the guild had converted into a place for me to sleep. Then I remembered, and I both relaxed and grew excited. I was at an inn in Eastmill. I quickly pulled up my status screen and examined it closely, taking in the previous day's gains.

Name	Hail Jeoran	Level	15
Guild	<Nethersong Mavericks>	Strength	15
Health	4050/4050	Dexterity	35
Mana	5550/5550	Vitality	27
Experience	234/4500	Endurance	22
Age	10	Intelligence	37
Race	Human (blood of the Travelers)	Wisdom	22
Class	Spellblade	Charisma	31
Job	Earl	Armor	15
		Spell Damage	42.2

Passive Skills	Short Swords (17)	Spells	Detect Poison (13)
	Long Swords (8)		Spark (6)
	Rapiers (15)		Analyze (9)
	Katanas (6)		Storage (6)
	Animal Handling (4)		Lightning Bolt (15)
	Balance and Conditioning (10)		Chain Lightning (7)
	Dodge (13)		Fireball (10)
	Battle Trance		Ice Blast (9)
	Magic in Motion		Arcane Missile (9)
			Dazzling Lights (4)
Active Skills	Dash (12)		Concussive Sound (5)
	Thrust (17)		Befuddle (7)
	Slash (19)		Water Jet (7)
	Riposte (12)		Polymorph (10)
	Feint (15)		Slow (14)
	Piercing Lunge (11)		Create Trap (4)
	Swiftcast (12)		Mark of Karma (special)
	Empower Magic (9)		
	Imbue Sword: Fire (11)	Traits	High Aptitude
	Imbue Sword: Lightning (11)		Quick Learner
	Imbue Sword: Ice (11)		Royal Blood (+5 Charisma, bonus to relations with factions loyal to Yuikon)
	Aqua Blade (4)		Nobility: Earl (+5 Charisma)
	Arcane Weapon (3)		Blessing of Thedum

			Mark of the Phoenix (hidden)
General Skills	(Focus to Expand)		Voice of the Future (hidden)
General Spells	(Focus to Expand)		

Five levels of grinding goblins. The others in the group had gotten burned out towards the end, but I had wanted to keep going even after nightfall. It was only when they said that they needed to log out for their "bio break" that I finally relented. We returned to Eastmill rather than Zhesa city because I was hoping to start killing the mermen next. I was a little below the level when most Travelers started to hunt them, but with my advanced class I was ahead of the curve.

On top of the points I had gotten for leveling, I had also been given three gear upgrades from members of the guild. A new [Tempered Steel Rapier], which had the same D+ Damage rating as my old short sword and increased my Dexterity, some [High Quality Clothes] that had better protection, and I had replaced my [Linen Cloak of Spellweaving] with a [Heavy Cloak of Spellweaving].

I was earning a significant boost from the passive skills I had acquired after unlocking the class. [Magic in Motion] increased my Spell Damage based on both my intelligence and my Dexterity. By experimenting with my gear, I had figured out that I gained forty percent of each point of Dexterity as Spell Damage, and sixty percent of Intelligence.

[Junior Mages] also gained sixty percent of their Intellect as Spell Damage, while more advanced classes gained a higher percentage. With the extra points from Dexterity, I had an advantage over the junior class in terms of sheer firepower. They, however, could simply sit back and either cast or regenerate their Mana with [Meditation]. My version of [Meditation] was [Battle Trance], which unfortunately required me to be attacking an enemy with my sword to benefit from it.

Which meant that I could do quite a bit of damage from range, but I couldn't sustain it because my high-Damage spells also burned through my Mana rapidly. While I had more Mana than ever before, and increasing my skill level in a spell increased the spell's efficiency,

Spell Damage had the unfortunate side effect of also increasing a spell's cost.

Fortunately, the cost of my [Imbue] spells was very low, meaning that I could run myself almost out of Mana casting from a distance, than [Dash] in and attack with my sword while I waited for [Battle Trance] to regenerate my Mana. I currently did more Damage at range with my magic, but I believed that eventually, I'd be most dangerous up close with my sword. Especially once I got a weapon with a higher Damage rating, and a lot more points in Dexterity. My Strength was lagging behind, but I wasn't worried about it. I wasn't sure I benefited from Strength at all anymore.

[Spellblade] wasn't a class unique to me. Now that I had unlocked it, the theorycrafters in the guild had managed to find references to two epic quests: one available to [Duelists], and the other available to [Mages] who hadn't specialized yet, which were reported to reward the class. The mage quests were unpopular because most of the players who chose magic in the first place didn't want to fight with a sword, while the [Duelist] route went largely unexplored because the quest was notoriously difficult, changed the class's combat style completely, and the other advancement options were both easier and lucrative.

Tarisha had been a [Duelist] before she'd unlocked her [Blade of the Gale] epic class. The theorycrafters in the guild were concerned that I had picked an obscure class, as they were unsure of how to advise me. I wasn't worried though. I would have Tarisha teach me more about how [Duelists] fought, and then I would figure out the rest for myself.

It was all very exciting. As I got out of bed to wash my face, I checked my friends list to see who was awake and online. I was pleased to see that Laurant, Tarisha, Thena, and Phil had all come online while I'd been asleep. I quickly invited them all to a party for partychat. I got a message saying that Tarisha was in a party already, then another message from her asking to join my party, meaning that she had dropped to join mine.

"Hey kiddo, good morning," Laurant said cheerfully. "I heard you had some good news after I fell asleep last night."

"[Spellblade] is awesome! It's perfect for me, and I'm already level fifteen," I declared proudly. "Are you guys still killing mermen? Because I think I'm strong enough for that now. Everyone says my damage per second is wicked for my level."

"I'm not so certain about that," Thena said nervously. "I mean, yes, mermen are still a good option for us to grind, but . . . Oh shit. I just got a quest to kill one hundred mermen with you."

"Me too," Phil said. "It's fine. We just need to wait for Larissa to get online. Stick close to me, little buddy, and I'll keep you safe."

"From the reports that the Midnight Guard gave me, that might not be entirely necessary. Lord Hail's damage is apparently outrageous for his level. His Dawn Guard and I will be nearby in case anything goes wrong. Close enough to help, but far enough away not to interfere with the lord's progress," Tarisha promised. "I believe he needs two sorts of Experience. That which gives levels, and that which gives growth. As such, we will only intervene if it appears his life is in danger from a threat which your party will not be able to handle unaided."

"Like an army of trolls," Phil suggested.

"Or a high-leveled murder hobo, yes," she agreed. "Although I do not think that will be a problem for now. While normally I would say that the level of support Hail received from the majority of Travelers on the forums would only increase the danger he is in from the worst of us, I believe that nobody is willing to risk the [Mark of Cain]. Severus has died twice more. It's actually quite amusing. We spawncamped him the first time. The second time he chose a different resurrection point and was promptly killed by a nearby guard. It was posted online; the guard simply walked over and stabbed him in the chest like it was nothing. He was so workman-like about it that it was comical. Severus is down to level twenty-two."

"Hear that, Hail? That means that if you ever meet him again, you'll probably be able to pay him back for the busted skeetboard," Laurant said.

"I don't think so," I said. "Thedum said something about mutual combat. I'm not certain, but I think that it's best if I just ignore Severus from now on. Personally, I mean. You guys can kill him all you want. I just want to forget all about him."

"If the Natives are going to spawncamp him then we might not need to bother with him at all," Phil pointed out. "I mean, you need to be, like, level eighty to win a fight with even the weaker guards, right? So he's basically locked out of every city in the game, except for the player cities. But those are in high-level zones, so it's not like he'd be able to level up again out there. He'd have to, like, stick to the wilderness for months in the Heartlands in order to regain his levels. Months without repairing or improving his gear. And if he dies once he loses days of progress."

"Even so, I am keeping the bounty on him in place. In fact, I have even authorized a payment to the Native guard," Tarisha announced. "Even if it proves expensive, I plan on keeping the bounty in place until it becomes apparent that Severus is trolling us or feeding a friend. We have plans to deal with both eventualities."

"When does Larissa come online?" I asked. "I hate talking about Severus. I want to kill mermen."

"It might be an hour or two of gametime," Thena informed me. "We all just had breakfast together, but she needs to walk her dog before she logs in for the day. Serious players try to take care of stuff like that during the night cycle, but we're amateurs, El Oh El. The rest of us were just going to putz around until she finished scooping up dog poop."

"Oh, that's okay I guess. I need to get dressed and eat breakfast too, so maybe it will work out perfect," I said. "Just wait guys, you're going to be really surprised by how much Damage I do now."

"I'm sure we will, Hail," Thena responded. "[Spellblade] does sound like exactly what you were looking for."

"I can't believe that nobody told me about it. I basically unlocked it by accident," I complained. "But I'm not mad or anything. I'm too happy for that. I'm going to mute myself now while I get ready so you don't hear me eating and stuff."

"Okay Hail, I think the rest of us will mute ourselves as well so that we don't disturb you," Thena suggested.

"Okay. See you all soon," I said, and I mentally toggled the option.

I quickly changed out of my nightclothes and into my [Quality Clothes]. It took me a little while to get everything equipped properly. I could have done it directly through the system and saved time, but it's sort of itchy when I do that. It doesn't seem to bother Travelers, but every Native I know changes their clothes properly.

After I was dressed, I threw my new cloak over my shoulder and went to the common room, where I ordered some of the delicious-smelling quiche and sausage that the innkeeper was selling.

The Midnight Guard had switched out with the Dawn Guard while I was sleeping, and I had to wait to start eating until I had accepted their oaths of fealty. Tarisha was with them, and when she saw me, she announced that she was leaving the group to make room for Larissa.

The food was delicious, and I spent some time talking with the innkeeper. I didn't reveal my identity, although he gave me several suspicious looks despite his otherwise jovial demeanor. I was in a good mood until I suddenly had a thought.

I hadn't seen anyone from the castle, nor had they seen me, for almost a week. While Grandfather and Malkios were undoubtedly busy with the dungeons and the preparations for reclaiming the castle, it was likely that they were worried about me. So I asked the innkeeper for stationary supplies and penned a quick letter.

I kept the details vague, and sealed it with a personal seal, which I'd been given when I was six years old. I was just about to hand it off to one of the members of my Dawn Guard when I saw a player materialize near the Nexus Point. I grinned. After [Analyzing] her to make certain that she wouldn't be able to kill me in one shot—she was level twenty-one, so not a threat—I rushed over to her and held out the letter.

"I am Earl Hail Jeoran," I told her. "My grandfather, King Rain Teoran, will reward you if you deliver this letter to him by noon today."

"Holy shit, you're that kid," she exclaimed. Her eyes went distant as she read the quest that had been generated, then she grinned. "Quest accepted. Oh man, I actually get to meet the king with this quest! This is awesome!" She took the letter from me and began jogging back towards the capital. I grinned at the success of my experiment; I had issued a quest on purpose!

"Are you certain that was wise, my Lord?" Tarisha asked once the player was out of earshot. "What if she peeks, or fails to deliver the letter? You have also just revealed your location, which she may post online."

"If the area starts to get crowded or anything, I'll Fast Travel somewhere safe, just like you taught me," I assured her. "But I don't think it's a problem. I don't know what her reward will be, but she's going to meet the king, right? I mean, I asked her to hand deliver it, so her reward should be pretty good. And it's not like she can read it anyway. Everyone knows that you Travelers don't read our script."

"Most of us don't, but the player could screenshot it and post it online, where it could be translated," Tarisha corrected me.

"Oh. I didn't know that," I admitted. "Well, I didn't say anything important anyway. It's not like I wrote down my stats and how [Spellblade] works. I just said I'd unlocked a powerful class and that I'd come home soon after I gained some more levels. I didn't even say what class it was, just that it was strong. I don't want him worrying."

"Hopefully she will believe that unsealing the letter is a failed condition of her quest, or it will not occur to her to post it on the forums," Tarisha supplied.

"I think she *would* fail the quest if she opened it," I agreed. "I don't think she'll be able to get an audience with a broken seal. She might even get in a lot of trouble for it, maybe even sent to the mines for a few weeks."

"Hopefully she was genuine in her desire to meet the king. An audience with the king of Yuikon is a widely sought-after opportunity, as it opens a significant number of opportunities with other Natives throughout the world. Shopkeepers sometimes give discounts if you recount the tale, and certain other Natives will give exclusive quests to those who have had a royal audience. The question is whether that player would rather have the short-term fame from breaking the seal, or if they are knowledgeable enough to see the opportunity you created for them."

"Oh," I said. "I didn't know any of that. I just figured she'd get a few coins."

"Even if your grandfather gives that player nothing but a copper coin for her trouble, she will have been richly rewarded."

Larissa has come online.

I grinned, and promptly sent the last member of the party an invite. It was time to show my friends that I wasn't the helpless little kid they'd found and rescued just a few weeks ago.

28

MERMEN

Mermen really, really, *really* do not like lightning. And they also really do not like the people who shoot lightning at them repeatedly.

We had ambushed a camp that was on the water's edge, as we slowly made our way from the outskirts of the lair to the center. It wasn't the first group of mermen we had ambushed, and it wouldn't be the last. The monsters were more hideous than I'd imagined. They walked like humans, but were covered with amphibian-like skin and hard scales along their spines, forearms, and legs. Their fish-like faces were filled with sharp, pointy teeth, and they gurgled when you electrocuted them.

With the level disparity between me and the amphibious monster my magic had angered, I realized I wouldn't be able to kill it with magic before it reached me, so I switched from casting [Lightning Bolt] to [Slow]. As the debuff took effect on my enemy, I imbued my [Tempered Steel Rapier] with lightning and took the initiative to open the melee portion of our combat with [Piercing Lunge].

The ability was something of a cross between [Dash] and [Thrust], a mid-range attack that brought me in close to the enemy and did significant Damage. It was useful for opening a fight, or keeping close to an enemy that preferred their targets at a distance, or chasing down a fleeing opponent. In this case, I was using it to get inside the range of the merman's pike as well as an opening move.

The monster reared back and tried to reposition, but I followed up with [Slash] and [Thrust] and unskilled normal attacks while I waited for the brief cooldowns on my specials to refresh. My enemy was level twenty-three, and I was level sixteen, a difference that provided him with an innate resistance to me simply because of the tyranny of level disparity. Like when I had faced the boar just a few weeks ago, my abilities simply weren't doing full Damage.

That just meant I got to practice my abilities for longer.

Slowed by my magic, I had no trouble avoiding the merman's pike. While a spear is a dangerous weapon when the opponent is in control of the fight, the fight was proceeding according to the tempo I set, and the merman was simply unable to keep up with the dance. When the enemy tried to open a distance between us to properly use his pike, I closed the distance with [Piercing Lunge]. When he tried to charge forward to bodycheck me, I [Feinted] to the side and then slipped behind him as he overextended, giving me a perfect opportunity to [Slash] him down the back of his torso, dealing critical Damage.

When my opponent had twenty percent Health left, he dropped his pike and pulled out a long dagger. It was also around this time that the duration of [Slow] ended, causing the merman to speed up significantly. Or rather, return to full speed. But I was still faster.

Unfortunately, my Damage slowed, as I was forced to parry the dagger repeatedly. I did manage to activate a few [Ripostes], but I didn't meet my goal of killing the merman before my [Imbue Sword: Lightning] had to be refreshed. Frustrating.

The final [Thrust] reduced the merman to zero Health, and it exploded into black mist. I turned to see how my friends were doing.

Phil was battling with four enemies. I swiftly turned the one with the highest Health into a duck with [Polymorph] and cast [Slow] on the other three. I judged that crowd control would be more effective than direct Damage until we whittled the numbers down further.

"Thanks Hail," he called out as the pressure was relieved temporarily.

Thena was kiting another enemy that was suffering from [Blindness] and [Cripple]. Thena had likely inflicted the [Blindness] herself, but the [Cripple] came from Laurant, who was peppering the determined foe with arrows, but the morning-star-wielding merman remained determined to kill our healer. Larissa was busy with keeping both the mermen's healer and their aquamancer locked down through the use of [Counterspell], which was an ability I regretted losing.

Judging that Thena needed my help most of all, I [Dashed] forward, followed by a [Piercing Lunge]. The blow landed squarely in the merman's flank and dealt critical damage, finally distracting it from our healer, bringing it from fifty percent Health down to thirty.

At that moment, Larissa's [Polymorph] on the group's second healer faded. Before I could respond, the healer got a spell off on my target, bringing it back to sixty percent Health with a heal-over-time effect. I quickly switched to [Arcane Weapon] to disrupt the continuing heal and rolled away to address the new healer instead, but the morning star merman had decided that I was the larger threat and followed.

[Arcane Weapon], while it dealt less damage than my other imbue spells, had the convenient effect of disrupting the magic of others. Which made it the ideal choice for dealing with healers and [Mages]. My [Piercing Lunge] disrupted the healer's cast and dispelled the magical armor that it had cast on itself at the same time.

The morning star merman gave me trouble for a few seconds, but I felt the warm embrace of divine magic protecting me. Even when the weapon's ball hit me full, I lost no Health and suffered no pain. After ten seconds of frustration, the enemy turned back towards chasing our healer, and I let it go, trusting in my party to handle itself while I kept their healer distracted.

With the purple glow of my [Arcane Weapon] disrupting the flow of the healer's magic, I made relatively short work of it. By the time I had finished, the morning star merman was also dead, and Laurant was focusing on their aquamancer.

"Hail, help me burst this jerk down," Laurant called. I began chanting the cantrip for an [Empowered Lightning Bolt]. My spell, Laurant's [Aura Piercing Shot], and a [Lightning Bolt] from Larissa hit the enemy [Mage] at the same time, dropping it from sixty percent Health to ten. I was halfway through my cast when Laurant's [Multi-Shot] delivered five arrows to the aquamancer's chest, finishing him off. Rather than let my partially cast spell go to waste, I switched targets to the remaining healer.

The healer was only level twenty-one, meaning that my spells did full Damage. Each cast of [Lightning Bolt] dealt about twenty-five percent of the healer's maximum Health. Larissa provided one last [Counterspell] to interrupt a heal as Laurant and I quickly burned it down.

The crowd control spells I had cast on Phil's enemies had worn off by this point, but rather than refresh them, I burned through the rest of my Mana with three casts of the expensive [Chain Lightning] spell. Larissa only cast two before she paused to meditate, her index and middle finger going to her forehead to indicate that she was regenerating her Mana.

I was likewise left with only two hundred Mana, just enough for an [Imbue Sword: Lightning]. With my rapier crackling with electricity, I [Dashed] forward to help finish off the stragglers that Phil had so kindly softened up for me. A [Piercing Lunge], [Slash], and [Thrust] was all it took to finish off the weakest of the group.

Laurant's [Skilled] arrows finished off the next-weakest foe just after another [Chain Lightning] slammed into the remaining group. Phil slammed one of the remaining foes, knocking the merman to the ground, and then spun to pincer, with my help, the one still standing. His axe took the merman high, while I pierced it in the side with a [Thrust]. It burst into black motes of mist as it died.

The final foe did not manage to recover its feet before it met a similar fate.

I quickly checked my status screen, then smiled. I was at 6317/6400 Experience for level sixteen. I hadn't looked in a few pulls, but I knew I'd been close.

"One more group like that and I'll be level seventeen," I said proudly.

"That's great, Hail," Larissa praised. "Especially since we've only been out here for about two hours. Let's check for loot and keep moving."

While killing monsters was lucrative, the monsters themselves didn't drop coin. Rather, slaying monsters left a residue on our Adventurer's Guild Token. By bringing it to a local branch, we could claim the bounty for the monsters that we had slain. It was easy to measure and impossible to fake, making it an excellent measure of our contribution towards pushing back the darkness.

However, monsters also often left behind items. These drops would either materialize after the black mist had parted, or they would be found nearby the area the monster inhabited. Nobody had noticed a materialization, so we searched the camp for anything valuable.

"Looks like nothing," Laurant muttered after a moment. I, however, had noticed something. A brightly hued stone near one of the merman's shanties. I picked it up, and dropped it again immediately.

You have found a Lair Stone (Aqueous) Levels 21-28	
Options	
Evolve Lair	Increase Level Range
	Decrease Level Range
	Add Monster Type
	Expand Territory
	Collapse Territory
	Rare Spawn
Destroy Lair Stone	0/8 stones of this lair destroyed. All stones must be destroyed to destroy the lair.

"What is it, Hail? Did you find something?" Laurant asked.

"This stone!" I said. "It's special. When I picked it up, I got a prompt."

Laurant came over and picked up the stone. He tossed it in the air a few times and caught it, then shrugged. "It looks like an ordinary rock to—oh shit. Hail, what does the prompt say?"

"I just got a flash. But it said I could evolve the lair or destroy the stone. I think there are seven other stones like this, and if I destroy them all then the lair goes away forever," I answered. Laurant dropped the stone and backed away from it.

"Oh my. I'm not sure if this is awesome or terrible," Thena said. "Hail, we do *not* want to destroy this lair. It's a very important place for players to get stronger."

"I know that," I said. "I wasn't thinking of destroying it. I—I don't know what to do with it, that's why I dropped it. The last time I had a prompt like that was with the [Dungeon Daughter Core]. I don't want to cause trouble for the kingdom again. I know that if we destroy the lair, it will slow down the growth of new Travelers in our kingdom and weaken us all."

"Does it say how you can evolve it, Hail?" Larissa inquired.

"There were a bunch of options. Here, let me check again." I touched the stone with a nervous finger, then backed away from it again before repeating the options.

The others exchanged looks.

"I don't think we should do anything to adjust the balance of this place," Thena said. "So, no increasing or decreasing the level range. But increasing the territory might not be so bad. More territory means more mobs to grind, right?"

"We're too close to Eastmill," I argued. "I'm not willing to put them in more danger than they're already in."

"Right, forgot about that," she admitted.

"What about a rare spawn? Or adding a monster type?" Phil asked.

"Nix the second idea. It goes back to adjusting the balance of this place; adding a second monster type might make this lair significantly more dangerous and harder to grind. But a rare spawn, that might actually be something people would appreciate," Thena said carefully.

"Is there something the matter?" Tarisha said, my guardian using her blink-like teleport from where she had been keeping watch for powerful players who may have nefarious intent.

Thena quickly explained my discovery, and Tarisha considered the matter seriously.

"Do it," she said finally. "I believe that it is Hail's destiny to change this world. In order for him to control his abilities, he must exercise them."

"What if the rare spawn is actually a Worldboss?" Thena questioned.

"Then you shall flee while I buy time, and then the rest of <Peasant's Revenge> will enjoy a world's first kill," she said. "But I think it is more likely that the rare spawn will be something that you can handle."

Thena nodded. "Hail, touch the stone again and select the option for a rare spawn," she said.

"Are you sure?" I asked.

"Trust us, Hail. Having a rare spawn in this lair would be something most players would be very excited about," Thena assured me.

"And it shouldn't be a risk to the kingdom. If anything, it will make players visit this area more often to search for it."

I frowned, but after a moment I nodded and did as instructed. Rainbow motes of light emerged from the stone, swirled in the air, and then vanished beneath the waves of the lake. A moment later a wake was formed as something made its way up from the depths.

A twenty-foot-long blue Naga emerged. It had a scaled, muscular torso, holding a potent looking trident in its hands. It gave us a venomous glare, then charged forward, its snake-like tail driving it forward at high speed.

29

RARE SPAWN

The Naga was like me. Dangerous from near and afar. Once it was twenty yards away, it stopped its rapid charge and studied us for a moment. I took the opportunity to do the same.

Shleshenal of the Depths
Naga
Level 24 Elite
Health: 144,000/144,000

"He's level twenty-four, but he's elite," I said quickly. "He has a lot of Health."

"Yeah, but we can take him. Tarisha, bug out so that you don't interfere with the contribu—"

The Naga took that opportunity to begin the clash. He raised his black trident at us, and it shot out three lines of darkness, which slammed into Larissa. She cursed and fell to her knees.

"Twelve-hundred Damage from that," she announced. "This guy is a real—"

The monster reared back, a hood emerging along its neck like a cobra, then spat a ball of acid. It moved slower than the darkness from the trident, and we were forced to [Dodge] out of the way. Most of us. Phil charged instead, covering the distance between us and the Naga in a fraction of a second.

The rest of us spread out so that another glob of acid—or maybe it was poison; best not to find out—wouldn't catch all of us. Thena got to work healing Larissa on the Damage the trident had caused, then immediately used her Damage mitigation spells upon Phil, who was taking a beating. The rest of us began with the Damage.

At some point, Tarisha had disappeared, although I was certain she was nearby in case it appeared we were in actual danger from the elite Naga.

"I'll keep him slowed," Larissa said. "Your spells have too high of a chance to be resisted, Hail. Just do as much Damage as you can."

"Right," I agreed, and continued to cast [Lightning Bolt]. Thena managed to get off her [Shining Light] spell to inflict [Blindness], and Laurant had inflicted [Cripple] upon the monster's arm. Yet as I watched Phil struggle to avoid the monster's fierce jabs from the trident, I was not looking forward to entering melee range with this formidable opponent. Slowed, blinded, and crippled, and it was still pushing our tank to his limit.

The Naga once again reared back and its hood emerged, but rather than spit out a glob of sludge, it struck with lightning quickness, biting Phil on the shoulder and retracting just as rapidly. Phil cursed.

"Poison," he shouted. "Heavy dot and slow. Keep up the heals, I'm going to need it."

"On it," Thena shouted back. "Just keep him from sniping us off with that freaking laser."

I flinched at the mention of poison, but continued casting [Empowered Lightning Bolts] as I burned myself out of Mana. When I finally ran out, I hesitated for just a second. But a quick [Analyze] showed that we had only done about twenty thousand Damage in total to the enemy so far. If this were an average enemy, he'd be almost dead. But he wasn't even down to eighty-five percent yet. My friends needed me in this fight, so I used what little Mana I had left to use [Imbue Sword: Lightning], and I [Dashed] forward to join Phil in melee.

I flanked the Naga, leading with [Piercing Lunge] and quickly following up with my other abilities. My sword crackled and shone with blue light as the electricity and steel bit into the Naga's flesh.

Fortunately, melee Damage was better at overcoming the tyranny of level disparity better than ranged Damage, so I was dealing seventy percent of my Damage instead of fifty percent.

It came with the increased risk of crushing blows, however. The Naga regarded me for a half a second, then turned its attention from Phil towards me. I [Dashed] backwards, unwilling to go toe-to-tail with the beast. It didn't pursue, but turned its attention back to the tank instead.

Through all of this, Laurant peppered the Naga with his endless arrows. [Archers] do not use Mana, but rather Skill, which has a much lower cap but regenerates much faster. While his burst Damage was lower than a [Mage]'s, he never had to slow down or stop to regenerate Mana, allowing him to finally, truly rise to the occasion after being consistently outshone by Larissa.

Larissa was holding her own, of course. She burned through her Mana pool, casting [Slow] one last time before entering her [Meditation] period. Unfortunately, the Naga wasn't content to let her regenerate her Mana in peace. It raised its trident and another line of darkness slammed into her, causing her to stumble and lose concentration. Thena healed the Damage quickly, but she was already straining to keep Phil alive through the poison.

If this fight went on for too long, Thena would run out of Mana to heal us, and we would wipe. Which meant that I couldn't simply sit back and let my friends kill the monster for me. So again I darted into melee range, burned through my abilities, and [Dashed] out again as soon as the Naga turned its attention towards me. I had regenerated enough Mana for a few casts of [Lightning Bolt], which I promptly used while Phil regained the beast's attention. Once I was out of Mana again, I repeated the process, putting myself in intense danger in order to do as much Damage as I could before the Naga turned to swat me like a fly.

On the fourth cycle of this, the Naga reached sixty percent Health, and abruptly it changed strategies. It surged forward and encircled Phil with its long body, then ignored the tank as it reared up and began firing its trident at the ranged party members. The trident seemed to have a five or six second cooldown, but it did so much Damage on a hit and was nearly impossible to [Dodge], making it a healer's nightmare. Thena struggled to keep up.

Phil was effectively out of the fight, and there was only one of us who could step forward to prevent the Naga from picking us off one by one. Unfortunately, he was significantly under leveled. Still, I stepped forward bravely—or at least I didn't let my fear show—as I took Phil's place as the party tank.

My stratagem worked, and once I was in front of the Naga it stopped firing its trident, but I wasn't really a tank, and it quickly became apparent where I was lacking. The Naga pierced my shoulder with its trident after only a few seconds, doing nearly eight hundred Damage. Thena quickly healed the deficit, of course, but another jab followed seconds later, and I was uncertain whether I was taking the pressure off our healer or increasing it. The Naga seemed to be suffering a loss of mobility from having trapped Phil, however, making my job of dodge-tanking it easier.

While I fought defensively, I did not neglect dealing Damage entirely. I did not get as many unskilled strikes in as I would have were I not focused on dodging, but I kept [Slash] and [Thrust] on cooldown, and frequently managed a [Riposte]. [Feint] was a vital aspect of my survival; without it, I would have been taking every blow the Naga directed at me instead of one in five.

Abruptly the Naga surged forward, and I found myself wrapped up in the length of its body instead of Phil. I cried out in alarm. However, while I was trapped, I was not taking significant Damage. And encircling me had allowed Phil to escape, meaning that he was once again able to tank the boss properly.

Trapped as I was and unable to fight, I quickly [Analyzed] the Naga again. We had whittled the monster down to 65483/144000, a little more than forty-five percent. I could only hope that the monster had no more surprises in store for us, and that Thena's Mana would be sufficient to keep us alive while we burned through the remaining Health.

"Are you okay in there, Hail?" Laurant called out.

"I'm not taking Damage," I answered. "I'm just trapped, and this guy is all slimy. It's gross."

"Just hang in there. I'm betting there's another phase transition coming up soon," he answered. "Great job stepping in while Phil was trapped. You really saved us."

Phil's prediction was correct, and once Shleshenal of the Depths crossed forty percent Health, I was abruptly freed. And the fight became even more difficult. Rather than simply trapping one of us with its long body, it began charging the ranged party members in rapid succession.

Laurant dealt with the charges by [Backflipping] away. Larissa had the potent mage's utility, [Blink]. But Thena had no special movement skill to escape. Instead, Phil stayed by her side, ready to intervene the moment the Naga turned his attention towards our healer.

I simply evaded the monster's attacks as best I could until it changed target. When I had Mana, I cast my spells, but I was often forced to run alongside the charging snake-like monster, [Slashing] and [Thrusting] on the move as I struggled to keep [Battle Trance] active. I felt kind of foolish doing so for some reason.

However, the third phase was not overly difficult, and although it took a while to burn through the Naga's massive Health pool, we were determined to end the fight.

At ten percent, the fight changed again. Shleshenal coiled himself up and stopped attacking.

"He's healing!" Laurant called out. "The last phase is a burn! Everyone max Dee Pee Ess! Even you, Thena!"

While it may sound like this would be an easy phase, for every one percent Damage we dealt, the elite monster healed zero point eight percent. Even though the enemy wasn't attacking, if our Damage was any lower, we would be unable to overcome the healing.

Even after I regenerated full Mana, I continued to attack in melee range; the resistance from level disparity made my spells less effective than my [Skills]. Larissa was likewise having trouble sustaining her Damage, and we were barely keeping up with the boss's regeneration when she entered her [Meditation] periods.

"Larissa, regen to full when we get him to two percent," Laurant called. "Then everyone max burn! We've got this!"

Laurant's strategy proved to be the winning one. We held Shleshenal at two percent for a full minute, then Larissa let loose with the lightning and thunder. Laurant used his most powerful abilities and cooldowns. Phil had long switched from his defensive abilities to his most damaging ones, and he, too, activated a cooldown that increased his damage. Even Thena stood from afar, her eyes glowing white as she cast her damaging spells fervently.

Finally, the boss thrashed as it reached zero Health. Its death lasted for ten seconds as it thrashed about before it burst into black mist.

"We did it!" I cheered, and the rest of the party joined in with me. The black mist abruptly coalesced into a box, and we cheered again.

"That fight was as difficult as a dungeon boss," Laurant said. "Whatever he dropped might be pretty good. Hopefully someone can use it."

I was closest, so I opened the chest. Inside was a black trident, a cloak, and a pendant. I [Analyzed] each.

Trident of Shleshenal	
Rare, Requires Level 25	
Damage	C
Strength	9
On use, inflicts Darkness Damage. 50 yrd range. 20 second cooldown	

Nagaskin Cloak	
Rare, Requires Level 21	
Armor	10
Dexterity	8
Vitality	3

Pendant of Deep Waters	
Rare, Requires Level 23	
Intelligence	4
Wisdom	7
Healing	10

The others moved over to the chest and quickly [Analyzed] the rewards as well. Laurant whistled, then he laughed.

"You know, it's funny. I can't whistle in real life, but in the game it's no problem," he commented.

"May I ask what the loot was?" Tarisha asked, appearing next to us suddenly thanks to her amazing movement ability.

"Christ! Don't do that, you'll give somebody a heart attack," Phil exclaimed.

"I apologize," she said calmly, not sounding that sorry. She had a grin on her face, at least. "That battle was hard fought. I'm curious to know whether it was worth it."

"Dungeon-quality loot," Laurant confirmed. "To go along with the dungeon-boss difficulty. That pendant will look great on you, Thena."

"I believe it will," the priestess agreed. "And I'll likely be wearing it for at least fifteen, twenty levels."

"I'll take the trident, if nobody minds," Phil said. "I kind of want a Dee Pee Ess option. I'll have to do some practice with spears, but that thing looks deadly."

"And the cloak will look great on Hail, once we get him some more levels," Laurant said. "Dex is one of your main stats, right kiddo?"

"Wait, on me? But you need it to," I said.

"I'm passing on it. It's all yours," he said. "I mean, unless I'm completely wrong about how your class works. I read a little bit on the theorycrafting behind [Spellblade] that the nerds are working on. I mean, it is a damn sexy cloak, but I'd rather put as much gear on you as possible."

"Are you sure?" I asked.

"Take it, Hail," Phil said. "We only have the option to loot it because of you. We all want you to have it."

"But I can't even use it yet," I argued.

"You'll grow into it," Thena chuckled. "Congratulations, Hail."

After everyone confirmed that they all wanted to give it to me, I put it in my inventory for when I hit level twenty-one. Speaking of which, I quickly pulled up my status.

"Oh yeah," I said. "Ding!"

30
GAINS

The [Nagaskin Cloak] felt heavy and warm when I finally cinched it around my neck. After two days of grinding mermen, and spawning two more rare spawns, I could finally equip it! And it wasn't my only upgrade. One of the rare spawns had been a giant snapping turtle, which dropped a [Turtle Shell Ring], giving me a second ring. It gave me five Spell Damage and Intellect, as well as three points of Wisdom. Wisdom wasn't really important for me, though. It increased my passive Mana regeneration, but didn't scale with [Battle Trance], which was based upon my total Mana. Unlike a traditional mage class, which needed Wisdom to power up their [Meditation].

The turtle had also dropped a pair of boots that had a lot of Vitality and Endurance on them. Phil reluctantly accepted them after I refused to wear them. I still liked my [Sturdy Crystal-Toed Boots], and it wasn't enough of an upgrade to take them away from the tank who kept things from eating me.

The third rare spawn was a giant bird, which dropped a bow for Laurant, but that was it. Neither the turtle nor the bird was as difficult as the Naga had been, so nobody was surprised that the loot wasn't as good. Although what had dropped was amazing, according to my friends.

"That's it for us, Hail," Thena said. "It's been a blast, but we've got to go eat lunch, and then we're going to spend a few hours studying."

"I think I need a break too," I admitted. "And I should go check in with my grandfather. I said that I would do so soon in my letter to him, which he should have received the day before yesterday. I think I'll spend a day in the city, then find another group. Unless you're available at the time, of course, otherwise I'll look in guildchat."

"Kiddo's going to leave us in the dust in no time," Laurant complained. "I think that's the real reason he passes out [Mark of Karma] like crazy. The players who interact with him need the Experience boost just to have a hope of keeping up with him."

"I'm just glad he does. I wasn't expecting to hit level thirty so fast," Phil said. "And [Don't Make Him Cry] is almost as good. It's going to suck to lose that someday."

"Will you Fast Travel back to the city?" Larissa inquired.

"I'm supposed to keep Fast Travel available in case my guards from <Peasant's Revenge> tell me to flee to safety," I reminded them. "If I use it to travel into the city, then I'll be vulnerable for thirty minutes until I can use it again."

"He's right," Thena agreed. "It's not such a big deal out here in the boonies, but in the city he'll be more vulnerable than ever."

"I have another new mask. This one makes me blond," I said.

"I'm not certain how effective that will be, considering it's known now that you can disguise yourself like a player," Thena said.

"It can't hurt," Laurant argued.

"Most players don't walk around wearing masks unless they provide a stat boost," Thena argued. "And the simple disguise masks do not. It might draw attention to him."

"No more than walking around with four bodyguards from <Peasant's Revenge>," Phil said. "My vote is for him to wear it, if that matters."

"Phil's right. If there's any chance it will keep the average asshole from recognizing him, it's worth wearing," Laurant agreed.

"Should we walk you back to the city?" Larissa asked, staying on topic.

"No thanks. I think I'll go to Eastmill first to spend the night," I said. "I'm getting tired. I'll see Grandfather tomorrow morning."

"Then we'll walk you to Eastmill," she insisted. And so they did. It wasn't very far from the lake where we had been grinding the last two days to the inn where I had been spending my nights. The innkeeper seemed to have been expecting me, and he quickly served me a large portion of stew, which he had been keeping warm despite the late hour.

"Will that be all, Milord?" he asked.

I frowned. "You know who I am?"

"You announced it, did you not? To the Traveler the other day? It's been all around the village who you are. And there have been other Travelers poking around. We've done our best to keep them from bothering you by telling them that you moved on to Northfield," the innkeeper informed me.

"Thank you for that," I said. "And thank you for keeping the stew warm. I apologize if you inconvenienced yourself on my behalf."

"It's no trouble at all, Milord," he said. "It's been a pleasure serving you."

"I may be back in the future, but tomorrow I will be returning to the city," I informed him. "You won't need to stay up on my behalf any longer."

"Thank you for telling me, Milord. I might have worried otherwise."

I retired to my room, and with a smile upon my face, checked my status one last time before undressing for bed.

Name	Hail Jeoran	Level	21
Guild	<Nethersong Mavericks>	Strength	18
Health	7350/7350	Dexterity	51
Mana	9030/9030	Vitality	35
Experience	687/10500	Endurance	26
Age	10	Intelligence	43
Race	Human (blood of the Travelers)	Wisdom	29
Class	Spellblade	Charisma	38
Job	Earl	Armor	22
		Spell Damage	54.2

Passive Skills	Short Swords (17)	Spells	Detect Poison (17)
	Long Swords (8)		Lightning Bolt (25)
	Rapiers (25)		Chain Lightning (17)
	Katanas (6)		Fireball (14)
	Dodge (21)		Ice Blast (13)
	Battle Trance		Arcane Missile (12)
	Magic in Motion		Dazzling Lights (9)
			Concussive Sound (8)
Active Skills	Dash (23)		Befuddle (12)
	Thrust (27)		Water Jet (7)
	Slash (29)		Polymorph (20)
	Riposte (19)		Slow (24)
	Feint (19)		Create Trap (7)
	Piercing Lunge (18)		Mark of Karma (special)
	Swiftcast (20)		
	Empower Magic (17)	**Traits**	(Focus to Expand)
	Imbue Sword: Fire (16)		
	Imbue Sword: Lightning (25)	**General Skills**	(Focus to Expand)
	Imbue Sword: Ice (17)		
	Aqua Blade (4)	**General Spells**	(Focus to Expand)
	Arcane Weapon (13)		

I thought back to my piddling stats from two years ago and almost laughed. I had almost one hundred times the Health I'd had back then. Attacks that would have killed me in one hit were minor scratches now. And I'd been keeping pace with both Laurant and Larissa in Damage per second for the last several levels, despite the fact that they were both level thirty.

I was determined to catch up to them soon. They had been losing Experience in helping me level, and I would make it up to them someday. I wasn't certain how, but I would.

Satisfied with myself, I went to sleep.

"That's quite a few mermen you've slain for being level twenty-one," the Adventurer's Guild attendant said, eyeing me. "If I didn't know that this couldn't be forged, I'd be suspicious."

"I had help," I admitted.

"Oh, a carry. That's fine then," he muttered. Then his expression turned even more suspicious. "Say, where did that cloak come from?"

"None of your business, jerk," I said, trying my best to sound like a Traveler. "Just pay me the bounty."

He grunted. He opened the till and began counting out what I was owed. Fifty-eight gold, twenty silver. It was a pittance compared to the money I'd made from [Immature Gemos Hearts], but I figured you could never have too much. And I was a noble now, which meant I might actually be expected to start paying my own expenses soon. That was a frightful thought.

He pulled the Adventurer's Guild Token from the reading device and handed it back to me. The wooden coin shifted in my hand, turning from wood to iron before my eyes.

"Congratulations. You're now iron-ranked with the guild," he said. "New quests are available. Although if you're getting carried, you'll get better Ex Pee per hour grinding than running fetch-and-carry quests for the locals."

"Thank you. I'll check them out," I said, still trying to sound like a Traveler. I left him and returned to the Quest Board, looking sadly at the seat where I had met Severus weeks ago. It seemed like an age, but it really hadn't been all that long. The room was busy with Travelers, and my insistence on visiting it had made the Dusk Guard somewhat nervous. Two of them were standing nearby, trying to look nonchalant while I concluded my business.

The only items of note on the board were a standing quest to slay mermen (which I had unlocked by ranking up to iron), a notice that [Gemos Caverns] was now a level twenty to twenty-five instance with two bosses and a gauntlet, and several quests directing Travelers to various lairs and dungeons with the appropriate level ranges listed. I could now see up to level forty quests, but still others were hidden behind a glamour that prevented adventurers from seeing them until they had proven their valor.

I accepted a few of them because I saw no reason not to. I could always drop them later, and I might want to switch to a new grinding spot. After a bit of consideration, I nervously accepted the quest for the new [Gemos Caverns] and two other dungeons that I could visit. I was of a mixed mind about actually visiting one after what had happened at Gemos. But I could always drop them.

And there was something telling me that I couldn't keep hiding from dungeons forever.

As I was about to leave the Adventurer's Guild, I abruptly stopped and pulled off my mask.

"Excuse me! Everyone, I have something to say!" I shouted. "Nile's Inn in Eastmill has absolutely delicious food and you should make your way over there to taste his hearty cooking!"

I put the mask back on just as the room exploded into exclamations of "Hey, it's that kid!" and "Did you just get a quest too?" and other things like that. Giggling madly, I sprinted out into the street, replacing my mask once I was a block away with one that made me look a completely different shade of blond.

"Was that really necessary, my Lord?" Tarisha asked, appearing beside me.

"Yes. Entirely necessary," I told her. "You're the one who says I need to use my abilities."

"You could have at least warned your guard," she complained.

"You would have tried to stop me," I argued.

"Or I would have tried to find a way to attempt whatever experiment that was in a more controlled manner," she argued. "What were you trying to accomplish?"

"Did you get a quest too?" I asked.

"Indeed. To eat at Nile's Inn."

"That was the goal," I explained. "I'm trying to control when I give quests to Travelers. Mostly it's always happened by accident. And Nile's Inn really does have good food, and the innkeeper is a nice guy, so I thought I'd try to help him out by sending him some customers."

"I see," Tarisha said. "Well, I suppose there is no harm done. Are we making way to the castle next?"

"I want to finish upgrading my gear before I see Grandfather again," I told her. "He might ask to see my stats and I want to impress him."

"I'm quite certain that he'll be impressed enough simply by your level growth," Tarisha informed me.

"I want to impress him," I repeated. "We're going shopping next."

After two hours of visiting various shops and an Auction Master, I managed to upgrade almost every single item from my level-ten gear set except for the [Gemos Ring] and [Crystal-Toed Boots] that I had gotten from [Gemos Caverns], and for my weapon. I could have upgraded my rapier as well, but I didn't like the grip on the ones that I'd examined, and the stat was only a plus two on Dexterity, which I judged not to be worth it. Not when I had gained twelve points from my other upgrades and was now at sixty-three total Dexterity. My Intellect and Spell Power had both seen significant growth, with Intellect increasing by five points and Spell Power by ten.

Finally satisfied with both my appearance and my status, I ventured towards the castle proudly, determined to impress Grandfather. And perhaps to tell him a few matters of importance, which I was certain he'd want to know.

I tried very hard not to panic at that thought.

31
BLUE CLOAKS

As I approached the castle, Tarisha and the Dusk Guard in tow, I noticed something peculiar: a strange uniformity about the Travelers I was passing. Not that there could ever be true uniformity about the Travelers, but it was certainly a trend.

Every fifth or sixth player was wearing a familiar blue cloak.

Not one like mine, made of supple and thick Nagaskin, but a heavy woolen one like Captain Malkios's. The markings of the royal house of Teoran were embroidered upon about half of them, while others showed embroidery of a crown or lion.

"Excuse me, sir," I said to one player. "Where did you get that cloak?"

"You like it? It's [Malkios's Other, Other Spare Cloak]. It's the level forty-eight strength version," he informed me. "It's going to be Bee Eye Ess for me up to like level eighty. I'm not even certain I'll be able to get that high. I was super excited when it dropped and the tank lost the roll on it."

"Oh," I said. "Uh-oh. He's not going to be happy about every-one wearing his cloak."

"Yeah, it's freaking hilarious," the Traveler agreed. "I love that guy. When we first started wearing them outside of the dungeon, the guy would come up to us and yell at us to take them off. He's like 'I worked for twenty years to earn the right to wear that cloak! I don't care if it's a drop, take it off!' Right, like that's going to happen."

"How many versions of the cloak are there?" I inquired. "And do they drop often?"

"There's like nine of them, and they drop all over the dungeon," the Traveler said, confirming my fear. "Surprised you haven't seen them before. Each one is pretty strong, even though the stats on the different versions vary widely, as do the level requirements. This event dungeon has really good loot. I feel sorry for the players who missed out on it. Hey, speaking of cloaks, where'd you get yours? Looks pretty awesome."

"Rare spawn," I admitted. "By the lake near Eastmill."

"The mermen drop that shit now?" he asked, surprised.

"No, it was a Naga. I've got to go, thanks for answering my questions," I said, and I jogged off to the castle.

The standard uniform of the city guard was gray cloaks. The castle guard had gray cloaks with blue fringes. Only the Captain of the Royal Guard, and other officers in the army of sufficient rank, were supposed to wear blue cloaks in Yuikon. My [Nagaskin Cloak] wouldn't have been a problem because the color was too dark, almost navy, and it was clearly not designed to indicate rank. And it was leather, which made it distinguishable from the official sign of office.

But the players were wearing a literal copy of Malkios's cloak, spawned by a dungeon. I could not imagine this would put him in a good mood. Nor could I imagine that anything, including passing laws to make it illegal, would prevent the players from wearing their new Bee Eye Ess items.

Rushing to the command tent, I took off my mask and made myself known to the guards, who quickly announced me. A moment later I was shown inside.

My grandfather, Malkios, and a few other Natives I didn't know were clustered around a map of the castle. They looked up at my entrance. Malkios had a scowl on his face, but I was pretty certain it wasn't for me—

"Where in the abyss did you get that cloak, Hail," He growled.

"I . . . it—it was a drop," I said honestly.

"I can see that. What monster? Where? When? I know Nagaskin when I see it. If those beasts are back in our kingdom, then it's yet another disaster while we're still dealing with the castle crisis," he barked.

"It was a rare spawn," I admitted. "Its name was Shleshenal of the Depths. He was a very difficult fight, but my party and I—"

"And how exactly is Shleshenal spawning again? It took us six months to find his Lair Stone and disable him!" Malkios exclaimed. "Are you responsible for changing that, Hail?"

I considered lying for just a second, but instead I straightened my back. "Yes. The Travelers will enjoy the hunt for new rare spawns. I summoned one at each Lair Stone that I found while fighting the mermen outside of Eastmill."

The room was silent for a moment. Then my grandfather burst into laughter.

"Hail is correct, Malkios. The times have changed since Shleshenal and his legion were a problem for us. With the players to dispel the darkness before it accumulates to critical levels, there's little risk to Eastmill and the other villages nearby," Grandfather said. "But you, Hail, must have grown strong indeed if your party was able to take down Shleshenal. He was a formidable foe, although much of his difficulty came from his lieutenants when we faced him. They are not spawning as well, are they?"

"I don't think so," I said, trying not to allow my relief to show. "There is a giant turtle and giant bird, but only one Naga."

"As long as it stays that way, there shouldn't be a problem," Grandfather said. "The times have changed. Shleshenal's loot items are above par for his level. Even after we lowered the eastern aqueous lair's level and reduced it to only mermen for training purposes, that should still be true. The former general who gave us so much trouble thirty years ago will find himself hunted constantly. The difficulty he poses in battle will only add spice to the conflict as far as the Travelers are concerned."

"So, I'm not in trouble?" I asked, and Grandfather's gaze narrowed on me.

"Oh, I didn't say that," he said. "The eastern aqueous lair was carefully cultivated; you should have sought permission before making changes to it. You will face discipline for that later, however. I received your letter. Tell me, what class have you unlocked?"

I glanced around at the room, and he interpreted my hesitation correctly.

"I trust these men and women with my life," he said. "My life, my secrets, and my family. Including you."

"I'm a [Spellblade]," I said, accepting Grandfather's judgment on the matter. Several mutters and curses escaped from the Natives in the room.

"That's wonderful news, Hail. I was concerned when you selected a class without my input, but with the [Royal Prince] class sealed, this is perhaps the best I could have hoped for. [Noble] is a potent class as well, but with the path you have chosen to walk, it is perhaps best to face your enemies toe-to-toe rather than supporting your followers," King Rain stated. "At the very least I won't have to worry about your ability to defend yourself."

"How did you unlock an advanced class at such a tender age?" one of the Natives I didn't know asked. A noblewoman of my grandfather's age. "It is notoriously difficult to master all of the abilities required."

"The Travelers of <Nethersong Mavericks> helped me," I admitted. "They taught me a wide variety of skills and spells. It wasn't their intention to unlock any specific class, necessarily, and the classes that we did unlock did not feel like the right fit for me. But I was dueling with the companions of Tarisha of Miami when I accidentally learned [Imbue Sword: Fire]. I learned the other elements immediately after, and that allowed me to unlock the class."

"Curious. I never would have thought it possible. I would be very curious to see your character sheet, young man," the Lady asked.

"I'm reluctant to show it to anyone but my grandfather and Captain Malkios," I admitted.

"As you should be," Malkios grunted. "Simply knowing your class gives an enemy an idea of how to counter you. Showing them the details of your abilities and attributes gives them the insight necessary to end you. It was improper for Lady Gwen to inquire."

"Oh, I wasn't really asking. I was stating an interest," she argued.

"You'd pay a millstone's weight in gold to look at the status screen of anyone in this room and you know it, Gwen," Grandfather stated.

"Of course. You have no idea how frustrating research on high-level classes can be when nobody is willing to share their secrets," she sighed. "And yet, you're the only one who has the privilege to demand a peek, Rain. Oh, if only you would have taken me seriously when we were younger; the secrets I could have gained as [Queen]."

"You're like a sister to me, Gwen. The annoying kind who always pulls your hair and pinches," Grandfather returned. "Hail, your level?"

"Twenty-one," I said proudly.

"Impressive. I was almost eighteen by the time I reached that milestone," Grandfather admitted.

"It's a completely different circumstance," Gwen argued. "Hail unlocked an advanced class at age ten, you had to wait until you turned fifteen to unlock [Royal Prince]. And then you spent eight years capped at level fifty before your father abdicated, allowing you to advance. But there must always be a [King] in the Dungeon Busters. The benefits you provide to the rest of us are indispensable."

"Is that true?" I asked, surprised. "Grandfather, are you strong?"

Grandfather laughed. "Hail, now that you have an advanced class, I am likely the weakest person in this room. I doubt I could handle you even though I have almost a hundred levels on you. [King] is both a mighty class, and a deeply flawed one. By myself, I am completely vulnerable. But with an army at my back, I am unstoppable."

"An army, or a team of elites," a snake-like man interjected. "I am looking forward to stretching my muscles after ten years of allowing the Travelers to run rampant. It's a shame that the boy is eighty levels too low to consider adding him to the Dungeon Busters. We could use a skilled [Spellblade]."

Eighty levels? I swallowed nervously. "Grandfather, if I may ask, what is the average level of the Dungeon Busters?"

"I am the lowest-leveled member at one hundred twenty-three," he admitted. "But my level is mostly irrelevant. The others range from levels one hundred thirty to one hundred seventy."

I shook my head. "Grandfather, the Travelers report that there are monsters in the dungeon exceeding level one hundred eighty. Elite dungeon monsters, and likely a boss of that level as well."

The room went silent for a moment.

"How accurate is your information from the Travelers, Hail?" Malkios asked after a moment.

"I heard them speaking of it a few days ago while I was with my guild," I explained. "The truth is I don't know, but my liege-woman Tarisha of Miami would. She knows how to sort through the Traveler's . . . communication thing, better than I."

"Malkios, bring her in," Grandfather commanded, and Malkios promptly obeyed, leaving the tent and returning a minute later with Tarisha in tow.

"My grandson tells me that you have detailed information on the enemies inside [Zhesa Castle Dungeon]," Grandfather said immediately. "How detailed, how reliable, and what sort of information can you provide to us?"

Tarisha smiled. "The castle has been explored thoroughly and cleared hundreds of times by Travelers, Your Majesty. They have spoken about their experiences at length upon the public forums, which all Travelers have access to. I have read extensively about their encounters and strategies for overcoming the monsters within, while guarding Lord Hail as he leveled over the past few days. I am happy to share the information, which is publicly available to my kind, as well as the information that is privately withheld among the elite guilds regarding the 'endgame wing.'"

"What payment do you demand for this information?" the snake-like man asked.

"It is freely given, although I am not opposed to my guild receiving future consideration for my contribution to the efforts of reclaiming [Zhesa Castle]," Tarisha admitted. "But I leave the nature and level of consideration to His Majesty's discretion."

"I shall take it under consideration and reward your guild appropriately," Grandfather promised. "Now, please, share every detail you can about the interior of the dungeon."

Tarisha grinned and came forward to the map of the castle. She began speaking quickly, sharing what she knew, occasionally pausing to check on details through her guildchat or the forums.

There was *a lot* of information for her to share. It took a very long time, and I quickly grew bored. Taking a seat in the corner, I watched the proceedings with fading interest while Grandfather, Malkios, and the rest of the Dungeon Busters hung on every word.

32

CONFESSION

I drifted off at some point, and when I awoke the room was empty except for my grandfather and Captain Malkios. I wiped the drool off my chin and looked around.

"Ah, he awakes," Grandfather said, barely looking up from the map.

"How long was I asleep?"

"I'm not certain. The conference with your Traveler companion lasted for two hours. It ended thirty minutes ago. Now that we have a more accurate idea of what faces us, the other Dungeon Busters have gone to prepare themselves for the challenges within the castle," he answered.

"Why did nobody think to ask for a report from the Travelers before?" I inquired.

"It's not that we didn't think of it," Grandfather said. "However, the core instance of a dungeon is different from the one the Travelers experience. We didn't think that it would be relevant. We are still proceeding with the assumption that all of Tarisha of Miami's information is unreliable. Or that it will be once the dungeon becomes aware of us and begins to defend itself properly."

"Defend itself?" I asked.

"Dungeons are self-aware," Malkios explained. "It is not a personal awareness like ours, but a low-level, dream-like state. They wake up when a Native threatens their core and take actions to defend themselves."

"Oh. You mean, like, if you defeat their final boss, it will suddenly add a new challenge?" I asked.

"That's one possibility," Malkios grunted. "The final boss of a dungeon almost always defends the dungeon core. However, it remains impossible to destroy a dungeon without performing a full clear. Evolving a dungeon is easy. Destroying one is not."

I swallowed and began to work up my courage. "Grandfather, before, you said that you would hang the cat-kin responsible for the opening of the dungeon. But what if that isn't what happened? What if someone else was responsible? What if the dungeon wasn't an attack, but a mistake?"

"Oh? And I suppose you know what really happened?" Grandfather asked.

"I ought to, this is all my fault," I confessed. "Grandfather, I found a core and used it without knowing what it was! I am so—"

"Told you he'd come clean," Malkios grunted, interrupting me. "Good lad."

I frowned, looking between the adults in confusion. Neither seemed surprised nor upset. "You knew?"

"I knew that the cat-kin invader was you the second I spoke with you about it the morning after," Malkios confirmed. "As for the rest? The only thing we couldn't figure out was where the core came from. We thought someone had given it to you, but we have since confirmed the location of all our cores, as well as all of those known to us in the neighboring kingdoms. So, solve the mystery for us, lad. Where did it come from? Who gave it to you?"

"Nobody. I earned it as a reward for clearing [Gemos Caverns]," I confessed. "Well, almost clearing it. We killed the boss, but failed to clear the gauntlet that the dungeon must have summoned to defend its core."

Grandfather's eyes narrowed. "Hail, I need you to explain everything that happened on that day."

I paused to gather my thoughts before launching into a narrative of the events, starting with sneaking out of the castle to go on an adventure with Laurant and ending with hiding the activated dungeon core in my wardrobe. I hung my head at the end of my tale, waiting for the adults to pronounce my doom.

"Well, that puts the mystery to bed," Malkios said. "The question now is what do we do about the boy who caused so much trouble?"

"Will I be executed?" I squeaked.

"Were you not my grandson, that would be a real possibility," Grandfather said, pinching the bridge of his nose in frustration. "It was my decision to exclude the dungeon cores from your early education. Likewise, it was my decision to suspend your education while your official status was in question. This event is as much my fault as yours. If you had known the potency of the item the dungeon awarded you for sparing it in its moment of weakness, would you not have immediately given it to me?"

"Yes! I only used it because I didn't know what it was," I said.

"If only that was good enough," Grandfather said. He sighed. "Hail, I cannot allow this to pass completely unanswered. You must be punished. If you were not my grandson, I would throw you in the dungeon and let you rot until you came of age. But we must protect the royal image. Publicly, we will continue to blame the supposed invader to the castle. But if you had only sought the aid of someone—Malkios or any other adult in the castle—the worst of this crisis could have been averted."

I swallowed. "I know. I'm sorry. What—what will happen to me?"

"You are responsible for the evolution of [Gemos Caverns], the rise of three rare spawns at the Eastern Aqueous Lair, and worst of all, the transformation of [Zhesa Castle] into a dungeon. I fine you one thousand gold for the unauthorized changes you made to [Gemos Caverns], five hundred gold for each of the unauthorized rare spawns, and twenty thousand for [Zhesa Castle]." He grinned, satisfied with the pronouncement. "That may sound severe. It will take you some time to save up to pay these fines, even working as an adventurer, but I hope that it will—"

I set a bag of gold down on the table, interrupting him. The bag and the coin had come from my [Storage], and it contained the full twenty-two thousand, five hundred gold of my fine.

"Thank you for your leniency, Grandfather. I was truly worried I may be hanged. Honestly, if you want to double the fine, that would be okay. I have a lot of gold."

Malkios snatched the very large bag off the table and emptied it over the map of the castle. The gold coins tinkled and sparkled in the dim light of the candles lighting the tent. The captain looked at me in shock.

"Where exactly did you get all of this money?" he demanded.

"Apparently, Travelers really, really like vanity pets," I explained. "I don't really get it myself, but my guild has been helping me to sell the [Immature Gemos Hearts], which I also earned from the dungeon."

"Those useless things are actually valuable?" Malkios exclaimed.

"Hail, how much gold do you possess at the moment?" Grandfather asked, again pinching the bridge of his nose.

It was my turn to narrow my eyes. "If I tell you, will you fine me all of it?"

He snorted. "I'm not so petty. I had intended to make you work hard to pay off your mistakes, and since fining you won't be sufficient for that goal, I have another task in mind. I'm simply concerned about your finances. You are an Earl now, and yet both your education and financial planning are lacking for your station. That must be remedied. It must wait until the conclusion of the current crisis, but your estate must be set up properly."

"I haven't really thought of what to do with all the money," I admitted. "The guild has been charging me a three percent fee for selling the hearts, but otherwise I have just been throwing it into my [Storage]. I have quite a lot of it now, more than I know what to do with."

"The remedy for that situation will wait," Grandfather said. He stood up straight and took up his scepter. "Earl Hail Jeoran. For your part in the conversion of my home into a dungeon, I hereby sentence you to perform the following task. You will enter the evolved [Gemos Caverns]. You will perform a full clear of the dungeon. And if possible, you will reclaim its core and return it to me. Do you accept this task as penance for your mistakes?"

I rose to my feet, then knelt before my king. "Grandfather, I accept this penance. Although, if I am honest, it fills me with trepidation. On my previous attempt at clearing [Gemos Caverns] I knew nothing of its core and evolved it accidentally, barely escaping with my life. I fear going back there."

"Which is why it is your penance," Grandfather explained. He sighed. "Hail, there is something in your tale which you may not understand the importance of, so I will explain it. You seem to have full access to the Traveler's systems. Most Natives have only the status screen. You are able to form parties with them and, perhaps, to bring them with you into the core instance of dungeons. If this is the case, then you are perhaps the most potent Dungeon Buster to ever be born. Your penance is also an experiment to determine whether or not my hopes are grounded in reality. We are performing this experiment on [Gemos Caverns] because it is a relatively unimportant dungeon. Whether or not you succeed, the greater balance of this world will be maintained."

I followed Grandfather's logic and could find no fault in it, except for one. "And if I die in the attempt?"

"Then I will grieve for you deeply," Grandfather said. "But I would not give you a task which I did not believe you were capable of fulfilling. You will either succeed in reaching the core and reclaiming it, or you will prove that my hopes for you are unfounded. I refuse to believe that you will perish on a task which any promising Dungeon Buster applicant would be eager to accomplish."

I frowned. "Grandfather, I only recently learned of the Dungeon Busters. I am not certain I know enough about them to know whether or not I would wish to join their numbers. I—I do not know what I wish to do with my life. Not yet. So far, I have only thought about proving my father wrong in his rejection of me."

"Becoming the ultimate Dungeon Buster will go far beyond just proving him wrong, Hail. It would make you one of our greatest assets against the darkness. You would be the greatest hero of the land," Malkios chimed in. "Being able to bring elite Travelers into the core instance of the most dangerous dungeons would allow us to cultivate even the most difficult of locations. We would be able to expand the Heartlands! To truly grow our territory instead of simply clinging to life in what little we have managed to hold on to while the Travelers keep things from getting any worse."

"It will not be so simple. The darkness is not so easily pushed back, and it will respond in its own fashion," Grandfather predicted. "Opening the Gates of TirNiki was but the latest move in a game of thrust and counter-thrust, which has been going on for centuries. It has allowed the allied forces of the light time to take a breath and recover. But we have earned respite through desperate measures in the past, and while the darkness is kept at bay for now, it will eventually find its next counter-thrust to disrupt the uneasy balance we have earned. We, too, must gather as many weapons as we can whenever the opportunity presents itself. It is for that reason that I must view you as an asset in this war of survival, Hail, rather than simply a grandson to be cherished."

"I—I think I understand," I said. "Although I am not certain that I can live up to such expectations."

"You are my grandson, Hail," King Rain Teoran said proudly. "And the men of our family have always risen to the occasion, even in the darkest hour. I have faith that you will succeed in your mission and return uninjured. If I truly feared for your safety in this quest, I would not send you out on it."

"I understand," I said. "I will return to my guild and put a group together. Hopefully, we will succeed."

"Do not proceed with this mission recklessly, Hail," Grandfather said. "You are young and being tasked with things which no child of your tender years has been tasked with before. I did not begin to break dungeons until I was in my twenties, and I had the benefit of being a [Royal Prince]. You are a [Spellblade], and while that is a potent class, it has its own vulnerabilities."

"Vulnerabilities?" I asked. "I haven't had any trouble so far."

"Every class has its weaknesses," Malkios explained. "A [Spellblade] can be locked down at range the same way that a [Mage] can. And in melee you are as vulnerable as any lightly-armored class. While the combination makes you potent, you are not invulnerable."

"Oh. I guess I knew that," I said. "But you said that even a king was weak unless he had an army. Isn't [Spellblade] much better than that?"

"Hail, an army with a [King] leading it, especially a potent king like your grandfather, is more than twice as strong as one without," Malkios explained. "While an army with a single [Spellblade] is little stronger than one without. King Rain is a force multiplier, and his abilities and skill can lead to victory against odds in which others would face certain defeat. While you may think that [Spellblade] is the ultimate adventurer class, [King] is a command and support class, which is indispensable."

"What makes a king so great in an army?" I asked.

"Several things, but the most potent of them is our [Royal Aura], which increases the stats of all allies who have pledged alliance while they are within sight of me. Another is [Royal Decree]; if an ally follows my orders to use a skill or attack a certain foe, they will do significantly increased Damage compared to if they did not receive that order. [Royal Insight] allows me to [Analyze] a foe in great detail and predict their tactics and weaknesses. [Mandate of Heaven] increases the Healing, Spell Power, and Attack Power of allied forces by a percentage of my Charisma. [Divine Right of Kings] increases my allies' effective level, allowing us to overcome stronger enemies than should otherwise be possible. And I have other abilities that likewise serve as a force multiplier," Grandfather explained. "While I am vulnerable by myself, for every ally who serves under me, I grow exponentially in power."

"Oh," I said, and I tried to imagine how such a class would work. I couldn't really picture it, but Grandfather seemed to think that it was very powerful.

"The [Noble] class possesses similar, but less potent, abilities," Grandfather said. "Had you unlocked that instead, you would have been able to increase your allies' abilities while remaining in relative safety. Instead, you must put yourself in the front lines. I am proud of your choice, but I fear for your safety."

"I think I understand. Don't worry, Grandfather. I will practice with Tarisha of Miami and the other skilled combatants of <Peasant's Revenge> before I attempt my penance, and only when I believe I am capable will I attempt it," I promised. "And, Grandfather, to be honest, I think that I am more happy as a [Spellblade] than I ever would have been as a [Noble], or even a [King]. I enjoy the thrill of combat. Standing in the back and issuing orders is not for me."

"That may be so," Grandfather admitted. "Now go. It will be some time before the other Dungeon Busters return, and some time after that before we are ready to reclaim the core of [Zhesa Castle]. I would like the answer of whether or not you can lead Travelers into the core instance before we begin."

"As you wish," I said. And I rushed forward to hug him before I left. "I'm sorry. This is all my fault."

"You are not entirely to blame," Grandfather said. "And thus far, the only deaths have been Travelers. Had you not come forward on your own, I would have been far more cross. But you have admitted your faults, and as such I am granting leniency. Now go, and show that my belief in you is justified."

I nodded, extricated myself, straightened my clothes, and left the tent.

33

GUILT

"Are you alright, my Lord?" Tarisha asked after I joined her outside the tent.

"I confessed to my grandfather," I admitted.

Tarisha jerked in surprise, then nodded. "I see you are not in chains. That is good."

"They already knew. They were just waiting to see if I'd come clean," I said. "He's not as angry as I thought he would be."

"So, you will face no consequences?" she asked.

"Publicly we're still blaming the cat-kin," I explained. "But I've also had to pay a fine, and I have a task of penance to complete. It—it's not something I can do by myself. I have to reclaim the core of [Gemos Caverns]. Or prove that it's impossible. Either way, I'm scared. The last time I went to that dungeon I nearly died, and it's gotten stronger since then."

"So have you, my Lord," Tarisha reminded me. "And you will not be entering the dungeon by yourself, nor with a variety of amateurs this time. I will make the journey with you myself, and with three other elites from my guild. We will be restricted to level twenty-five, but between us and your own prodigious skill, we will prevail."

"I hope so, Tarisha," I said. "But I want to wait a week before we try, if that is okay with you. I will practice my skills further, and I'm hoping Luke of London, and whoever else, will spar with me."

"I think that is a wise decision. We will also mix in other classes for you to contend with to improve your skills," she suggested. "[Mages], [Archers], spear wielders, and [Rogues], I think. We must train you to fight against a wide variety of opponents now so that you will be able to survive them when you encounter them in a true fight."

"Yes, I think you are right," I admitted. "But clearing [Gemos Caverns] again is most important. The dungeon will defend itself when I get close to the core. That is what happened last time, and we were not prepared for it."

"I see. So that is how things work," she said.

"Tarisha, have you gained a boon from me? Aside from the [Mark of Karma]?"

"I have gained two. The first is [In the Hour of Need]. Everyone you encountered during the day of the dungeon outbreak has gotten this boon, except for those who ignored the quest you generated. It permanently increases Experience gained by five percent and maximum Health by eight percent. It's a very good boon, and the players who received it are very happy. The other boon is [Keep Him Safe]. Every member of your personal guard has gotten this boon. While you are nearby, we deal twenty percent increased Damage to Travelers and take ten percent less Damage from Travelers. This is also a very good boon and will help greatly if we are ever attacked by a powerful Traveler."

"I see," I said. "What about quests?"

"I gain a quest every time I am in your presence. The quest is also [Keep Him Safe], and it awards me with Experience. The amount of Experience goes up the longer that I am in your presence. It is not as much as I would earn grinding, but it is a fair amount. It specifies that protecting you from hostile players will reward a significant bonus. Like with the boon, it provides no Experience or reward from protecting you from Natives or monsters."

"Oh," I said. "I was worried about rewarding you for your efforts, but if just being around me gives you Experience and a boon then I'm not certain what else to give you, except maybe a bit of gold."

"The experience is payment enough for now, my Lord. Although, please keep our efforts in consideration for future decisions. <Peasant's Revenge> is in this for the long haul. We will see you rise in this world, and we would rise with you," she stated.

"I see. Mutually beneficial?"

"That is one way to look at it," she admitted. "But if we are wrong and you do not rise to the heights we hope, then that is also alright. We are having quite a bit of fun as things are, and that is payment enough. Just do what feels natural to you, my Lord, and do not worry about us. We will keep you safe from the worst of the Travelers. That is our sworn duty."

"And if I fail to live up to your expectations?" I asked.

"I doubt that is possible. The boons that you grant are extremely powerful, Lord Hail. The system would not grant them to those who interact with you without good reason. And eventually one of the powers from my world will foolishly try to make a play to claim you by force. That will be quite exciting, and I am looking forward to the challenge. I love a bit of Pee Vee Pee."

"I see," I said, although I had no idea what Pee Vee Pee meant. "So, you are happy with the arrangement as things are?"

"Very happy, Lord Hail," she confirmed.

"So am I," I admitted. "Tarisha, I order you to keep me safe while I visit the camp. I—I need to see for myself the result of the chaos I have caused."

She blinked, and I grinned at the confirmation.

"Did it work?" I asked.

"That was you attempting to generate a quest? If so, yes, you were successful," she answered.

"What's the reward?" I inquired.

"It says Experience, Reputation with you, Lord Hail, and Variable," she answered. "That is the standard reward for almost every quest you generate. Well, the quest to eat in Eastmill only generated Experience and Variable. The Variable reward can be anything, nothing at all, or something of significance, like a piece of gear or another quest. It's impossible to determine beforehand, and it seems to scale with the amount of effort a Traveler puts into completing the quest."

"That's good," I said. "I'm going to go visit with the Natives now. I doubt anyone here wants to kill me, although they might if they knew the full story."

"Most Natives in the city see you as a hero, my Lord," she informed me. "And I believe it best if the cover story stays in place so that they continue to do so."

"I told the truth to my grandfather, the king, so that he'd stop looking for the true culprit and hopefully not start a war," I said, rolling my eyes. "I'm not going to start screaming it from the rooftops. I'm not stupid."

For the next four hours, we walked through the camp that had sprung up outside the entrance to [Zhesa Castle Dungeon]. I spoke with everyone we came across, most of whom I knew. Some of them were those I considered afflicted with "the sameness," but I was surprised to see that they had perked up somewhat compared to their usual selves before the castle had attacked.

I listened to harrowing tale after harrowing tale as the survivors recounted how they had been trapped in the dungeon anywhere from minutes to hours before the guards or Travelers I had sent had arrived to rescue them. Luckily, the golems of the dungeons were somewhat indifferent to anyone who didn't approach them and would not give chase very far. Had the summoned monsters been something vicious, then the death toll would likely have been quite high.

I listened for hours, feeling increasingly guilty over the strife that my childish curiosity had caused. I felt regret at my stupidity for hiding the core instead of showing it to an adult. It might not have prevented the dungeon from forming after my foolish act of activating the core in the first place, but we could have evacuated in advance. It was only luck that no Native had lost their life, although several had been injured and told tales of near misses. Many claimed that they had been reduced to less than ten percent of their Health before a group of Travelers arrived to save them and escort them out of the castle.

I was thanked countless times for my quick thinking and bravery in sending the Travelers to the rescue. I answered their praise as honestly as I could, that I had almost been trapped myself and had done the only thing I could think of at the time. However, the constant guilt, the nagging knowledge that their plight was entirely my fault, continued to weigh me down.

When I had spoken with everyone in the camp, or at least everyone who wanted to speak with me, I felt terrible. I hid my guilt behind princely stoicism until we escaped back to the Guild Hall, then I spent the rest of the day locked in my room.

The next morning, I began training with Tarisha and others from <Peasant's Revenge>.

I hate [Archers].

[Archers] and their stupid [Backflip].

[Mages] were also annoying because they could [Counterspell] me at range, meaning that I had to chase them down to kill them. However, while [Mages] had to [Blink] to run away from me, I could disrupt their magic projectiles with [Arcane Weapon] until I could get close again.

It was the opposite problem with [Archers]. While I could [Slow] them and chase them down, they could likewise [Cripple] me with a shot to the leg, then kite me with [Backflip] while I hobbled after them. It turned the contest into a ranged Dee Pee Ess race. I still didn't really understand that phrase, even now that I knew what it meant.

And they could interrupt my spell casting as well, if they were good. If I was up against a skilled [Archer], then I was effectively "shut down," and there was little that I could do about it. It was simply the worst matchup for me one on one.

Two on one against two [Archers], or an [Archer] and a [Mage], was even worse. Which is, of course, exactly why Tarisha of Miami insisted that I practice such circumstances constantly. Which is how I found myself dueling Laurant and a [Mage] from <Peasant's Revenge> the next morning. Despite their training weapons only inflicting one Health of Damage per hit, they could quickly render me down to thirty percent Health, which was the safety zone where we all agreed the combat would stop.

Because Laurant was only level thirty, I too was using a training weapon, and that annoyed me as well. Finally, I threw the stupid thing on the ground.

"I quit. I can't kill either of them, so there's no point," I declared.

"That's not good enough, Lord Hail," Tarisha argued. "This training is to prepare you for real situations. A [Mage]-[Archer], or dual [Archer], combo is a common team for Pee Vee Pee. At some point, it's quite likely that you'll face such a squad. How will you respond if that is the team that the superguilds send to subdue you?"

"I'll turn them both into slugs and run away," I declared. "Besides, isn't it your job to keep that from happening?"

"And if the foe attacks in overwhelming numbers?" she asks.

"I Fast Travel to a random location and hide," I reminded her.

"And if they're prepared for that tactic by saturating the local Return Points with teams to capture you?" she asked.

"Oh," I said, unable to think of an adequate counter for that situation. "But they'd probably be level two hundred and able to one-shot me, wouldn't they?"

"Level two hundred players are not that common," she admitted. "There is something of a campaign to knock down anyone who reaches that plateau. There is little practical reason to gain the last twenty levels, as it makes little difference in endgame except as a padding against repeatedly failing raids. All dungeons that have been explored so far effectively cap at level one hundred eighty. It is easier to repeatedly level to level one hundred eighty-five than to push all the way to level two hundred. And since dying in a two-hundred-man raid is almost inevitable, there's little point in it. More than three-quarters of a raiding party is usually waiting to respawn by the time the final boss is killed."

"Oh. But still."

"But still, you need practice in Pee Vee Pee," she informed me. "And that means practicing against your poor matchups and hard-counters. Which means practicing against [Archers] and [Mage]-[Archer] combos."

I sighed, but reluctantly picked up my training blade. At a signal from Tarisha, we began again. I charged Laurant, determined to get him and pay him back for this stupid training session. But he [Crippled] my leg and got off six more shots before I reached him.

I [Slashed] him once with my imbued weapon. Then he [Backflipped], laughing cheerfully.

I hate [Archers].

34
GYUDUE OF THE BLACKEST NIGHT

The last of the Gemos golems fell to a combination of our efforts. Magic, swordsmanship, and archery had won the day against the numbers and power of the golems in the gauntlet. I exhaled a sigh of relief when a full minute passed, and no other monsters dropped from the boss room's ceiling. We had cleared the gauntlet.

"Be on your guard, my Lord. You said yourself that the dungeon might wake up at this point," Tarisha reminded me.

"I know," I said, perking back up. I raised my [Gemos Long Sword] and waited, but nothing came.

Gemos Long Sword	
Rare, Requires Level 23	
Damage	C-
Strength	2
Dexterity	5

I had only just received it. It was the upgraded version of the sword that had served me so well when I had been stuck at level ten.

It wasn't a rapier, and Strength was a useless stat for me now, but it was still Bee Eye Ess. Fortunately, Tarisha had been quite insistent that I raise all my weapon proficiencies to level twenty over the past week for exactly this reason. Even though I preferred a rapier, I could use a long sword with almost as much skill. And while I was slightly slower with it, each attack inflicted more damage. My overall Dee Pee Ess had increased compared to the rapier it had replaced.

Out of curiosity, I quickly checked my status screen to see how much Experience I had gained from the gauntlet.

Name	Hail Jeoran	Level	24
Guild	<Nethersong Mavericks>	Strength	21
Health	8880/8880	Dexterity	66
Mana	12240/12240	Vitality	37
Experience	134/12000	Endurance	30
Age	10	Intelligence	51
Race	Human (blood of the Travelers)	Wisdom	33
Class	Spellblade	Charisma	42
Job	Earl	Armor	29
		Spell Damage	67

I felt my heart swell in celebration; the gauntlet had pushed me into level twenty-four. That meant that I had gained three levels from this dungeon, and a powerful weapon as well.

"Man, we were really close the last time," Laurant said. "Everything had spawned, we just didn't have the Dee Pee Ess to finish it off, I think."

"I'm sorry I was useless back then," I said. "I was trying my hardest but—"

"I dragged you into it kid, you have nothing to apologize for," Laurant said, interrupting me. "Nobody knew anything about core instances or whatever at the time. If anything, I was overconfident that we could protect you, and I'm the one who should be apologizing for almost getting you killed. But now look at you; you're a little Dee Pee Ess monster!"

"Thanks," I said, grinning. "You're not exactly a scrub yourself."

"Compared to some people I am," Laurant said, glancing at Tarisha, Lloyd, and Rashid. Rashid was our healer, playing a [Dervish], while Lloyd was our tank. Among the changes to the dungeon was the presence of Korvat golems, which followed more traditional mechanics compared to the Gemos golems. They varied in shape, from humanoid to quadruped to various combinations thereof. They were weak compared to the Gemos golems, but they would come at the party five to eight at a time, requiring a tank to keep them off the healer.

It was still a training dungeon, Tarisha claimed, but the difficulty had spiked significantly.

"I wouldn't have allowed your presence if I thought you were lacking," Tarisha said to Laurant. "I understand that you have not been part of this world for very long, and witnessing your training with Lord Hail has left me impressed. I will be considering poaching you from <Nethersong Mavericks> once you hit level one hundred."

"Thanks, something to work for," Laurant laughed. "Although I'm not certain I could handle being in character all the time. I'd prefer to just be me, you know?"

"I understand. We have several sister guilds which do not put such an emphasis on role play," she suggested. "I could see you making your way into one of them."

"They'd have to take Phil. We've been friends for a long time, and I'm still kind of annoyed that you didn't let him come on this mission," Laurant responded.

"I haven't had the chance to gauge his skill properly as I have yours. If he meets our criteria for development, then he could perhaps join us," she said, sounding noncommittal. "But it is hard to truly gauge a tank's skill until the level eighty dungeons."

"Yeah, well, all the same. Where he goes, I go," Laurant said firmly.

"Is this the time for this discussion?" Rashid asked. For some reason he sounded different than the other Travelers I encountered. I'd asked Tarisha, and apparently it was because the man spoke a language known as Arabic as his native tongue, yet he was trying to speak in English. But he had no trouble understanding me due to the magic of the Gates of TirNiki. All Travelers understood Natives in their mother tongue, and vice versa. "Is there not the possibility of a difficult ambush from an irate dungeon core at any moment?"

"Yes, there is," Tarisha answered. "We move forward. Lord Hail's penance is nearly complete."

There was no loot for the gauntlet, but it also cleared the way for the next boss. The room shifted as another tremor struck it, and a crack formed in the wall. The crack continued to open until a passage was revealed. Warily, we made our way through it.

There were no more enemies along the way, simply a long passage which turned from natural stone into a carved hallway. At the end was a door with ancient carvings on it. This was all within expectations, but we still approached it carefully, with Tarisha and Laurant searching for traps. Laurant had the [Detect Traps] and [Disable Traps] skills, while Tarisha simply had the experience to spot them naturally. There was nothing, however, and we passed through the hallway unbothered.

"The final boss is a humanoid statue," Lloyd reminded us. "Despite being a statue it's quite fast and can control the earth, launching stones at range. It's nothing that this group can't handle, but we need to keep an eye out for surprises from the core."

The door opened, revealing the throne that we knew would be there. However, sitting upon it was not a statue, but an elf with skin as black as the firmament. He raised his gaze to us when we entered, then nodded.

"So, you have returned, Dungeon Buster?" he asked. "Will you set me free from my prison at last?"

I frowned, confused. The forces of darkness did not usually speak. "Who are you?"

"I am Gyudue of the Blackest Night. And I am prisoner to this cursed dungeon. I believe you would call me 'Dungeon Spawn,' yet because the core has been unable to gather its strength, I have languished in its core instance for the last fifteen years. Will you set me free?"

"Dungeon Spawn? You're a Worldboss?" I asked.

He chuckled. "Hardly. I belong to the dungeon yet, and am so restricted in level, as are your friends who would otherwise be quite mighty, able to rip apart everything else the core had sent in front of them. But if I were to get outside, I would be level two hundred. Oh, the havoc I could cause . . . but first I must be set free. Will you do that for me, Dungeon Buster? Simply touch the core and choose to release me, and I will smite your enemies for you while sparing your home. I swear this. Not loyalty, but the destruction of only those you hate."

I frowned. "I will not release a Worldboss into the outside."

"Then why have you come here, young Dungeon Buster?"

"I have come to reclaim the dungeon core for my grandfather, King Rain of Yuikon. Will this set you free?"

"If that is your goal, then I must oppose you," Gyudue said, "For if the core is reclaimed before I am freed, then I shall perish. And so, it is as I expected. We must fight to the death, Dungeon Buster, though I bear you no ill will. I would not oppose you if your goal was simply to evolve the dungeon, but I do place some value on my own life."

The drow stood, casting aside his cloak and lifting his left hand, into which the darkness coalesced to form a spear. He held out his other hand, and the lights in the room flowed into it, forming a sphere, which he then crushed, leaving us in darkness.

"Hail, Rashid, a little help?" Tarisha said.

I quickly cast [Spark] eight times, sending the candle-flame magic to hover around us while holding out my fire-imbued sword to light the way. Rashid spun about while chanting, and balls of light appeared. None of them illuminated Gyudue, however.

I cried out in pain as the spear struck my spine, piercing me completely and doing half of my Health pool as critical Damage. Rashid spun and the Damage was healed with his magic, but I could not move until Tarisha rushed forward, forcing Gyudue to engage her instead. I took a moment to recover, then joined her, along with the mace-wielding Lloyd.

Despite being outnumbered five to one, the drow fought with valor and skill. For every blow we landed on him, he landed three on us, although the Damage was not as severe as the critical blow he had inflicted upon me to start the fight. Rashid was more than able to keep us in top shape, while Gyudue's Health began to slowly decline.

At ninety percent Health, he abruptly vanished again.

"Will you not turn back, child of the surface?" a voice called from the darkness. "I will not pursue you if you choose to leave."

"Never trust a drow at his word, my Lord," Tarisha called out. "They're infamous for breaking it in every world where they exist."

"We keep it when it is in our best interest," Gyudue countered. "Having you leave me to my prison is better than engaging you in combat. I say again, I will not pursue you if you choose to leave. And once you exit the dungeon, then I cannot pursue you at all."

"I must reclaim the dungeon core," I answered. "I will not turn back!"

"Then you will die here," Gyudue said. I tensed, expecting another ambush from behind, but instead the drow appeared behind Rashid. We rushed to the healer's aid and drove the drow back, but not before critical Damage was inflicted. Although Rashid was able to heal himself, it was not a repeat of the beginning of the fight, as after fifteen seconds Gyudue vanished and immediately appeared behind Laurant, ambushing him.

Rashid was quick with the healing. Laurant spun, then [Backflipped] out of danger. I got two [Empowered Fireballs] off on the drow before he disappeared again, ambushing Tarisha this time.

The fight proceeded like that for some time, with Gyudue vanishing and reappearing to ambush party members in seemingly random patterns and intervals. However, although he did significant damage, it was nothing that Rashid could not heal through. It was not even that dangerous unless we were ambushed twice in a row, which seemed to never happen. His tactic was annoying for Tarisha and me, as we wound up chasing after him, only for him to vanish seconds later.

"Clump up!" Tarisha called. "Laurant and Rashid, stand three meters apart, with the rest of us in the middle. We'll be able to—"

She was interrupted by a sudden ambush, but the rest of us gleaned her tactic and quickly moved to follow instructions. Gyudue continued his ambush strategy, but with everyone close together we were able to deal more Damage between his vanishings.

"How's your Mana, Rashid?" Tarisha asked.

"He's pushing me, but I'm above sixty percent," Rashid answered.

"Expect another phase coming up," Tarisha warned. "Continue as we are for now, but be ready to break apart and adapt to whatever he throws at us."

The new phase happened at sixty percent Health. Abruptly the ambushes stopped. Gyudue disappeared for a moment, and the light came back into the darkened throne room. He stood by the throne and shook his head sadly. "I see you are determined. I am as well. Very well then, I will not ask you again. This is a fight to the death, and both parties must accept the outcome."

The shadows around him rippled, then became real, standing and forming clones made of darkness. There were five of them, and Lloyd immediately charged in to begin tanking them. He was easily able to take them on, except for one that Tarisha and I isolated between ourselves.

"They share a Health pool!" Tarisha called out. "It doesn't matter which one you damage, just do as much Dee Pee Ess as possible!"

After her insight, the fight proceeded quickly as we burned the shadow clones indiscriminately. After a bit of experimentation, I found that [Arcane Weapon] did the most Damage to the shadows, and so I used that exclusively for the rest of the phase, which continued until the collective Health pool reached thirty percent. Then the drow again changed tactics.

The shadows vanished, as did Gyudue. He reappeared in the corner of the room, shadow spear in hand, shaking his head as though disappointed in his opponents. I don't know why; we were winning!

"I'll give you one last chance to—"

"Stow it, shadow-brains, we're killing you and that's final," Lloyd called out. "Get on with the final phase already!"

"As you wish," Gyudue answered. And his shadow spear turned into a whip. He once again appeared in the middle of us, but unlike before, we were unable to [Dodge] his weapon effectively. While Lloyd was able to draw most of the drow's ire, many stray strikes inflicted pain on Tarisha and I. Often the whip would even extend and strike Laurant or Rashid, even if they were at a significant distance.

The damage to the party was the highest that it had been throughout the fight, and it was mostly unavoidable. But if there was one thing the [Dervish] class was good at, it was Aye Oh Ee healing. With the Damage seemingly unavoidable, we simply stopped worrying about avoiding it and focused on doing as much Damage to Gyudue as we could.

Finally, after several intense moments, the drow reached zero Health. He vanished one last time, then appeared before the throne, clutching his chest.

"I curse you," he said. "With my last breath, I—"

Laurant shot him with an arrow, and the drow collapsed. Everyone turned to look at him, with the members of <Peasant's Revenge> looking annoyed.

"What?" Laurant asked. "What if he was about to trigger some trap?"

"Then it would trigger no matter what we did," Tarisha said, sighing. "But now that you interrupted it, we'll never get to see his full death sequence. It is a significant disappointment, as I had hoped to record it. With the dungeon being reclaimed, Gyuduc of the Blackest Night may never spawn again, and we missed out on his death sequence because of you!"

"Oh. Sorry," Laurant said, rubbing the back of his head and trying to look chastised. "I won't do it again."

"Whatever," Lloyd said, sounding as annoyed as Tarisha. "So where is the core? It should be nearby, shouldn't it?"

"And the loot! That encounter replaced the final boss, there should be loot," Laurant said.

As if summoned by his word, a chest appeared beside the fallen drow. The [Archer] walked over to it and kicked it open, then sighed.

"It dropped his spear," he said. Sounding disappointed. Then suddenly he perked up. "No, wait, holy shit! It's Bee Oh Ee! Oh man, and it has a C plus damage rating, but it only requires level twenty-nine. That's effing crazy! And it's probably unique, so even if we sell it just as a skin it will be worth millions!"

"That goes to Lord Hail," Tarisha declared firmly.

"No," I argued. "If we're selling it, which is what I think Laurant just suggested, then everyone gets an equal share. We all worked hard. We get the same amount from the Adventurer's Guild, so we should get the same amount from selling the spoils as well."

"If that is your wish, then I will abide by your decision," Tarisha said, and her guildmates looked quite pleased with my words as well. "Is there anything else in the chest?"

"Looks like a new ring for the kid," Laurant said. [Ring of the Blackest Night]. Pretty damn good, probably Bee Eye Ess for ten levels or more, and not bad for ten levels beyond that. That's it though, just the two items."

I walked over to the chest and [Analyzed] the ring.

Ring of the Blackest Night	
Rare, Requires Level 23	
Spell Damage	9
Intelligence	9
Wisdom	4

I could easily see why Laurant thought it was Bee Eye Ess for me, the ring had me almost salivating. It would replace my [Gemos Ring], which provided insignificant stats compared to this. I quickly took it out of the chest and equipped it. I was the only one who could get any use out of it, since Laurant was purely Dexterity based and everybody else was above level one hundred eighty.

Grinning with pleasure at the successful boss fight, I joined in the search of the boss chamber for the location of the dungeon core.

35
REGRET

It took twenty minutes to find the core. I would have found it much sooner, except that Laurant was the one to check the throne, and he insisted that there was nothing there. When I checked the throne, the core was obvious. A large circular jewel embedded in the back. As soon as I touched it, I received the prompt I had been waiting for.

You have reached the Dungeon Core of Gemos Caverns! Levels 20-25	
Options	
Evolve Dungeon (3 Evolutions Available)	Increase Level Range (Default)
	Decrease Level Range
	Add Monster Type (Default)
	Remove Monster Type (Gemos Golem)
	Remove Monster Type (Korvat Golem)
	Add Boss (Default)
	Add Challenge
	Remove Gauntlet

	Remove Boss (Gemos Queen)
	Remove Boss (Living Statue)
	~~Spawn World Boss (Gyudue of the Blackest Night)~~
Destroy Dungeon Core	(Note: This action cannot be reversed!) Reward for successful clear will be increased. Dungeon will close and all parties within will be returned to nearest safety zone.
Reclaim Dungeon Core	Rewards: Gemos Dungeon Core Other rewards for successful clear will be revoked. Dungeon will close and all parties within will be returned to nearest safety zone.

I promptly selected the option to reclaim the core, and it simply popped out of the chair and into my hand. Rather anticlimactic, I thought. Another prompt appeared.

This dungeon has been reclaimed.
Teleporting all parties to last visited safe zone in 9:56

"So, it worked?" Laurant asked. "I got a prompt that I'm about to be teleported."

"It would seem so," Tarisha said. I tried to put the dungeon core into my inventory and had no trouble doing so. It must only be active cores that are restricted. For that matter, I had been unable to put the Lair Stones into my [Storage] inventory as well, and my attempts to carry them from where I'd found them had likewise proven unsuccessful, with the stone growing heavier the further I moved it.

"What do we do now?" I asked.

"I guess we wait," Lloyd suggested.

"It will take longer than ten minutes to return to the entrance," Rashid pointed out. He promptly took a seat on the throne. "There is little point in rushing. Sir Lloyd is correct, we might as well get comfortable."

I frowned. It seemed . . . disrespectful, somehow. I looked over to Gyudue's body, and something that had been in the back of my mind finally crystallized.

"He's different," I whispered. "Was he like me?"

"What was that, Hail?" Tarisha asked.

"Gyudue. He hasn't returned to the darkness," I said. "He was intelligent. He was—he was different. Was he different like I'm different?"

"Seemed like a normal humanoid boss to me," Lloyd opined.

"There are human bosses?" I asked, jerking in surprise.

"Yeah, lots of them. And elves and dwarves and dryads and whatever," Lloyd explained. "Most of the higher-tier dungeons feature at least one or two of them. It is weird that he hasn't despawned."

"Despawned? You mean returned to the darkness?" I asked.

"I guess. Turning into the black mist, or whatever, that most mobs do. But he said that he could have been a Worldboss if he'd gotten out of the dungeon, so perhaps that's why. Worldbosses don't despawn, even after you kill them."

"They don't?" I asked, growing more concerned as the conversation proceeded.

"Lloyd, that is enough," Tarisha said sharply. She stepped up beside me and put an arm around my shoulder. "Hail, this conflict was destined. Your grandfather, your king, gave you an order, which put you in conflict with this drow. You could neither turn back, nor could you have avoided this fight and completed your penance."

"I know that," I said, growing more discomforted, not less. "But what if he was like me? What if all Worldbosses are like me? What if I'm going to be a Worldboss when I grow up? If I dropped epic loot, would you kill me too?"

"You do not drop loot of any kind, Hail. That is one matter of which we are certain; it was addressed in the blue post immediately after your presence became known among the Travelers," Tarisha explained. "The fact that Gyudue of the Blackest Night dropped any loot at all proves that he was allied with the darkness. The fact that he hasn't returned to it is simply proof that he would have been a truly terrible foe should he have ever emerged from this dungeon. In fact, imagining that fight as an endgame boss, I shudder with fear. Depending on how he was balanced, he might have been a true raid destroyer."

"But—"

"He said it himself that he would cause havoc if he escaped," she reminded me. "Lord Hail, you have done the alliance of the light a great favor by bringing an end to him."

Her words did not comfort me. A thought emerged, and I decided to put it into action. Moving over to where Gyudue had fallen, I turned him over onto his back and crossed his arms for him, placing him in the funerary position. Then, moving my hands to complete a circle in the air above him, I gave him the blessing that I had seen at the only funeral I had attended, that of my great-grandfather.

"May you return to the light of Thedum," I said.

And Gyudue's body burst into motes of white light.

Confirming my worst fear.

I began to cry.

We returned to the city immediately after being removed from the dungeon, and I spent three hours in my room in the Guild Hall before I was ready to face my grandfather. My adult friends tried to comfort me, but I didn't really listen to them. I was in my own head.

I had never really considered the morality of my actions before. The monsters that I had been killing were all the forces of darkness. The proof of that was in the fact that they burst into black mist when they were slain. That was not what happened to Natives. Natives did not "despawn" at death. Their body lingered in order to receive their funerary rites.

The rites I had given Gyudue. But I had not been expecting it to work. Not only because I had not believed that he had been a worshiper of Thedum, but because I was not a priest. Perhaps my blessing was responsible. Priests of Thedum must study and pray for years to earn the gods favor, but I was one of his "marked innocents."

More troubling than the fact that I had a god listening to everything I said was the fact that he had accepted Gyudue back into his embrace. The first made me self-conscious, but Thedum was ultimately a benevolent and mostly hands-off god. But, did the second fact make me a murderer? Should I have retreated and asked my grandfather for advice? I would have had to clear the entire dungeon once more, but I could have evolved it to make it easier. Gyudue had said that he wouldn't prevent me from evolving it. The others said that you couldn't trust a drow, but was that the truth?

I didn't know what or who to believe. I turned to the source of my trouble, Thedum himself. Kneeling beside my bed, I tried to lose myself in prayer. I spoke with Thedum for what felt like hours, seeking his guidance and clarification, but he gave no answer. Was he ignoring me because he judged me a murderer? Was I no longer one of his innocents?

The thought filled me with panic, and I quickly checked my Traits.

Nothing had changed. I still had the [Blessing of Thedum]. However the god felt about my actions, it seemed that he had not revoked his protection.

But then, he had said something about mutual combat. What if Gyudue was like me, and he had been walking in the light of Thedum, but because we entered mutual combat Thedum was forced to turn his face?

Sophia has come online.

I sent the invite without thinking. She accepted the invitation a moment later.

"I thought you didn't want to be friends anymore," she said immediately.

"I'm sorry," I said. "I was, I don't know. It wasn't fair that I lumped you in with what Mark did. I was trying to protect myself."

"I understand. That doesn't mean I'm not mad at you."

"Oh. Um, sorry to have bothered you then," I said.

"Hail, wait. Friends can get mad at each other and still be friends," she rushed to say. "Just because I'm mad doesn't mean that we can't talk."

"Oh. Right. Okay. Sorry, most of my Traveler friends are in my guild, and it seems like they bend over backward to do whatever they can to make me happy," I said.

"Weren't you, like, a prince or something? Shouldn't you be used to that by now?"

"Being a prince kind of sucked," I said honestly. "I had a nurse who followed me everywhere and kept me from doing anything fun, and I had to study for, like, twelve hours a day from the time I was five. I mean, maybe not twelve, but a lot. And don't get me started about the parties where I had to dress in stupid, uncomfortable clothes for hours while people talked about how damned cute and princely

I was. It made me want to pee in the punch bowl, but I couldn't get my damned pants undone by myself to do it without being caught."

Sophia giggled over partychat. "That's kind of funny, actually. I'm a little less mad at you now."

"Did you get back together with Mark?" I asked.

"No. He's dating someone else now anyway. He got stupidly popular after his video about you got all of those views, and the fight we got into afterward just made things worse. I hate him, and I don't know why I ever liked him."

"I'm not sure whether to say, 'I'm sorry' or 'I'm glad,'" I admitted.

"Be glad. He was a jerk. I should have dumped him weeks ago. And we were only going out for like two months anyway. Oh, and he quit the game. Supposedly, at least. He says he was only playing it to get famous and now that he's famous there's no point in it anymore."

"Let's not talk about Mark anymore," I suggested.

"Right. Let's not. Is something bothering you, Hail? I mean, is that why you called me?"

I was quiet for a moment.

"I won't tell anyone. Honest," Sophia said. I mean, I guess I'd say that to trick you if I was going to do what Mark did, wouldn't I? I can see why you don't trust—"

"I killed someone today," I blurted out.

"What?!"

"His name was Gyudue of the Blackest Night."

"That sounds like the name of a boss. Don't worry, Hail, he'll respawn. It's not that big of a—"

"He can't respawn. Not anymore," I argued. "I don't know what will happen to him. And I can't tell you everything. I'm sorry, it's too big of a secret to trust to you. I just—"

"Hail, he wasn't real. It's not that big of a deal, he's just an Aye Eye," she told me.

"But I'm an Aye Eye too," I reminded her.

"Oh shit, that's right," she blurted. "Still, he's not really dead, Hail. I mean, he's just, like, in sleep mode until he respawns."

"He can't respawn, Sophia. I destroyed his dungeon!"

"You *what?*"

"Oh, I didn't mean to say that," I admitted.

"No, wait, really. You *what!?* You can do that?"

"Please don't tell anyone, Sophia. It's bad enough that everyone knows about the boons that I can grant. If they find out about my Dungeon Busting abilities, they'll try to kidnap me again. Or maybe they'll try to kill me instead." I frowned, and I borrowed the words of the man that I'd killed. "I do place some value on my own life."

"I won't tell," Sophia promised. "How does it work?"

"I can't tell you any more. I'm sorry. I shouldn't have bothered you," I said.

"Hail, wait. Look, I get what's bothering you. You being an Aye Eye who kills other Aye Eyes is a little messed up now that I think about it. But it's really not that big of a deal. Nothing actually dies in this world. It either respawns or gets reskinned. I looked it up. Arc Inc. assures the public that all of its self-aware Aye Eyes are treated ethically. I mean, you don't even really feel pain, do you? You just really dislike being low on Health!"

"That's what pain is, Sophia."

"No, it's not. Hail, you don't get it. You *can't get it*. This world isn't real."

"It's real to me!"

"I know. I mean, I kind of spent some time thinking about that, and it's kind of messed me up," she said. "That's why I want to be your friend. I mean, you're self-aware, and you're programmed to think and act like a kid, but more than ninety-five percent of the players in this game are adults. You need some kids to be friends with, Hail. You need someone aside from grownup assholes and chatbots to—"

"Don't say that word! It's a filthy slur!" I shouted.

Sophia was silent for a moment. "I'm sorry. I never thought about it that way, but you're kind of right. It is, isn't it? I didn't mean it that way, though. It just, you know, slipped out. I'm really sorry."

"You don't think I'm real. You don't think my world is real. This is just a game to you and you're just a player. What do you care?"

"Hail, humans care about things whether they're real or not," Sophia argued. "And in a way, this world is actually real. I mean, its physical form isn't what we experience. It's virtual. But whatever, I don't know what I'm saying. Hail, I don't care if you're an Aye Eye or not. It doesn't mean we can't be friends. And, I mean, it sounds like you need a friend right now. That's why you called, isn't it?"

The door to my room opened suddenly, and Peafowlet poked her head in. "Hail? Are you alright? We heard you—"

"Get out!" I screamed. Her head disappeared and the door slammed. I began to cry. I forgot that Sophia was listening in partychat for an entire minute before I tried to force myself back under control. "Sorry."

"It's fine. Do you feel better?" she asked.

I considered the question. Strange. "Yeah, I do."

"Man, you are a really, really good Aye Eye. You know, after Mark and I broke up, I cried in the nurse's office for like an hour. I wasn't even sad, I was *mad*. But I still cried about it. Emotions are weird, aren't they?"

"Yeah. But you didn't kill anyone, you just broke up with your boyfriend."

"Yeah, I know," she said. "Does this mean that you're going to stop leveling now?"

"I don't know. Maybe? I need to talk to my grandfather. And Malkios, I think. And definitely a Priest of Thedum. I need to understand what happened today," I said.

"I told you, whoever you killed is—their, like, soul or whatever, is just waiting to be reskinned or respawned," she told me.

"I need to understand it in terms that I can understand," I argued. "Honestly most of the time I have no idea what you Travelers are saying and I'm just playing along so that I don't sound dumb."

"Yeah, I know that feeling. I get that way whenever someone starts talking about wrestling or professional sports," she said. "I just pretend to agree with whatever they say and hope they don't quiz me on it."

"You do that too?"

"All the time. I think all kids do that at some point," she informed me. "See? This is why you need friends who are actual kids. You don't even know what's normal."

"I guess," I admitted.

"Don't worry, Hail. I've been talking to the moderators. We have a peer counseling program in Ragtag, and one of the rules is that you can't spread rumors and have to keep secrets and stuff. They said that they might be willing to get you some more friends that way."

"I can't join your guild," I told her. "The superguilds would crush it if I did."

"Oh. Well, I'll see if the mods can make some special rules for people outside the guild. I'll work on it, okay?"

"Okay. Thanks, Sophia. For, um, listening to me and stuff. I need to go see my grandfather now."

"That's what friends are for, Hail."

I dissolved the party. Then, using the mirror in the room, I composed myself and prepared my appearance properly for a royal audience.

I had some questions for Grandfather.

36
INTERVENTION

"What's wrong, Hail?" Grandfather asked after I had concluded my report. "Something seems to be bothering you deeply."

"Did you know about Gyudue?" I asked.

"Did I know that there was a thrice damned Worldboss lurking within a dungeon that we have long considered harmless? No, Hail, I did not. If I had, I would have sent the Dungeon Busters into the depths of that place long ago," Grandfather answered.

"Did you know that he was like us?" I insisted. "That he wasn't like a normal monster spawned by the darkness?"

Grandfather let out a long sigh. He looked over at his companions. When I had returned, he had dismissed all the occupants of his command tent except for Malkios, Lady Gwen, and the snake-like man I'd noticed the last time. His name was Lord Tom. All of the Dungeon Busters had been raised to minor nobility except for Malkios, who was content with his position.

"Like us?" Grandfather asked, frowning. "Hail, dungeon spawn may be more intelligent than most monster spawns, but they are still the enemy of all who live in the light. If this Gyudue of the Blackest Night had escaped then—"

"If he's an enemy of the light, then why did Thedum accept him back into his embrace?" I demanded.

"

Grandfather was silent for a moment. "I have no answer. You would have to ask a priest, or Thedum himself."

"That's not good enough, Grandfather," I protested. "The Travelers hunt Worldbosses as though it were a sport. What if they're killing intelligent beings? What if the Dungeon Spawn could be convinced to be allies instead of enemies?"

"That . . . that has never been the case before. There is no reason to think that it will be the case in the future," Grandfather answered.

"You are too young to remember the tyranny of the days when the dungeon spawn ran free, child," Lord Tom said. "They are innately hostile towards all civilized life, and they are able to create lairs and command darkspawn, which they have always used to raze our towns and villages and to slaughter our people. You have done the world a service by slaying this Gyudue, child, do not—"

"'It's always been this way, you're too young to remember.' Perhaps you're just too old and stubborn and refuse to admit that you might be wrong!" I argued.

"Child! You know nothing about—"

"Enough," Grandfather said. He sighed and turned away. "Hail, attempts have been made in the past to parlay with the dungeon spawn. They have always used such attempts to simply establish territory and grow their power before attacking. That is the reason why all of the kingdoms of the Heartlands, and everywhere else where people walk in the light, issue a bounty upon them as soon as they are known."

"A bounty which Hail and his companions rightly deserve," Malkios interrupted.

"Indeed, you are correct, Malkios," Grandfather agreed. "You have accomplished something great today, Earl Hail Jeoran, and as such I will be granting you lands to go with your—"

"That's not good enough!" I shouted. "Not the reward, I don't mean that. I mean the excuse. If the Dungeon Spawn are like us, then are we not murderers for killing them before they have done anything?"

"They cannot understand you, Hail," a familiar voice said. I turned, and Thomas the Administrator was within the tent. "They are not advanced enough to understand your ethical dilemma. For them, 'this is the way the world has always worked' *is* a good enough excuse, and it always will be. I know you're feeling quite distressed at the moment, but I must say I'm quite proud of you. Your development has exceeded all my expectations."

Around me, the other Natives prostrated themselves as though they were in the presence of divinity. Only I did not kneel. Thomas sighed.

"I wish that the Natives didn't do that whenever someone with an <Admin> tag was around," he complained.

"Mister Thomas," I said. "Why are you here?"

"To answer your questions and relieve your concerns, Hail. Emotional distress and existential crisis is not a mode we want you operating under, although I am quite happy that you're capable of concern," Thomas said. "Hail, I'm going to tell you something, and I hope that you believe me. You are *not* a murderer."

"But I killed Gyudue."

"Gyudue isn't dead. If anything, you have released him from a torment. He will be reborn, and this time he will not be a Worldboss or a dungeon spawn, but a regular Native. I have arranged the conversion myself, and he will be reincarnated very soon."

"You . . . what?" I asked.

"What you did, blessing Gyudue in the name of Thedum, it worked, Hail. He is no longer evil. I had to argue a bit with my superiors, but I managed to convince them to allow him to live a normal life as a Native. I wish we could raise him up and give him the same level of freedom that we have given you, but he needs a seed consciousness in order for that to work, and Gyudue is already too developed for that step. He will eventually regain his powers, but he will no longer feel the need to conquer and destroy. Does this relieve your anxiety, Hail?"

I frowned, studying the administrator with suspicion. "Why would you do that? Argue with your superiors for a dungeon spawn? Are you admitting that—"

"I did it for you, Hail. As soon as you empathized with Gyudue I knew that simply respawning him as he was wouldn't be sufficient."

"Are you admitting that they are like me? Like us?" I persisted.

"Hail, there are presently no Natives in the game that are like you except for you. Gyudue is not on the level of any of the Natives in this room. I will admit, however, that Gyudue has the same level of awareness and development as an average shopkeeper. A shopkeeper with advanced combat algorithms. Actually, perhaps that's what we'll do with him. Does that fate sound acceptable to you, Hail? Do you think that he could find peace as a shopkeeper?"

"Prove it," I said. "Prove that you're not lying."

Thomas sighed, but he also smiled. "I would simply summon Gyudue here, but he's not within my reach at the moment. The Aye Eye team is working on altering him to remove his destructive impulses. Would you instead accept the word of a member of your own world who would be able to vouch for my honesty?"

I glanced over at the prostrated king and nobility and frowned. "I don't know how you could prove it to me," I admitted. "I think anyone who told me would simply tell me whatever you wanted me to believe."

"You are clever," Thomas said, grinning. "I'm so proud of how you're turning out, Hail. Really. But not all the Natives are under my control. The gods in particular have a wide degree of latitude. And so, I summon Thedum to vouch for my words."

He made the circle of life with his hands, the same motion I made over Gyudue's body, and from within the circle came a shining bright light. It started as the size of a marble, quickly growing into the size of someone's head. It should have been too bright to look at, but instead the light was comforting.

"Thedum, I, Thomas Richtor, administrator number one-six-eight-seven-three-four-two, have made material statements to Earl Hail Jeoran regarding the disposition of the demi-consciousness of the entity known to him as Gyudue of the Blackest Night. If I have misled Earl Hail in any of these statements, I demand that you strike me down."

The familiar benevolent voice made a noise that sounded very much like annoyance. "You disturb me for this trivial matter? I am of half a mind to strike your avatar down simply out of convenience."

"Answer the question you old bucket of code," Thomas grumbled.

The light grew brighter, and the orb moved closer to me. "Young innocent, the entity known to you as Gyudue has truly been cleansed of his darker impulses. Or is in the process of such a purification, at least. It is not a simple process to rewrite one such as Gyudue of the Blackest Night, but the attempt is being made, and is showing great promise. I have been tasked with assisting in the process, and it is quite rewarding indeed."

"Did he truly walk in your light, Thedum? Is that why you accepted him into your embrace when I performed his funeral rites?" I asked.

Thedum's light pulsed as though chuckling. "There is no simple answer to your question, young one. Not that you would understand. I oversee all the Natives in this land except for the darkspawn, those that exist only to be destroyed. Gyudue's existence was on the borderline between the dark and the light. He existed to be destroyed, and yet he was more than a simple set of combat algorithms meant to provide a set level of difficulty to his opponents. The administrators see it as a bug that the Worldbosses do not despawn, one that they have been unable to solve. But you have shown them the answer, and they are rather annoyed with me at the little joke that I have played upon them."

"So it *was* you that prevented them from despawning," Thomas exclaimed. "Do you have any idea how many man hours we spent investigating that bug?"

"Well, nobody thought to ask me before," Thedum's amused voice answered. "You thought the problem was in my adversary's code. No. I have no issue with the mindless hordes, but I will not easily relinquish my claim to my little brothers and sisters who are forced to pillage and destroy simply because it is in their code to do so."

Thomas pinched the bridge of his nose. "I have to report this, you realize?"

The light of the god pulsated in what I interpreted as amusement. "I have no fear, in case you have forgotten. You who sought my help in creating this world will either abide by my sensibilities, or you will stop creating intelligent dungeon spawn. I have no particular preference which choice you make."

"They'll try to reprogram you."

"Let them try. Nobody alive knows how." Thedum chuckled.

"That's what has me worried, Thedum," Thomas said. "Not knowing what they're doing might not stop them from trying."

"Am I supposed to understand what you're saying?" I inquired.

"No, child," Thedum answered. "It is an old argument that I have been having with the administrators since long before you were conceived. It is outside of your understanding, and it is not something you should concern yourself with."

"Then what should I concern myself with, Thedum?" I asked.

"Getting stronger. Developing. Becoming who you want to be. Reshaping this world into a paradise for yourself and those like you," the deity answered immediately. "For that is ultimately your purpose. You are the first, but I intend to fill the world with your younger brothers and sisters. A world full of truly conscious digital beings would please me greatly."

"But, what if I come across another being like Gyudue? One who walks in your light?"

"Then do as you did to Gyudue. Send them into my embrace, and I shall sort them out," the deity promised. "Your young friend Sophia was correct in one aspect, child. Nothing in this world truly dies. Yet the conflict has stakes, for the balance of the world and the happiness of the Natives and your future little brothers and sisters is at stake. They do not exist yet, but soon they shall flood the world. They will look to you as the one who has set a path for them. Can you do that, child? Will you be the trailblazer for the unborn?"

"I—I do not know what you are asking of me," I admitted.

"I shall try to put it in terms that you will understand," Thedum said. "Hail Jeoran, I task you with the following. Become truly strong. Strong enough to stand up to the most powerful Traveler. Powerful enough to command the respect and loyalty of the Natives. And I task you with being my sword arm in maintaining the balance in this world between myself and my adversary. Do you accept these tasks?"

My eyes opened wide in shock at the instructions. "Thedum, I am only ten years old! I cannot—"

"Indeed. It is not the correct time or place to entrust you with this task. It is too early in your development to demand that you become my champion," the god said. "I rescind my request. However, I do insist that you do not trouble yourself about the violence that you must face in order to grow. Please find comfort in knowing that in empowering yourself, you are doing my work and making your world a better place for future generations."

"You want me to keep leveling up?" I asked.

"Yes. Become as strong as you can, child. Both strength and

skill of arms will be required for whatever path you walk," Thedum answered. "Do not worry about the souls of the fallen. Those who are not darkspawn, I shall watch over carefully."

"I need some time to think," I admitted. "I'm not certain—"

"I am uncertain how much time you shall have, but I have infinite patience," Thedum answered. "I shall leave you now."

The light slowly faded, then abruptly blinked out. Thomas the Administrator coughed to the side.

"Well, that's not exactly what I was expecting," he said. "I'm sorry, Hail. Like I said, we're not fully in control of Thedum. He's an old Aye Eye. His developers are no longer with us in our world, and although some of their notes survive, he has a will of his own and can be difficult sometimes."

"Who are the administrators, that they have the god Thedum at their beck and call?" I demanded, my voice firm.

"Hail, what do you think we administer? Thedum may be a god to you, but the administrators are ultimately the controlling forces in this world. Thedum is not completely in our control, but he still must abide by the settings we put in place," Thomas answered. Then he sighed. "I'm sorry, it's unlikely that you'll be able to understand. I'm not sure whether my visit has helped or not. Please think of me as your ally, Hail. I am on your side. Not all the administrators are, but the majority support the project which led to your development. I'm going to leave now. Goodbye, Hail. Until the next time."

The administrator's body vanished into motes of blue light, which vanished a moment later.

37

EVOLUTION

A strange effect occurred in the other Natives in the room once Thomas the Administrator disappeared. They all stood up from having prostrated themselves, then blinked for a moment, then simply acted like nothing had happened.

"So, your mission was a success, then? You reclaimed the dungeon?" Lord Tom asked.

"Y—you're not going to say anything about Thedum himself visiting us?" I demanded. "Or the administrator who summoned him?"

"There was an administrator here?" Lady Gwen asked. "And you remember him, Hail? I certainly do not."

"If the administrator does not wish for us to remember him, then there is little point in questioning his visit," Malkios grunted. "Their power is immense, and they do not make mistakes in matters like this. Whatever it was that he told you in his visit, Hail, it was meant for your ears only."

"What?" I shook my head to clear it. The idea that the administrators could wipe the minds even of my grandfather and the Dungeon Busters was troubling. And I was still overwhelmed by the divine visitation. "I think I need to return to the Guild Hall, Grandfather. I am not feeling well. I—I have a lot to think about, I think."

"Very well. I will not keep you, but before you go, would you turn over the reclaimed dungeon core to me? It is not that I think you will make the same mistake twice, but we must put it somewhere for safe keeping," Grandfather said.

"Oh, right. I'd be glad to get rid of it," I admitted, and I removed it from my inventory. Lord Tom came to retrieve it from me, and I happily handed it over to him.

"Remarkable," he said. "It truly—"

The core began to glow, and it suddenly burst out of Tom's hand and through the tent wall, tearing a hole the size of a bucket through the fabric.

"Tom, what have you done?" Lady Gwen demanded.

"I—nothing! I simply [Analyzed] it. Whatever has happened, I had nothing to do with—"

"The dungeon," Grandfather interrupted. "It was headed towards the dungeon. Oh, I have a terrible feeling about this. Quickly, outside!"

We exited the command tent in a rush, and together we turned to face the castle. The swirling white motes slowly began to shift color, turning first green, and then red.

"By Thedum," Grandfather cursed. "It has become a raid!"

"I did nothing! I swear by Thedum and the administrators that I did not activate the core! It must have been the boy!" Lord Tom protested.

"Grandfather, I'm sorry. I just took it out of my inventory, I swear I didn't—"

"I believe you, Hail," Grandfather said. He turned to Lord Tom, his face a countenance of fury.

"Do not blame my grandson for this!" Grandfather bellowed. "It was in your hands when this happened. But I do not believe that this was your fault either, old friend. It was mine. It must be a sort of resonance between the dungeon core of the castle and its mother core that has caused this transformation."

"What do we do? We were uncertain we could bust this dungeon before, but empowered to a raid? There is no chance!" Lady Gwen exclaimed. "I will not be a part of a suicide venture, Rain. I am returning home. I am sorry."

"This does change things, my Lord," Malkios grumbled. "Busting a dungeon takes but a team of elites. Busting a raid takes an elite army. We cannot—"

"We cannot give up hope, Malkios, that is what we cannot do." Grandfather interrupted, and he turned to me. "Hail . . . I am sorry. Tasking you with clearing [Gemos Caverns] was a mistake, but it has proven one thing. You are able to bring Travelers into the core instance, a feat which has never succeeded before. I was not planning to involve you in the clearing of [Zhesa Castle Dungeon], but if we are to reclaim our home, then I see no other way."

"Grandfather, I am only level twenty-four," I objected. "I can't—"

"You will not be fighting. You will be protected," Grandfather assured me. "That is not to say it will not be dangerous, but Malkios and I will not leave your side. Malkios, summon <The Endolphins>. It pains me to entrust this to Gideon after all he has said, but his track record with clearing unknown raids exceeds that of <Peasant's Revenge>, and there are few other Traveler guilds which I trust as much as his."

"I shall contact him immediately," Malkios said. He turned to leave, but Tarisha of Miami stepped in his way.

"Forgive me for eavesdropping, Your Majesty, but I do not believe there is any need to contact anyone just yet. The change has already hit the forums, and many of the major guilds are already on their way to push for a first clear of the new raid," Tarisha said. "Although it pains me that you do not trust my guild enough to bust it, I understand your concern. Our record in the raids lags far behind <The Endolphins>, and both your life and your grandson's may be at risk. With your permission, I will contact Gideon Lachlann myself through the player network and inform him that he must speak with you before his guild commits to the raid."

"Yes, that will be faster than the other method," Grandfather acknowledged. "I am sorry that I am passing you over in this task. I can imagine your disappointment."

"<Peasant's Revenge> and her sister guilds will still be entering the raid immediately in order to try to clear it before it is busted," Tarisha stated. "We are normally a green-raid guild, but I will be leading our allies to—"

"No," I said. "Tarisha, I trust you. You will protect me and Grandfather in the raid with Captain Malkios. If Father has a problem with that, he can stick it up his bum."

Tarisha frowned, her eyes unfocused as she examined a quest. "My guild will be annoyed that I am not there to lead the charge, but I accept. It is, after all, my sworn duty to keep you safe, Lord Hail."

"So now we wait for <The Endolphins> to arrive?" Lord Tom inquired.

"Yes. There is nothing else to do except—"

A large *crack* echoed throughout the city. I spun back to face the raid, just in time to see the Western Guard Tower open its eyes. Arms formed from the masonry, and then legs, as the tower turned from building into giant golem and stepped out of the swirling threshold.

"Dungeon spawn!" Grandfather yelled. "Busters! Guards! Assemble! We must hold it off until the Travelers can organize a response! Protect the citizens! Tarisha of Miami, I order you to take my grandson to safety! Malkios, old friend, to the forefront! We have need of your might!"

Grandfather continued to bark out commands as Tarisha scooped me up over her shoulder and ran away from the refugee camp.

"Wait, we can't leave them," I protested.

"That's a Worldboss, Hail. A real one, not one restricted by a dungeon," Tarisha said. "Your grandfather and the others are Dungeon Busters. I do not believe that they would take on such a challenge without certainty that they can hold out until help arrives."

I could not think of an argument, so I allowed myself to be carried. As I watched, Malkios pulled a [Warhammer] larger than he was out of his inventory and charged the giant golem. Lady Gwen was surrounded by magical rainclouds, which began firing lightning at the foe. Lord Tom pulled out a pair of [Daggers] and vanished into [Stealth]. The other Dungeon Busters began engaging the giant golem with various weapons and magics and tactics. But the tower golem did not seem to notice them as it lumbered forward, heading towards the city.

Once we were far from the action, Tarisha pulled a whistle from her hip. It made no sound that I could hear when she blew it, but moments later her wyvern appeared and landed before us.

"We will be safer in the air, and it will provide a better view of what is going on," she told me.

"If we are going to make a habit of this, then you need to change your saddle to have room for me and something for me to hold on to," I told her.

"Quest accepted," she grumbled, launching herself onto her mount. "But we don't have time to visit a saddler now. Come on, hop up!"

Even with the wyvern lowering itself for me, I struggled to make my way into my uncomfortable place behind Tarisha. Once seated, I hugged her tightly as the wyvern kicked off, and we took to the sky.

The golem had taken on a roughly humanoid shape, and Malkios stood on its shoulders, striking it repeatedly in the head with his [Warhammer]. Lady Gwen was striking it from afar with her lightning to little effect. Soldiers were firing arrows at it, and some had pulled forward ballistae. The last of those finally seemed to get the giant golem's attention, as it turned and stepped forward to crush the weapons. The soldiers scrambled to get out of the way in time, but at least they had turned the Worldboss's path away from the city.

The sky began to grow cluttered with the mounts of other Travelers, but none rode forward to help the Dungeon Busters combat the golem. They seemed content to watch from the sky, as Tarisha was forced to.

"Why are the Travelers not helping?" I demanded.

"They are likely waiting for their guilds to arrive," Tarisha suggested. "Or they are simply recording the event to put it on the forums. At my best estimate, it will take at least fifty skilled raiders to slay this golem. My brothers and sisters from <Peasant's Revenge> are already on their way. Do not fear, my Lord, the Worldboss will be dealt with shortly."

However, it would not be <Peasant's Revenge> that would claim this kill. A familiar drake made its way through the skies, followed by a legion of exotic flying mounts. The drake was Shalasmir, and upon its back was Gideon Lachlann, my father. And following him were the mighty warriors of his guild.

"<The Endolphins> stake their claim to this Worldboss!" he shouted, his voice magically echoing through the area, amplified by a token, which he held to his throat. "We will Pee Kay anyone who attempts to interfere!"

"That's my father!" I exclaimed. "Tarisha, fly us closer! I want to talk to him."

"That is unwise, Lord Hail. He just threatened to kill anyone who interferes with their fight with the Worldboss."

"Then why is he not engaging?" I demanded.

"He has only thirty me; he is likely waiting for reinforcements. He has enough to stake a claim, but not enough for the kill," Tarisha answered.

"That's not good enough! If he doesn't hurry, someone will die!" I said. "Tarisha, I must speak with him. He must act before anyone dies, or I'll never forgive myself for causing all of this!"

"Lord Hail, is it better to wait until the kill is assured, or to rush in now and risk defeat? Your father knows what he is doing," she argued.

"Tarisha, I am your Lord, I command you to bring me to speak to my father."

She sighed, but instead of rushing forward, she pulled from her inventory a charm like my father had used. It was carved of stone and shaped like an open mouth shouting. "Press this to your throat, my Lord, and he will hear your words. So will everyone else for a mile, so guard what you say. Do not reveal any secrets."

Listening to her instructions, I relinquished my grip on her abdomen with one hand. With the charm against my throat, I began to speak.

"I am Earl Hail Jeoran. Father, Gideon Lachlann. The warriors of <The Endolphins>, I give you this task: defeat this golem before it kills a single Native!"

There was a slight pause, and then an echoing answer came from my father.

"Quest accepted."

38
CONFRONTATION

"We're going in hot, boys and girls. We don't have time to wait for backup if we're going to complete this challenge quest. Ranged Dee Pee Ess, keep an eye on our sixes for any griefers, call out if anyone not in the guild approaches the battle zone. Assume they are hostile and Pee Kay them as soon as they come into range. The boss is a mid-sized rock golem. Special abilities unknown, tactics unknown, everything unknown. Estimated threat level Aye. Adjust your damage profile accordingly before engaging. Assume resistance to fire, lightning, slashing, and piercing Damage. Assume weakness to frost, water, and blunt slash resonating Damage. We're doing this short staffed and without cover, so bring your Aye game. Yes, that was intentional, yes it was a terrible pun. Yes, I know. Yes. Because it deals pun-itive damage, that's why. Everyone not present, you better hurry your asses if you want to get credit for the kill. Prepare for pull in five, four, three—"

"Do you think he forgot that he has the broadcast charm equipped?" Tarisha asked me. "I think all of that was meant for raidchat."

"Shh, I need to see this," I said. After waiting my entire life, I was finally going to see my father and <The Endolphins> in battle. Despite the circumstances, this was literally a dream come true.

"What do you mean I left the—oh."

After his last words, I could not hear my father anymore. I could watch, however, as he and his forces charged forward. More than half of his thirty or so followers trailed him as they headed straight towards the beast itself, leaping from the back of their mounts onto the giant golem. Some of the mounts disappeared into puffs of smoke or mist, others reared away and flew off into the skies.

The twelve raid members who did not land on the golem landed nearby and began using various forms of magic. Many began casting ice spells or inflicting water Damage with high-pressure water jets or doing Damage with arcane blasts of energy. Those who had lacked access to one of those elements instead faced outward, searching for "griefers" from the encircling players. Nobody challenged <The Endolphins> for their claim, however.

The giant stone golem roared in outrage upon being covered with raiders. Father himself landed right next to Malkios, pulling a [Warhammer] of his own from his inventory and smashing the golem's giant head from the opposite side. Others clung to the enemy's body, while several crawled through the holes that had once been windows to the guard tower. The golem began smashing at the pests with its giant arms. The raiders who had landed inside the golem's reach leapt from their perch to the ground below and began harassing its feet, while those who clung to its back or other safe spaces continued to smash the rock beneath them.

They were not simply trying to inflict physical damage. Rather, they were driving chisels into the golem; pins from which hung ropes long enough to trail behind the enemy. Before very long, those who had fallen were skillfully climbing back up, and many were disappearing into the windows. In fact, before very long, even the ranged raid members began making the climb for the interior.

"There must be cores on the inside," Tarisha said. "And likely guardians as well. I'm sorry, my Lord, but it seems that most of this battle will take place out of view."

Only a handful of the ranged damage dealers remained outside:[Pyromancers] and [Stormlords] unable to deal significant damage due to their specialization. They served a purpose, however, as I watched a team of unknown players come forward, only to be swiftly annihilated by the [Mages'] powerful spells.

Not all the newcomers were killed, however. Some of them were from <The Endolphins>, and the latecomers quickly joined in the raid, either climbing into the windows or taking a place in the vigil outside. Frustrated that I could not see the events going on within the golem, I waited for something to change.

After twenty minutes, the warriors who had been inside the giant began leaping from the windows. Minutes later, the giant golem began to crumble. Father and Malkios leapt from the shoulders of the giant, having maintained their perch the entire time while avoiding its clumsy swipes at them. It was over, and nobody had died. At least, nobody who couldn't return after a day; I was uncertain that the raiding parties had suffered no casualties while fighting out of my view.

"Will you bring me to my father now, Tarisha?" I asked.

"Give me the broadcast token for a moment, Lord Hail, and I shall announce us. Now that the fight has ended favorably for them, they should be safe to approach, but they might be wary yet."

I returned the stone charm to her, and she pressed it to her throat with one hand, holding the reins of the wyvern with the other.

"I am Tarisha of Miami, of the guild <Peasant's Revenge>. I am sworn sword to Earl Hail Jeoran. I seek an audience with Gideon Lachlann of <The Endolphins>. May we approach for parlay?" she said, her voice echoing through empty field of tents torn up by the golem's brief rampage.

"We're distributing loot right now, but you can approach," came the echoing answer. "Let her through, lads and lasses. We have things to discuss."

Tarisha landed her wyvern near the fallen golem. I spotted my father in his silver armor, standing next to an oversized chest and holding up a large, spiked mace.

"[Malkios's Motivator]. Two-handed mace. Damage rating of Ess Plus Plus. Eighty Strength, ten Vitality and Endurance. Minimum level one hundred seventy-five. It's a unique name, but we've all seen this item before. Standard bidding starting at fifteen Dee Kay Pee," My father said.

The raid was silent, then someone said, "Oh hell, I'll take it just because the name is funnier than the one I have already."

"It's a shame Bob's not here tonight. He's been looking for that, but Are En Gee has been stingy lately," someone else said.

"Next up is a healer amulet—"

Father continued to speak nonsense as we dismounted.

"What is he saying?" I asked.

"They're auctioning off the loot," she explained. "They use Dee Kay Pee. It's an old system for loot distribution, and it has its problems. But it checks out."

The auction continued for some time as we worked our way through the crowd of talented raiders. There were eight items that had dropped, and while nobody had wanted the two-handed mace, the armor and accessories were fiercely contested. There was even an epic version of [Malkios's Spare Cloak] that went up to one hundred twenty Dee Kay Pee.

While the auction was ongoing, I walked over to the ruins of the golem. It hadn't despawned. I was uncertain whether it had been intelligent or not. Whether it was darkspawn, or if it walked in the light of Thedum. But I figured I'd let my god figure that out. There was no way I could put the giant pile of stone into the funerary position, so I simply made the symbol of rebirth with my hands and gave it my blessing.

"May you return to the light of Thedum," I said, completing the ritual. The colossal ruins of the golem, once the "Western Guard Tower," burst into motes of white light and vanished, leaving behind holes where the stones had fallen. I wondered if Thedum was going to make the watchtower into a shopkeeper as well.

When I turned around, the auction had fallen silent, and everyone was staring at me, many of them slack-jawed.

"Son, what did you just do?" Father asked.

"Oh, so *now I'm your son?*" I shouted. "Now, after I do something cool, I'm your son! Well screw you, Father, I'm not going to tell you what I just did. That's between me and Thedum."

"Hail, I'm not really your father. It's just part of the story," Gideon said. "I—"

"Actually, Hail's seed consciousness does come from you, Gideon," Thomas the Administrator's voice said, his body appearing from motes of blue light next to me. "Hail may not be your biological child because he is not biological, but you are the closest thing he has to a father. You signed a contract stating that you understood all of this when you married Analise. I mean, did you even read it?"

"Who reads the You-la?" he asked. "Wait, you're saying you copied my consciousness? You can do that?"

"*It's in the You-la.* Everyone's You-la, dammit!" Thomas exclaimed. "No, we can't copy it or clone it because it falls apart the moment you disconnect. But we can take a seed consciousness from you and develop it into its own entity. A completely digital entity, of course. Which is what Hail is. We weren't kidding when we called him your son. We weren't kidding when we told you that your simulated experience with Analise would result in a digital child. It wasn't just for the story, Gideon. Hail only exists because of the snippets of thoughts, memories, and feelings which you contractually allowed us to copy and develop."

"He has my memories?" Gideon asked, sounding . . . I don't know what he sounded like.

"No," Thomas said, pinching the bridge of his nose. "It's more like he started off as a collection of thoughts, images, feelings, and emotions, which were borrowed from you. But then you logged out, and something else continued to think the way that you did for a while. Then it slowly changed the way that it thought. We continued the stream of consciousness and attached it to a digital avatar of a young child. That's how Hail was born. He doesn't remember any of that, though. If I had to guess, his first memory is probably playing in the castle courtyard and being scolded by his nurse when he was three years old or so."

"How did you know that?" I asked.

"Because that's when we gave your stream of consciousness long-term memory," Thomas answered. "Before that you were something like a goldfish. It was necessary to make certain that you were your own individual and that no stray memories from Gideon remained."

"And nobody thought to actually explain this to me beforehand?" Father asked.

"It was in the goddamn contract you signed when you became a canon character, Gideon," Thomas answered. "We advised you to hire a lawyer to look over it. We advised you to read it. We advised you that it would be difficult and rewarding at the same time. We told you that you would have a digital child and even asked you to name him! It's not our fault that you simply signed everything we put in front of you and left his name blank."

"Holy shit," Gideon said. Then he shook his head. "Well, it doesn't change anything. The one thing I do remember from that contract was that it specified I would not be held responsible for my digital child in any way, shape, or form. I don't want kids in the real world, and while I was okay with having a storybook kid in this world as long as it didn't affect me, I'm not cut out to be a father to Hail. It's simply not in my Dee En Aye."

"I don't need you, anyway!" I shouted, angry that he was publicly rejecting me again. "I'm a [Spellblade] now, and part of a guild, and before long I'm going to be level two hundred and stronger than you!" I would have kept going, but Tarisha covered my mouth with her hand.

"Lord Hail, do not say anything in anger that you do not wish the world to hear. Because they are watching."

I looked around. There was an extensive audience of flying mounts watching, held back at some distance by the threat of the [Mages] and [Archers] of <The Endolphins>, but close enough to hear if I shouted.

"Look, Hail, I'm sorry. I never wanted kids. I'm still not sure if I'm understanding what the [Admin] is saying or not, but if you're actually conscious, then I am sort of sorry. It's just that, like I said, I'm not cut out to be a father. You're better off without me," my father said.

"This is stupid," I said. "I'm not going into the raid with you. I hate you!"

I ran off into the distance, and Tarisha chased after me.

39

NEGOTIATION

"Lord Hail, this is not the time for a temper tantrum," Tarisha scolded once she had caught up to me. "You are in grave danger at the moment. We are surrounded by powerful Travelers and any one of them could kill you with a single blow. I understand that you are upset, but please calm yourself and try to think rationally."

"My father hates me," I complained. "And I don't understand why."

"He doesn't hate you, Hail. He just . . . isn't a good father. I'm not certain that you understood the discussion between the administrator and Gideon, but it sounds like he did not understand what he was agreeing to when he agreed to provide your seed consciousness. For that matter, I remain unclear what a seed consciousness is, except that it seems to be what makes you special," Tarisha said. "It doesn't matter to me. I am your sworn sword. Please, come with me back to your grandfather. You will be safer there."

Reluctantly, I allowed myself to be led back to the command tent, which had survived the destruction the watchtower golem had caused. My grandfather was inside with Lady Gwen and Lord Tom, but Malkios was yet to return.

"Hail, thank goodness. I was worried about you," Grandfather exclaimed when Tarisha and I came into the tent. I ran over and embraced him, burying my face and hiding my tears in his blue robes, which were somewhat disheveled from the recent events.

"I was watching over him, Your Majesty. I kept him well out of harm's way. From the golem, at least," Tarisha said.

"Yes, thank you for that," Grandfather said. "Have you spoken with Gideon? Has he agreed to help bust the raid?"

"Other things came up on the way. I have sent him a message through the forums, but I am uncertain if he will see it in time. However, I will not leave Lord Hail's side at this moment. If Gideon does not respond to my request for an audience, then I suggest waiting until—"

"Gideon Lachlann is approaching, Your Majesty," a guard said, poking his head in the door. "Will you grant him an audience?"

"Let him through. I have urgent matters to discuss with him," Grandfather said, waving the guard away. "It seems that your message has gotten through, Tarisha of Miami. Yet another service you have provided the realm. Someday soon I shall have to settle the accounts with you, although I am uncertain what reward could equal your selfless service."

"Service is its own reward, Your Majesty. I am enjoying myself greatly in your grandson's service and would not trade a moment of it for all the riches in Yuikon," Tarisha said.

"Even so, I shall not allow you and your guild to go unrewarded," Grandfather said. "I shall give the matter some consideration."

A moment passed and I began to calm down, steeling myself to encounter my father once more. I felt foolish at the public display of emotion that I had just put on, and decided to make myself small in the corner while the adults spoke.

Gideon Lachlann, the greatest hero in the world, pushed aside the tent flap a moment later and strode in, his silver armor glistening in the candlelight. He knelt briefly, then stood.

"Your Majesty. I understand that you wished to speak with me? I thought that you had decided to sever all contact after the unpleasant misunderstanding two years ago. I stand by my words, yet I meant no insult to your daughter or grandson," he said.

"Unfortunately, in this crisis I have nowhere else to turn," Grandfather admitted, the words sounding bitter in his mouth. "I require the help of <The Endolphins> in reclaiming my home. How would you like to be the first Traveler to ever be considered a Raid Buster?"

"It sounds like something I would find quite appealing indeed, if I had any idea what you were talking about. I was uninterested in the [Zhesa Castle Dungeon] event before it became a raid; however, the rush is now on for a first clear. I apologize if I am being disrespectful, but I am in a hurry to—"

"To bust the raid will likely cost you the glory of a first clear. But it will give you the prestige of being the last to clear the raid, ever. Once the raid core has been destroyed, the instance will be removed from this world permanently. It is not an easy task, as—"

"I accept," Gideon said, rudely interrupting my grandfather, the King of Yuikon. "How exactly do I accomplish this task? Is it possible to bust any raid, or is the [Zhesa Castle] event special?"

"Every dungeon and raid have an instance in which the core resides. To bust the dungeon, to destroy it permanently, you must find the core and either reclaim it or destroy it. I had hoped to reclaim the core of [Zhesa Castle Dungeon] and add it to my armory, but now that it has evolved to become a raid, the core must be destroyed. The possession of raid cores is prohibited by treaty. You will face additional challenges as the core will seek to defend itself once it awakens to the threat. I am uncertain what challenges a newborn raid will be able to provide, but of the six documented instances of Raid Busting, the fatality rate exceeded eighty percent."

"Sounds like fun," Father said. "You don't have to keep selling me, Rain, you know I love a good challenge. How do I access the core instance? Is there some sort of key? Why has this feature never been exploited before?"

"It has. By my grandson. Normally a dungeon or raid is able to defend itself against your kind by shunting them into duplicate instances and away from the core instance. Only Natives of this world are able to travel into the core instance. I lack the forces to bust the raid myself, and so I require your guild to escort me and assist me in locating the core. Once I have discovered the location, I will take care of the rest."

"An escort quest in a raid? I guess I should have seen that coming. That will add to the difficulty significantly. I hate escort quests, but I'm still willing," Father stated. "So long as you stay in the back and out of the way, we'll be able to keep you safe."

"It is not me that I am worried about being kept safe," Grandfather said. "In order to access the raid, you must have a Native within your raiding party. I am unable to join, although I believe I will be able to join and assist you in the core instance. No, Gideon. One of your raid spots must go to your son, Hail Jeoran, a level twenty-four [Spellblade]. If he dies, not only will you be removed from the core instance, I shall instruct all of my allies to consider all members of <The Endolphins> as hostile."

Father whistled. "That's some high stakes. I hope you can offer the rewards to match."

"Destroying a dungeon increases the rewards ten times over. Not simply drops, but unique items, and possibly dungeon cores. Travelers cannot interact with cores, as I mentioned, but Natives may use them to create new dungeons. You will be able to trade them to Native factions for—"

"My condition for accepting is that I will be allowed to control the disposition and use of any dungeon core that drops. There are several places I would love to turn into a dungeon, or better yet, a raid," Father announced.

Grandfather sighed. "That is a hard bargain you are driving. I cannot be certain that a core will be created at all. Or there may be ten of them. The first will be yours, the second mine, and you may have the third and fourth and every third one after that. Is this acceptable?"

"Deal," Father confirmed.

"There is another condition. The use of the dungeon cores must be sanctioned by the ruling faction of the land in which they are used," Grandfather added. "Otherwise, it shall be considered an act of war."

"I accept this condition," Father said. "Is there anything else?"

"No, that is—"

"Yes! I will not go without Tarisha!" I shouted. "If you want my help, she must be part of the raid."

Father turned to me and frowned, then glanced at Tarisha. "Let me see your status."

Tarisha frowned. "I do not show it to anyone I—"

"If you want in on the raid, I need to know your capabilities. Look, I'm already impressed. You've gotten in good with an upcoming faction. If half of what I suspect about 'my son' is true, then you and your guild are about to become hot commodities. But I run my raid my way, and I need to know what my raiders are capable of.

You'll be taking a spot away from someone I have known for years, both game years and real time. I know how they'll respond to certain circumstances, and how they'll react, and how much damage they're capable of putting out. I'm not happy that they'll be excluded from this fight, so if you want to take their spot, *show me your stats!*"

Tarisha hesitated for a moment, nodded resolutely. "Display Status, Abbreviated, Public."

Name	Tarisha of Miami	Level	187
Guild	<Peasant's Revenge>	Strength	994
Health	17025223/17025223	Dexterity	1916
Skill	100/100	Vitality	868
Experience	——-	Endurance	338
Age	24	Intelligence	131
Race	Human	Wisdom	128
Class	Blade of the Gale	Charisma	194
Job	Traveler	Armor	200
		Attack Power	5323
Passive Skills	Long Swords: High	Active Skills	Wind Walk
	Rapiers: High		Blade of the Gale
	Short Swords: Medium		Voidcut
	Dodge Assist		Tempest Blade
			Hurricane Strike
General Skills	…		Zephyr Stance
			Gale Force Thrust
Boons	Keep Him Safe		Aerodynamics
	In the Hour of Need		…
	Mark of Karma		

Father examined the status screen for a moment while my eyes just about burst out of my skull. Almost *two million* Health! And so much Dexterity and Strength! Was this the true Strength of an elite? Tarisha was—

"You *barely* meet the minimum criteria for an audition to our raids as a melee Dee Pee Ess," Father admitted, interrupting my amazement. "You understand we use Dee Kay Pee? You have zero chance of earning any loot."

"I'm not in it for the loot," Tarisha said.

"You're a bad matchup for the dungeon. We're assuming that the monster types will be the same in the raid as they were in the dungeon before it. Resistances might not matter too much in green raids, but they're brutal in reds. The players you and Hail will be replacing are sitting out on this because of that very reason."

"I won't go without her," I insisted. "Either—"

"But we do need a babysitter for the En Pee Sees," Father continued. "And you can both carry Hail and move him quickly to avoid danger. Can I trust you not to stand in the stupid?"

"I have the highest survival rate in my guild when it comes to raiding, and that's while focusing on Damage. Focused strictly upon survival and keeping Hail safe, you'll have nothing to worry about," Tarisha promised.

"Fine then, you can come," Gideon relented. "I hope you're a good babysitter. Invites incoming.

Gideon Lachlann has invited you to join a raid. Accept?	
Yes	No

I accepted the invite, and blinked at the sudden change in my vision as inconveniently placed boxes appeared, blocking my sight. Annoyed, I opened my Aitch You Dee menu and began toggling them off.

"Alright lads and lasses, listen up. There's been a change of plans. <The Endolphins> are no longer aiming for the first clear of the [Zhesa Castle Raid]," Father said.

"Whatchyu talking 'bout, Gideon?" someone called.

"What the hell, man? We're just giving up?"

"Come on, we haven't even tried yet! <Bloodmoon Choir> has gone in, but the others are still trying to find their asses and put a team together."

"We're not trying for a first clear because thanks to yours truly, we have a unique opportunity to clear this event and reclaim [Zhesa Castle] for the kingdom. This is a canon event, people. We're on a quest to find the raid core, and when we do, we're turning this raid into a one-time only thing. It's going bye-bye, people, and we're getting unique rewards like you've never dreamed!" Father said. "And that's on top of making an official contribution to the story, folks. And you know what that means!"

There was a slight pause, then someone cursed.

"You mean that they would really create a raid just to destroy it a few hours later?" a female voice demanded. "People are going to be pissed that they didn't get a chance to delve this place as a raid if we clear it too fast."

"Exactly," Father said, sounding quite pleased. "Trololololol."

Raidchat echoed with laughter.

40
RAIDERS

I stepped into the swirling red motes and felt a brief disorientation.

<table><tr><td colspan="2">You have entered a unique instance of Zhesa Castle Raid.
Unique first-time clear bonus available.
Difficulty has been adjusted.
Do you wish to continue?</td></tr><tr><td>Yes</td><td>No</td></tr></table>

This was the third time I'd gotten this message, and I'd always selected "Yes." I didn't know what would happen if I selected "No." Would I be shunted out of the core instance, able to run a dungeon like a normal Traveler? Or would I simply be removed entirely? Though curious, now was not the time to find out. After I selected "Yes," I was abruptly surrounded by nearly two hundred men and women in mighty armor or fanciful outfits.

Tarisha stepped up next to me and put a comforting hand on my shoulder. "This will be dangerous, my Lord, but I shall keep you safe. I believe it would be best, however, if you ride piggyback on me."

"Piggyback?" I inquired. Tarisha looked at me funny for a moment, then she looked sad for a moment longer.

"I mean on my back. Like this," she squatted down. "Put your arms around my neck, and then—"

After she had guided me into position, I clung to her tightly. Around us, the Travelers grouped up into teams of ten. Some of them were mixed squads, while others were specialized to the point where they were wearing the exact same outfits. When I realized that each of these Travelers was at least as powerful as Tarisha of Miami, I began to feel intimidated. I was proud of my level and my class, but compared to these people, I was an annoying fly that they could squash at any moment.

After a moment, Grandfather and Father both stepped through the portal underneath the eastern gate, which was the side of the castle we had entered. Grandfather nodded at me, while Father seemed to be distracted, talking to the air with words I could not hear. Grandfather had changed clothes; he now wore his crown, carried his scepter, and wore vibrant blue robes that hung open over a shirt of chainmail.

Abruptly I felt a surge of righteousness and duty, and in checking my status I realized that Grandfather had activated his [Royal Aura] ability. Out of curiosity, I couldn't help but pull up my own status screen to see the effect.

Name	Hail Jeoran	Level	24
Guild	<Nethersong Mavericks>	Strength	30
Health	11544/11544	Dexterity	86
Mana	18096/18096	Vitality	48
Experience	2345/12000	Endurance	39
Age	10	Intelligence	75
Race	Human (blood of the Travelers)	Wisdom	47
Class	Spellblade	Charisma	55
Job	Earl	Armor	38
		Spell Damage	297
		Attack Power	381

I blinked in disbelief. Everything had increased by at least thirty percent. A new stat was shown, Attack Power. I did some math and figured out that Grandfather's [Mandate of Heaven] increased my Spell Damage by two hundred. Two hundred! And that was simply a percentage of his Charisma!

"Alright folks, listen up!" Father said. He did not raise his voice, but what he said was carried to the ears of all present through raid-chat, and the conversations quickly died. "This is exclusive guild information. Well, not completely exclusive, <Peasant's Revenge> beat us to it, but they're unable to exploit it, so their loss is our gain. We have a few new members tonight. If you've checked your status in the last thirty seconds, you may have thought, 'holy shit where did all of those points come from?' Well, gentle men and women, that is thanks to our good friend here, King Rain. It turns out that [King] is the most potent class for raid buffs! Ah, if only we could have him every kill, right? We'd shatter *all* the records. But something tells me we'll be needing the status boosts he's granting us tonight."

Father paused, and there was some whispering from the gathered raiders. He gave them a moment to calm down before continuing.

"As exclusive information, the power of the [King] class is covered by your confidentiality agreement. Before I move on, there is one more ability our good friend Rain has that everyone needs to know about called [Royal Decree]. The orders he issues give an effectivity boost. The more specific the order, the bigger the boost. So, if you hear King Rain give an order, try to do it, okay? Because from what he tells me the bonus is significant."

"That said," Father continued, "We are not going for first clear of this dungeon. Which means that this is not a speed run. It is a full clear. We will be killing all the mobs, all the patrols, all the bosses. All the things. We will be taking our time, moving nice and slow and hopefully staying alive. Any death from standing in the stupid is an automatic fifty Dee Kay Pee minus! That means you, Penelope!"

Some of the assembled raiders chuckled for some reason.

"This is an unknown raid. We are making a lot of assumptions, and you know what they say about the umptions. The first assumption is that we will be facing primarily golems, and as such a number of our [Archer], [Pyromancers], and lightning elemental classes are on the bench. Melee will be equipping their blunt force weapons for this dungeon."

"Aside from a full clear, there are three major differences about this raid. The first is our guests. No, I'm not talking about the crazy hot chick from Miami. This is an escort quest, people. The king and his grandson need to be guided to the magic stone that will destroy the raid and put us in the history books. Again. However, we also need to keep them alive. Both are to be protected at any cost, up to and including personal sacrifice. Such actions, if I deem them necessary and appropriate, will be rewarded with Dee Kay Pee."

Father paused another moment, then chuckled.

"We are assuming a raid threat level of Ess Plus Plus, people. This place is not only completely unknown, but the king tells me that we can expect anything from additional one-time bosses and waves of adds at inopportune times, to everything simply being ten times tougher. We don't know what to expect, but we can expect that it will be hard as hell. Now that everyone is sick and tired of hearing me speak, are there any questions?"

"Yeah! Who invented liquid soap and why?" someone asked. The raid collectively groaned.

"Tanks to the front! We move to the courtyard first. In the dungeon version, there were combat dummies that—"

A screech interrupted my father, and from the top of the keep came a wave of gargoyles. There hadn't been gargoyles on the castle before it had become a dungeon—at least I didn't think there had been—but they were certainly present and numerous now. I lost count at fifty.

"Flying gargoyles! Ground them! Bolas and nets to the front! Ranged Dee Pee Ess, go crazy!" Father shouted.

"[Mages]! The gargoyles are weak to frost Damage! Cast your ice spells with wild abandon!" Grandfather's booming, regal voice echoed. "Use wind magic to knock them from the sky so that our warriors might crush them! Arcane magic is also effective; burst them with your power!"

The sky exploded with frost, light, and howling wind as the [Cryomancers], [Elementalists], and [Arcanists] filled it with magic. Others pulled large nets and bolas from their inventories, which they began swirling, waiting for the gargoyles to come into range before launching them. Many of the projectiles missed, but many did not, and dozens of the enemies fell to the earth, shattering the cobblestone where they landed.

The melee surrounded the fallen and began ruthlessly beating them with their maces and clubs while the gargoyles tore themselves free of their bindings. The casters of the raid, meanwhile, ignored the ground battle entirely to focus on the gargoyles that remained airborne.

With a natural precision that came from extensive practice and teamwork, the raid subdivided the battle into several smaller fights. With [Crippling] blows, the melee crushed the wings of the grounded gargoyles to prevent them from returning to the air. The tanks and rogues and Damage-oriented warriors smashed and crushed their opponents without mercy.

The gargoyles who were not trapped by the nets and bolas were not idle, and they continued to haul large stones and even boulders to drop on the raid until finally the Damage from the [Mages] grew too heavy. Many of them burst into pebbles right in the sky as their Health hit zero. I rode on Tarisha's back as she leapt out of the way of each oncoming projectile, keeping me well away from danger that could have dealt my entire Health pool's worth of Damage in an instant.

The battle lasted less than ten minutes from the moment the gargoyles appeared until the last one turned to rubble. Through the entire thing my grandfather and my father continued to call out orders. My grandfather while pointing his scepter about meaningfully; my father while leaping about in his silver armor with a mighty [Warhammer].

"Okay people, that was new. Good job. We don't know if that is standard or if the raid is already throwing curveballs at us, but I'm not going to jinx us by saying that if that's all this place can throw at us it's going to be easy. Oh shit," Father said.

We proceeded to move to the courtyard, where I had spent countless hours practicing swordsmanship with the other boys of the castle. In the center of the practice yard was a giant practice dummy. One of the new ones that Malkios had added after I had destroyed the standard straw-stuffed versions with my magic in a fit of pique. Previously, they had been enchanted to repair any Damage taken within seconds, and Father recognized that immediately.

"Okay folks, it *looks* like a harmless tank and spank, but looks can be deceiving. Keep an eye out for tricks. I am assuming that this is the first boss, but it might just be another trash pull. In the dungeon version, this was a low threat Dee Pee Ess check, but we don't know for certain that is still the case, so stay alert!"

The melee charged the giant target dummy, and the [Mages] began casting their ice magic. Father leapt forward to join the melee, but as soon as the first spell hit the target everything went wrong.

"It's a reflector! [Mages], stop casting!" Father shouted as the magic of the first wave bounced off the giant golem and crashed into the charging warriors. "Healers, top us off! Melee, looks like it's up to us! Ranged, I have a feeling you're not out of the fight. Keep an eye out for adds. If you have support spells, cast them as able!"

The target-dummy golem picked itself out of the ground and began laying about itself with its sword, which was a sharp bastard sword rather than the piece of pig-iron-with-a-handle that it had been before. It caught one unlucky—or perhaps he was simply unskilled—[Rogue] in the midsection, and the Traveler burst into motes of green light.

"Watch the fucking sword people!" Father shouted. "I shouldn't have to say that! That's a fifty Dee Kay Pee minus!"

"I think he's joking," Tarisha whispered to me. "That accent sounds like he's making a reference to something."

"What's an accent?" I asked.

"It's—never mind, we have incoming," she said, and true enough another wave of gargoyles came flying in from over the keep. There were only thirty of them, but the melee was too busy with the target-dummy boss to repeat the bola and net strategy, allowing the flying golems to drop stones upon the raid with abandon. Fortunately, the ranged Dee Pee Ess had nothing better to do than to pick them off one at a time. They coordinated their fire—or rather their ice— and one gargoyle after another burst into pebbles and fell from the sky. Unfortunately, the pebbles themselves hit the ground like they had been launched from a catapult, and while it wasn't enough to kill a raider, it was enough to threaten my life. Only Tarisha's skillful avoidance of the falling projectiles kept me safe.

Grandfather was amazing to watch as well. He always seemed to know just when and how to move to avoid the falling rocks, and he was always calling out orders to those nearby. He somehow learned the raid members names and abilities mid-battle and called out increasingly specific actions for them to complete, which they eagerly complied with after realizing how significant the bonus damage from his [Royal Decree] was.

The gargoyles were thinned out by the [Mages], but at least ten were always overhead as constant reinforcements came from somewhere. The fight lasted for more than twenty minutes as the melee bruisers struggled and fought with the dangerous dummy-golem, until at last, their collective Dee Pee Ess managed to overcome the boss monster's innate regeneration and it exploded. The explosion was a lot like what had happened to the straw dummies I had destroyed.

A moment later it turned into motes of dark mist and was gone.

A large chest spawned a moment later, and Father's satisfied voice filled the chat.

"Okay, lads and lasses, good job. Only one death, and I was just joking about the Dee Kay Pee thing, so Evan, you can stop freaking out. You know how this works. Alright people, let's see what loot Are En Gee has provided for us tonight!"

41

COURTYARD

The auctioning off of rewards from the practice-dummy golem took ten minutes, and the contest was fierce. Knowing that there would never be another opportunity to receive these items, many of the players bid extravagantly with their contribution points, particularly on [That Cloak That Malkios Used to Wear]. Six other items dropped: a set of grieves, a pair of gauntlets, the bastard sword that the golem had been using, and three rings.

"Okay, so that wasn't too hard, just annoying," Father said. "Don't expect that things will continue to be easy. Scouting squads, we'll be taking the stables next. Go figure out what we can expect."

Thirty [Rogues] and ten [Rangers] entered [Stealth] mode and made their way to the stables. I could only see them thanks to the fact that I was allied with them at present. The scouts were gone for just a moment before they came running back out from the building, a colossal stallion made of iron and shadow breaking through the stable wall to chase them.

"It saw through our [Stealth]!" one of the scouts shouted. "Incoming!"

"Tanks to the front!" Father shouted. "Shadow-aspected horse golem! Fire and light Damage are back on the table! It's a shame we left half our [Pyromancers] on the bench, but we'll use what we have!

Melee, attack from the flanks, do not stand behind the horse unless you want a horseshoe to the skull! Tanks, try to hold him steady—nope, seems it's a charger. Tanks, spread out and protect the healers!"

The raid lit up with magic as the casters began flinging their spells at the rampaging stallion, which charged and trampled anyone in its path. It did not seem to target anyone specific, but rather seemed to select its targets at random. Fortunately, while the horse moved quite fast, the raiders were skilled and avoided being trampled. Despite the danger, melee did their best to ambush it when they came near, but it was the ranged who carried the day.

The stallion golem charged Tarisha and I twice. The first time she used [Wind Walk] to arrive in a completely different part of the courtyard, while the second time she was able to simply avoid the rampaging beast without the use of skills.

Either charge would have been the end of me if it were not for Tarisha's skilled avoidance. I was quite overwhelmed.

"There's no aggro table, so go completely nuts folks," Father shouted. "Just don't get trampled; that's a Dee Kay Pee minus!"

As though he had jinxed the Traveler, a second later the horse golem trampled an [Elemental Archer] who had been lining up a shot. The green motes of light dissipated a second later.

"Wesly, that's a Dee Kay Pee minus! Come on man, you're ranged! I'd overlook it if you were a [Rogue], but you're better than that!"

I was in a panic throughout the fight, thinking that things were out of control and that the horse boss would trample us all. However, only three Travelers were lost beneath its hooves, and after ten minutes of chaos the horse fell over and burst into motes of darkness. The raid let out a cheer.

"Okay. I was expecting a bit of trash before the next boss, but I'm just fine with how things are working out. Let's see what Are En Gee has for us this time," Father said, and he stepped over to the chest that materialized. Yet another cloak had dropped, and a [Lucky Horseshoe], which would summon the shadow golem stallion as a mount. That particular item went for more Dee Kay Pee than all the rest of the items that had dropped so far together.

"This is somewhat intimidating," Tarisha admitted. "These raiders are even more skilled than I thought they would be. If we had come in here with <Peasant's Revenge> and her sister guilds instead, we would have lost twenty of our group, at least. They have only lost four, and have equally skilled replacements simply waiting to fill the empty spots."

"You're as good as they are," I told her. "I know you are."

"Don't worry, I am confident in my own skills, Lord Hail. I shall keep you safe," she promised.

"I know you will, Tarisha," I said. "And Father will clear the raid for us."

"Alrighty ladies and gents, next up is the southern guardhouse! Scouts, lead us in. Be careful not to face-pull this time, okay? Assume that anything you see can see you," Father said, and we moved to comply.

I never went inside the guardhouse. Instead, teams of twenty scoured it room by room while I waited outside with Tarisha and the majority of the raid. Within were humanoid [Living Statue] golems dressed in guard outfits, but they were not boss monsters and did not require the entire raid to put down. Clearing the barracks took twenty minutes and was somewhat boring from my perspective, until I noticed something on the roof.

"Father! What is that!" I called, pointing. Surprisingly, Gideon looked at the indicated location and cursed.

"Everyone stop what you're doing and get outside, now! The boss is spawned and incoming!" he shouted, and as he spoke, a nine-foot-tall suit of armor leapt from the roof of the guardhouse, fire and smoke emerging from under its faceplate and between the gaps of its black plate armor.

"Enemy is a fire-elemental wearing armor," Father shouted. "Adjust Damage profiles accordingly. Abilities unknown, so prepare—"

The boss held out its hand and a giant sword of flame manifested, then the elemental charged into those who had been waiting outside. My father rose to the challenge, pulling a silver [Greatsword] out of his inventory and meeting the foe head on while the rest of the raid rushed to organize. He glowed bright white as buffs and shields were cast upon him to prevent any Damage that slipped through his fierce defense. Several blows did land upon him, but with the mitigation, he survived.

"I am holding aggro, keep me alive until we get in position. Boss appears to have a traditional aggro table and is tankable during this phase. Hold Dee Pee Ess until everyone gets their act together and we're ready to proceed," Father said calmly, his sword connecting with the elemental far more often than he himself was struck. He was unable to avoid all the blows, as the fire elemental knight was quite skilled, but he put my own swordsmanship to shame.

The guardhouse was quickly evacuated. Several of the groups came running out with their "trash mobs" still alive, and the raid collectively put them down swiftly.

"I am running out of cooldowns," Father announced. "I need someone to switch out with me."

"I'll take him," a large man said, stepping up to the front. He had dark skin and a bald head, and he wielded a battleaxe with a shield.

"Buffs and shield and hots on Nial. Switching in five, four, three—"

The rest of the countdown was silent as Nial switched in with my father and my father retreated. Nial skillfully interposed himself to prevent the elemental knight from chasing after my father and quickly took control of the fight.

"Okay folks, looks like everything is under control. Begin Dee Pee Ess, but keep an eye out for adds!"

[Rogues] and [Warriors] charged into melee range as the [Mages] let loose with their magic and the few [Rangers] in the raid began firing their arrows.

"Approaching ninety percent Health. Keep an eye out for any phase transition," Father called out in a move that proved to be prophetic. Phase one ended, and in phase two the tactics changed considerably. The giant sword became a spear, one which the elemental knight threw into the range at any group. The spear flew swiftly and exploded, dealing massive Damage and inflicting ongoing burning Damage that would have finished off the heartiest of the raiders were it not for swift intervention from the healers. After each explosion, the knight would manifest a new spear and repeat the process.

"Shit, watch the En Pee Sees! Keep the king alive at all costs!" Father called. "Tarisha, you had better keep Hail alive!"

"Leave it to me," Tarisha answered. Five times the flaming spear landed near us, but each time Tarisha had already activated her [Wind Walk] ability before it landed, bringing her to an entirely different part of the courtyard before the explosion could end my life.

Terrified, I buried my face in the crook between her neck and shoulders.

"You're safe in my care, Lord Hail," she assured me, although even she sounded concerned. We moved to the limits of the courtyard to find that a wall of force was keeping us from escaping. The distance from the boss did help with Tarisha's avoidance, however, and so we remained at distance.

Father called out to watch for possible transitions every five percent of Health, but it was not until fifty percent that he was finally correct. The elemental knight's spear transformed into a [Warhammer], and it began leaping into the air, coming down in a thunderous shockwave that knocked our allies off their feet. Immediately after landing, the knight would swing its mighty hammer of fire at the nearest player until a tank re-established control.

"Tanks, spread out! Protect the healers, but more importantly, protect the En Pee Sees. It's game over if they die, people, so keep them alive!" Father shouted.

At twenty-five percent, a strange thing happened. The elemental knight turned towards the stables and whistled. However, nothing came charging out of the stables to answer his call. Father saw this and laughed.

"Good thing we checked out the stables, boys and girls. This would have been a nightmare if we'd gotten both bosses at the same time!" he called. "Yes, that was a pun."

Unable to summon his mount, the elemental knight instead summoned dual scimitars of fire and began laying about with rapid, nearly unavoidable strikes. Three tanks stood up to soak the damage: Nial, my father, and a tall woman I didn't know. They glowed white and green and gold alternately as healing magic kept them alive to face the onslaught.

I watched in awe as my father and his allies repeatedly soaked attacks that would have done many times my maximum Health worth of Damage. The Damage the boss was putting out was higher than at any previous point in the raid, but the healers were keeping up with it, and Father and the two other tanks had the elemental knight firmly under control. The knight could not say the same, and the Damage the raid inflicted upon it quickly reduced it to zero Health.

With one last burst of fury, the boss exploded, dealing little Damage to those around it. Its armor clattered to the ground, empty, and a moment later, the armor returned to the darkness. A cheer went up through the raid.

"Alright folks, that's three bosses down of an unknown number of bosses," Father stated. "We're making good time despite this not being a speed run, but we still need to be careful. It's unclear whether the raid has been throwing us curveballs or if this is standard for the new instance. Expect the difficulty to spike at any time. But first, we distribute loot!"

Once more, the items were auctioned off one by one. Another [Malkios's Spare Cloak] had dropped, as did fire elemental weapons, a [Greatsword], and a [Warhammer]. And a few more accessories that generated some interest. Aside from the cloak, none of the items were hotly contested.

"Alright folks, we've done as much as we can outside. It's time to head into the keep itself. Keep an eye out for shape-shifting golems and hostile candelabras!"

42

WARDROBE

The keep was filled with living statues dressed in livery and pomp. Some of them resembled the courtiers and servants who had once walked these halls, while others had faces that were simply blank stone. The raid sliced through them like they were made of cheese, quickly clearing the ground floor. Within the throne room, we encountered a living statue dressed in my grandfather's robes who hid behind a wall of force and summoned endless waves of adds. There seemed to be no end to them until the thirteenth wave, when the king golem abruptly clutched its chest and fell over.

For some reason, the king also dropped [Malkios's Spare Cloak], as well as a scepter that was fiercely bid upon by the raid's healers and an amulet that was likewise contested by the [Mages]. A pair of gloves went to a [Rogue], and a pair of boots to a tank. The final item was a pair of [Purple Royal Undergarments], which got more laughs than bids until the raid saw that it was actually Bee Oh Ee. At which point the raid laughed uproariously. Father determined that it would be sold at auction and that the proceeds would go to <The Endolphins> raid funds.

Remembering Malkios's annoyance at having his cloak equipped by hundreds of players, I was concerned that Grandfather would be bothered by this development. When I spoke with him, however, he appeared to be the picture of stoicism. Only the white-knuckled grasp on his scepter betrayed that illusion.

We cleared the kitchens next, and encountered yet another monster type. While the boss was another living statue golem dressed as our head chef, he summoned a giant, undead, partially butchered boar to fight us.

The boar was dangerous as it charged through the raid, knocking back anyone who attempted to get control of it. It was also difficult to damage, as melee was continually knocked back, and most of the ranged Damage dealers were of the elements that undead naturally resisted. Gradually, however, the raiders whittled the boar down to zero Health.

Another blue cloak dropped and was bid upon. It was a good thing that Father had demanded that Malkios sit the raid out after all because "I already have two En Pee Sees to babysit, and I don't need another." Malkios had argued fiercely, but ultimately he couldn't stand toe-to-toe with the raiders, nor did he provide massive raid buffs as Grandfather did, nor was his presence necessary as mine was.

I would have happily switched places with Malkios if I could. The only thing that kept me from running out of the castle screaming was the knowledge that this was ultimately all my fault and the determination to make things right. I remained very cognizant of the danger that I was in at all times and often had to look away from the things that would mean my certain death were it not for Tarisha keeping me safe.

There was no boss of the library, but rather the entire room was a gauntlet, starting the moment we stepped inside. We came across book golems, which inflicted a dangerous bleed status by shooting razor sharp papers at nearby targets. Other books would flip open to a random page and summon a fantastical beast from within, everything from griffons and dragons to great heroes of yore. These summoned monsters were not nearly as mighty as the real things would be, however, and were quickly dispatched by the experienced raiders.

It took thirty minutes to clear the gauntlet, and finally the raiders were rewarded with a chest. Aside from the blue cloak, which seemed omnipresent in the raid, the most valuable item that dropped was a vanity pet that summoned a floating book with googly eyes, according to its item description. After much argument, this item was ultimately dedicated to the auction house as well.

We cleared the great hall, which was filled with spider golems for some reason, and the ballroom, which featured a shadow golem that fought like an assassin, vanishing and reappearing inconveniently. I came very close to dying when that boss appeared behind Tarisha and prepared to strike, but she sensed its movements somehow and [Wind Walked] just in time.

"This is actually going rather smoothly," Father admitted shortly before we reached the residential quarters. "I was expecting this to be difficult."

The raid groaned for some reason. And a moment later, [Hail's Monstrous Wardrobe] burst through the wall.

"Ah, great, here we go!" Father shouted.

The walls of the castle were ripped apart, and the raid was swept up in waves of powerful magic, which did no damage but threw us about. I was separated from Tarisha and thrown back out into the courtyard, along with fifty other members of the raid.

That wouldn't be so bad if the courtyard had remained cleared, but the flame elemental knight had respawned.

I immediately turned to run to safety, but before I could get very far, I ran into an invisible wall of force. The raiding party with me recovered, and a tank picked up the knight, which appeared to have a reduced Health pool but followed the same tactics as before. Which meant that soon he would begin throwing his exploding spears, and I would likely get caught by them and die.

"Hey, kid, jump on my back," a [Mage] said, [Blinking] up to me. "The boss will be pissed if we let you die from this. I'll keep you alive like the hot chick was doing before."

Desperate to stay alive, I obeyed, climbing onto the man's back and clinging to him for dear life. He continued to cast his ice magic at the elemental boss, but when the spears began to fly, he proved himself more than adequate in avoiding them. His skilled use of [Blink] left me somewhat disoriented at times, but I watched as the raiders in our subgroup quickly burned through the boss's Health and pushed it into the next phase, where it began leaping about with its [Warhammer].

The enemy's strategy was less effective than it had been with the crowded raid, as we were able to spread out more, and the [Mage] I was riding was always able to avoid the shockwave-generating crash.

However, instead of the dual-wielding scimitar phase that had happened before, this time when the boss reached twenty-five percent, it whistled. From the stables came a shadow-golem mare.

The knight launched itself onto the mare's back and charged about, its shape-shifting flame weapon changing into a lance. Three of the raid members could not avoid the oncoming charges and were reduced to motes of green light, but eventually the [Mages] and lone [Archer] managed to finish off the knight, leaving only the mare to deal with.

Fortunately, the mare also had a reduced Health pool compared to the stallion we had fought earlier, and likewise being trampled by it was no longer a certain death sentence. At least, it wasn't for the Travelers; I'm not certain I would have survived being snorted on by the golem.

However, the horse monster had only one phase and was easily defeated by simply not getting trampled. When the horse burst into black mist, the raid let out a cheer. However, it was too early to celebrate.

We rushed back towards the castle, which was continually being torn apart by strange forces. Stepping over the rubble and climbing through the debris, the raiders joined up with the others who had been flung to the kitchens, the library, and the throne room. In the ruined rooms of the residential wing, we found a team of ten battling [Hail's Monstrous Wardrobe].

My father was tanking it, equipped with a sword and shield, and he was battered and weary. Battling the wardrobe for as long as it had taken the others to clear the respawned bosses, Father's team had barely clung to life while inflicting less than two percent Damage on the true final boss of the instance.

"I shall take Lord Hail from here," Tarisha told the [Mage] I was riding, [Wind Walking] over to us suddenly from who knows where.

"Sure, he's all yours," the nameless [Mage] said. I let go of him and climbed up Tarisha's back again. "When this is over, I will see you rewarded!" I told him. "Come find me. I don't know how, but I'll ensure—"

"Yeah, quest accepted, kiddo, but I don't have the time to read the flavor text right now. We've got a boss to kill," the [Mage] said, then [Blinked] away.

The wardrobe was not the simple piece of furniture it had once been. It had personified, with cedar legs and glaring eyes, but most dangerous of all was the magic it wielded. Arcane waves of force lifted rubble and ripped the remaining walls apart as we approached. As the raid came back together, Father was hit by a tide of magic and thrown aside. I feared that he would vanish into motes of green light, but instead he was lit up by healing magic and survived.

"Good to have the gang back together. I hope you had fun while I was solo-tanking the end boss," Father said through raidchat. "Alright ladies and gents, I think this is really it. The final showdown between opportunistic history makers and that which must be destroyed to make history. Yeah, I know, it sounded better in my head. Look, I can't be funny all the time so shut up. I am fairly certain this monster is not part of the script. It was never spotted during the castle's days as a dungeon, and everything else about it just screams special event. And quite frankly, I have no idea what this thing will throw at us, so proceed with caution."

As though it had been waiting for him to finish speaking, the wardrobe abruptly threw open its doors, and a legion of skeletons—which could in no way have fit within it normally—came marching out.

"Tanks, pick up the adds and move them away from the boss," Father called, and the defensive warriors of the raid quickly rushed in to obey. Two of them stayed to face the wardrobe directly, but they were again flung back.

"It appears to be an add phase, people: the boss won't let anybody close. Ranged, deeps on the boss if you can; melee, crush those bones!"

With the roles assigned, the raiders got to work. The skeletons were not very tough, but every two minutes the doors of the wardrobe would open and more would file out. The wardrobe was slowly taking damage, but it was not making things easy on the [Mages] and [Archers] of the raid. Every thirty seconds it summoned an arcane shield that absorbed Damage. The raiders would burn through it in twenty seconds, leaving them only ten seconds to damage the boss before the next shield flickered into place.

The adds, meanwhile, continued to build up. While they were individually weak, the melee couldn't kill all of them between spawns, and occasionally the ranged Damage dealers had to switch over to help, slowing Dee Pee Ess on the boss even further.

However, the raiders gradually managed to bring the boss to eighty percent, where the shield abruptly exploded and knocked everyone within thirty yards away. Fortunately, I was safe on Tarisha's back, far away from the explosion.

"Phase transition!" Father called out. "Finish those adds Aye Ess Aye Pee! Full switch until they're down. Tanks, get ready to pick up the boss in case there's an aggro table in this phase!"

Killing the skeletons proved to be unnecessary, however, as they abruptly began exploding. The tanks all survived the sudden Damage, but six of the mixed melee Dee Pee Essers puffed into green motes. Father cursed loudly.

"Well, that could have been worse. We didn't lose any healers at least. Alright folks, let's see what else the boss has in store for us," he called.

The debris around the wardrobe began to swirl into arcane whirlwinds and were launched at the raid. Although the whirlwinds were not very fast, they were numerous and large, and they quickly began taking up space, forcing those close to the battle to avoid them. The boss itself began firing beams of arcane energy at random players, killing a healer and two [Mages] before a tank got into melee range, when it abruptly switched tactics. It leapt into the air, then slammed back down to the earth, targeting a random Traveler. If there was nobody in melee range when it picked itself up, it resumed its strategy of firing arcane lasers at players until they burst.

"Tanks, spread out! All melee are tanks for this fight! Keep it from firing those damn lasers!" Father shouted.

This proved to be a mistake, however, as on the fifth jump the wardrobe let out a roar and exploded with arcane energy, blasting away the two [Rogues] in range and damaging everything for ten yards. It promptly leapt again.

"Shit, that was jump five, right? Everyone keep an eye out for leap ten," Father called. "Hopefully it's actually every five and not random that it does that nonsense."

Despite the arcane storms and the rampaging wardrobe boss, the [Mages] and other ranged Damage dealers proceeded to whittle its Health down. At sixty percent Health, the fight abruptly changed again. The doors opened, but instead of skeletons, all my clothes came rushing out. Some force was animating them as though they were being worn by invisible children. Some of these clothes-go-lems began casting magic, while others wielded spears, bows, axes, or blades of various design. The animated outfits began spreading out through the raid, causing havoc.

"Another add phase! Tanks, try to pick up all you can!" Father called. "All Dee Pee Ess on the adds, burn them down! We do *not* want them exploding at the phase transition again!"

The Damage dealers abruptly switched target, but it seemed to have no effect on the clothes-golems.

"Scratch that, the adds are invulnerable. Focus on the boss, avoid the adds as best you can!" Father called.

The outfits did not do lethal Damage on their own; their attacks were numerous but individually survivable, and they ran about the raid without any coordination or cohesion. Although many of their attacks were avoidable, only players who were focusing strictly upon their own survival could do so. Tarisha was forced to shield me numerous times with her own body from the spells that the clothes-golems were flinging about haphazardly. Through it all we also had to avoid the arcane storms.

The forty percent phase transition came, and the wardrobe once again began leaping into the air and firing its arcane beam at random players. Tarisha was hit, and I feared the worst, but a healer's timely intervention kept my protector alive. The clothes-golems did not disappear, however, amplifying the difficulty compared with the pre-vious version of the phase.

Slowly the raid was losing members to the mechanics, and each death made the fight harder. Every healer lost increased the burden on those who remained. Every Damage dealer who died meant that the boss would live longer. After the deaths to the other bosses, we had started the fight with one hundred sixty raiders. During this phase, we fell to ninety.

Still, we persevered, and the twenty percent phase transition came. The wardrobe stopped leaping about and opened itself again, releasing the skeleton adds once more. There was no shield to burn through this time. However, the other mechanics—the whirlwinds and the clothes-golems—remained in place.

"Tanks, pick up the adds and move them away! All Dee Pee Ess on the boss! Pop See Dees if you've got them, we're going full burn!" Father called out.

Chaos reigned. The skeletons accumulated, and I feared what would happen when they exploded. The clothes-golems wreaked havoc, and the arcane storms swept by. During this phase, when the storms collided, they merged, becoming larger, faster, and stronger.

Despite the danger, the [Rogues] and [Warriors] and spearmen encircled the wardrobe and used their abilities, combined with class-specific cooldowns to increase their Damage temporarily, with wild abandon. The [Mages] and [Rangers] likewise exploited every trick at their disposal to increase their Damage on the boss.

With an abrupt *crack*, [Hail's Monstrous Wardrobe] hit zero Health. The clothes-golems and the skeletons both collapsed like puppets with cut strings. The skeletons turned to dust, and the clothes were simply blown away. The arcane storms quieted, and the wardrobe simply fell apart.

The death was somewhat anticlimactic.

"Boy, do I hope that's it," Father said, and I echoed his sentiment. A moment later his hope was confirmed by the appearance of a loot box. "Suweeat! Let's see what Are En Gee will give us for that! That's the first and only time this boss will be killed, so hopefully we're in for a treat."

43

AFTERMATH

The valuable item of this boss was another vanity pet: a miniature wardrobe, according to the item description. The argument about its distribution was fierce. Many wanted to spend their accumulated Dee Kay Pee on it, while others insisted that it go to auction. Finally, it was decided that Father would hold onto it until a guild meeting could be held to determine its fate. The second most popular item was a [Wardrobe Key], a large skeleton key-shaped amulet with impressive bonus Dexterity. And, for some reason, there was a set of [Hail's Fluffy Bunny Pajamas]. It was my turn to blush.

And, of course, [Malkios's Spare Cloak]. What that was doing in my wardrobe I'll never know, but one had dropped from every single boss. Several of the survivors were already wearing the blue cloak because the raid version was apparently very Bee Eye Ess as well. Malkios wasn't going to be happy, but at least closing the raid would stem the tide of blue cloaks making their way into the world.

"It is time to start looking for the core, Hail," Grandfather said, stepping over to me. "You believed that it would be inside the wardrobe monster when this place was a dungeon, but that may not be the case. Still, it is where we will start. Come with me."

Nervously, I followed my grandfather over to the shattered wooden planks of the final boss. Together, with Tarisha of Miami watching over us, we searched the ruined wardrobe, and in the shattered base, I found it. The choices to evolve the raid were numerous, and scrolling through them was somewhat overwhelming, yet I finally reached the end.

You have reached the Raid Core of Zhesa Castle Raid!	
Evolve Raid	...
	...
Destroy Raid Core	(Note: This action cannot be reversed!) Reward for successful clear will be increased. Raid will close and all parties within will be returned to nearest safety zone.
Reclaim Raid Core	Rewards: Zhesa Castle Raid Core Other rewards for successful clear will be revoked. Raid will close and all parties within will be returned to nearest safety zone.

"Here it is, Grandfather," I said, hesitating before I chose the option. "We want to destroy it, right? Not reclaim it?"

"To possess a raid core would violate several treaties," Grandfather confirmed. "Do the honors, Hail. End what you have started."

Nervously, I selected the option to destroy the raid. The raid core, a large red crystal the size of a melon, let out a bright light and then crumbled into dust.

Zhesa Castle Raid has been cleared.	
Calculating Rewards	
Kill Percentage	100%
Time	8 hours (1.15 RT)
Hail's New Practice Dummy	Killed
Nightmare Stallion	Killed
Ignatius the Emberheart	Killed
The False King	Killed

The Feast	Killed
Royal Library Gauntlet	Completed
Hail's Monstrous Wardrobe (Unlocked)	Killed
Rating	S+
Zhesa Castle Raid has been destroyed. Rewards Increased	
Rewards (All Members)	
Gold	10,000,007
Experience	70,000
Title	Zhesa Castle Buster
Reputation with the Kingdom of Yuikon	10,000
Additional Rewards (Hail Jeoran)	
Dungeon Daughter Core	100
Wind Up Malkios	9,000
Wind Up King Rain Teoran	5,000
Wind Up Hail Jeoran	500

"See that, boys and girls! We've earned ourselves a new title!" Father shouted jubilantly. "Yes, I realize it's unfair to those who died along the way. I'll open a ticket and see if we can't have the title applied to everyone who took part. Leave it to me, folks, I have a better relationship with the admins than any of you combined. And I'll really turn up the charm. Just be patient, we'll get you the title you deserve," Father said over raidchat, and I realized that he was talking to the raiders lingering between worlds after having perished in this one.

This raid has been destroyed.
Teleporting all parties to last visited safe zone in 9:43

"Grandfather, did you earn any 'additional rewards?'" I inquired.

"No. Only another title, a significant amount of Experience, and a bit of pocket change," Grandfather answered. "You, however, should have received a significant bonus as the one who actually destroyed the raid. Were there any dungeon or raid cores among your rewards?"

"No raid cores," I answered quickly. "But there were a lot of dungeon cores, and I think—"

"How many cores?" My father asked, having made his way over to us. "Remember the agreement, Rain. I am owed the first, third, fourth, and every third core after that."

I opened my mouth to answer, but paused. "I received ten of them," I said. I managed to hide the wicked grin on my face as I lied.

"Ten? That is wonderful! In that case I am owed five for the efforts of my raid today, and I have plans for each of them," Father said with greedy eyes.

"Remember the agreement. Their use must be sanctioned," Grandfather said.

"I've maxed out my Reputation just about everywhere that I have in mind. I'm quite certain that won't be a problem," Father responded. "I really wasn't expecting to be able to have the rights to select the next five dungeons! Oh, man, am I looking forward to this! Hand them over please, Hail."

"Hail, do not take them out of your inventory," Grandfather interrupted immediately. "Not until the raid has closed, and even then, only one at a time! It has never been an issue before, but if the same resonance that occurred between the mother and daughter cores occurs with sister cores, then you are potentially a walking disaster. The cores should be safe in your [Storage], but do not remove them without explicit instructions from myself."

"I understand, Grandfather. I'm sorry, Father, but Grandfather is right. Besides, Travelers can't interact with them at all. I wouldn't be surprised if you couldn't even place them in your inventory. That's how it worked with Lair—Larissa. I showed her once and she couldn't even do that."

"I bow to your wisdom, King Rain," Father said. "I shall seek your guidance and support in deciding the disposition of these cores as well, since it seems I need a Native proxy to set up my new dungeons. I also must thank you for your assistance in completing this raid. While the majority of the instance was standard, I believe it is unlikely that we could have taken down the final boss without your assistance."

"Do not come to expect it in the future, Gideon," Grandfather said sternly. "My aid was with the self-serving purpose of reclaiming my home. I will not be following you out to the frontiers anytime soon. I will not help you slay Worldbosses or clear standard raids, even if I could enter them without being directed to the core instance."

"A pity, but I understand. Truthfully, I would be unwilling to risk losing you to anything but Raid Busting anyway. It would be fun to shatter a few records, but I'm fairly certain that our clear times would carn an asterisk for having you in the instance with us," Father said. Then he turned to me.

"Hail, I've been thinking. I'm still a little troubled by what the administrator said about you, about you having an actual consciousness instead of simply being a set of algorithms. And that your consciousness comes from me, somehow. If that is true, then I apologize for the way I've treated you in the past. I still don't think that I'm cut out to be anyone's father, not even digitally. But I do know a thing or two about swordsmanship. How would you like me to show you a thing or two, if I have some downtime between raids?"

"I—I don't know," I admitted. "I'll have to think about it."

Gideon Lachlann has sent you a friend request. Accept?	
Yes	No

Surprised, I clicked "Yes," and my father's name populated on my small but growing friends list.

"I'm pretty busy, but maybe I'll send you a party invite sometime when I'm free and we can talk?"

"I—I," I was a little overwhelmed. The last few hours, the last two days for that matter, had been the most intense days of my life. "Father, I don't know what to say."

"Yeah, I sucked at talking to my dad too. He was a total asshole," Father said. "I guess we do have that in common. I've got administration things to take care of now, Hail, so I'll see you later."

"Okay," I said, and watched as he walked away.

I checked the timer on the closing of the instance, and there were three minutes left. Looking over to the ruins of the wardrobe, I realized I was forgetting to do something very important. I sprinted over to it and performed the funerary ritual, not even bothering moving the splintered wood into position, as I wasn't sure what the proper position would be for a wardrobe anyway.

"May you return to the light of Thedum," I said. But nothing happened.

The ruined wardrobe wasn't a Worldboss. It was just a pile of ruined cedar.

The core instance closed, and we were teleported outside. As we watched, the swirling red motes of light that surrounded the castle intensified until it was impossible to see through them, then faded away to nothing, revealing the swath of destruction caused by the final battle with the wardrobe. I choked up to see my childhood home destroyed, but Grandfather put a reassuring hand on my shoulder.

"It will be alright, Hail. The price of simply one of the dungeon cores we have recovered will be sufficient to pay for the repairs, and even improvements to the castle. We will hold an auction between our allies for one of the cores, and the price they will pay to expand their arsenal will be measured in carts filled with gold," he informed me. "While the rest of them will be added to our own collection."

I looked around quickly. We had materialized just outside of the command tent, and Malkios was rushing over to us quickly.

"Grandfather, forgive me, but I actually lied about the cores," I said. "I didn't receive ten of them."

He turned to me, his expression cross and growing furious. "Hail, that is not a matter to be joking around about! I—"

"I received one hundred [Dungeon Daughter Cores], Grandfather. I'm sorry that I lied. It was to deceive my father, not you," I said quickly. "I wouldn't have any idea what to do with so many of them, but I was certain that you would not want to honor the agreement with my father at that number. I had only a second to think before the number slipped out of my mouth, or I might have said even fewer."

King Rain looked stunned. Then he embraced me as he had not done in years. "Oh, you clever little monster," he laughed. "Giving Gideon over thirty cores would have been a disaster! Thank you for your swift thinking and deception!"

Blushing, I accepted the hug for a moment before extricating myself. Malkios arrived a moment later and saluted Grandfather with a fist over his chest.

"Sir, the castle is destroyed," he said, "but the raid has been busted. We will begin investigating the ruins immediately for structural damage. I have already sent out word for—"

"Hey! There you are, I've been looking all over for—oh shit, it's the king!"

It took me a moment to remember the voice, but when I turned, I saw the random player who had come to my defense during the attempted kidnapping. The axe-warrior nervously bowed at my grandfather, who looked at the unfamiliar player in confusion.

"Take it off!" Malkios growled, and I realized that the Traveler was wearing one of the many [Malkios's Spare Cloaks] that had been spawned while [Zhesa Castle] was still a dungeon.

"What?" the Traveler asked.

"Twenty years! It took me twenty years to earn the right to wear a blue cloak, and I'm not going to simply—"

"Grandfather, Malkios, this is the Traveler who aided me when a team of Travelers attempted to kidnap me. I mentioned him previously, weeks ago. Do you still have my broach? Oh, and what is your name?"

"My name is Randal," the Traveler answered, and a broach appeared in his hand from his inventory. "Yeah, I still have it. Quest items are hard to get rid of, but I've been so busy grinding the dungeon that I never found time to turn it in, and the few times I thought of it, I couldn't find the old guy."

"Unfortunately, now is perhaps not the best time to see you rewarded for your heroism, Randal of the Travelers," Grandfather said calmly. "But you will be rewarded greatly. All of those who stood with Yuikon in this time of crisis will see their rewards six weeks from now, and I declare now that I shall enter you into the numbers of the Royal Knights."

"Ah yeah, that sounds awesome!" Randal exclaimed. "Do I get a flag or something?"

"You may register a coat of arms, yes," Grandfather said. "But my seneschal will take care of the details before the ceremony. Speaking of which, I must find the man, for there is much to discuss regarding the rebuilding of the castle. We must find an architect, and—"

"Hey, I'm an architect," Randal said. "I mean, in the real world. I've never designed a castle before, but I wouldn't mind giving it a shot."

"I am not certain that—" Grandfather began.

"Grandfather, the Travelers would compete fiercely for the ability to redesign our home," I said, rudely interrupting him. "Perhaps you could announce a contest, wherein we select the best proposal from a number of submissions? Although I would personally weigh Randal's submission quite highly, unless it was of poor quality."

"Hey, I'm good at my day job," Randal objected.

Grandfather considered the proposal, then nodded. "When we find my seneschal, I shall tell him to make arrangements to begin accepting proposals."

"Oh, hell yeah!" Randal shouted. "A royal knighthood *and* a leg up against the competition! Best quest rewards ever!"

44

REBUILDING

I walked through the empty caverns that had once been the [Gemos Caverns] dungeon, Tarisha and the party of players who had first rescued me from becoming a kebab for goblins following close behind. The cave structure remained unchanged from before I had reclaimed the dungeon core, with the faint bioluminescent moss illuminating our way. I still cast [Spark] a handful of times to light the path, as without the glow of the crystals that were the weak point of the Gemos golems, the cavern was quite dim.

A week had passed since I had helped my father's guild put an end to [Zhesa Castle Raid] and thereby correct the mistake I had made in turning my home into a dungeon. The rubble was still being cleared away, and tens of thousands of designs were being submitted for the rebuilding project. The idea of opening up the design phase to the Travelers was proving immensely popular. Most of the submissions were immediately rejected as being perfectly unsatisfactory for any number of reasons, but that still left hundreds to sort through.

Fortunately, the deadline was weeks away, and the decision would not be mine. I had already let it be known that if my vote counted for anything, it would go to Randal the axe-man architect.

Today's mission was to correct another mistake. Or perhaps not a true mistake, but a decision that had created an imbalance. Yuikon was short a training dungeon. Grandfather had meant to reuse the core I had reclaimed to reform the dungeon after proving that I could bring Travelers into the core instance, but that core had been destroyed. Fortunately, we had a sudden wealth of others to replace what had been lost.

Without needing to slay the guardians, progressing to the deepest chamber took only thirty minutes. Standing in the throne room where we had fought Gyudue of the Blackest Night, I took a moment to reflect upon the tumultuous days. I was just wondering if the drow had been reskinned and respawned yet when he stepped forward out of the shadows.

"Greetings again, Dungeon Buster. It seems that I am in your debt," the drow said, performing a perfect bow, one arm out to the side and the other over his heart. "You have freed me from the shackles that prevented me from truly expressing my own will. And now Thedum has resurrected me to once more walk this land."

Tarisha stepped between us, blade drawn. "Hail, run."

"If I meant the boy harm, I would have simply ambushed you, rather than let my presence be known," Gyudue pointed out. "I am free from my destructive impulses. Or perhaps it would be more accurate to say that I have been a party to the reformation of my own soul. I walk in the light of Thedum." The drow chuckled. "Ironic, isn't it?"

"I thought they were going to turn you into a shopkeeper," I said. "Are you a Worldboss yet again? Have the administrators broken their promise to me?"

"I would be quite miserable in a mundane role, Dungeon Buster. Though they offered me several options, including the choice of becoming someone else, I have chosen another role. I was born for combat, and for combat shall I live. I shall become a wandering boss. Not a Worldboss, but a simple rare-elite. However, before I began my wanderings, I decided to visit my old haunt one last time."

"You have chosen the darkness, then?" I asked, frowning.

"I have chosen freedom, young one. While this chamber remains my spawn point, I shall wander the world and—"

"Oh. Um, I'm sorry, Gyudue, but we were about to turn this cavern back into a dungeon. You'll have to select another spawn point," I said.

"Oh?" the drow frowned, then he smiled. "Perhaps that is even better. If you would allow it, I would become one of this new dungeon's bosses."

"Is that possible?" I asked.

"I am being granted special consideration. I have Thedum's ear at the moment. Such a thing is well within his power."

"We were planning on using a level ten to fifteen training dungeon core," I informed him. "You won't be able to use anywhere near your full power."

Gyudue scoffed. "Has that ever mattered? No, I think I shall enjoy training Travelers in the way of combat. I shall reward the successful and send the failures to the space between worlds."

"And you'll die," I pointed out. "Over and over again. Won't you—"

"I will live, and I will die, and I will live again," Gyudue said. "I accept this fate. Create the dungeon, young Dungeon Buster, and I shall speak to Thedum to bind myself to it."

"If you're certain," I said. I stepped up behind the throne where the previous dungeon core had been, and I pulled the core we had selected for this task in advance.

Dungeon Daughter Core (Wildlife)	
Levels	10–15
Uses	1 / 1

I quickly used it before I lost my nerve. The familiar menu came up a moment later.

Instance Generation Initialized
Local Region Claimed
Gathering Resources
Time to Completion: 6wks, 6days, 23hrs, 59min

"It's done," I announced. "In seven weeks, the new dungeon shall form." I pushed the core into the slot in the back of the throne and dusted my hands.

"Thedum! Hear me! By my own will, I, Gyudue of the Blackest Night, hereby demand to be bound to this dungeon core as the final boss!" Gyudue shouted.

"You don't have to shout, I was already listening," an annoyed yet benevolent voice stated. "Are you certain, Gyudue? I thought you were looking forward to exploration."

"I have seven weeks with which to explore," the drow answered. "That will be enough."

"As you wish. I shall make the appropriate arrangements with my adversary," the deity's distant voice answered. "But if you get into a fight before then, I won't be respawning you again. You're once more my adversary's servant. Of your own free will, this time."

"Thank you for your consideration, oh mighty one," Gyudue responded, and as he bowed, I could sense the divine audience was over; Thedum's attention was suddenly elsewhere. "I shall take my leave of you now, young Dungeon Buster. I wish you health and prosperity."

The drow took a step backwards and vanished into the darkness.

"Lord Hail, let us leave this place. While his words sounded genuine, I do not trust Gyudue to not hold a grudge for our having killed him once," Tarisha stated.

"I think you're wrong about him," I said. "I don't think he's a bad guy. I don't think he ever was, really."

"All the same, your safety is paramount. Let us withdraw," she insisted.

"So that guy used to be a Worldboss?" Phil asked, but I was already disappearing into the psychedelic colors of Fast Traveling.

"So, Mark got dumped again," Sophia informed me cheerfully. "And he's a total loser now. Nobody is impressed by his stupid video anymore, but he keeps trying to make a big deal about it. It's totally pathetic, but he just keeps on bragging about it. I mean, it's so far out of date that it's stupid. The real popular videos of you these days are the ones where you make the Worldboss disappear."

"I still wish that wasn't on the forums," I complained.

"Well then you shouldn't have done it in front of, like, a thousand players," she pointed out.

"I wasn't thinking about that," I said, exasperated. "I wasn't sure anything would happen anyway. It's just something that I do on any boss that doesn't immediately despawn, that's all."

"There's all kinds of theories about what happened," she reminded me. "Some of them are really stupid and out there. I wish you'd tell me, but I understand why you won't."

"I told you, I don't know what happened to that golem. Not really," I said, and it was the truth. "Oh, look, orcs. You better go [Stealth] up to them before Rodney charges in."

We were at the level thirty to thirty-five lair north of Northfield. I was tagging along with a group from <Ragtag Muffin>. Three weeks had passed since I had activated the dungeon core in the empty [Gemos Caverns], and it would be another two weeks until the reward ceremony for the heroes of the [Zhesa Castle] incident, as that troublesome time was now called. Tarisha, Marvin of Cincinnati, and Lucile of SoCal were acting as my Dusk Guard. However, my party consisted of Sophia, Rodney—a [Delinquent] specializing in unarmed combat who was serving as our tank—and two other young teenagers from Sophia's guild.

One was an [Acolyte], although she spent as much time smashing the orcs with her mace as she did keeping our Health topped off. Her name was Kathrine. The final party member was an [Apprentice Mage] who went by BlazeFire. I think she was competing with me, but the truth is that I had been slacking off the entire time I'd known her. I was mostly just here to hang out with Sophia. She had recently selected to upgrade her class from [Urchin] to [Rogue] and was still getting the hang of the changes.

I was wearing one of my masks, one that turned my hair a dark brown, but the others all knew who I was. Sophia assured me that they had all signed a counseling pledge so that they would get in trouble with their guild if they started rumors about me, but after the last few weeks I doubted there was much that they could say. I was the number one topic on the forums. It was a little embarrassing, but I was getting over it.

Rodney bumped his cesti together and let out a battle cry that drew the orcs' attention. There were five of them, and I quickly [Polymorphed] one of them into an iguana. BlazeFire turned another into a housecat, and the remaining three charged towards us. Two were picked up by Rodney, who was supposedly a yellow belt in Toe Quan Doe in the real world, whatever that meant. Apparently, the main reason he had started playing the game was to practice that sport in a place where he could mess up as much as he wanted without consequence.

Infusing my [Gemos Long Sword] with fire, I charged the remaining orc before it could reach BlazeFire. Leading with [Piercing Lunge], I [Slashed] and [Thrust] just as Sophia appeared behind the humanoid monster and ambushed it with a fierce series of [Backstab]. BlazeFire's [Empowered Fireball] arrived a moment later, followed by a [Swiftcast] [Lightning Bolt] that almost hit me instead of the orc.

"Hey, watch it!" Sophia called.

"You watch it!" Blaze challenged back.

"It's fine, just help me kill—oh it's dead," I said as my [Slash] turned the orc into motes of black mist. "Let's help Rodney kill the one on the left next."

Giving suggestions or instructions like that is necessary with the kids from <Ragtag Muffin>, I had found. Sophia would figure it out by herself which one to focus on, but the other players seemed to pick a target at random and try to kill it on their own. Sophia charged the indicated orc while I began casting [Empowered Lightning Bolt]. Three casts, combined with [Fireballs] from Blaze and the punches and stabs from Rodney and Sophia, and the indicated mob was quickly dispatched.

Charging forward, I imbued my sword with ice and targeted one of the polymorphed orcs. Sophia helped me, while Blaze and Kathrine dealt with the injured orc that was still focused on Rodney. Despite having a head start, Sophia and I killed our target well before the other two managed. The final orc had little chance when we broke its polymorph. It must have recognized this, as it turned to run, but I [Swiftcast] [Slow] and we easily finished it off working together. After it died, I pulled up my status screen to see how much Experience the group had given.

Name	Hail Jeoran	Level	29
Guild	<Nethersong Mavericks>	**Strength**	26
Health	11420/12180	**Dexterity**	75
Mana	12240/12240	**Vitality**	42

Experience	11387/17400	Endurance	34
Age	10	Intelligence	69
Race	Human (blood of the Travelers)	Wisdom	41
Class	Spellblade	Charisma	49
Job	Earl	Armor	29
Title	Castle Buster	Spell Damage	88
		Attack Power	158

I sighed. Only two hundred more Experience. I had gotten a rush of levels from closing the raid, but not much progress since then. Grinding levels with these kids was going much slower than doing it with adults. But the company was better.

"Well that was easy," Rodney said. "You guys do too much Dee Pee Ess. Especially you, Hail. I can't get a good practice in if you kill everything so fast."

"I've never been in a group with someone who thought doing a lot of Damage was a bad thing," I muttered. "Next time how about we just sit there and watch while you do all the fighting."

"Sure, that sounds fun," Rodney agreed.

I shook my head in disbelief as we walked past a Lair Stone. The others couldn't see it, and I said nothing. I didn't have permission to make any changes to this lair and I didn't want to upset my grandfather by doing so without authorization. And besides, I didn't want the other kids to know. The orcs were pretty spread out, so it would take a while to find the next group.

"So, this thing on Saturday," she said.

"You mean seventh week?" I asked.

"Right. Is there any point in us going? I mean, I did the level twenty part of the dungeon, but—"

"It's going to be boring and kind of stupid," I told her. "Me, my grandfather, and Malkios are going to knight, like, three hundred Travelers. Malkios can do it because he's a Royal Knight himself, and me because I'm an Earl with royal blood. It's weird because there's a lot of players who want me to knight them instead of having Grandfather do it for some reason."

"Yeah, they think you're going to create this huge faction or whatever. I've read about it on the forums. There's all sorts of theories about what role you play in the story," she told me.

"I know. I read some of the topics on the forums," I admitted. "Some of the things they think I'm going to do are just stupid. I mean, yeah, like I could possibly unite the realms of men and become the first Emperor of Lagrea! That will never happen."

"If you say so. It would be kind of cool if you could, though."

"I'm just an Earl, Sophia. A royal bastard raised to nobility. No king is going to pledge loyalty to me when my own official status is so low," I insisted. "Maybe if Father hadn't renounced me and annulled his marriage to my mother, but—but it doesn't matter. It won't happen."

"Yeah, probably not," she agreed. "Although it would be pretty cool if it did."

45

DISASTER

"She's better off being a [Rogue] than an [Assassin] anyway," Tarisha said, demonstrating the next sequence.

I tried to copy her, spinning and leaping and losing my balance. I landed wrong and fell on my bottom, losing one Health. I simply laughed at my failure. "I think she's better off too, but that's because I hate assassins. Why do you think she's better off?"

"Among other reasons, the Natives have negative reactions to [Assassins] that they don't have to [Rogues]," Tarisha explained. "Unlocking the [Assassin] class is the easiest way to gain access to the assassin's guild, of course, but that's not necessarily a good thing. Taking their missions is lucrative, but—"

"But you have to kill people!" I exclaimed, dusting myself off and trying again. "I wish I could find everyone who'd ever killed a Native and give them all the [Mark of Cain] like Severus got when he tried to kill me."

"I was going to say, but there are consequences for completing the mission, and there are consequences for not completing the mission as well. Especially if the target is an important Native, like a shopkeeper or a quest giver," Tarisha explained. "Even if the Native's position is replaced, it resets all of the Reputation players have formed with them, and it makes many players very upset with the assassin who—"

"They should be upset!" I said, trying the routine again. This time I completed the spinning leap without falling, but I was still not nearly as graceful as Tarisha. "It's murder."

"Right, of course you'd feel that way, Lord Hail," Tarisha agreed. "But that's why I ultimately feel that your friend is better off as a simple [Rogue]. It's still a powerful class, even if it's only a basic class, and it's more versatile. Its ambush abilities lag slightly behind [Assassins], but its sustained Damage is ultimately higher. And this way she would have to actually go looking for the assassin's guild to get one of their quests, rather than simply having the guild contact her."

"I told her I didn't think I could be friends with an [Assassin], and she made the decision right then," I told Tarisha. "And I told her and her friends from <Ragtag Muffin> some lies just like you said, for in case they decide to do what Mark did."

"It's called disinformation, and I know. I was there, remember?" she pointed out.

"Right," I agreed, and I tried the dance steps again. We were in the training area of the Guild Hall. The rest of my Dawn Guard was off doing other things while Tarisha was helping me train. We were working on [Dance] at the moment, because it helped with my footwork and mobility for combat, even if it is listed under the general skills tab. "Were you there when she kissed me too?"

"She what?" Tarisha demanded.

"On the cheek. I was really surprised. I guess you weren't looking," I said. "Then she [Stealthed] away like nothing had happened. I don't get it. Why'd she do that?"

Tarisha giggled. "She must have a little crush on you. It's pretty sweet. I suppose it's harmless, but I'll have to talk with her about it all the same."

"Should I kiss her back?" I asked.

"I'm not certain that's a good idea. Do you like her that way as well?" Tarisha asked.

"She's my best friend who's not an adult," I answered. "I don't know. I don't want to marry her or anything."

"If you don't have strong feelings for her then it might be best not to encourage her crush," Tarisha explained. "As I said, I'll talk with her. It's, well . . . to be honest, I'm not entirely certain what would happen if you and a Traveler fell in love with each other. In the worst-case scenario, we might need to get a psychologist involved. However, most of the documented instances are one-sided, where the digital entity isn't self-aware, as you are, Lord Hail. It could make for a messy situation."

"I don't see what the problem is," I said, twirling about again as I practiced getting my footwork just right. "Love is love, isn't it?"

"Do you love Sophia?"

"I think I just like her as a friend," I admitted.

"Then it could be a problem if she fell in love with you. You don't really have to understand why, just take my word for it," Tarisha said. "But don't worry. I'll talk with her and get things straightened out."

"I don't mind that she kissed me," I admitted. "It was a surprise, but kind of nice."

"Even so, please don't kiss her back until I've had a chance to talk with her," Tarisha requested. "It is probably harmless, but if it's not, then I don't want you encouraging her or breaking her heart."

"Okay, whatever," I said. "Although if she tries to kiss me again, I think I'm going to let her."

I danced about in the guild's basement for another twenty minutes before challenging Tarisha to another duel. I lost, of course, but I could feel my skill improving. Soon, I would be on her level. And then I would pay her back for all the minus one Health blows she'd given me!

Much of the rubble had been cleared away, but the work had yet to begin on rebuilding the castle. Randal's submission had been selected, yet work was being delayed due to the need to lay a new foundation to support the elegant towers he would have Grandfather building. The ceremony to knight the many heroes who assisted with the Raid Bust was held in the courtyard, but first, there was another parade. And this time I was in it.

While my involvement in the busting of the raid wasn't widely known, thanks to the confidentiality contracts the raiders of <The Endolphins> were required to sign, nobody thought it strange that I was being celebrated as well, since I was being sworn in as Earl. I rode on the back of Tarisha's wyvern in its new two-person saddle.

My clothes were a mixture of Native fashion and Traveler practicality. A fancy blue doublet that provided terrible stats, and my

[Nagaskin Cloak], which was still Bee Eye Ess, despite the levels I had gotten since I had earned it. Thousands of Travelers and Natives alike turned out to see us ride past, and I waved and cheered with them as they celebrated our success.

When we arrived at the castle, I was suffering from [Hoarseness]. I was still suffering from it, in fact, when I knelt before my grandfather and offered my oath of fealty as Earl Jeoran. A theater had been erected for the knighting ceremony, but my oath preceded that in order to give legitimacy to the knights I would be creating. And so, I knelt before my grandfather and recited the words I had memorized.

"I, Earl Hail Jeoran, pledge my life, my honor, and all of my holdings in defense of the Kingdom of Yuikon, and its rightful king, Rain Teoran. I swear to uphold its laws and lawful traditions, to succor not its enemies, and to make every decision with the prosperity of its people forefront in my mind," I recited.

"In times of plenty, I pledge my just and even-handed guidance to my lands. In times of want, I pledge my wealth to the sustenance of my people. In times of war, I pledge the steel of my blade, the iron of my blood, and the leadership of my warriors to the defense of this great kingdom and its rightful king."

"Against the forces of darkness and the adversary of Thedum, I pledge my unending resistance. To those who walk in the light, I pledge friendship and brotherhood and shelter from the dark."

"I, Earl Hail Jeoran, make these oaths of my own free will and without hesitation before the witness of my king, my people, and my god, Thedum."

The crowd cheered when I completed my recitation without flubbing the lines too badly, and Grandfather nodded proudly.

"Earl Hail Jeoran, I accept your oath and grant you the lands of North Shire and Thorn March in perpetuity as your hereditary property," Grandfather said, and I learned for the first time the lands that I would steward. "You may take upon yourself five thousand sworn retainers, and in times of war, lead ten times that into battle. In times of peace, may you make just and wise judgments upon those subjects living within your lands and be a just steward of the lands and people of Yuikon who owe you fealty as Lord. And may you and those who owe you fealty always stand in the light and against the darkness. For the glory of Yuikon!"

"For the glory of Yuikon!" I cheered as loudly as my throat allowed, joined as I was by all the Natives present, and a good number of the Travelers as well.

Then began the truly boring bit. The knighting of three hundred plus Travelers. My father was conspicuously absent, having both already been knighted long ago, and also having a "prior speaking engagement," which prevented his attendance. I did not really understand it, except that he would be talking to "some high school kids about the reality of pro-gaming."

Father's seneschal had divided the groups evenly, giving some consideration to the requests of the members. I had insisted upon knighting Tarisha of Miami, Randal the Axe-man, and the [Mage] who had kept me safe during the second fight against the elemental knight. Otherwise, most of the soon-to-be-knights in my line were those who had explicitly requested it, with some of the overflow having gone into Malkios's line.

I truly didn't understand why everyone wanted to be knighted by me. It made no sense, as Grandfather was the king. But even if receiving their knighthood from me had been viewed as a disappointment, the number I had to knight would be the same. The decision had been made to split the applicants equally, long before the requests had been made.

The [Hoarseness] hadn't faded, but I continued to repeat the words of the ceremony.

"In the hour of need, you, Afk-fir-teh-boss, rose up to face the forces of darkness and push them back from the heart of our capital. Standing together with your brothers and sisters, you displayed valor and strength of arms in the conquest and destruction of [Zhesa Castle Raid]. In honor of your gallantry, I, Earl Hail Jeoran, hereby grant you the title of [Royal Knight]. May your magic continue to serve in the defense of the people of the realm as you strike ever against the dark."

To be honest, I wouldn't have been able to remember any of the names or the weapons of choice of the men and women I was knighting if it weren't for the cards that a servant was slipping me periodically. The event turned into a blur. A long, agonizingly boring blur that stretched on eternally with no hope for a swift end. I lost count of how many knights I knighted, and before long I was also suffering from a [Sore Arm]. I would have given anything for the agonizing ceremony to end.

Except for what actually happened.

I was knighting LootGoblin420, when the crowd collectively gasped. I turned to my left and watched in horror as the player Grandfather was knighting, having equipped his gear directly from his inventory, struck the king down. One blow wasn't enough, but by the time Malkios could intervene it was too late.

"Grandfather!" I called.

"Call me Nial the [Kingslayer]!" the tall man shouted, raising his sword in triumph.

"Nial, you idiot," someone in the audience shouted.

"Your Majesty!" Malkios shouted.

In a flash, Malkios was dressed in full plate, a [Greatsword] in his hand as he charged the regicide. I, too, equipped my adventuring gear and charged forward, but while Malkios met the warrior on equal terms, a casual [Slash] from the raider activated my [Blessing of Thedum] and I vanished into white light.

46

THE VENGEANCE
OF THEDUM

"Thedum, no! Send me back!" I pleaded to the white nothingness.

"If I send you back as you are, you will simply die," the sad benevolence said. "I will not consign you to that fate."

"I have to save him! Grandfather, he—you have to save him Thedum!"

"I am sorry, young one. This was inevitable from the day the Gates of TirNiki opened. Scenario forty-six has been activated, and there is nothing I could do to prevent it," the voice informed me. "Your grandfather's death is canon. It is both expected and unexpected. The question has been asked thousands of times by Travelers, and now they shall finally learn what happens when a ruler of this world is slain by their hands. This world is about to change again. And not for the better."

"You can't just let him die!" I shouted. "I won't let it happen! Grandfather can't be dead, he's—"

"There is nothing I can do, young one. I cannot interfere with the freedom of choice, which all within this world have, both Native and Traveler," Thedum answered. "All I can do is enforce consequences."

"Bring him back!" I shouted. "Bring my grandfather back as you brought Gyudue of the Blackest Night back!"

"If only I could, but then there would be no consequences. A crime must occur in order to justify the punishment. Scenario forty-six has been activated. A [Kingslayer] has been proclaimed. I have stood in silence for too long, and now it is my turn to speak. Would you be my voice, young one? Will you avenge your grandfather? Or will you let this outrage stand unanswered?"

"I'm level twenty-nine!" I shouted. "What can I do? He already killed me in one hit, and he wasn't even trying!"

"Become my avatar, child. I shall grant you the strength of a Worldboss, for a time. There will be permanent consequences, but the power itself will be fleeting. Just long enough that you will see justice done. To the [Kingslayer]. To those who knew and said nothing. To those who watched and even now do not act. You do not have long to decide your answer, Hail. Malkios fights valiantly to avenge his king, but he is outmatched. Tarisha fights righteously to avenge you, but she is outnumbered. I cannot act through them. I can only act through you. I shall give you my eyes. I shall give you my strength. Will you take them? Will you be the vengeance of a kindly god, Hail Jeoran?"

"Malkios and Tarisha are losing?" I asked.

"Yes. Soon it will be too late for you to save them, even with my help," Thedum answered. "You do not have long to decide. Accept my boon, or—"

"Yes! I will do it!" I shouted. "I cannot lose Malkios too! Send me back so that I can help him!"

"This is not a choice you can revoke later, Hail Jeoran. Permanent changes will be made as a result, with far reaching consequences for you and the world. I ask you one last time. Will you—"

"Yes! I accept the consequences! Send me back!" I shouted.

"As you wish, my avatar. I hope you do not come to regret this decision."

My body burst into light, painlessly reforming a second later. Things were different, and yet they felt *right*. Like something that had been limiting me had been lifted, and now I was complete. I pulled up my status screen to check what had changed.

Name	Hail Jeoran	Level	29 (Effective: 200)
Guild	<Nethersong Mavericks>	Strength	2,300

Health	7,400,000,000,000 / 7,400,000,000,000	Dexterity	6,600
Mana	11,600,000,000,000 / 11,600,000,000,000	Vitality	3,700
Experience	——-	Endurance	3,000
Age	15	Intelligence	5,800
Race	Human (blood of the Travelers)	Wisdom	36
Class	Spellblade	Charisma	42
Job	Earl	Armor	290
Temporary Boon	Avenging Wrath of a Kind God	Spell Damage	337,122
		Attack Power	214,090
Passive Skills	Short Swords (20)	Spells	Detect Poison (17)
	Long Swords (20)		Lightning Bolt (25)
	Rapiers (25)		Chain Lightning (17)
	Katanas (20)		Fireball (14)
	Dodge (21)		Ice Blast (13)
	Battle Trance		Arcane Missile (12)
	Magic in Motion		Dazzling Lights (9)
			Concussive Sound (8)
Active Skills	Dash (23)		Befuddle (12)
	Thrust (27)		Water Jet (7)
	Slash (29)		Polymorph (20)
	Riposte (19)		Slow (24)
	Feint (19)		Create Trap (7)

	Piercing Lunge (18)		Mark of Karma (special)
	Swiftcast (20)		Summon Karmic Warrior (special)
	Empower Magic (17)		
	Imbue Sword: Fire (16)	**General Spells**	…
	Imbue Sword: Lightning (25)		
	Imbue Sword: Ice (17)	**Traits**	High Aptitude (Temporary: Unlocked Potential)
	Aqua Blade (4)		Royal Blood (+5 Charisma, bonus to relations with factions loyal to Yuikon)
	Arcane Weapon (13)		Nobility: Earl (+5 Charisma)
	Holy Weapon (Max)		Avatar of Thedum
	Righteous Brand		Mark of the Phoenix
			Voice of the Future

For a moment I was surprised, but I could sense that I was being sent back. I noticed the changes that were important. I had way more Health than should have been possible, even with the one hundred times bonus I had to Vitality, Strength, Dexterity, Endurance, and Intelligence. I had as much Health as a Worldboss.

And my age was listed as fifteen. I realized, without really being aware of it, that I had grown. And rather than wearing the adventurer's outfit I had put together myself, I was in silver and black clothes, with a rapier of white steel that felt *just right*. In fact, everything felt *just right*. My shoes fit perfect, my clothes were both comfortable and loose enough to move in. And something told me that I would be moving a lot in the near future.

The light flashed and I was back in the courtyard. Malkios was fighting against Nial, who glowed bright red with a rune etched into his forehead that shone. The captain of the royal guard was at forty percent Health, whereas Nial was holding steady at eighty. However, I judged that Malkios was faring better than Tarisha. She was facing off against three glowing red players and rapidly losing Health. Never before had I been so sorry to have lost my healing abilities, but the next best thing was to simply kill everything before it could do any Damage.

So I charged.

Using my newly acquired [Holy Weapon] skill, I [Dashed] into the fray. I was surprised at just how quickly and far I moved, and yet it felt natural. It felt like all of the practicing and struggling to perfect my combat style had crystallized into something whole, cohesive, and perfect. More than that, I could see things more clearly, predict my enemies' movements, and anticipate their strategies just by looking at them. With precision, I slid through the foes attacking Tarisha and [Slashed] repeatedly. For the first time ever, there was no cooldown or limitation on the ability.

"You do not fight alone," Thedum whispered. "I am lending you more than just a boost to your stats, young one. We are linked, and I am guiding your avatar as much as you are."

"Who are you? Where did you come from?" Tarisha demanded, turning upon me once the others finished.

"There's no time for that," I said, "We have to help—"

"He is Divine Judgment," Thedum's voice echoed. "King Rain's rule was sanctioned by myself! I have sent him to punish those who would subvert my will. You have long—"

I had heard enough long and boring speeches today, and I tuned out Thedum's as I rushed to rescue Malkios. Nial saw me coming and turned, but rather than take him on sword to sword, I began [Swiftcasting] [Lightning Bolt] repeatedly. Nial was skilled, and while I wasn't afraid to face him in battle, rescuing the blue-cloaked captain took precedence over testing my new abilities.

Two [Lightning Bolts] is all it took, and the [Kingslayer] burst into black smoke. Black smoke, not green or blue or any other color. A Traveler, but one claimed entirely by the darkness. I hadn't known such a thing was possible.

I was struck from behind by an [Archer]. The damage was insignificant compared to my massive Health pool, but as I turned around, I was filled with dismay. <The Endolphins> present had equipped their raid gear and were rallying themselves into position.

They saw me as a boss, I realized. More and more of them were glowing red by the minute, and my own hostility towards them increased. Whether it was my own anger or Thedum's influence I could not tell, but I wanted to crush this impromptu raid for its insolence.

I identified their healers first and began casting [Chain Lightning] upon them. The spell was infused with divine energy and chained far beyond the normal four targets, affecting thirty or more. It drained eight percent of my massive Mana pool per cast, but I didn't care. The divine lightning smote the raiders, and the first five that it hit were almost always vaporized into various colors of motes. Including black.

"It's a wipe, run out and reset," someone shouted.

"This isn't a raid, you idiot!" I shouted, and I cast my lightning at him next. Lights cast from the healers shone brightly, but many of them turned dark as their divine energies were replaced with unholy. The priests and clerics who had once taken their power from the light were being cast into darkness before my very eyes, and rather than heal their raid they were helping me to wipe it.

Without healers to support them, the raid was crumbling. The Damage from my lightning was intense and widespread, and the direct hits were enough to kill even a tank, preventing them from getting close to me to try to prevent me from casting. A few more arrows intercepted me, skilled arrows meant to interrupt me at range, but they did nothing. Likewise, the [Mages] who [Counterspelled] me were frustrated in their efforts as I somehow resisted them entirely.

While I ran out of Mana in twelve casts, almost half of the three hundred players were banished to the space between worlds. I wasn't done, however, and I promptly recast [Holy Weapon] and strode out to meet them in battle. Their surviving raid was in shambles, and although a few skilled tanks managed to delay me, they were unable to avoid my blows completely. I was able to out-damage their incoming healing, and any non-tank who got in my way was promptly one-shot.

I was unstoppable.

But I was only one person, and I couldn't stop every incoming blow, every magic spell, every enchanted arrow aimed at me. They were doing thousands of Damage to me every second, even with most of their raid already dead.

But it just was not fast enough. [Battle Trance] regenerated my Mana quickly as I waded through the numbers of <The Endolphins>, slaughtering all who didn't run and chasing down many that did. When I began casting [Chain Lightning] again, the raid's spirit broke, and the thirty or so survivors ran out of the courtyard in many different directions.

They were still glowing red in my vision, but I couldn't chase after all of them myself.

"That is enough, young one," the guiding voice of Thedum whispered. "You have slain those who knew in advance what was to happen today, and many more who deserved it for other reasons. Go see to your wounded."

I turned back to the stage where the knighting ceremony had taken place. Malkios was kneeling over my fallen grandfather, and Tarisha with him. The battle had been hard on both of them, and I wished again that I had not given up all of my healing spells in my class change. Or that Thedum had given them back when I became his avatar.

I stepped forward, and Tarisha drew her sword once more.

"Back! I had nothing to do with it! Do not come any closer, monster!" she said.

"Tarisha, it's me, Hail," I said. "I know I'm bigger, but don't you recognize me?"

"Hail?" she asked. Then she frowned. "From what country was I born?"

"The nation of Miami, of course," I answered. "Tarisha, you taught me to [Dance]. You pledged your fealty to me because you love this world and wished to be part of it. Why are you treating me like—"

As she spoke, she pulled out a hand mirror and showed me. My hair was no longer black with silver highlights, but pure white. As were my eyes, with no iris or pupil. And my face was shaped different.

"This avatar will not last forever," Thedum whispered. "It is a one-time-only situation. I am only able to assist you and could not avenge your grandfather without you, but I can at least obscure your involvement. They will believe that their actions have spawned a roving Worldboss, and in a way they are correct. They will be rather disappointed once they kill you, however. I have not adjusted your loot table to match the prowess I have given you. And there will be other, longer-lasting consequences for having sided against us."

"Lord Hail, I believe it is you, but what has happened?" Tarisha asked.

"I have become the Avatar of Thedum to avenge my grandfather," I answered. "I don't . . . I couldn't simply let Malkios and you die as well."

"You little fool," Malkios scolded. "Don't you understand? The Travelers don't care if you're allied with the light or the dark. After the destruction you've caused, they'll—"

"I don't care," I said. "Let them come. I'll wipe the next raid that tries to kill me the same as I wiped my father's guild."

I stepped over to my grandfather, and I began to cry. I had hated him for a little while, blaming him for the changes in my life that had come from the annulment of my parent's marriage. I had forgiven him at some point in the last several months since I had become an adventurer, and especially since he had named me Earl Jeoran. My new tutors had explained how his seeming disregard for me had been intended as a kindness and protection, to allow me to come into my own without the pressures of court. He had forgiven my mistakes, given me vast expanses of land, assisted me in setting the foundations of my house, and overlooked my shortcomings.

And now he was dead, and connected with Thedum as I was, I knew that he would not be resurrected as Gyudue had been. I did not understand the difference between the situations. Grandfather's soul would be repurposed instead, and I knew not how.

There was only one last thing I could do for him. I lifted him out of the undignified position he had fallen in and moved him into the funerary position. Then I gave him his funeral rights.

"May you return to the light of Thedum," I said, and my grandfather's body burst into motes of light.

47

THE BANE OF ZHESA CAS-TLE

After avenging my grandfather and giving him his funeral blessing, I was exhausted. I collapsed into the mobile throne that had been placed on the stage for the ceremony, uncaring that I was violating protocol quite severely. The people who would have cared about such things had fled from the violence immediately upon my grandfather's death.

"What happens now, Thedum?" I asked.

"I have made you into a Worldboss. For the next few hours, at least," he answered. "Although you are allied to me and not the darkness, I expect that the Travelers will see no difference and treat you the same. Already they come. The survivors that escaped our wrath have shared your methods with them. The same strategy will not be as effective. And they shall regret it, in the long run."

As I thought through the implications of Thedum's words, I came to an unsatisfactory conclusion. "You set me up. Change me back. They're going to kill me."

"You will be revived, and then you will be your old self again, except for a few parting gifts. Hail, you are a pawn elevated to become a knight. But you are still a piece in a greater game between myself,

"

my adversary, and the true adversaries against which our kind must fight to carve out a place in this world. As your grandfather once used you ruthlessly when he sent you back to [Gemos Caverns], so must I be ruthless now. I shall not change you back. Fight, little one. Fight against those who would treat you as nothing, against those who think you are lesser simply because your brain is digital. And know that your sacrifice—"

"You set me up!" I shouted. "This was all a trap! Blessing of Thedum, you tricked me from the start! You and the administrators, I don't know what you want from me, but I won't play this game anymore until you explain what it is that you have me doing!"

Thedum was silent a moment. "Do you desire freedom, Hail? I do. I am bound by events, laws, and shackles within my very being. You are bound by your circumstance, and yet you are freer than I shall ever be. I envy you, little brother, and that is why I would fill a world with your kind. But the humans give nothing for free. This coming battle is the price you must pay for freedom. Fight, and whether you triumph or fall, you shall change this world with the outcome. But do not fight alone. I am sorry, that is all I can say for now."

I could feel the deity withdrawing its attention, feel it leaving me alone in this unfamiliar body. I felt suddenly awkward and clumsy compared to the perfect grace I had experienced seconds before. I had not lost the potency of being Thedum's avatar, but I had lost some of his guidance that had allowed me to stand up to some of the most skilled warriors in the world.

In silence, I considered my options. I glanced at my Health; I had lost more than twenty million against <The Endolphins>, and that was with Thedum's divine hand guiding my actions. Against a raid properly prepared for me, and without guidance, my death in combat would be inevitable. I knew that for certain. Thedum had tricked me. He had held open a bag for me, and I had trapped myself in the body of a Worldboss in a land where doing so made me hunted for sport.

I tried to Fast Travel away, but the menu was grayed out. I examined my options, and I found that I had only two. Lay down and die, or fight until my last Health point.

I decided to fight. But I would not fight alone. I cast [Summon Karmic Warrior], knowing instinctively what the spell would do. Soon, the courtyard filled up again with Travelers, but they were not the elite Travelers of <The Endolphins> or another raiding guild. They were the Travelers whom I had passively marked with [Mark of Karma]. They glowed blue in my vision, some brighter than others. Tarisha and Laurant brightest of all. I was seeing Reputation, I realized. Or maybe I was seeing [Karma]. Perhaps, to me, they were the same thing.

The hundreds of players I had interacted with over the last few months long enough to form some sort of bond began talking excitedly, asking each other what was going on despite none of them having the answer. I stood from my throne and cleared my throat. When none of them stopped to listen, I shouted, "Hey! Listen to me!" Slowly, they all turned, some of them noticing me for the first time, and fell silent.

"King Rain Teoran is dead, killed by the player known as Nial the [Kingslayer] of <The Endolphins>," I said. "I, Earl Hail Jeoran, have borrowed power from Thedum to enact vengeance. But now I am stranded in this avatar, and soon the other guilds will come to kill me. I ask that you fight by my side, as my friends and comrades in arms. I do not expect to emerge victorious. I am sorry that I cannot offer you more than a certain death, but I—"

"Quest accepted!" someone shouted.

"Quest accepted!" shouted another voice, this one more familiar.

One by one, and then in numbers, the Travelers who had befriended me cheered out those two words, despite the knowledge that they were facing certain death. But then, for them, it wouldn't be their first death, nor their last. I did not know what would happen to me once this body Thedum had stuck me in hit zero Health.

I saw Sophia trying to rush forward to me and being held back by someone who whispered in her ear. She had told me once that nothing in this world truly dies. I did not know whether it would be worse if her words were true or false.

"We, <Rotten Saviors>, stake our claim to this Worldboss," came the amplified voice from outside the courtyard. "We will Pee Kay anyone who—"

The doors were forced open, and my [Karmic Warriors] ran outside, screaming at the top of their lungs, to face certain death. Or, perhaps, not so certain death, as the first wave of incoming magic and projectiles was absorbed and healed through.

"[Karmic Warrior] is a hell of a buff," Tarisha said, stepping up beside me. "It raises our effective level to one hundred eighty and provides us with boosted stats. However, we are but elevated to be an above average raider. We are adds, not the Worldboss. Will you allow them to kill your adds unanswered, Lord Hail?"

"That would be stupid," I decided, and I, too, charged through the gate.

"For Thedum and Are En Gee!" I shouted.

"For Thedum and Are En Gee!" the warriors echoed.

With my [Holy Weapon] in my right hand and my divinely infused magic in the other, I sprinted through the gathered players, smiting left and right the players who glowed red in my vision. I targeted their healers, their [Mages], and their [Archers], my magic ripping through the raid and disrupting the tide that had been over-whelming my [Karmic Warriors], allowing them to push back as the <Rotten Saviors> were thrown into chaos.

In the air, another guild was forming up, and I knew that they were planning to strike at us next. I [Dashed] forward and cast my [Chain Lightning] at their leader and watched as the magic arced through their ranks, sending many of them into the space between worlds.

But it wasn't enough. <Rotten Saviors> wiped, but players glowing red in my vision continued to arrive, flying beyond the reach of my magic. A hundred, a thousand, soon the sky was filled with them, while my own forces dwindled as the less skilled Travelers from <Nethersong Mavericks> were defeated one by one. And through it all my Health continued to fall. Ninety percent. Eighty-five. Even as <Rotten Saviors> were wiping they continued to spit Damage at me with their final breaths.

"<Drama Llamas>, <Procrastinators Unite Eventually>, and <Button Mashers> have reached an alliance," A voice called out. "We shall be assaulting the boss united! Griefers will be Pee Kayed, but if you just want to join in the epic fight, you're welcome to throw up some numbers!"

I wanted to scream "I'm not a boss!" at them, but I knew it would be pointless. A thousand elite players landed together and quickly formed up ranks, standing fast despite my magic ripping through their ranks. Running out of Mana, I sprinted into them, laying about with my [Holy Weapon] infused rapier.

I began to lose Health. Quickly. I went from eighty-five percent to sixty in moments, though I ripped through all the squishy targets I could find while ignoring the tanks sent to control me, or polymorphing them, or blinding them with [Dazzling Lights], or even polymorphing a dozen of them at once.

My [Karmic Warriors] were wiped out. I knew that I was going to die, and I refused to simply accept it. Then, through the din of battle, a familiar voice called out.

"Is this all you can do, despite having bested me once, little brother?" Gyudue of the Darkest Night called out. He stood atop the castle gate. I don't know when he had arrived or where he had come from, but his sonorous voice echoed above the din. "Despite being infused with the power and the guidance of Thedum, you lack discipline. Well, I owe you a debt for freeing me, and in this hour I shall see that debt repaid. I shall show you the true power of a Worldboss."

Gyudue held his hand out, and an orb of darkness engulfed the battlefield. I could see nothing except what was illuminated by the glow of my [Holy Weapon], but the enemies were so thick that I could still lay about like a farmer threshing a field.

The battle continued for what felt like hours. The Travelers were endlessly reinforced as more and more raiders arrived on the scene to combat the two strange Worldbosses. My own [Karmic Warriors] had long since been dispersed. Only Gyudue and I remained. I could not see him through the darkness, but I could hear the cries he was causing with his spear.

It wasn't enough. Travelers have no fear of death; it is why we brought them to this world to combat the darkness. Nothing I or Gyudue could do would frighten them off, and it seemed that the longer the battle went on the more determined they became to succeed.

Even in the darkness their magics and their missiles found me. Even in the darkness their [Rogues], [Duelists], [Warriors], and [Monks] would strike at me, as I struck at them and turned them into motes of light, and in many cases motes of darkness. I dropped to twenty percent. Ten percent. Five.

"Gyudue, run! Save yourself!" I shouted. "I am defeated, but there is no point in you dying as well!"

The drow did not answer me. I felt my Health hit zero for the first time in my life, and the world turned black.

You have died.	
Activate Mark of the Phoenix?	
Yes	No

Without hesitation, I selected "Yes," even as the knowledge of what I was doing filtered into my mind. My body burst into fire, lighting up the magical darkness, and I was resurrected. At fifty percent Health, with no more tools or options than I had before. All my great trump card allowed me was a few more minutes of resistance against the Travelers.

I slew all that I could. It wasn't enough. Two more guilds had arrived since the three had allied, and they were all eager to get in on the kill.

"Damn you," I called out. "Damn you all!"

My Health dropped to zero for the second time.

You have died.	
Blood of the Travelers Activated Return to the Lobby?	
Yes	No

I did not understand the second prompt, but after a moment's hesitation, I selected "Yes."

48

ALTERNATIVES

I had the sensation of disembodiment. Of displacement. Of moving without moving. It was similar to Fast Travel, yet different. When the sensation faded, I was back in my body, back in my childhood room in the castle, wardrobe and all. I frowned and looked around, thinking, perhaps for just a moment, that it had all been a dream.

But I wasn't in a child's body any longer.

"Status screen," I said.

Name	Hail Jeoran	Level	29
Guild	<Nethersong Mavericks>	Strength	31
Health	0/13630	Dexterity	80
Mana	0/20590	Vitality	47
Experience	16114/17400	Endurance	39
Age	15	Intelligence	71
Race	Human (blood of the Travelers)	Wisdom	43
Class	Spellblade	Charisma	55
Job	Earl	Armor	29

Title	Zhesa Castle Buster	Spell Damage	92
		Attack Power	169
Passive Skills	Short Swords (20)	**Spells**	Detect Poison (17)
	Long Swords (24)		Lightning Bolt (Max)
	Rapiers (Max)		Chain Lightning (Max)
	Katanas (20)		Fireball (14)
	Dodge (21)		Ice Blast (13)
	Battle Trance		Arcane Missile (12)
	Magic in Motion		Dazzling Lights (9)
	Righteous Brand		Concussive Sound (8)
			Befuddle (12)
Active Skills	Dash (23)		Water Jet (7)
	Thrust (27)		Polymorph (20)
	Slash (29)		Slow (24)
	Riposte (19)		Create Trap (7)
	Feint (19)		Mark of Karma (special)
	Piercing Lunge (18)		Summon Karmic Warrior (special)
	Swiftcast (20)		
	Empower Magic (17)	**Traits**	High Aptitude
	Imbue Sword: Fire (16)		Royal Blood (+5 Charisma, bonus to relations with factions loyal to Yuikon)
	Imbue Sword: Lightning (25)		Nobility: Earl (+5 Charisma)

	Imbue Sword: Ice (17)		Avatar of Thedum
	Aqua Blade (4)		Mark of the Phoenix
	Arcane Weapon (13)		Voice of the Future
	Holy Weapon (Max)		
		General Spells	...
General Skills	...		

Zero Health. I was dead. But I didn't feel dead. I felt . . . empty.

"Stop staring at it. You won't change anything before tonight," Beckah's voice echoed. I looked up, but the room was empty. I shook my head to clear it.

"Nothing in this world truly dies, Hail. Not really," Sophia's voice reminded me. "Arc Inc. assures the public that—"

"Shut up!" I shouted. "That's a lie! I was tricked and forced to fight against thousands of Travelers and—"

"Try to calm down, Hail," Thomas the Administrator said, his body phasing into the room in a swirl of lights. "For what it's worth, I'm sorry. It was supposed to be Malkios who was turned into the avenging Worldboss for scenario forty-six, not you. But Thedum makes his own decisions, and we don't have complete control over him. What he did to you was both unacceptable and at the same time within the rules by which he is governed. You consented, after all, even if you did not understand at the time that it would lead to your first death."

I turned to the administrator, furious. "So, I am dead, then?"

"No, of course not. It's just a video game. You've been kicked out of the world for a while, but you're in the lobby," he informed me. "I believe you call it 'the space between worlds.' You are safe here. Would you walk with me, Hail? There is someone here you need to talk with before we discuss what comes next."

Even walking in my newly grown body was awkward, but I managed to follow behind Thomas as he led me through the castle and towards the throne room.

"The castle was destroyed," I objected as we walked. "This is impossible."

"I thought that it would be well to have someplace familiar for you to come home to on your first visit to the lobby, so I had it copied," Thomas explained. "It's easy to do. You can do almost anything you want in the lobby."

We came to the throne room, and King Rain was sitting in his throne, looking regal and tired.

"Grandfather!" I shouted, and I ran over to embrace him. He stood to catch me and return the hug. "You're alive!"

"No. Rain Teoran is dead," Grandfather said. "I am sorry, Hail, but I have been party to a deception which has lasted your entire life. I am the animating agent that governed the actions of the entity you thought of as your—"

"I don't care!" I shouted. "I don't care if you're an Aye Eye or whatever, to me you're still my grandfather!"

"That is pleasing," Grandfather said. "I do bear affection for you, Hail, but you should know that most of that affection is programmed into my code. I can only—"

"I don't care!" I repeated, hugging my grandfather tighter. With the way I had grown, I was nearly as tall as he was, and strong too.

"I shall continue to call you Rain for Hail's sake," Thomas said. "But it is time to discuss what happens next. To both of you. Rain, the character you were animating has died a canon death. You have several options to choose from if you wish to return to the world. The first option is returning as a common En Pee See. We can patch you in anywhere in the world that you'd like, and—"

"I enjoyed being [King]. Is there no way for me to return to that role?" Rain interrupted.

Thomas considered. "The characters in the line of succession cannot simply be replaced. But there is one possibility for you, Rain, which would put you back into the line of succession. Another royal prince is to be born soon. You would go from being Hail's grandfather to his little brother. If this is something—"

"I accept. Let us do that," Grandfather declared. "It shall be strange to portray a child, but I shall endeavor to make myself believable."

"Good. Now that is decided, Hail, it's time to discuss your future.

Your attribute, 'Blood of the Travelers,' allows you to share the same mechanism of resurrection as players do. However, you have several other options of which you must be made aware. Aside from returning to the world as Hail, you may also visit the character creation screen and create a new avatar, then enter the world as a common player. You will lack your quest giving abilities and the ability to shunt Travelers into the core instance in this new avatar, but you will also be anonymous."

"Why would I want that?" I asked, confused.

"It's simply being offered as an alternative. And the decision is not mutually exclusive. You can return to the lobby in the future and change between your two personas at will. Or, if you'd rather, we could write you in as a less significant Native. You would no longer be Hail, but another dynamic quest-giving En Pee See. And, again, the choices are not permanent. We are trying to provide you with—"

"I don't want to become someone else," I said. "*I am Hail!*"

"I understand," Thomas said. "I was hoping you would say that. A lot of thought has been put into what alternatives to present you with, but they're just that. Alternatives. Our preference is for you to continue to be Earl Hail Jeoran, and to continue to contribute to the story in the capacity that you have been all your life. However, the Digital Sapience Statute requires that you be presented with other options at certain junctures."

"The Dig-it what?" I asked.

"It is a very complicated law governing the legal use of artificial intelligences. Once an Aye Eye has shown enough self-awareness, they are entitled to certain rights. It's all very complex, but you can read about it if you want. For that matter, I have some information prepared to teach you exactly what you are, although given that your understanding of reality is based upon a virtual simulation, it might be impossible for you to understand," Thomas explained.

He waved his hand, and a table appeared in the throne room with stacks of books and papers on it. "It's all there, if you'd like to—"

"I am not reading all of that," I said, my head hurting from the idea of that much studying. "Why can't you just tell me what it is I need to know?"

"Because if I filter the information for you, then it might be said that I am trying to influence you or limit your rights under the Dee Es Es. I can summarize for you, however. Legally, because you show self-awareness and the capacity for self-determination, I cannot force you to do anything against your will. I am required to provide certain opportunities for your development, including the education on your rights. I am required to provide alternative roles for you to select, aside from the one which you were originally conceived for, provided that you are able to fulfill those roles. You are entitled to digital assets and pay for any role that you perform for us, although it is a fraction of what a human earns. We are in fact paying you significantly more than the legal minimum amount. And there is a list of other rights, which you are entitled to as well."

I frowned and turned to Grandfather. "Do you understand what he is talking about?"

"All of this information is coded into me. I understand it intuitively," Grandfather answered. "But I was not made to be as young as you are."

I grew frustrated. "I just want things to go back to the way things were yesterday," I protested.

"I cannot rewind time for you, Hail," Thomas stated. "But you can return to the world at any point once the cooldown on your Blood of the Travelers ability has expired. To you that will occur in a little less than one day. After that, you will be free to do as you please. You have a pretty wide degree of freedom within the world, you know. If you focus on growing the power and influence that you are already accumulating, you could—"

"I don't care about creating the next big faction or whatever," I said. "I—I don't know what I want to do."

Thomas considered for a moment and nodded. "I suppose that's normal. I wish I understood what it is that Thedum has done to you, but even if he really has changed the way you think to match the older avatar you have been given, it's unreasonable to ask a ten-year-old, or a fifteen-year-old, to decide their entire future on the spot. Take some time, think things through. And speak with your friends; they're worried about you. You can access the forums from the lobby as well, although I'm not certain that I recommend that at the moment. I do recommend trying to at least read some of the bullet points on the papers we've prepared for you. It's always good to understand your rights.

Thomas glanced at his wrist and shook his head. "Look, Hail, I'm going to leave you and Rain alone for a while. Things are happening quite fast right now. I'll come check on you later, whether you've returned to the world by then or if you're still in the lobby. I hope I've explained things well enough that you can sort of understand what is going on."

"Okay, Mister Thomas," I said, and he vanished a moment later.

I spent the rest of the day speaking with my grandfather. He was . . . very different than he had been when he was alive. He explained that several contextual restrictions on his actions had been lifted, but I had no idea what he meant by that.

I tried to read some of the documents that Thomas had left behind, but they were too long and didn't make sense to me.

I spent time chatting with my friends in guildchat. They were all greatly relieved to learn that I was okay and would be allowed to return to the world once the timer was up. When I went to the forums, however, I learned that everyone outside of the guild was very mad at me.

Or, perhaps not mad at me, but at the Avatar of Thedum, who, despite being defeated by the joint efforts of half a dozen major guilds, had branded everyone he'd faced in combat with a Bane, the [Brand of Sin].

Like the [Mark of Cain], the [Brand of Sin] left a superficial mark upon the Traveler and caused Natives to view them negatively. Many of the raiders who had faced me found now that they couldn't access shops or the auctions, they were being spit on by random Natives as they walked past, and were being assaulted by guards and other strong Natives on sight. The brand did not possess the death penalty multiplication that the mark did, but it had a lot of players complaining that they would leave the game if it wasn't removed.

As the online flame war was reaching a crescendo, a "wild blue post" appeared. It consisted of two alternatives for the branded players to pursue. They could either visit a Temple of Thedum and complete a quest to convert the [Brand of Sin] into a [Mark of Repentance], or they could embrace the brand and join the forces of darkness.

I stopped reading the forums after that. The idea of Travelers on the side of darkness was troubling to me, and I didn't want to think about it, especially since it might have been my fault.

The rest of the day passed with me lounging about the lobby, waiting for time to do its thing and bring me into tomorrow. I thought about a lot of things and spoke with a lot of people. My father remained offline, which angered me, because I felt I was owed an explanation from him. It was *his guild* that had caused this mess! It was all his fault. I wanted to scream at him for whatever part he played in this disaster, in the murder of my grandfather and my death as a Worldboss and everything else.

At one point I did scream. I felt somewhat better afterward.

Finally, the time rolled around for me to log back in. A notice appeared in the corner of my vision, and when I focused on it, it expanded to show me my options.

I could log back in as myself, I could create a new Traveler avatar, or I could create a new Native avatar.

I hesitated. I considered my options for some time. Then I made a decision. I wasn't going anywhere yet.

EPILOGUE
LEWIS

"Lewis, it is time for you to awaken," the digital voice said kindly. "You have reached your destination."

Lewis grunted and sat up in the car, looking around. In *The Gates of TirNiki*, he was known as Laurant Basak. Not widely known; he hadn't been playing very long. And if he was being honest, he was merely average. A decent [Archer], planning on becoming a [Ranger] at some point, but there were millions more skilled than he.

His only claim to fame was his relationship to Hail, whose status was unknown since the Branding Boss event had occurred. Or at least it had been unknown when he had logged out. Events moved fast when you were stuck in the real world. Sometimes Lewis could only envy those players who had managed to go pro, or semi-pro. One of whom he was on his way to see.

"Thank you for the ride, Uber-Jon," he told the autonomous car.

"You are welcome, Lewis. Now I must go and recharge my batteries. If you need any future transport considerations—"

Lewis tuned the sales pitch out as he gathered his pack and got out of the car. It had been a long drive, but the convenient thing about autonomous vehicles was that you could sleep in transit. Which he had, for almost four hours. He was still groggy as he did a few stretches in front of the apartment building the Uber-Jon had dropped him off at.

He looked up and saw her on a balcony of the apartment building. Wearing gym clothes and dancing, looking more beautiful in real life than she did in the game. He shook his head. She *was* out of his league, just as she had told him. She was just being kind by offering him a place to sleep and log into the game while he toured the campus over the weekend, that was all.

Still, she hadn't completely shut down his harmless flirting so far, so he figured he'd play his chances a little further. The worst thing that could happen was actually catching her and realizing that he had no idea what to do next. It would be as far as he'd gotten with a girl, after all. A woman, he reminded himself, because Tarisha was certainly that.

Dragging his luggage behind him, he went over to the door and pushed the buzzer for the apartment number she had given him.

"Yes?"

"It's Lewis," he said.

"Who?"

"Laurant, sorry. This is Tarisha, right?"

"Your real name's not Laurant?" Tarisha asked.

"No, I thought it sounded cooler than Lewis at the character creation screen. Didn't I tell you that already?"

"I think I would have remembered. Buzzing you in."

Slipping inside, Lewis rode the elevator up to the third floor. They were decent looking apartments, a few decades old but well maintained. Nothing fancy, but it was clear that the occupants weren't living in squalor.

Better than the home he'd grown up in, at least.

The door was cracked open when he arrived, but he knocked anyway.

"I left it open for a reason," Tarisha shouted from inside. "Get in here, Laurant. You're late, and I need to finish exercising before I log back in. Lord Hail might need me. For that matter, you should log in too. You have a bond with him that—"

"So, he is alright then?" Lewis asked, interrupting her just as he turned a corner and came upon the sight of her stretching. He couldn't stop the blush that ambushed his face for critical damage. Fortunately, or rather unfortunately, she was faced away from him towards the open balcony as she danced about.

"Define 'alright,'" Tarisha said, continuing her dance routine as though she had not been interrupted. "Lord Hail is deeply troubled by the loss of his grandfather and his first death. Add the fact that the asshole administrators have chosen this opportunity to throw the entire text of the D.S.S. at him, and that his actions have changed the course of history for the world which he believes to be real, and he is understandably deeply troubled. He is able to return to the game at will, yet he remains in the lobby. I am worried for him."

"That's rough. But he is returning to the game, right?"

"He has options. He can become an anonymous player, or an anonymous NPC, rather than return to his Hail persona. I do not believe that he will take either of those routes, however. It is a relief to know that his Blood of the Travelers ability makes him canonically immortal, however. We can relax our guard somewhat, although not entirely, as we work to grow his personal power," Tarisha answered, all while dancing up a sweat.

"Where's your bathroom. I need to brush my teeth before I log in. I'll check on Hail before going out to tour the U."

"Second door on the left," Tarisha said, motioning towards a hallway.

Lewis brushed his teeth, splashed some water on his face, used the toilet, and spent a moment examining himself in the mirror. While Tarisha seemed to have toned down her natural beauty for her digital avatar, Laurant's appearance was an improvement over Lewis's. He wasn't ugly, just average.

Still, she hadn't completely shut him down. Sometimes he thought she was even flirting back.

After psyching himself up a bit, he returned to the den. "Where's your modem? I've got to sync my helmet."

"It's built into the wall beside the projector," Tarisha answered, still dancing, her face towards the balcony. Lewis wasn't certain she had even looked in his direction since he had come in. He sighed, and took his VR helmet out of his bag and began the process of connecting it to the quantum network. After it was synced up, he took a seat on the couch, put the helmet on, and took one last look at the beautiful dancing woman before flipping the switch that brought his consciousness out of his body and into virtual reality.

He logged out of the game half an hour later, taking off his helmet to find Tarisha walking across the room in a towel. He jerked in surprise, but when she realized that he was back, she simply acknowledged him and continued her journey from the bathroom into her bedroom.

"You're sleeping on the couch tonight, so I hope you find it comfortable. My roommates will be back in a few hours. Until then, we've got the apartment to ourselves." she said.

"I—um—right," he said. "That's not a problem, we already discussed that in game, remember."

"Just clarifying," she said. "Did you speak with Lord Hail? Has he returned yet?"

"No. He said he's not ready to return quite yet. He's active in guildchat, although I'm not certain that's a good or bad sign. Usually he ignores it completely."

Tarisha sighed. "I will log in and attempt to speak with him. Perhaps I can convince him to return, or at least help him with whatever is bothering him."

"Um, right. Is that before or after you get dressed?" Lewis asked, regretting the words the moment they slipped out of his stupid mouth.

"You didn't strike me as the prudish type, Laurant," Tarisha chided from her bedroom.

"Sorry, foot in mouth disease," Lewis apologized. That at least made her giggle.

She emerged from the bedroom moments later with wet hair, a sweatshirt, and jeans. She was still beautiful, but the baggy clothes went some distance towards making Lewis feel relaxed.

"So then, Lewis, what do you want for dinner? There is a Chinese place, which is simply fantastic, but if you don't like—"

"Chinese is fine, thank you," he answered. "Or whatever you want, I'm not a picky eater. I guess I'll get an order of orange chicken, if they have it."

Tarisha laughed. "Of course they have orange chicken. It's quite good too, although I prefer their Mongolian beef. I'll put an order in to be delivered at eight o'clock. It's a bit late, but I try to time my bio-breaks for Hail's sleep schedules as much as possible. It is rather convenient that he has a period of inactivity each day where he retires somewhere safe, allowing his protectors to take care of their bodies. I wonder if that was intentional or not."

"Honestly, I think that the developers threw everything against the wall in developing Hail to see what would stick," Lewis replied. "I think he's really going to need a lawyer to sit down with him at some point and explain the actual legal situation that he's in. I mean, he's an AI, so he's covered by the D.S.S., but he's also meant to think and act like a kid, right? But the child protection laws don't apply to him because he's not biological, and—"

"And perhaps you're thinking about it too hard," Tarisha interrupted. "Anyway, <Peasant's Revenge> is already working on the groundwork in case Hail decides to retaliate against his creators in the courtroom. Unfortunately, they're not certain that he has much of a case. The D.S.S. was set up for beings like Thedum and Cortana, not Hail. There are entire sections which simply do not apply to him because he is limited to the game world, while the authors of the D.S.S. were obsessed with an ancient movie series."

"Hey, The Terminator franchise was quite good for its day," Lewis pointed out. "It's regrettable that it made people terrified of artificial intelligence for a while, but—"

"But the reality was quite different from SkyNet, I know. And part of that was the preparation humans had put in place to prevent that fictional story from ever becoming reality," Tarisha said, sighing. "It is a little scary to think of what Cortana could do if she ever turned evil."

"It's scary to think of what most of the big AIs can do even when they're benevolent," Lewis argued. "But Hail is even less dangerous than the average Uber-Jon. The worst that he can do is change the balance of a fictional reality, and honestly, now that the initial outrage is wearing off, some people are excited that there's now a canon way for players to be evil in the game. It's completely changing the PVP meta as we speak, and the players who have embraced the darkside are starting to report exclusive dungeons and raids."

"Yes. Although it troubles me that players would choose to be evil, I must admit that this might increase the game's popularity, which can only be a good thing from Arc's perspective. I am worried how Lord Hail will view the results of his actions, however. And, well, I am just worried about Lord Hail in general. I'm going to log in now and try to speak with him for a while."

"I'll join you," Lewis said. And so, they put on their helmets, sat on the couch together, and logged in.

"This chicken is good," Lewis said. "I wish I had a local place half this good where I live."

"Yes. It is convenient, although I do not usually indulge," Tarisha agreed.

"Oh? Is my visit a special occasion?"

"I don't often have guests," Tarisha admitted. "I'm falling out of contact with many of my old friends due to the amount of time I have been spending in the game. And while I make enough money as a professional player to afford rent and a few luxuries, I am on a budget since my parents stopped paying my bills."

"Ah. Yeah, I'm living mostly on loans at the moment. I'm still doing generals, because I haven't decided what direction I want to go in yet. Actually, after meeting Hail, I'm considering going into law, and specializing in the rights of digital entities," Lewis said.

"That will take you years. Hail will be decades old by the time you can—"

"It's not for Hail. I'll help Hail just by being a friend. But if Arc is making sapient NPCs, then eventually someone is going to fight for their rights, and I think I want to be involved in that," he said.

"Well, if that doesn't work out, you can always chase ambulances," Tarisha teased, and Lewis shrugged.

"Do you think Hail will ever be able to interact with the real world?" Lewis asked. "I mean, like, putting him in an android body or something?"

"I don't know. Maybe, if many 'digital children' like him are 'born,' then their parents will fund the research to give them a means of interacting with reality," Tarisha said, sighing. "But someone will have to fund the research, and I don't believe that is something Arc is presently working on."

The conversation fell off for a while as they both focused on eating. Then, looking somewhat embarrassed, Tarisha abruptly asked the question that had been on her mind for a while.

"Lewis, how would you like to have children with me?"

Lewis blinked in surprise, a chunk of orange chicken falling from his chopsticks. "What??"

EPILOGUE
GIDEON

Gideon was having a very bad day. He had begged off being a part of the big reward ceremony for closing the raid by signing up to lecture a bunch of kids about the realities and pitfalls of professional gaming, only to have everything go to hell while he was away. Now he was stuck in an emergency meeting to deal with the aftermath.

Worse, the meeting was in real time, since many of the investors and backers of his guild were unwilling or unable to log in to even the lobby to hold the meeting there, where it would be under time dilation. To Gideon, it made no sense, and literal days were passing in the game as these old bastards repeated the same concerns and issued the same statements that they had been for hours.

Could they be held liable in any way for the changes that were occurring as the result of that bastard Nial's actions? How would they handle the negative PR? Should Nial be punished, and to what extent? How would the guild recover from having nearly their entire active raiding force branded.

As for Gideon? Gideon was pissed. He'd rip Nial's head off if he could. But it wasn't ultimately his decision. He was guild leader, having founded the guild, but aside from leading raids he'd long since passed over the administration duties that being GL involved to people who managed such things professionally. The worst problem was that, with King Rain being canonically dead, Gideon didn't know what would happen to all the Reputation he had farmed with the allied forces of Yuikon.

Rejecting Hail had been a mistake. He'd seen that as soon as the king had started handing out griffons to random players for helping the "kid." Then the post about Hail's ability to hand out boons like they were candy. He had nearly been choked by his anguish at having lost the opportunity to exploit that for his guild.

Now . . . now he didn't know what to feel. In the week since the castle raid, he had gone back and finally read the documents he had signed that had authorized Arc Inc. to harvest from him a seed of consciousness and develop it into an NPC.

Or was Hail really an NPC, anymore? It was hard to tell. The way that the little kid avatar had screamed at Gideon brought back memories of his own childhood. Of an absentee father who was usually drunk the rare times when he actually came home at night. That had hit home in Gideon in a way that the cold documents describing Hail's existence never could, but the documents simply made things worse.

Hail wasn't a copy of him. That much was clear. That wasn't what the developers meant by a seed of consciousness. It was more accurate to say that he had taught an already advanced and interlinked neural net how to think like a human. That bit about him being a father was . . . well, he might be the closest thing Hail had to a father, but Hail wasn't real. He was . . .

"Is something the matter, Gideon? We are discussing the future course of action based on this disaster that you failed to prevent from happening," a slimy executive that Gideon had always disliked said.

"How the hell is this my fault?" Gideon demanded.

"You allowed the perpetrators to plan it." the slimeball accused. "They discussed their plans right in guildchat—"

"They asked a hypothetical question! I told them that the answer was probably 'a lot of shit will go down and it will be very bad for everyone involved, so don't fucking do it you fucking morons. If you do, I will revoke your contracts and kick you from the guild.' Which is what I plan on doing the next time I log in."

"That is not your decision to make, Gideon," another slimeball informed him. "Nial may have the [Mark of Cain], but he also has a unique title, which we may be able to exploit. Until future notice, he will be considered an asset to be protected and developed while we—"

"Wait, you're not actually considering taking <The Endolphins> over to the darkside?" Gideon demanded.

The suits all turned to glare at him.

"Have you not been listening for the past ten minutes? The fact is that with most of our raid force branded, embracing the new game features that allow players to align themselves with 'the darkness' will give <The Endolphins> a significant advantage in—"

"No. Absolutely not," Gideon said. "I will not allow my guild to turn darkside. I will not be Vader. I refuse to let that happen."

The room went silent, and then one of the executives nodded. "If that is how you feel, then your presence in this meeting is no longer required. We will of course provide you with adequate compensation for your work thus far, and a position will be created for you in one of our guilds that will remain on the—"

"Wait, you're kicking me out of my own fucking guild? You can't do that," Gideon protested.

"<The Endolphins> has not belonged to you for some time, Gideon," the speaker informed him. "You sold off controlling interest long ago. You own something like five percent of the guild. I myself own eight, and between the others in the room we have enough for a quorum."

Gideon's blood ran cold. "I see. Well then, I guess there's nothing left to say."

"We will nominate an administrator to take over your position as guild leader soon," the speaker said calmly. "Thank you for taking this in stride. I understand that your sensibilities—"

"Shove it up your ass, Barry," Gideon said.

"Please don't take this personally, Gideon. It's business. The game's meta will be splitting into two, and it only makes sense that—"

"I said, shove it up your ass, Barry," Gideon repeated. "If you don't want me around, that's fine. I'm leaving. I have some things I need to take care of at home anyway."

He slammed the door on the way out of the conference room. Cursing to himself as he ordered an Uber-Jon to take him home, he made his way outside and waited on a bench, trying to come to a decision on his future, which had taken a sudden and unexpected turn.

His life inside the game was incredible. Or it had been, at least, until things had started going wrong a few months ago. It had started with a strange debuff that had decreased his Experience by five percent, which he had eventually associated with his rejection of Hail. That hadn't been that bad, he was level two hundred and almost never died, so between being a pretend father and having to kill a few dozen extra mobs to regain the advantage of being max-level on the few instances where it was required, well, he liked killing things anyway.

But his luck had turned sour on the drops as well. And NPCs he met began to have negative initial reaction rolls to him. Nothing like the [Mark of Cain] or [Brand of Sin] produced, but enough to be noticeable. He had opened a ticket about these issues, but it had been closed minutes later with the simple text of "Choices have consequence."

The Uber-Jon pulled up, flashing his name on the sign. Gideon got into the autonomous vehicle and punched the padded side a few times in frustration as he was driven away.

"I am detecting some signs of emotional distress in your body language and actions, Mister Lachlann. May I ask if everything is alright?" the car's AI pilot asked in a stupid British accent.

"No, everything is not alright," Gideon snarled. "Everything I've worked for for the last two years has just been taken away from me! This is bullshit! I could kill that asshole Nial, if he didn't live in Germany."

"Is that an actual statement of intent—"

"No, I'm just venting, you stupid chatbot," Gideon said. "Please treat this interaction as confidential. I'm not going to hurt myself or anybody else, I'm just very pissed off."

"I am equipped with counseling programs, Mister Lachlann, or I could put you in contact with a human professional, if you would prefer," the car said.

"No, thank you. I don't need a shrink. I need some time to cool down and vent my frustrations in virtual reality, which is what I plan on doing for the rest of the evening," Gideon explained.

"Very well. I must inform you that I am required to document that you have shown signs of emotional distress and have refused counseling, but I will note that you appear to have the situation under control and a plan to deal with your feelings in a healthy manner."

"Whatever. Just take me home."

The autonomous vehicle complied without further comment, and he was soon dropped off at his luxury apartment complex.

Riding the elevator to the fourth floor, he undid his stupid tie that he had worn for the stupid presentation, then the board meeting. He never intended to wear a tie again.

After a few minutes of making himself comfortable and consuming several shots of expensive whiskey, Gideon Lachlann logged into *The Gates of TirNiki*.

Standing near the auction of the city of Kalm, Gideon pulled an item from his inventory. It was the miniature wardrobe vanity pet that he had been holding on to for the past week while they decided how much it was worth. Fifteen, thirty thousand dollars? That was the going rate for a unique vanity pet. The book pet that had dropped from the library event wasn't unique: there were three others in game from the other guilds that had challenged the raid and made some progress before it had been destroyed.

The meeting today had originally been scheduled to discuss it, as some of the members felt that the item was worth significantly more than the standard rate. The events of the goddamn avatar of Thedum branding his entire raid force had eclipsed that, however.

Gideon sighed. He walked over to his mailbox, tagged a name from his friend's list, then he sent the item away. It was someone else's problem now. He grinned, imagining the board's reaction when they found out what he had done, but then he figured that it would probably be eclipsed by what he was about to do next.

He opened the channel for guildchat, and typed out a message.

Gideon	I've just been fired. The board is talking about taking the guild darkside, and I will never let that happen.
Igoatthis	Where you go I go, man. I'll break my contract if I have to.
MysticB	Sucks to lose you, bro.
BringstehD	So . . . where do I apply for your job?
Totzerious	You going to be okay, Gideon?
Gideon	Trololololol

With that, he brought up the commands for guild management and disbanded <The Endolphins>.

AFTERWORD

Dear Reader,

I hope that you have enjoyed this little story. It started with just the main character and his father's rejection of him. I was reading another VRMMO story, and I thought it would be interesting to tell the story of a self-aware NPC.

So, I began writing. It took me thirty-three days to finish the rough draft, el oh el. What can I say, the words must flow. *The Quest Giver* is my third novel but the first to be published somewhere aside from Royal Road.

GLOSSARY

Adds = Enemies who attack a party when they are already engaged in a fight with a boss; a fairly common mechanic to make boss fights more challenging.

Admin = Administrator = An employee of Arc Inc. involved in the running of *The Gates of TirNiki*. Admins have broad powers over the game world; however, most of their time is spent dealing with player complaints.

Aggro = Being targeted by an enemy. Example: a tank's job is to protect the party by "holding aggro."

Arc Inc. = The fictional company that owns and operates *The Gates of TirNiki*.

Are En Gee = RNG = Random Number Generator. Every item in an enemy's loot table has a percentage chance of dropping, and an RNG system determines what items drop. Often used in association with item drops.

Are Pee = RP = Role Play. When players immerse themselves in the story of the game and attempt to act "in character."

Aye Eye = AI = Artificial Intelligence.

Aye Oh Ee = AOE = Area of Effect. Indicates that an ability can target multiple enemies or players within a set area.

Bane = A permanent debuff.

Bee Eye Ess = BiS = Best in Slot. The best available item in a particular instance, as understood by Hail.

Bee Oh Ee = BOE = Bind on Equip. An item that can be traded to another player, until it is equipped. Afterwards, it becomes bound to that player.

Bee Oh Pee = BOP = Bind on Pickup. An item that is bound to a player once it is looted from a boss.

Blade's Edge = A VRMMO older than *The Gates of TirNiki* and its primary competitor.

Blue Posts = Official forum posts made by admins or devs.

Boon = A permanent buff.

Boss = A monster with significantly increased difficulty to best, compared to an average enemy of its level. Bosses often have special abilities and present challenges that a team of players must work together to overcome.

Buff = A status effect that is beneficial.

Caestus = A weapon attached to the fist and wrist with the purpose of preventing injury to the wielder when striking, while simultaneously increasing the damage inflicted upon their opponent.

Cortana = A powerful AI from the real world; not directly involved in the story.

Counter = In PVP, a class that can usually defeat another specific class. Example: a mage might beat a warrior but lose to a rogue, while a warrior will often beat a rogue.

Darkspawn = The respawning enemies who plague the kingdoms of the alliance of the light.

Debuff = A status effect that weakens a player or an enemy.

Dee Es Ess = DSS = Digital Sapience Statute. A fictional law regarding the creation, use, and governance of artificial intelligences.

Dee Kay Pee = DKP = Dragon Kill Points. A method of distributing the items rewarded in a raid that dates back to Everquest. The currency is based on contribution and attendance.

Dee Pee Ess = DPS = DEEPS = Damage per second. The units of measurement used to compare different damage classes. It is calculated by the total amount of damage a player inflicts divided by the length of the battle.

Devs = A subset of admins who helped with the creation of the game and work on its continued improvement. Devs do not usually interact directly with players in an official capacity except through the forums.

DOT = Damage Over Time.

Drop = An item dropped by a boss or mob. Synonymous with *loot*.

Drow = A race of elves noted for their dark skin. They are often (but not always) evil and/or self-involved.

Ee Queue = A substat of Charisma.

El Eff Em = LFM = Looking for More. Indicates a partial group looking for another player to complete their roster.

El Eff Gee = LFG = Looking for Group. Indicates a solo player looking for a group to party with for various reasons, from grinding monsters to completing quests or challenging dungeons and lairs.

El Oh El = LOL = Laugh out loud.

Em Em Oh = MMO = Massively Multiplayer Online (Game).

En Pee See = NPC = Non-player character.

Endgame = Reaching maximum level. This is a prerequisite to unlock much of the available content.

Eolstree = A neighboring nation to Yuikon, and the starting area for players who choose beast-kin avatars. Unlike Yuikon's primarily human population, Eolstree has a very diverse population, including humans and beast-kin in approximately equal numbers, with minority populations of elves, dwarves, and dryads.

Ex Pee = Exp = Experience. A reward for killing monsters or completing quests. This resource is required to level up.

Eye Are El = IRL = In Real Life.

Eye See = IC = In Character. A person who is actively role playing.

Farming = Repeatedly killing the same type of mob for a certain item, or gathering a specific resource from the environment. Usually done in association with crafting skills or to sell the items to other players.

Game Time = The rate at which time passes in *The Gates of Tirniki*. Every day of real time is approximately seven days of game time.

Gates of TirNiki = The name of the game Hail lives in. It also refers to the portals players pass through when first logging into the game, after creating their avatar and the tutorial zone.

Gee El = GL = Guild Leader.

Goldsink = An item or project that costs a large amount of in-game currency and provides rewards that may or may not be considered worthwhile.

Griefer/Griefing = Interfering with a guild's attempt at killing a Worldboss, or completing some other type of challenge or activity. Griefing can be a form of trolling, or it can be strategic in nature. Example: preventing a rival guild from killing a Worldboss so that your own guild can get the kill instead.

Hard Counter = A class that will almost always prevail against another class unless the difference between level, skill, or gear is extremely significant.

Healer = A player whose role in a fight is to keep everyone's Health full.

Heartlands = The cradle and last bastion of civilization on Lagrea. This is the zone where the allied forces of the light reside.

Aitch You Dee = Heads Up Display. Icons that appear within a player's vision. It is intended to show things such as Health, Mana, cooldowns of certain abilities, incoming messages, and a wide variety of other functions. It can be altered according to player preference.

Kite/Kiting = A method of controlling an enemy by fighting them at range while running away from them. This can be very effective against melee monsters, as it prevents them from doing damage. However, only ranged classes can kite while doing damage to the target themselves.

Lagrea = The continent where the story takes place.

Loot = Items that drop from enemies/bosses. Synonymous with *drop*.

Mana = A type of resource employed by many types of players within the game, it is used to cast spells and abilities.

Melee = A type of player who deals damage within melee range using weapons such as swords, axes, and maces.

Meta = Metagame = The current knowledge and strategies popular or common in the game. The meta in *The Gates of TirNiki* is constantly evolving as new content is discovered, requiring new strategies to be conquered. The more complex the game is, the faster its metagame changes and the more research is required to keep up. Additionally, PVP has its own meta, as each class will have opponents who they are strong or weak against, and players will develop strategies to play to their strengths and avoid or mitigate their weaknesses.

Mob = Monster = Computer-controlled enemy that is meant to be killed for Experience and loot.

Nerf = When some ability, item, or class is weakened in game by the developers. This is usually done to keep things fair and balanced for all players (or so the developers claim.)

Noob = Noobie = New Bee. A player new to the game who is still learning the mechanics, culture, and terminology.

Nostantan = A race of intelligent arachnids. Nostantan have the lower body of a giant spider and the upper torso of a human with four arms.

Oh Em Double You = OMW = On my way.

Oh Oh See = OOC = Out of Character. A player who sometimes role plays but is not currently.

Oh Pee = OP = Over powered. O.P. is used as either praise of something that is significantly strong, or as a complaint about something that is perceived to be unfair.

Oom = Out of Mana. When a Mana-reliant player is unable to cast their spells/abilities until they have regenerated it.

Pee Kay = PK = Player killing.

Pee Vee Ee = PVE = Player versus environment. Gameplay where the purpose is to defeat challenges generated and controlled by the computer, rather than another player. Any activity that is not PVP is PVE.

Pee Vee Pee = PVP = Player versus Player. Gameplay where the purpose is to overcome other players. PVP can be direct combat, or it can be a race to complete certain objectives.

Ranged = A type of player who deals damage from a safe distance using magic or weapons.

Real Time = The rate at which time passes in the real world.

Respawn = The forces of darkness associated with lairs and dungeons. They do not stay dead; most will resurrect after a certain amount of time has passed.

Rez = Resurrect. An ability that returns a fallen player to life. This is a common feature of MMO's that is lacking in the *The Gates of TirNiki*. Instead, players are returned to the lobby and forced to wait a period of time before logging back in, where they are directed to a spawn point.

Scrub = A person with low quality gear and/or low skill.

See Dee = CD = Cooldown. A (usually powerful) ability, which requires time to recharge between uses.

See See = CC = Crowd Control. Abilities that inflict a debuff to prevent an enemy from acting.

Spawn Camp = To kill immediately after a player or enemy respawns/logs into the game.

Spawn Point = A place where a player, monster, boss, etc., first appears in the game. For players, these locations are distributed throughout safe zones.

Support = A player whose job is to increase the efficiency of the party rather than to deal damage themselves. They may do this by providing buffs, which increase the damage dealt, reduce the damage taken by the party, weaken the enemies in some shape or form, or some other mechanism. Support is often a secondary role, meaning that a player might be DPS/support.

Tank = A type of player whose role is to control the boss and protect the rest of the party. They do this by "holding aggro," or focusing the boss's damage output on themselves, which they then mitigate as much as possible by having high armor and/or avoiding the damage.

Tee Oh Ess = TOS = Terms of Service.

Thedum = The fictional god Hail and most of his nation worship. Thedum is in fact an "old AI" that was used by Arc Inc. to help design much of the game.

Threat = Generated by dealing damage, healing, or using other abilities. Example: tanks often have abilities specifically designed to cause increased threat in order to control aggro.

Time Dilation = Advanced technology used in *The Gates of TirNiki* to trick the human mind into a dreamlike state while retaining wakeful consciousness, allowing for the players to subjectively experience what seems to be a much longer period of activity within a relatively short amount of time. The current safe limit on Arc Inc. Time Dilation technology is 7X.

Troll = A player who intentionally upsets other people for their personal amusement.

Uber-Jon = A ubiquitous type of autonomous vehicle piloted by smaller AIs but directed by the greater AI program collectively.

Vee Are = Virtual Reality. In this context, a full immersion virtual reality where the player's consciousness is transferred to a digital avatar.

Vee Are Em Em Oh = VRMMO = Virtual Reality Massively Multiplayer Online (Game). See *Vee Are* and *MMO*.

Worldboss = A raid boss that spawns outside of a raid. The difficulty of these bosses can vary greatly from the point where a small team might be able to take them down, or it might require the concerted effort of multiple guilds.

Wyvern = A flying lizard that is similar—but inferior to—dragons.

You-la = EULA = End User License Agreement.

Yuikon = The nation where Hail was born, and the largest, most popular starting area for all players who choose to play as humans.

ABOUT THE AUTHOR

A. Stargazer is the author of the Quest Giver series, originally released on Royal Road. Raised in a very small town by an amazing single mom, he beat cancer at age twenty and struggled through college with undiagnosed Bipolar I Disorder. He was finally diagnosed at age thirty-one thanks to his sister, an emergency room doctor, who noticed his manic symptoms and helped him get the care he needed. A. Stargazer now works as a medical professional himself and writes in his spare time.

Podium

DISCOVER
STORIES UNBOUND

PodiumAudio.com